THE COMPLETE ADVENTURES OF BELLOW BILL WILLIAMS, VOLUME 3

Ralph R Perry

SHARK TRAIL

THE COMPLETE ADVENTURES OF
BELLOW BILL WILLIAMS, VOLUME 3

RALPH R. PERRY

ILLUSTRATED BY

SAMUEL CAHAN

COVER BY

PAUL STAHR

STEEGER BOOKS • 2021

PUBLISHING HISTORY

"The Scar" originally appeared in the June 2, 1934 issue of *Argosy* magazine (Vol. 247, No. 3). Copyright © 1934 by The Frank A. Munsey Company. Copyright renewed © 1961 and assigned to Steeger Properties, LLC. All rights reserved.

"The Jungle Master" originally appeared in the July 14, 1934 issue of *Argosy* magazine (Vol. 248, No. 3). Copyright © 1934 by The Frank A. Munsey Company. Copyright renewed © 1961 and assigned to Steeger Properties, LLC. All rights reserved.

"Blood Payment" originally appeared in the October 6, 1934 issue of *Argosy* magazine (Vol. 250, No. 3). Copyright © 1934 by The Frank A. Munsey Company. Copyright renewed © 1961 and assigned to Steeger Properties, LLC. All rights reserved.

"The Rats of Mahia" originally appeared in the December 1, 1934 issue of *Argosy* magazine (Vol. 251, No. 5). Copyright © 1934 by The Frank A. Munsey Company. Copyright renewed © 1962 and assigned to Steeger Properties, LLC. All rights reserved.

"Fangs of the Fetish" originally appeared in the February 23, 1935 issue of *Argosy* magazine (Vol. 253, No. 5). Copyright © 1935 by The Frank A. Munsey Company. Copyright renewed © 1962 and assigned to Steeger Properties, LLC. All rights reserved.

"The Golden Oyster" originally appeared in the May 25, 1935 issue of *Argosy* magazine (Vol. 255, No. 6). Copyright © 1935 by The Frank A. Munsey Company. Copyright renewed © 1962 and assigned to Steeger Properties, LLC. All rights reserved.

"The Atoll of Flaming Men" originally appeared in the October 19, 1935 issue of *Argosy* magazine (Vol. 259, No. 3). Copyright © 1935 by The Frank A. Munsey Company. Copyright renewed © 1962 and assigned to Steeger Properties, LLC. All rights reserved.

"Shark Trail" originally appeared in the March 21, 1936 issue of *Argosy* magazine (Vol. 263, No. 1). Copyright © 1936 by The Frank A. Munsey Company. Copyright renewed © 1963 and assigned to Steeger Properties, LLC. All rights reserved.

"About the Author" originally appeared in the August 23, 1930 issue of *Argosy* magazine (Vol. 214, No. 5). Copyright © 1930 by The Frank A. Munsey Company. Copyright renewed © 1957 and assigned to Steeger Properties, LLC. All rights reserved.

TABLE OF CONTENTS

THE SCAR

Only natives stole the heads of murdered men—but about
this victim Skipper Bellow Bill Williams was not so sure

CHAPTER I

HOLOCAUST

OUT OF THE dark and moonless sea Bellow Bill Williams's pearling schooner glided into the circle of red glare cast by a yacht which was ablaze from truck to waterline. The rigging was gone. Blazing masts swayed, ready to fall. Fire spouted from every porthole and roared from every hatchway. The yacht was a furnace—yet every lifeboat still hung in the davits. Not even the head of a swimmer was visible in the red glare.

"Ahoy!" Bellow Bill thundered. "By the blue hell, couldn't one of you jump?"

From far away he had watched the first gleam of fire break out, small as the sudden flare of a match in the night. For long minutes he had cursed the light breeze which prevented prompt investigation or rescue while he watched the fire spread with sinister rapidity. An oil boat might have wrapped itself in flame with such speed, but a yacht? Wood does not burn faster than lifeboats can be launched. Here was a vessel, secretly abandoned and set afire by her own crew—a case of barratry—or worse.

There was no response to his hail, but on the yacht the sides of the deck house bulged and collapsed, all at once. The roof slanted toward him, fiercely illumined by the gush of flames, and a corpse which had been lying upon it slid slowly to the burning deck. That corpse—lacked a head!

For an instant Bellow Bill could only stare. Vast and incredulous amazement held his breath in his great chest. Then he jumped, turning his back on the yacht to scan the dark seas

*It was a
small but
deadly krait*

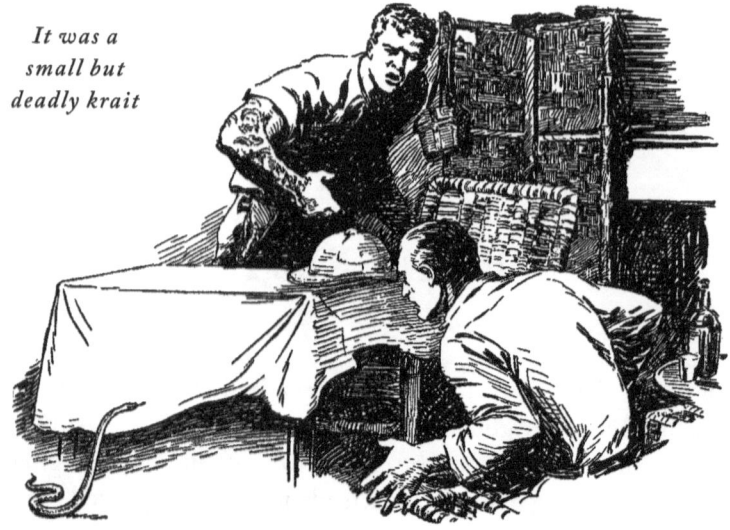

around through glasses. He was looking for a prau or a sampan, gliding toward the land with the loot of the yacht, and for the heads of the passengers and crew.

Twenty miles away lay the northwest coast of Borneo. Time was when the Bajau tribes had been head-hunting pirates and no ship sailed these waters without boarding nets out and loaded guns in the rack. Those days were passed? So Bill had believed.

There was a British resident at Jesselton, thirty miles away. British planters raised tobacco, in stations scattered along a shore that were still lonely and wild. The Bajaus had abandoned the sea and had become plantation laborers who amused themselves by stealing water buffaloes.

So men said, and so Bellow Bill, who knew the South Seas better than any official, would have sworn. But a headless corpse was proof to the contrary. Natives, not white men, take heads. Not even white murderers do that. Somewhere on that dark sea was a boatload of savages who had thrown back to the blood lust of their fathers. They could not have sailed far, in that gentle breeze.

Nevertheless, darkness hid them. Bill's glasses revealed only a tiny white blur against the black water, three hundred yards off to windward. He put the schooner about, and soon identified the object as a face. And gliding alongside, he discovered that the body was that of a girl. She floated high in the water, supported by two pillows into the loops of which her arms were slipped. Her shoulders were bare. A white dress billowed around her, and in the flickering light of Bill's lantern she seemed young. The boathook which he had ready in his huge tattooed hands dropped to the deck. He heaved the schooner to and dove over the side that he might bring her aboard unmarked. Gently he laid her beside the lantern, just in front of the ship's wheel.

She was in evening dress. Under the heart there was a slit in the silk, still tinged by the stains of blood, despite her immersion. Stabbed, the body left with the head intact because she was a woman. Women's heads have no value because women are easy to kill.

She was beautiful. The bobbed hair was an intense, glossy black. The nose had a saucy tilt. She had loved life, and laughed at it. She— Bill started. The red stain on the dress was spreading! She was still bleeding—*she was alive!*

BILL SWUNG down to the cabin, and a moment later was back with blankets and a bottle of whisky. The latter he dared not use at first. She did not seem to breathe. He could scarcely feel the beating of the heart as he dressed the wound, using strips of his shirt for bandages.

The gash bled profusely. Too freely, he realized swiftly, to be very deep. He staunched the flow, bathed her temples with whisky, and started to chafe her hands. When a hint of color crept into her cheeks, Bill poured a drop or two of whisky between her lips.

Her eyes opened. Slowly at first, and then with the quick and hideous fixity of terror.

"No!" she moaned. "I'll kill myself!—There!"

She tried to move, but she was too weak.

"Steady!" Bill boomed.

His great voice rumbled over the sea. Bill was a gigantic man, six feet three, and two hundred and forty pounds of hard muscle, tattooed from wrist to shoulder and neck to waist. With his shirt off, in the flickering lantern light, he might have resembled a native.

"I'm white. You're safe!" he added.

But the terror in her eyes did not diminish.

"White?" she gasped. "So was the man who slaughtered us. He was white! And that mark—that mark on your chest—is the same as his!"

"Easy!" Bill rumbled.

A chill ran down his spine. This must be hysteria and delirium. Yet she was so positive, and so completely terrified. He glanced down, and observed that the armholes of his sleeveless singlet revealed part of the sails and yards of the full rigged ship that was tattooed on his chest. What the girl saw was three parallel lines in blue ink.

"Never mind," he soothed. "Look around you. This is a pearling schooner. I'm the skipper. Don't try to talk. Close your eyes."

"I can't!—We had finished supper. We were sitting under the stars on deck—laughing. *Laughing!*" The girl choked with the horror of the memory. "My father—my mother—all my best friends! Am I the—the only one who—?"

"Yes," said Bill.

His booming voice was gentle and grim. He rose and trimmed the sails for the race to land, swiftly scanning the darkness again.

"Don't think about that," he urged. "Wait until morning. You'll be calmer."

"I'm not hysterical!" said the girl. Her voice had steadied, and the hysterical fixity had left her eyes. "I *must* tell you—while every detail is still vivid. It's so horrible, and incredible! The lookout sighted a canoeful of natives, sinking, he said. We stopped the yacht and took them aboard, but suddenly they drew knives and guns. It was all so quick—"

"I see," Bill rumbled.

Almost as though he had been an eye witness. The crew and the guests in evening dress, crowding solicitously around the natives whom they had rescued. The gasp at the sight of weapons, the shout that changed to a scream; and afterward the horrid yelling of savages mad with bloodshed, and the different screams as the few who escaped the first rush were dragged from their hiding places below decks and butchered, one by one.

"You say the man who followed you below was white?"

"Yes. He was breaking down the door of my room with an ax. His skin was dyed brown, and he wore a loin cloth like the rest. On his chest was a mark, like—like that." She touched Bill's chest. "Only his was a scar, black and raised higher than the flesh. I threw all my jewelry to him, but that wasn't enough. So I stabbed myself. I only had a corn knife, but it was razor-sharp. I don't understand why—"

"You need strength to drive a knife home," Bill rumbled. "But you say the man was white. Why are you so sure of that if he was disguised?"

"By the shape of his head. Though his eyes were light, too."

BELLOW BILL started violently, and reached to his hip for the fine cut chewing tobacco which was his solace whenever his head whirled. If this girl had given any reason for the identification other than this bizarre and seemingly irrelevant matter of the shape of heads! For South Sea natives do occasionally have blue eyes, but the Polynesian and Melanesian skull differs from the Caucasian—only slightly, but invariably.

This slip of a girl could *see*—had seen.

"By the blue hell, I'm beginning to believe you!" he muttered. "Would you know this man again?"

"Anywhere!" She shuddered.

"And he had this queerly shaped scar on his chest?"

"It wasn't queer! Every one of the others had a scar just like it. Like a brand! A brand out of hell, there on the right side of the chest!"

Bill almost swallowed his quid. Once again the girl had scored. She *had* seen—accurately.

"There were other white men?" he asked, though his mind was elsewhere.

"I saw only one."

He nodded.

"What was the name of the yacht?"

"The South Wind. I'm Alstair Potter. My father—"

Bellow Bill nodded again.

Charlie Potter, multimillionaire on a round-the-world cruise with his family and seven guests. Yachtsman, polo player, an ambassador, middle-aged. A famous and popular man who had been fêted in London and Sydney. The jewels alone of the women aboard the South Wind would have been worth a king's ransom. The cash in the safe would have amounted to a fortune, in the South Seas. The yacht was undoubtedly a prize to tempt a white pirate—and who save a white man would have known when to expect the craft? Natives do not attack ships that are passing out of sight of land.

"You had better go below and get some sleep," he boomed. "We're sailing faster than a canoe can paddle. We may intercept that gang."

Bill had little hope that he spoke the truth. A white man would have discounted the chance of a passing vessel, and taken precautions for a quick escape. The girl, however, understood that he wished to ask no more questions.

She let him carry her below, and if she did not sleep, she at least made no sound throughout the rest of the night.

The pearler steered toward the land, thinking and planning. At dawn, with the port of Jesselton in sight, he slipped the wheel in the becket and went down to the cabin to awaken Alstair.

"Miss Potter," he began, "you've told me an amazing story. I believe every word of it.—Now I'm going to make you an amazing proposition. I want you to think it over. Not as long as I've been thinking, which is all night—but just as hard. First, there's some facts I want you to take my word for. That scar—the scar of hell, as you called it—is the ordinary tribal mark of a certain branch of the Bajaus. At least five hundred men carry it. It looks like this."

On the cabin table he drew with a pencil three parallel vertical strokes.

"That's unfortunate," Alstair said. She received the disappointing news like a thoroughbred. "Even so, that does localize the search for the pirates, doesn't it? And it does help to identify the white leader?"

"Of course. There aren't more than five white men living in the district occupied by that tribe. Of those five, only two have been there long enough to be adopted, and of the two, perhaps one has personality enough to turn the tribe back to the old ways."

ALSTAIR'S EYES were as dark as her hair. She looked at Bill steadily and long.

"After what I saw, nothing is so important as justice," she said. "That's all I can do for my father—and the others. You mean you really think you know the man?"

"Suspect, not know!" Bill boomed. "All I'm saying is that in the jungle we whites know one another as though we lived in the smallest of small towns. If our man is ever arrested, I suspect that his name will be John Mageen. A big man, with a high forehead, and hair getting a little thin."

"That description fits," Alstair nodded. "Yet you say 'if.' Surely the government officials will help me all they can?"

"They will. A navy, and every district officer within a hundred miles, will be at work within an hour after you've told your story.—But I meant 'if,' " Bellow Bill rumbled. "Because our man expects that search. He would never have dared to attack the yacht unless he had provided himself with an alibi or some other means of making the search fail."

Bill paused.

"Some secrets are too startling to keep," he went on. "That a white man should turn native and lead a native tribe back into piracy is one of them. Granted that the officials, like me, believe you. And even though the weakness of the British official is that he is slow to believe that anything which has never happened before is happening now. Even so, the news goes out by wireless and over party telephone lines to dozens of officials, every one of whom has a native servant at his elbow.

"My opinion is that the news is bound to leak out, and once a native learns it, it will spread among them faster than electricity can carry it from official to official. By grapevine telegraph, and by drums that beat out a warning from village to village. 'Men are looking for a white man with a Bajau mark on his chest,' they will say. Since our man is hand-in-glove with the natives, he'll take the warning and disappear in the jungle. Maybe the British will find him, some day. They are good at that, given time. But they won't find him quickly, and I don't think you will care to stay in Borneo for months, or even come back, months and possibly years later, to testify."

"No," said Alstair thoughtfully. "But you haven't drawn that scar exactly right. The ends were broader. Like this."

She placed six small, knob-like ends on the three parallel lines, then she laid down the pencil.

"I understand what you are driving at. Yet what else can we do but tell the officials?"

"The knife of the medicine man often slips," Bellow Bill rumbled. "Tribal scars are bound to vary in minor details."

He ran muscular fingers through his hair and grinned with a reckless challenge.

"My proposal is that you keep the news about the white man to yourself for twenty-four hours. Tell about the piracy, and then pretend that you are exhausted and have to go to bed, under a doctor's care. Early to-morrow—let the cat out of the bag."

"But why?"

"So that I can get to Mageen's station before the news breaks!" Bill boomed. "I think I'll pretend I want to buy a plantation, so that all five of them will be around trying to sell me something when the drums start to talk. I want to watch them when they discover that instead of committing a perfect crime they've left a witness alive. And I'll promise you that any planter or stranger in that district who starts to run will find me right on his heels. Think that over. In my opinion, it is worth the twenty-four-hour delay that I'm asking."

"Why—you're grinning!" exclaimed Alstair. "You really want to be alone with that tribe—and those planters—when I explode my evidence!"

Bellow Bill grinned more broadly.

"All right," Alstair said. "I'll pretend to be overcome by shock for a day. God knows it will be a slight enough pretense!"

CHAPTER II

THE BORNEO PLANTER

"**LISTEN TO THE** drums!" Bill boomed. "I speak most of the Melanesian dialects, gentlemen, but I can't savvy any of that lingo." In his deep voice he parodied the sound beating through the jungle and across the cultivated fields of tobacco—"*Ta-ump! Ta-ta-oom!* Hear the change? That's speech, gentlemen! Vowel, a short beat to indicate a consonant, and a change of pitch. The three elements of Melanesian speech. And important news, too, from the way the other drums are picking up the beat!"

The five planters sitting at tiffin on Mageen's veranda stopped talking for an instant, out of politeness. The hot and oppressive air of mid day throbbed with the beat of drums which echoed a short refrain monotonously from hill to hill.

Swiftly Bill glanced around the circle.

Sweat stood out on Mageen's broad forehead and trickled in the deep cleft of his chin, yet there was no heat flush on his bronzed, leathery skin. The pale eyes had a glitter on the surface, like balls of glass, but they were withdrawn. Mageen was listening. The others had merely stopped talking.

"No more can I," Mageen replied. His voice was unpleasantly high-pitched and sharp. "Nor Conklin here, for all that we've lived fifteen odd years among one Bajau tribe. Nor any white man.—Don't hurry to get up, Williams. I've hung up half a dozen bottles of beer in a wet sack. It will just about be cool."

"You keep the good news for the last."

Bill grinned, but he could feel the pulse beating in his temple.

10

Mageen lied. The four other men were talking now, and he listened. Conklin, heat-withered and dry, past middle age, and with the bitterness born of failure graven in the downward twist of his lips, drank the cool beer indifferently. McNab, red and rawboned and new to the tropics, finished quickly, and spouted figures to prove to Bill that a plantation was profitable if the owner could get the best of fever. McNab couldn't, so he'd sell at a bargain. Hammond, equally new, but English, and very pink in the heat, tried to interrupt. Harris was experienced, but his chin receded, and malaria made him listless. He merely praised the beer, and Bill excused him mentally, along with the two younger men. These three last were not criminals. They lacked both character and strength.

The throbbing of the drums ceased. Mageen drained his glass with a gulp.

"You haven't seen Harris's plantation yet, and you said you favored rubber," he remarked. "So I won't see you again till supper, I suppose?"

"Rubber, did I say?" Bill rumbled. He recalled no such remark. "No, Mageen. Trees are too easy to stick out. You've pretty well sold me on tobacco, and yours is the best place."

"Quite so! Obviously," the planter retorted. "Well, you've seen my whole station, except the new fields I'm clearing. We'll look at those.—Boy! Two ponies!"

Though he raised his voice, not a muscle of his face changed. He did not signal the thick-set Bajau who brought the two ponies around to the veranda, nor even so much as look at him. Bellow Bill made sure of that. Mageen might speak casually and seem to acquiesce in Bill's wishes, but the pearler had been in danger too often to be deceived. He could feel that the duel had begun, though all he had seen was beads of sweat on a face which was pale.—And—and a tribal scar, slightly thickened at the ends, on the chest of the Bajau servant. Slightly reddened, too, that scar was, which was a fact for which Bill could not account.

"You carry a sheath knife as well as a revolver," Mageen was saying. "Isn't that unusual?"

"Diving knife," Bill corrected, tapping the heavy blade. "Where would a sailor be without a knife, in case of squalls? Being a planter, you've got a loaded riding whip under your arm. All habit."

MAGEEN SWUNG into the saddle, and Bellow Bill followed, a length behind. Where the path cut through jungle he watched every leaf, fortunately motionless in the mid day heat. At the turns in the trail he quickened the pace of the pony, lest Mageen, who was by far the better rider, should make a dash to escape.

Yet nothing appeared to be further from the mind of the planter than flight or ambush.

The drums were talking again, but Mageen's talk was of seed and cultivation and drying-sheds, the relative intelligence and cheapness of Bajau, Mantu, and coolie labor; the question of whether it was more profitable to clear new land or fertilize old.

"Fact is, I use both methods. Two strings to the bow, eh?" he broke off, drawing rein at the edge of a clearing.

Axes were ringing. A score or more of Bajaus were wielding heavy iron field hoes, grubbing up the undergrowth as the trees were felled. The ponies picked their way amid the litter, and Mageen began to lecture on clear line, while Bellow Bill studied the tribal marks on the naked, sweating chests. Every scar that he could see was normal—three straight, clean lines, such as he had drawn for Alstair the day before.

A native cried out shrilly. The top of a tree in front of the white men trembled as it commenced to fall.

"Bill! Spur!" screamed Mageen.

His own spurs went home; his pony leaped—straight at the falling tree!

For one split second Bill was motionless. The warning and the quick movement were wholly unnecessary—till in that instant a moving shadow slid over Bill and his pony. He glanced upward—at the vast bulk of a second tree, sweeping down upon him, faster and faster. And in the same breath he vaulted from the saddle.

Spurs he had none. The pony he forgot. Sailor-like he trusted to his own feet; and despite his size, Bill had the agility of a cat. He was on the ground before Mageen's pony had made a second jump. His man was escaping, and so Bill lunged and caught the pony's tail. He was all but jerked from his feet; he caught himself with a wrench that all but halted the pony, and ran on.

The tips of falling branches whipped around his head. From behind him came an appalling scream, cut short by the snapping of tree limbs and the thud of a heavy trunk into the earth.

Mageen checked the pony.

"Your horse!" he exclaimed.

"Aye! That was my horse that was killed!" Bill thundered.

His grip shifted from the tail of the pony to Mageen's stirrup.

"Funny I could run out, but my horse couldn't!" he said.

Sweat trickled into the cleft in the planter's chin.

"Why—what can you mean?" he demanded shrilly.

"I aim to see," Bill rumbled. "Let's go back together, eh?"

He lifted the planter from the saddle and drew his diver's knife. Swiftly he hacked a way back through the foliage. A huge limb had knocked the pony down, and, snapping as the tree fell, had impaled the animal. The carcass was not pretty to see.

"It was confused, with its rider gone!" Mageen shrilled. "Damn you, were you too yellow to stick to your mount?"

"I stick to men!" Bill growled. "And lucky for me, too!"

WITH THE heavy knife he pointed to the rear hoof of the dead pony, about which a green jungle vine, strong as a rope and almost as flexible, was noosed.—*Noosed,* not twisted. To a sailor, the turns of a slip knot were unmistakable, and though a pony might trip over a twisted vine, no vine ever tied itself into an intricate knot.

Bill waited grimly for Mageen to explain. The planter merely wiped the sweat from his face.

"It beats me!" he said. "I—I don't know how you feel about this, but I could use a drink. Shall we go to the bungalow and get one?"

"Whatever you say," rumbled the pearler.

He refused to admit to himself that the idea was welcome, and yet Mageen had *not* addressed a word to the laborers; and unless it was with his eyes, he had not signaled them. Nevertheless, an assassination had been planned and had been adroitly executed. Any man accustomed to horses would have been pinned to the earth with his mount, or in case he had been lucky enough to be simply knocked out of the saddle, he might have been beaten to death as he extricated himself from the tangle of limbs.

There were natives enough at hand to do that, Bill reflected grimly. And the bruises left by clubs do not differ from those inflicted by the limbs of a falling tree. The job was neat, and it would have been easy to explain as an accident. Yet how had the orders been given? Not by Mageen, Bill was sure. And how by an accomplice, assuming that there was one? For no messenger had passed Bill and Mageen on the trail.

The drums were muttering again in the still, hot air. The sounds seemed to come from far away, but Bill was well aware that that might be but an auditory illusion. A native drum that can be heard miles away is sometimes all but inaudible close by, and the contrary is also true.

Tam-tum-a-oom! A-a-a-oom! A message throbbing through the heat which all natives could understand. Telling—planning—what?

Bill filled his cheek with fine cut and spat grimly.

"Hot, ain't it?" he boomed.

"Think so? I'm used to it, I guess," Mageen rasped.

He plodded along the bridle path without more words.

When they reached the bungalow at last the pearler was scarcely surprised to find the four other planters gone. All had promised to wait. No matter. That throbbing drumbeat had done its work. There remained only the Bajau house boy, who came onto the veranda noiselessly in his bare feet.

"Soda and the whisky, Poapi!" Mageen rasped.

He led the way into the inner room and dropped into a long cane chair, motioning Bill to take another. The pearler, however, perched himself lightly on the edge of a table. Recline? Not in this room—or company. The roof might come down or a spear fly through the door—yet all that would come was Poapi, with the decanter, soda, and glasses on a brass tray.

Bill made himself a drink, with the intention of spilling it, but he seized the opportunity to look closely at Poapi's tribal scar. He thrilled at the discovery that the shape had been altered. The three straight lines were old. The enlarged ends had been incised with a knife point, much more recently. Their reddish color was due to newly healed scar tissue. Which meant what? A new clan within the tribe? A new secret society? Or had Poapi won some honor, of which this was the visible mark? For the present, such questions must remain unanswered.

"Drink hearty!" said Mageen, unpleasantly.

AS BILL lifted his glass his ears, tuned to identify every slight sound, caught the faintest of slithering noises. Even so, the snake almost reached him before he could move. It came straight and swift, as though it followed Poapi's footprints, passing the chair where Mageen reclined without turning aside. It was small but deadly—a krait.

"Shoot it!" Mageen shrilled. "For God's sake shoot while I get a shotgun!" He sprang toward a double-barreled weapon leaning in a corner.

Shoot a writhing streak two feet long and less than an inch thick?

Bellow Bill seized the table and snapped it bottom up with a flick of the wrists. *Wham!* he slammed the table down upon the snake, and leaped upon the table bottom to crush the snake with his weight in case the blow had failed. The thing was done far more quickly than it can be told.

Then the gun flashed into Bill's hand—to cover Mageen!

"Enough of this!" Bill thundered. "Gimme that shotgun, you—you pirate! Butt first—and clamp both hands around the front sight!"

Mageen had lifted the weapon. Yet he obeyed, in the instant that Bill's finger was tightening on the trigger, in the belief that the planter was about to shoot it out. As the shotgun was passed to him, the sailor broke it open; and the shells which dropped out he ground under his heel to expose the loads. It was birdshot, and Bill swore aloud.

"Buckshot was what I was looking for," he rumbled. "Still, at twenty feet, birdshot can blow a hell of a hole in a man, eh?—Poapi!" Bill bellowed.

Poapi appeared in the doorway.

"Are you mad, Williams?" Mageen shrilled. "Pirate, you call me!"

"I'm arresting you for the piracy of the yacht South Wind!" Bill rumbled. "By the blue hell, there's a limit to what I can take!"

Mageen stared, pale to the lips, yet not incredulous, merely withdrawn.

"Piracy?" he repeated.

The moment of self-communion passed. The pale, blue eyes lost a little of their glassy glitter.

"So that's what happened! Good God, I wish you'd taken me into your confidence sooner! You'd have saved yourself a lot of suspicion, and two mighty distressing accidents. Piracy was the one crime I didn't suspect!"

"No?" Bill boomed sarcastically. "Talk all you like, but don't move!"

Mageen shrugged.

"You've got the drop on the wrong man, Bill," he said steadily. "Nevertheless, it happens that I can take you to the right one. He was still alive last night, when you arrived."

CHAPTER III

THE PIRATE AND THE SCAR

"STILL ALIVE?" BILL sneered. "You'd better hope he's alive yet! A strange white man gets wounded, suspiciously, and none of you five planters mention it? The hell you say! Take off your belt."

With the planter's belt, the pearler strapped Paoli's arms behind his back. Since Mageen was forced to hold up his trousers with his hands, he was hobbled whether he elected to fight or to run. The attitude of the planter was therefore faintly ridiculous, but the expression on his face was not.

"Do you want to see this man, or don't you?" he demanded. "You said you came here to buy a plantation, and none of us were going to admit that the natives were making trouble unless we had to. The fact is, this man was washed ashore clinging to the broken mast of a schooner, during the big gale two weeks ago. He gave the name of Smith, which was his business. I offered to put him up at the bungalow, but he preferred to live with the Bajaus in the young men's house.—That was his business, too. What's the use of arguing with a stranger who wants to go native? He got along with the natives all right. I'll say that for him."

"He must have," Bellow Bill rumbled.

"Last night," continued Mageen imperturbably, "he and the young men took out the big canoe. Fishing, they claimed. When they got back, shortly before dawn, Paoli brought me word that there had been a quarrel over a woman, and that Smith had been stabbed. As a matter of fact, I found him stabbed through the chest and deep into the lung, too badly hurt to bring here. Moving a lung wound around is too liable to induce a hemorrhage. So I bandaged him up and left him in the young men's house. He's there yet. I didn't question the story of a quarrel, but if there was a piracy off the coast last night I guess that was the sort of 'fishing' that was done. The wonder to me is that it doesn't happen oftener. A desperate white man with nothing to lose can hop up a bunch of natives with *blang* and lead 'em to hell and back."

"Frank, ain't you?" Bill rumbled. "All right, let's go. And I'll blow your ribs out, if anything starts to look like an 'accident.'"

Bill did not believe the story. Mageen, he figured, was merely inventing a yarn for the purpose of luring him away from the bungalow and into the native village. Nevertheless, an attack which must be made more or less in the open was far more to his taste than the tricky attempts at murder which he had recently survived. If an attack occurred, he meant to settle very promptly with Mageen.

Almost to Bill's disappointment, there was no attack—not even a suspicious looking incident. His prisoners led him for about a quarter of a mile down a broad trail to the beach. They passed the Bajau village, where men and women dashed out to stare and chatter at the sight of Mageen tramping along with a revolver nudging his spine, but that was a reaction altogether to be expected.

A LITTLE farther on was the clubhouse of the unmarried men, a large oblong structure roofed and walled with thatch, and situated in a bowl-shaped depression, in order that the veranda where the young bachelors lounged, and the stone-paved clearing where they danced, might be out of the sight of the women in the village. The Bajaus believe that young men should sow their wild oats with the minimum of open scandal.

Bill had seen such clubhouses a hundred times. Nothing about the exterior distinguished this one, and the interior was just as standardized, from the geometrical decorations painted on the rafters in white and black and red to the floor of slats, raised above the earth on piles, which bent and creaked under his weight.

On the other hand, there were but two young men in the house, though the hour was close to sunset, and one of these two seemed to be dead. Moreover, the tribal scar on the breast of the clay idol was slightly thickened at the ends, and so was the scar on the chest of the young man who squatted by a pallet spread in the corner of the big, dimly lighted room.

"He is dead, *tuan*. Even now, he died," said the young native to Mageen.

Bellow Bill had prepared for that news, since he had seen that there really was a stranger in the clubhouse. He strode forward, alert to discover marks of foul play—and felt a cold shock as he gazed at the body. Had he deceived himself?

For though the dead man was white, his skin had been stained brown and on his chest was that slightly altered tribal scar, so newly incised that the flesh had barely healed. He was past middle age, with thin hair. The staring eyes were a light blue.

Bill reached grimly for his fine cut. Though the stranger did not look at all like Mageen, the features had a rough similarity.

"He wasn't a beach comber," the pearler growled. "There are the marks of glasses on the bridge of his nose."

"All I know is what he said," Mageen retorted indifferently.

Bill was unwrapping the bandage around the chest. The body was warm. The wound had punctured the lung, and the man had died within an hour or two. But whether the wound had been inflicted then or a day earlier, as Mageen claimed, only a physician could tell; and in the steaming heat of Borneo, any evidence of healing around the edges of a wound would vanish before a doctor could be summoned.

"THERE'S NO dark, dried blood on these bandages," Bill rumbled.

"Why, of course not," Mageen retorted. "My God, Williams,

can't you get the idea that I'm a pirate out of your head? Why make a mystery of something simple? Conklin wasn't at my bungalow, was he? Of course Conklin came down here and changed the bandages! He'll tell you so at my bungalow to-night, when he comes back with the others for supper."

"We won't be there," Bill rumbled. "I'm going to take you to Jesselton right away—as a witness."

Mageen caught his breath. For an instant his features twisted, and the leering, misshapen face of the clay idol over his head was no more malign than his.

"That means neglect and ruin for my tobacco!" he began, only to pause abruptly at the sound of shouting from the native village.

For a second or two, the men measured one another as the clamor moved toward them. Then they relaxed as they caught a few of the Melanesian words.

"White officials!" Mageen snarled. "I've you to thank for them, too, eh? Thank God they'll be honest, sensible English-men, and not more gun-toting, crazy Yankees!"

"Aye, that'll be the constables," Bill rumbled. "They've started quick, and come fast."

He was not prepared, however to see Alstair Potter enter on the heels of a district officer and six native police with rifles. The girl gave him a swift glance of gratitude and relief and pointed at Mageen.

"That's the man!" she cried.

"Consider 'self un' arrest," snapped the official, stammering from excitement. "Anything say—used 'gainst you!"

The doors of the clubhouse were crowded with natives. The armed policemen wheeled to face the mob. Only Mageen himself was unmoved. His head shook slightly from side to side, but he showed no other sign of tension.

"For piracy, I assume?" he demanded shrilly. "Don't be excited, Bates! I'm glad to be arrested, legally. A couple of Americans have simply—made a mistake." He looked from the district officer to Alstair. "Before you commit yourself any further," he shrilled, "look at this man!"

He pointed to the corpse.

"Here's the pirate you saw, Miss!" he said.

Alstair took three steps forward. Her face went pale, as white as it had been when Bill lifted her from the sea.

"He's not the pirate," she whispered.

The natives were crowding into the house as far as the line of police would permit.

"You're the pirate!" she went on. "But—I do know this man. He was the treasurer of my father's company."

"Oh, but I say! A friend? What?" Bates cried.

Alstair smiled bitterly.

"No friend," she admitted. "He robbed my father to save his own investments when the market was crashing. Father might have put him in prison; but instead, he forced him to leave the country. To get out of American business altogether, if you understand. His name is Kaffery. He had a nice wife, and three fine boys. Father was sorry for him."

"Then, I say, he was an enemy! Eh?"

"But Mageen was the pirate who broke down your door on the South Wind!" Bill thundered. "Stick to the point, Bates! This girl can *see*, I tell you! Make Mageen take off his shirt and show you the scar!"

"Yes, make me!" shrilled Mageen.

With both hands he ripped shirt and undershirt apart, and faced them, grinning. His chest was unmarked.

CHAPTER IV

BILL IS CARELESS

"OH, BUT I say! You were mistaken about that, weren't you?" Bates said brightly. "You're quite sure of the face, still? Deuced serious matter to make a mistake about, you know!"

"Quite sure!" said Alstair, dully.

Bates shrugged, and walked forward to examine the body; but Bellow Bill spat out his quid with a curt finality and moved over beside the girl.

She could *see*. She had not erred even about the shape of the tribal scar. As far as Bill was concerned, Mageen had carried a scar on the preceding night. How he had faked the mark—for faked it must have been—was inexplicable. So were several other things which the planter had accomplished recently.

Already, he was recounting to the district officer his story of the stranger. From time to time, Bates nodded. Two Americans. Personal hate was the motive. Natives are easily influenced.

"Kid, I believe you, but the judge won't," Bill rumbled to the girl. "You can't convict Mageen now by an identification alone. One error makes everything doubtful."

"I suppose so," Alstair agreed. "But I am *not* mistaken! Can't we get corroboration from the natives?"

"Hard to make them hang their own sons and brothers," Bill said. "No, it ain't by what they say that we'll trip him! But would you be willing to run a little risk?"

"Would I!"

She stared, for Bill had winked, and then lifted his voice in a

22

language which she did not know. The words boomed through the house like thunder.

"About the native witnesses, Bates," Bill was roaring. "Here's how to get the right men to hang, and the men who know! They all belong to a new secret society, and you can pick them because their tribal marks are blurred at the end by fresh scars!"

In the densely packed crowd of natives there was a sudden swirl. The thatch crashed as it was wrenched apart, and through the door—through any hole they could find or tear—a score of young men dove for the safety of the darkness which was swiftly sweeping across the land as the sun set. Fathers and brothers blocked the rush made by the police to catch the fugitives, and for ten seconds the end of house was pandemonium.

"You bloody fool! Must you yell out things like that in Melanesian?" Bates screamed.

"I'm not after black tools! To hell with them! Let the rest go!" Bill thundered.

Despite the confusion Mageen had made no effort to escape. Once more, the pearler had been out-generaled. But before the district officer could protest further, the planter whirled and burst through the thatched walls of the clubhouse, tumbling to the ground below exactly as the guilty blacks had done.

An angry shout from Bates followed him; an order to halt or be fired upon. Bellow Bill grunted contemptuously, and ripped trousers, singlet, and shirt from his body. Rolling away from the white clothing, he smeared his face and body with damp, black earth. Beyond him was a patch of light that came from the hole he had made in the thatch. Bates's shadow darkened it. He was leaning out, revolver in hand.

"Deuced suspicious, what?" the district officer was saying. "First he keeps the news from us, and now he scatters the witnesses! I'll be damned if I'll let the other natives go!"

Bill grunted with disgust. Bates's mind was hopelessly single-track. He was honest enough, brave enough, but blind except to the obvious. He would be satisfied to march Mageen back to a probable acquittal at Jesselton. Swiftly, the pearler crawled across the clearing to the rim of the depression in which the clubhouse stood and curled up under a thicket of pandamus from beneath which he cold see the lights of the village.

THE INACTIVITY was irksome. Drums were banging over in the village. Was it to summon courage or cover the retreat of the guilty? Bellow Bill could not tell, nor did he greatly care. *For the first time that day he was merely an observer.* For the first time, his movements could neither be foretold nor calculated. All day, events had gathered around him in a baffling manner and had been suddenly shot at him as at a target. Now he had withdrawn. The visible bull's-eyes were Bates and Alstair Potter.

To obtain this advantage, Bellow Bill had engineered the escape of the Bajaus marked with the thickened scar, trusting to the rifles of the constables to protect Alstair. Mageen had baffled him. Mageen's assistants might be less expert; and Bill was just as positive that the planter had assistants as that he was guilty. Not once, during the day, had he taken the aggressive personally. Throughout, he had relied, and by his refusal to escape he was still relying, upon an organization which seemed able to execute his commands as though it was able to read his mind. Bellow Bill hoped that he could watch the machinery at work, instead of being confronted, time after time, with a finished product.

The village was quieting down. Inside the thatched clubhouse Bates was preparing to defend his prisoners, during the hours of darkness. The light which had been burning in front of the idol was extinguished.

One by one, the constables took their rifles and dropped to the ground beneath the building.

For a long time the night was breathless and hot, and so still that Bill could hear the floor of the house creak whenever one of the prisoners changed his position.

The silence helped him. On a windy night he might not have been aware that the house was being surrounded. The first of the Bajaus sifted through the bush like ghosts. A twig cracked.

Leaves rustled here and there around the clearing. One man squirmed to the edge of the depression, within twenty feet of him; but despite Bill's vast experience in the bush, that one Bajau was all that he could locate. Instinct, as much as hearing, warned him of the others.

By contrast, the second wave of the attack was clumsy. While they were still at least a hundred yards away, Bill was aware that a small group was advancing from the village. They came purposefully, but at the rim of the little depression they halted.

The stillness was broken by the soft throb of a drum. Bellow Bill tensed for the charge. He meant to charge himself and cut through the natives from the rear—but not a Bajau stirred! The stillness following the drum beats was nerve racking. Even the defenders in the house expected an uproar, for Bill could hear the floor complain as some man shifted his weight.

Creak-creak! Creak! A pause. *Creak-creak! Creak-creak! Creak-creak!*

Again the throb of the drum. And again the man in the house stirred in response.—*Response!*

Bellow Bill started. He barely muffled an oath. Tag ends of knowledge unused since the World War, and now half forgotten, flashed through his mind. The creaking of the floor, with its single and double beats, was spelling words to answer the questions tapped out by the drum!

That was no nervous defender, but Mageen himself! So this was the way in which Mageen had given secret orders all day? By the tapping of a finger on the saddle horn; by the tap of a toe on the bungalow floor. The messages of the drums were incomprehensible; but having learned the wig-wag code in the war, Bill could make out the responses.

Two-one. Two-two-two.—That meant "No?"

"No," Mageen was telegraphing. "No... No... I will... Not alone... With gas... Yes... Yes."

THE MESSAGES ceased, leaving Bill little wiser. The noisy group retreated, and for a few minutes Bill hoped that Mageen had ordered a general retreat. The Bajaus, however, never stirred, and very soon the other group was back, panting in the stillness, staggering under a heavy load. They halted fifty feet from Bill, quite invisible, but through the dark came the unmistakable soft, hollow *blong* of a wrench against a steel barrel.

Bill set his teeth. "With gas" must have meant, With gasoline. The idea was characteristic of Mageen. Simple, and diabolically effective. A trickle of liquid down the slope beneath the thatched house, the touch of a match, and a river of flame would spread to the building and force the defenders to charge across the clearing and into the pitch black undergrowth where the circle of Bajaus waited with knives and spears. Bates and the six constables would be lucky if they as much as laid eyes on the natives who would butcher them. To escape, once the gasoline was lighted, would be impossible—and already it must be gushing from the barrel.

No time to give; no hope that Bates would understand a shout of warning. Bellow Bill roared as he leaped to his feet and charged, but it was the roar of a lion that turns on the hunters, all fury. A native rose in Bill's path, to scream and pitch back as a swing of Bill's heavy diver's knife ripped his chest.

The flash of a revolver stabbed through the bush, guiding Bill. He was hit as he made out the dim forms of a half a dozen men, but the shock of the bullet failed to stop him.

Before all could fire he was among them, flailing with knife and gun. He was hit again, as he burst through the group; but he hammered down one enemy with the revolver, and left two more on the ground, screaming from what his knife had done. Whirling, Bill charged back for the barrel. Men jumped aside for room to shoot. He let them go.

Quickly, he tipped the barrel over on its side so that the liquid sloshed out upon the ground and sent it rolling in the direction of the village, leaving a trail of gasoline behind it. Firing his gun off once more, with the muzzle close to the ground, he ignited the gas, so that it made a blazing path through the brush.

A bullet raked his side. Bill sprang back from ground that was aflame, to drop flat in the poor shelter of a bush.

Bullets from the clearing ripped the leaves around him. The constables were shooting wildly and recklessly.

"It's me—here!" Bill thundered. "Bates! Save your lead! Stand by for a rush!"

"Cease firing!" was the answer, clipped and incisive.

In the sudden silence, twigs snapped everywhere in the brush around the clearing.

A revolver was fired at Bill, missing him by inches.

"I say! You'd better retreat yourself, what?" shouted Bates, coolly enough. "Crawl in, old man. We'll cover you."

But in the flames that licked smokily from the damp earth, Bill could identify the three men he had dropped in his first rush. Their skins were stained brown, but they were white, and there was a scar on each chest! Conklin and Harris were dead from knife wounds, but Hammond, who had been felled by the gun, was unmarked. Hammond and Harris, the new-chums, men of whose innocence Bill had been positive. Grimly and in silence Bill waited for the gasoline to burn itself out. Bates called to him, and receiving no answer, ordered his constables to fire at will. In the undergrowth, the enemy with the revolver waited for Bill to move. That would be the Scotchman, McNab, who had been so anxious to sell out, and who was now more anxious to prevent Bill from making a prisoner of Hammond.

THE SMOKY flare of the gasoline was slow to disappear. Bill was bleeding severely. He expected at every instant to see a bullet crash through Hammond's brain, and he was a little surprised because none came. No wonder Alstair had observed that the pirates were armed with guns as well as knives! No wonder the planters had failed to wait, but had vanished that afternoon! All five of them were guilty; but with Conklin, Harris, and Kaffery dead, the survivors had more scapegoats to blame for the piracy.

No evidence connected McNab with the crime. The evidence against Mageen depended upon the credibility of Alstair and

Bill. Which was not enough, Bill decided. Who but himself had intercepted the message telegraphed by the creaking of the floor? Who would believe that a planter had mastered the language of the drums, which every scientist in the South Seas had tried in vain to learn?

To obtain a capital sentence against an Englishman, from an English judge, two strangers required evidence more tangible than a glimpse of a man's face and the creak of a bamboo slat in the darkness. Bill had promised Alstair speedy, intuitive American justice; not the deliberate process of British law, which might be satisfied with jailing Mageen as an accessory.

Ten feet away lay Hammond. McNab lurked only a few yards beyond. The flames continued to curl from the gasoline-soaked ground; but before the light flickered out the natives, momentarily shaken by the death of the planters, might rally.

The enormous strength of Bellow Bill made him deadly, in hand-to-hand combat, but he had never been an expert shot. Nevertheless, he rose to his full height, out of the brush, and leaped astride of Hammond's body, revolver raised, grimly determined to squeeze, not pull, the trigger.

McNab fired. Bill swayed as the bullet struck him. Mud-smeared, his naked, tattooed body was awful to see in the flickering light. His answering shot was slow, but he squeezed the trigger. His bullet cut through the leaves directly under the flash of McNab's gun—and the Scotchman did not fire again.

Slowly the pearler stooped.

"Fire high and fast, Bates!" he boomed. "I'm walking back—with a witness!"

Bill swung Hammond onto his back, and in that instant he experienced exultation and despair. Exultation because the flickering light revealed that the scar on the chest of the new-chum was false—built up of a dark, sticky gum which adhered to the skin. The gum, most likely, from a peraminium nut. Despair because for once Bill's vast physical strength, great enough to keep him on his feet after taking a bullet at close range, had betrayed him. The blow of Bill's revolver had crushed in the side of Hammond's head, and the witness was dead—as McNab had been able to see, though Bill had not.

CHAPTER V

HALF LIGHT

THE PEARLER HAD meant to swing Hammond onto his back. Instead, after the briefest hesitation, he hugged the limp body against his chest, covering the face with one huge, tattooed arm. Grimly he strode across the clearing, covered by the fire from the rifles. The natives had not rallied yet. Perhaps partly frightened by the sudden explosion of the empty gasoline barrel as the trail of flame caught up with it in the village.

A flickering greenish light still filtered through the underbrush against the broken thatch of the house walls, however.

"I say! A witness? How do you know he's a witness? Let me have him!" Bates ordered excitedly. "Unconscious, eh?"

"Oh, quite!" Bill rumbled.

With his knee he thrust the district officer back.

"You'd better stay and steady your constables. The natives aren't done. Where's Mageen?"

"Topside. Bound.—I left with girl guarding him, with my revolver. Needed every rifle—"

"Oh, quite!" Bill boomed. "Here—crape with your fingernail at the scar on this chap's chest"

"I say! It comes off!"

"Right!" Bill rumbled. "Put it in your pocket."

The pearler swung the limp body to the floor above, and heaved himself after it. "I'm hit, Bates," he explained. "I want the girl to bandage me. Be back in a minute."

The floor of the guest house was not as dark as the space

beneath. Patches of greenish light seeped through the rents in the thatch. Bill held Hammond against his chest and creaked across the floor toward Mageen, who reclined against the base of the idol with his hands bound in front. A yard away, Alstair sat cross-legged, a revolver in her lap.

"Hurt badly—Bill?" she whispered.

"Not bad enough," the pearler rumbled. "Never mind me. Get some water."

"There's none here!"

Bellow Bill was well aware of that. He was demanding water as an excuse to send Alstair away—and as a test. He stood just beyond a shaft of greenish light which crossed the room at the height of his waist. It revealed a dark stream of blood which trickled down his leg, and the limp, dangling arms and legs of Hammond. Above was dense shadow. Bill swayed.

"Get a canteen from one of the constables," he choked. "This chap I'm holding is a witness, and we've got to bring him to and make him talk!" Bill held his breath.

Alstair could see. Never yet had she missed a visible detail. Would she protest now; cry out that Hammond was dead and beyond aid?

She rose instantly, and started across the creaking floor.

"Wait!" Bill gasped. "Come back! Pull one of the scars off this chap's chest for me! I don't want to lay him down! That's right! Now hold the scar in the light, where Mageen can see it! That's fine! Look at it, Mageen! Look hard! This is Hammond I'm holding; and when the water gets here he'll talk!"

In suspense, Bill squeezed the "scar" till the stiff gum oozed around his finger tips. But the planter only snapped his teeth shut, and Alstair, by far the better observer, only turned away to get the water—though hesitantly.

"You're badly hurt, Bill!" she whispered. "Are you sure—it's all right?"

"Give me the revolver!" the pearler gasped. "Aye, it's all right! Don't hurry! I'm stronger than hell! I'll last!"

Alstair turned, but as she crossed the floor she ran. Bellow Bill staggered back a pace, and cocked the revolver.

"This is Hammond, Mageen!" he repeated hoarsely, as though he had not gasped out the same news before. "I heard you signal, too—with the floor—Gas, eh? You—like to play with fire—eh? Too bad for you—that I was too hard to kill—too hard…"

THE RUMBLING voice died to a croak. The limp body slipped from Bill's arms. He staggered and swayed, leaning farther and farther into the shaft of lurid light, his mouth open, fighting for balance, his eyes staring, striving at the last to pull the trigger of the gun. Instead, he crumpled on top of Hammond, at Mageen's feet.

With bound hands, the planter snatched the revolver.

"God! What to do!" he breathed fiercely. "They'll shoot me if I try to cross the clearing. This big tattooed ape lasted long enough to beat me! Even if I kill him and his damned witness! No—no, by God! He hasn't! And they won't shoot, the fools! God, if I had a knife, too!"

Mageen kicked Bill savagely, but the pearler never stirred.

"Dead!" Mageen gloated. "But I'll blow your head in to make certain—and Hammond's, too!—Ah!"

Alstair was running back with the canteen. She halted with a sharp cry of alarm as Mageen levelled the revolver at her breast.

"Scream all you like!" he snarled. "I'll drop you if you move! Bates, do you hear? I've got the gun! I'll kill the girl if you move—and if your men move."

There was an oath from below.

"I say! Can he?" Bates grated.

"Yes!" whispered Alstair.

"Walk forward!" Mageen snarled. "Take that idol in your arms. I'll need it. Do you hear, Bates? I'm going to fire two shots as a signal to you. Then I'll jump down into the clearing with the girl, and run with her into the bush. I'll let her go there—but if you shoot at me on the way, it's your own gun, full cocked, that's against her back! I'll kill her, even though there's a bullet in my own brain!"

"I shan't shoot," Bates answered steadily. "But I'll run you down and hang you later!"

"Will you?" Mageen shrilled. "You conceited fool! I know more about natives than any man living! What other white man has ever formed a native society of his own? I did! First for profit, and then for power—and you never heard a rumor of it in Jesselton! Even my white neighbors dared not speak, when they went to town, for at first they were afraid of what I would do to their friends, left here behind when I heard that they had snitched. As I would have heard, too, and did hear! And later, they joined me—because I gave them a choice of joining or being killed…

"Run me down?" Mageen laughed jeeringly. "You won't be able to get a native to admit that he has seen me, though I passed months ago. They *fear* me—fear me, Bates! It amuses me to be feared; to be a king and a half God, beyond any law. Why, I have killed natives as I pleased.

"Even that sport grew tame, when a wandering white man hinted at a better game—a yacht. That would prove my power, and I needed money. You wouldn't have heard a whisper of that, either, Bates, if Hammond hadn't turned soft-bellied. He pulled me away from the girl, and—I thought the fire would make her safe enough. I would have been all right, except for this tattooed sailor, who had more courage than brains—and who wasn't so hard for a bullet to kill, as he boasted!

"Are you ready, Bates? I'll fire two shots as a signal. And remember, nothing—not even the arrest of a pirate—is worth the life of a white girl!"

Mageen pressed the revolver against Bill's head and pressed the trigger.

There was no report, but the touch of steel galvanized the pearler into action. A tattooed fist crashed against Mageen's jaw, hurling him backward, consternation stamped on his features.

The clay idol slipped from Alstair's grasp, and breaking, spilled the money and jewels taken from the yacht over the two men.

"But he didn't shoot!" Alstair cried.

"How the devil could he shoot, when I packed the frame of the gun full of paraminium gum, between the hammer and the firing pin?" boomed Bellow Bill, sitting up.

"*I* tried to pull the trigger before I let him have the gun, and I couldn't! And I'm a damned sight stronger than he!—Carry him out where his natives can see him, Bates, and tell them that his own scar of hell is the thing that will hang him. They'll run away—if *I* know natives!" Which Bellow Bill did.

THE JUNGLE MASTER

*Bellow Bill Williams, South Seas pearler, enters the bush
for a finish fight with a deadly master of jungle craft*

CHAPTER I

THE BLOODY HEAD

NAKED BLACK CANNIBALS with brutish faces and enormous mops of frizzled, kinky hair waded from a schooner to the beach, each man bowed beneath the weight of a steel pipe to be used for hydraulic mining. The savages lived in a huge communal longhouse thatched with the sun-dried leaves of the sago palm. Their most precious possessions were human heads. They fought with stone axes, poisoned darts, and spears horribly barbed with hardened wood and bone. The pipe they carried was the most modern, up-to-date product of the draughting rooms and furnaces of Birmingham.

And that contrast was New Guinea.

Down the hillside to the beach pressed the jungle, matted, steaming in the heat, fecund; so thick that it seemed that it would crowd the narrow strip of sand back into the sea. Yet on the beach stood a slender, middle-aged little white man with a clear cut, intellectual face, and a girl whose hair was a warm brown, like oak leaves touched by the autumn frosts.

Similarity of feature marked the pair as father and daughter. Both wore patched and threadbare khaki; yet despite the shabby clothing they carried themselves like a king and his princess. The pipe was theirs. With it they would rip gold from the jungle first, and in the end make jungle and cannibals leap ahead to civilization.

And that was New Guinea, too. Stanley Morrison and his daughter Peggy looked feeble in contrast with the savages. Easy to kill—but while they lived they would conquer. The look that marks the true pioneer was on each face.

Bellow Bill Williams, leaning on the rail of the schooner, knew that look. He was a pearling skipper and a sailor, mostly. He stood six feet three in bare feet, and weighed two hundred and forty pounds, all hard muscle. Tattooing covered him from wrist to shoulder and chin to waist. Outwardly he was not at all like the Morrisons. To see the savages grunt under lengths of pipe that couldn't weigh much over a hundred and fifty pounds amused him, but at the scanty heap of supplies piled on deck to be carried ashore he was not amused at all.

This man Morrison had spent the last of his dust on machinery. There wasn't even enough tea in the supplies to last a month, and there hadn't been enough gold dust left after he'd paid Bill the freight to color the palm of the pearler's huge hand. The lean little guy was gambling with the jungle to the last pinch of his resources, and the girl was backing him up.

Bellow Bill liked that. In the long run, what does grub amount to? A pioneer can pull a belt tight. For the machinery which conquers the jungle there is no substitute. This jungle would be licked—because a slender little man and a young girl dared to match what they knew against starvation and fever and loneliness. Why, they had eyes for nothing except their precious pipe! They were smiling at each other like happy kids!

Bill did not feel a stranger to the pair at that moment. He liked to see people like that; and because he was watching, not day dreaming, he was the first to see the other New Guinea cannibals who leaped out of the jungle.

THEY RUSHED without warning, eight or ten blacks, shoulder to shoulder, brandishing clubs of stone. The porters dropped the steel pipes and ran. Morrison had only time to step in front of his daughter. The savages broke over the little man like a wave. A pile of black bodies and swinging, jabbing clubs sprang up where he had stood. One black bounded on, caught the girl by the throat, and flung her heavily to the sand.

*Like an ant heap
the cannibals
rolled apart*

Bellow Bill roared. That booming, deep-throated war-cry awoke the jungle echoes a mile away. It was no more to be ignored than the roar of a charging lion. The savage bending over the girl looked up. His club was raised, but Bill had vaulted the rail, dashed through the shallows, and was sprinting along the beach with a speed amazing for so big a man. The huge tattooed hands swung empty—until at full stride Bill snatched a length of pipe from the sand and heaved it over his shoulder as though it weighed no more than a pole.

With a shrill howl the savage raised his club to parry. As well attempt to parry the swing of a derrick boom!

"Ha!" Bill roared. He scarcely felt the impact of the pipe on the woolly skull. The weight of his own blow spun him clear around, the pipe swinging in the air—but the savage was stretched flat, head cracked like an egg.

"Ha!" Bill thundered. Digging in his heels, he swung ponderously at the heap of men who covered Morrison. Two savages had the misfortune to be on top of the pile. The pipe mashed the face of one, and sent the second sprawling with a broken neck.

Like an ant heap the pile rolled apart. One savage, in sheer panic, leaped at Bill. The pearler kicked him back with his knee, and whirled the pipe for a third blow—only to let it fly from his hands because none of the cannibals were still within its sweep. Even Bill's strength could not hurl such a missile far. It struck no one, but the thud of the weight on the sand lent wings to the flight of the savages. They dove into the jungle.

Three were left dead on the beach. One, whom Bill had kicked, lay writhing. The writhing annoyed Bill. With a stone war club he tapped the man over the head, just hard enough to stretch him senseless, and knelt beside the girl.

HER EYES were wide with horror and amazement, but she tried to smile and pointed to her chest. She would be all right when the breath knocked from her lungs returned. Morrison, however, was badly hurt. Both arms were broken, probably because he had thrown them over his head to protect himself from the clubs. The act had saved his life, but he had taken a terrible beating. There were bruises on the lean chest and body that made Bill look grave.

"Peggy?" Morrison gasped.

"She's all right. Lie still, old-timer," Bill rumbled. His speaking voice had the deep bass note of a far-off surf. "I'll carry you aboard the schooner. It'll be three days' sail to a doctor, but I can set your arms."

"No. Can't leave—yet!" whispered the little man. "My partner and his mate—Cogswell and Fitch—are back in the bush at the diggings. Can't leave—till I find out—about them."

"I get you," Bill rumbled. "Though you mean your partners, don't you?"

"Partner," Morrison insisted. He was gray with pain, but his eyes were steady. He knew what he was talking about. "Cogswell made the discovery. Fitch wasn't with him at that time, so Cogswell wouldn't give him a share, though they usually work together. I bought a half interest. With my last shilling… Peggy! Please go away a moment. I must talk to this sailor—alone!"

"You can talk right out, dad. I also noticed that the savages who attacked us were from the same tribe—the same men, in fact—who were working peaceably for us at the diggings this morning." She smiled at Bill. "Though I don't suppose the skipper here realizes what that implies."

"I do, though," Bill rumbled. "They attacked your partner and his buddy, and, being savages, decided to take your heads too. Or—"

"Or they took our partner's money. A few ax heads and a bolt or two of calico is a cheap price for Cogswell to pay for two murders that would give him a gold mine," Peggy finished quietly. "That's what you didn't want me to hear, wasn't it, dad?"

The injured man stirred.

"Partly," he admitted. "I'm not a fool. Cogswell's got my capital. I'm an engineer, and he's had the use of my brains. I've built the dam, and surveyed the pipe line. Any jungle prospector can bolt the pipe together. I'm not needed any more. And yet I can't accuse him until I go and see. If he did lose his temper and shoot a native or something I can't desert him!"

"Cogswell," said Peggy earnestly, "knows the jungle. We're new-chums compared to him, dad. He's mastered every trick. For fifteen years he claims he's been a prospector among cannibals. I believe him, too. He told me once he was going to get enough gold to live like a lord for the rest of his life. A lifelong spree—and he knows how much money that would take. Lose his temper? Not he!"

PEGGY PAUSED. "But what can you do?" she demanded. "You may be injured internally. You can't wait long, even though the skipper here can set bones like a surgeon."

"Not far from it. I've had the practice in that sort of doctoring" Bill rumbled.

"I must wait!" said Morrison. He could not even raise himself on an elbow, but with his eyes alone he seized the center of the stage. "If I die, the Resident may do something for you, Peggy. Though damn, damn little! What can the law do in the jungle? I can't die, and I won't! Will you wait here, skipper, till my arms knit? I'll charter your schooner for a month! I've got to go into the bush and fight it out with Cogswell! I've got to *know* whether he's double crossing me or on the square!"

"Why?" Bill boomed.

"Because my last shilling is locked up in gold that's still in the dirt," said Morrison. His teeth were clenched, but his voice was even. "I won't go to a hospital and run up a big bill. I won't leave Peggy alone and broke in the South Seas, with that bill to pay as best she can!"

"I'm not afraid!"

"Women that aren't afraid are hurt worst of all," said the father briefly. The eyes were on Bill.

"You understand, skipper. Sooner or later I've got to go into that jungle and find Cogswell, or his head! The jungle is fighting for him, and knowing the bush like a book, as he damn well does, he damn well knows it! He can wait till I come to him. If I come back with police he can wait till they leave, and then shoot me in the back. He figures I'm afraid, and I'll damn well stay here in your schooner and prove to him I'm not, till I'm strong enough to prove it on his bearded face!"

"You'll never be strong enough," Bill rumbled. "Brave women ain't the only ones that get hurt worst." The eyes of the helpless man glared. The deep, rumbling voice softened. "Sometimes nerve is no good without heft," said Bill. "I'm granting you nerve, mister. I watched you step out to die not fifteen minutes back. No man could have moved more prompt. My point is that not even to save your life and the girl's here could you have picked up one of those pipes."

Bellow Bill reached to his left hip pocket and filled his cheek with fine-cut tobacco.

"You're plain damn right and you're plain too damn little!" he growled. "If your partner and his buddy are square, we've got to get to them; and if they ain't, we've got to find them double. So I'll put you on the schooner and doctor you up, and come dark, I'll hit the trail. If I ain't back by the next sunset you ought to be able to sail to port somehow. All you got to do is follow the coast."

Morrison stared upward, speechless. Peggy leaped to her feet.

"But you're a sailor! Cogswell knows the jungle!" she protested. "Don't you understand? Why, by killing these natives you've involved yourself in a blood feud with the whole tribe! Any man of them will kill you on sight! It's—it's not your place to go!"

"You've mentioned that Cogswell was a master of the jungle till it's kind of gotten my goat," Bill boomed. "I ain't followed the sea all my days myself… Blood feuds? Why, sure, I know. You'll need to hire a different tribe of savages anyhow to get out that gold."

"But what do you want? What share?" snapped Morrison.

"I never reckon profit in advance," Bill rumbled. Slowly he grinned. Golden lights were beginning to dance in his eyes, but he spoke with embarrassment. "I guess I want to see fair play, mostly. You've got nerve, you two. I'd like to see you have the chance to use it in the kind of fight you're fitted for, and understand. Now tell me: what kind of hombre is this Cogswell, and what's the lay of the land? Who's Taipi? Is there one tribe of cannibals hereabouts, or several? Their clubs I've seen, but do they use bows and arrows, or poison darts?"

CHAPTER II

THE BARB ON THE SPEAR

AT MIDNIGHT BELLOW Bill hit the trail. That bushmen as expert as Cogswell and Fitch had been unable to reach the sea after so long a delay was evidence that they were either in league with the natives or had been killed. Bill's task was to discover which. He was also resolved to give the tribe which had assaulted Morrison such a lesson that in the future attacks on white men would be tabu.

While waiting for darkness, Bill made Morrison comfortable, put the schooner in such shape that Peggy could defend it, and learned all that he could about the locality and the white and black men in the jungle.

The gold diggings and the Papuan village of which Taipi was headman were in a bowl-shaped valley about a mile from the sea. A stream ran through it, dammed at the head of the valley to provide power for the hydraulic monitor. Off to the left, or west, was a much smaller Papuan village, of which Peggy knew nothing save that the name of the headman was Pahea, since Taipi had refused to share the profits of labor at the diggings with a rival tribe.

Both Cogswell and Fitch were tall, sinewy, fever-bitten men, but Cogswell was bearded, Fitch clean shaven.

"Cogswell," said Peggy evenly, "never looked at me as though I were so much flesh when he thought I was watching. Fitch never stripped me naked with his eyes at all. He's much nicer than Cogswell, really, but he's not a leader. Just the partner. The lieutenant. If double crossing was done, Cogswell did it, and Fitch merely backed the play, just as he'd agree to anything Cogswell proposed.

"Though after all that doesn't really tell you very much about them, does it?"

"More than you might think!" Bill rumbled. "And the Papuans use clubs, spears, and poisoned darts, eh? How often did Cogswell, or Fitch, clean his gun?"

"Why—never, that I can remember!"

"Then neither of them fancies himself as a shot," Bill rumbled. "I don't clean my firearms often either. I never could hit anything at long range anyhow, so what difference does a little rust in the barrel make? You better use that sawed-off pump gun, if you have to use anything."

The pearler rose and went below to make his preparations.

To Peggy these were strange to see. Despite the sultry heat, Bellow Bill appeared most anxious to protect himself against cold!

When he came on deck at midnight he was wearing heavy trousers of blue serge, a thick woolen coat, and over all, like a cape, a dark blanket, one corner of which was sewn into a pointed hood.

On his back he strapped a five gallon can of gasoline. In his pocket he put a half stick of dynamite, capped and fused. For arms he took a foot-long deep sea diver's knife, a revolver—and a four-foot length of chain, with strips of cloth drawn through the links so that it would not clink when he walked.

"You'll melt carrying all that!" Peggy protested. "That is, if you don't die first of prickly heat. For heaven's sake, why the chain?"

"All your doing, gal," Bill grinned. "You've given Cogswell such a reputation I figure I'd better sweat water than blood. The chain? Why, the blow of a club can be parried. If I hit with a chain, though, the end curls over the edge of a shield and cracks the head behind it."

"And you're lugging all that paraphernalia for some definite reason like that?"

"Every piece of gear is the master notion of some uncommonly able scrapper that I've met and suffered from," he purred. "It's the fruit of fifteen years and more of South Sea trouble that I'm packing on my back. Anything less would be disrespectful, since I'm callin' on the headman of a big village and a master of the jungle."

WITH THE utmost cheerfulness Bill swung himself over the rail of the schooner, carrying the heavy load like a feather. Peggy could see him while he waded to the beach, but once he crossed the sand he vanished, for the dark clothing merged with the night black foliage.

He avoided the beaten trail. Twisting through the trees, 'dark as a hole, and scarcely wider than his shoulders, the trail put him at the mercy of any savage who chanced to be squatting beside it, and also advertised his coming, for he would be unable to avoid brushing against the leaves.

Bill's road was the stream. Here there was more light, or rather a strip less dark overhead, for the jungle grew to the very bank, like a wall. At night the stream was a black cañon some twenty feet wide. Bill could not be reached by a spear, and the tangle of vines which laced the trees together prevented a concerted rush such as had overwhelmed Morrison.

The vines were his allies. Any movement in the jungle below would be communicated to the tree-tops. He advanced slowly, head thrown back. Jungle flowers have no perfume, but on a sultry night the unwashed bodies of cannibals smell. In a jungle duel the fatal indiscretion is to walk, unwarned, within arm's length of your enemy.

For nearly a mile—which required an hour of slow advance—not a leaf stirred. The stream began to flow faster. The black walls of vine shrouded trees drew closer together. Bill decided he was close to the bowl-shaped valley and the village. Ahead, against the sky, a branch swayed suddenly and dipped toward the earth.

It was enough. Bill stopped, snuggled his head deeper into the hood, and drew the blanket closer around his shoulders. Step by step he retreated, angling toward the opposite side of the brook. He meant to squirm through a gap in the foliage, to count his enemies as they crossed the stream, and to scatter them if they dared to follow him up the bank.

He found a suitable gap in the vines. The opening was barred by half a dozen of the terribly barbed Papuan spears, the butts driven into the bank, the points slanting toward him.

For an instant the sweat which bathed Bill turned cold. A new-chum might have been tempted to push those spears aside. Not he. The barbs were too likely to be smeared with poison. His path of retreat from the ambuscade which had been laid ahead had been blocked in advance—which was better tactics, much better, than Papuans usually displayed. They left him the choice of running the gantlet ahead or toddling back home.

He did neither. He strode to a bowlder near the center of the stream and squatted down beside it, wishing grimly that the water were deep enough to cover all of him but his nose. Beneath the blanket he gripped the revolver, and the length of chain. They would wonder what he was doing, squatting down like a frog in the middle of a brook. They would also have to chose among their weapons. Which?

Along both banks a quiver ran through the vines. Huddled beneath the blanket Bill felt a succession of impacts light as the touch of a moth's wings. He shivered, sunk his hooded head against his breast, and pressed his bare hands between his knees. Poisoned arrows! Blow gun darts, thorns tipped with fluff, dozens and dozens of them, burying smeared points in the thick wool.

Years ago he had escaped death in such a fusillade because he had happened to be wearing a coat. The blanket was better protection than a coat, but to wait, to crouch in the water while the darts struck, took all his nerve. Sweating, he counted seconds. The poison would act instantly. Eight... nine... ten...

THOUGH HE had felt no thorn-prick, he kicked out spasmod-ically, cried out, and let himself slump flat in the stream with a hollow groan. That flight of darts would have killed any Papuan warrior. These savages would be expecting him to die. The brav-est of them would come out to take his head.

One was already writhing through the vines into the stream. Another followed, and another. They had almost reached him when he hurled the blanket aside and leaped up at their feet. The chain and the knife each claimed a victim. The third warrior turned with a howl and sped upstream.

Bill charged after him. For the first ten yards he was careful not to overtake the man. Afterward his heavy clothing and the weight of the gasoline on his back let the warrior gain. At the point where he had seen the branch move a spear flashed by his head, but that was the only attempt at counter attack. In the rear the Papuans were yelling—to keep their own courage up. They were squirming through the vines into the stream, but they were not pursuing. They had shot poison into this huge enemy, and he had risen and slain their bravest. For a time they would be satisfied to yell—and stay where they were.

The pearler scrambled up a ridge of stone over which the stream tumbled. Right and left the jungle opened out. Close ahead were three small tents, farther off a dark mass toward which the warrior pursued by Bill fled, yelling at every jump. That must be Taipi's village.

A torch was kindled, throwing a red glare in the high arched entrance of the longhouse of the warriors. The savages were wakening, answering shout with shout. Bill sprinted toward the tents. A glance inside each was enough. Nothing had been looted, though to Taipi's savages a steel pickax or even the tin cans scattered about represented a fortune. There had been no fight at the diggings. Cogswell and Fitch were, in all probabil-ity, still alive.

Promptly Bill retreated, seeking the path that left the valley on the left. He no longer ran. In the darkness a faint foot-trail would be hard to find. Around the longhouse the yelling was gaining in volume, and in courage. The survivors of the ambuscade were joining their kinsmen, but though another torch had been kindled, neither light was moving out into the fields.

Bill skirted a patch of stunted sugar cane. The valley was small, scarcely two hundred yards in diameter, rimmed by cliffs, but he trusted to the concealment of darkness, forgetting the tin can on his back. The flash and bark of a rifle from the sugar cane and the whine of a bullet past his head revealed his error.

Bill emptied his revolver at the flash, backing toward the brush.

There was no answering shot. Bill crouched and reloaded his gun. Nothing moved in the sugar cane. In the longhouse the shouting ceased momentarily. Bill grinned. Inch by inch, on hands and knees, he continued to circle the valley until he found the path mentioned by Peggy.

Once he was in the jungle again, where the path began to climb toward the valley rim, he rose. It would be a brave man indeed, white or black, who dared to follow him down this tunnel twisting through the darkness. He hoped he had killed one of the prospectors. Preferably Cogswell.

CHAPTER III

THE SURVIVOR

AS HE groped his way forward he also hoped that the rival Papuan villages were not at all friendly, and yet not so recently at war as to have man-traps dug in the path. There was no longer an alternative route, nor a practical retreat, for that matter.

Bill was gambling on the fact that Papuan villages are usually hostile, even when they are located close together. Very often they will speak languages that are mutually incomprehensible, using words of similar sound with meanings that are totally different. With Taipi's warriors Bill had a blood feud. In Pahea's village that fact, if it were known at all, would mean precisely nothing. Bellow Bill would merely be a strange white man.

From the jungle he emerged at last into a small clearing. A longhouse loomed beyond, dark as ink, but Bill did not deceive himself with the belief that all these warriors were asleep. Rather, as he crossed the open ground and halted fifty feet from the gaping entrance, he wished that he still had his blanket.

"*Sambio!*" he bellowed in his enormous voice. "*Sambio!* Peace!"

There was no answer. Bellow Bill expected none. There was no flight of darts, either; no spear flung.

Only silence. Fifty feet away naked men were gripping weapons, wondering whether this stranger who hailed them was weak enough to be killed in safety, or whether, if he were strong, he did come in peace.

Bill unscrewed the cap of the can on his back and scattered gasoline in a ring. He flung down a lighted match, and stood the next instant in a circle of leaping flame. From the longhouse came a guttural exclamation.

"*Sambio! Dim-dim puri-puri!*" Bill rumbled, which meant that he came in peace, and was a white magician. "*Sambio—Pahea!*"

The name of the headman brought an answer.

"*S-sambio!*" came a voice out of the dark; nervous, but unwilling to confess fear. A torch, thrust into the embers of the longhouse fire, commenced to spark and flare. The instant there was light Bill vaulted onto the platform of poles which stretched like a porch in front of the arched doorway. Behind a screen of palm leaves crouched a score of Papuans. Spears were leveled. Had Bill hesitated the spears would have met in his body. He shouldered toward the headman. Big as Bill was, the can on his back made him seem larger. Not until Pahea recoiled a pace did he halt. Then he held out a fistful of the fine-cut chewing tobacco, and filled his own cheek. Hesitantly the cannibal accepted the gift. Face to face they stood, spitting in turn. The circle of warriors squirmed nearer.

"Me cross along Taipi!" Bill boomed. "Me make *dim-dim puri-puri* along him. *Puri-puri* make Taipi and fellow belong along Taipi run seven bells! You fellows come along me, spear Taipi, spear fellow belong Taipi when they run. You fellows get tobacco, get ax, get calico."

In the torchlight the warriors grinned. Bill was promising easy victory, loot, and riches, Pahea, however, looked doubtful.

"Taipi *kai kai* too many fellows belong me," he objected. "Me fright along him too much! Too many fellows belong Taipi for *puri-puri.*"

Gravely Bellow Bill spat. He could hardly blame the headman for doubting that any magic could make an entire village take to its heels. Yet allies he must have to mop up in case he won a victory.

"What name!" he scoffed. "You fellows walk about along me. Watch *puri-puri. Puri-puri* too much, spear Taipi. *Puri-puri* no good, you fellows run back here little bit!"

No risk, and an easy retreat. Significantly he shook the can on his shoulders. The gasoline sloshed. To Bill's delight a warrior in the circle spoke up, urging acceptance, by his tone. At once one of the interminable arguments which precede action by savages was in progress.

IGNORANT OF the language though he was, Bill could follow the round. There were only a few ideas, repeated over and over by different individuals. He was undoubtedly a most potent magician. Yes, but was he potent enough? They wanted the trade goods, and to eat Taipi. Yes, but Taipi might eat them. No, for Taipi could not catch them.

Bill relaxed, and squatted on his heels. Though Pahea was still opposed to the expedition, some of the warriors would be sure to join him when they had talked themselves out.

Talk, talk, talk. The torch spluttered and dripped sparks. A second was kindled. Talk, talk, talk.

"Ahoy there!" rang a voice out of the darkness—speaking English.

Bill leaped up, dominating the circle of savages.

"Who is it?" he roared before Pahea could reply.

"Cogswell!" came the answer. "For God's sake, mate, don't keep me out here!"

With Pahea watching him, Bill could not show either amazement or anxiety. He motioned for the torch to be moved to the edge of the platform.

"Walk into the light, then!" he boomed. "And move slow!"

It was Cogswell. A brown beard covered his face. He walked with bent knees, and long arms swinging from powerful shoulders, like a gorilla. His clothing was in rags. He was hatless, and—without a weapon. He swung himself onto the platform, a pipe gripped in his bearded lips, and started toward Bill, apparently oblivious of the spears, and of the fact that the pearler's hand was on the butt of a revolver.

"Sit down!" Bill rumbled. He motioned to the opposite side of the circle. "Where's Fitch?"

"You ought to know. You shot him," Cogswell muttered. "Thank God I got to you! That longhouse is howling hell. Taipi's taken Fitch's head, an' they're having a dance before they eat him. I skipped when they brought him in, before they could remember that two heads would look better than one."

"That so?" Bill rumbled.

Cogswell scowled and chewed on the empty pipe.

"I'm here, ain't I?" he said. "If you don't believe me you can go to hell, sailor! I guess I can make the beach. I've lived in the jungle since I was a kid, and I know a few back trails that ain't watched."

"Why didn't you use them?"

"Gor'bli'me!" snarled the prospector violently. "Are you getting the wind up? Because I know what happened down on the beach this afternoon, that's why! When the war party came back—them that could move—Fitch told me. Over a gun. We was working on the claim and he held me up. He had no share in the mine, and he figured he was going to get one."

"Why didn't you give him one at the start?" Bill rumbled. "There was enough gold."

"The hell there was! There's never enough!" Cogswell snarled. He leaned forward in the torchlight, the pipe hanging from his teeth. "I've prospected the jungle fifteen years. I've cleaned out plenty of pockets in my time. I've figured I was a millionaire, and wot happened, eh? The vein pinches out, or I wash the gravel to bed rock! I live like a lord a few months, and with the taste of real living in my mouth I come back to the bush again! Gold enough, hell! There's enough while it's in the ground, and when it's out how can I know it'll be enough? I want all I can get! I found this claim. Fitch didn't. Why should I give him a cut?"

"I get you," Bill boomed.

"Well, did you think I was a preacher?" Cogswell snarled. "Morrison's nothing but a toff! If Fitch had scragged him he could have had his share. He didn't, and he's long pig now. Fineesh. Wot I want to know is, 'oo's share did Morrison give you for coming in here? Mine, I'll lay!"

"We didn't decide," Bill rumbled.

"Gor'bli'me, you'd have decided damn soon if I'd hit the back trails alone!" Cogswell growled. "I'm no fool! Fitch and me was mates. Naturally anybody'd figure we was working together. It's my gold I'm thinking about. I got to do something to prove this was Fitch's show, and I figure guiding you back is it." He paused, the pipe working in the heavy, bearded jaws.

" 'Ow you got through I can't see. Fitch wasn't a new-chum. Don't know that I've ever seen a cove like you, anyhow. That can, now. Wot's the lay?"

"Why, come along and see," Bill invited. "Either you're telling the truth or you've got nerve, mister. I don't know which, or greatly care. Back trails and gold claims don't matter to-night. Neither you nor Morrison is going to work that valley now that Taipi's topped off a blood feud with long pig."

"A squad of police an' a little dynamite will fix that!" Cogswell scoffed.

"A black with a spear along a trail you pick will fix me," Bill rumbled. "Dynamite and a rush at dawn might fix a girl, too. I'm playing too chancy a game to be sensible, mate. I'm right obliged that you joined me. You'll help me a lot by coming along with me—with your hands tied."

"You've got a gun," Cogswell scowled. "Gor'bli'me, I never did meet a cove like you! Think you can get these blacks to back you and wipe Taipi out, wot?"

"Sure. It's no great trick to lead savages to war and loot once you get them talking," Bill rumbled.

Cogswell shrugged, leaned forward, and drew a deep breath. Of acquiescence, Bellow Bill believed, confident in his arms and his vastly superior physical strength.

Sharply Cogswell blew through the pipestem. A cloud of red pepper flew into Bill's eyes.

BLINDLY BILL hurled himself at the spot where Cogswell had been sitting. As he leaped he collided violently with the prospector, and realized that the latter sprang as instantly to attack him. They fell together, but Cogswell squirmed out of Bill's grip. The stuff in Bill's eyes burned like acid. He was sneezing in paroxysms. Blindly he flailed his arms, not daring to use knife or chain in that crowd of sneering natives.

One wild swing struck Cogswell—in the shoulder, but it knocked him sprawling.

"Spear one dim-dim fella!" Bill thundered.

One of the savages must have tried, for there was a curse, a thud of feet as Cogswell leaped from the platform to the ground, and a few seconds later the crack of a rifle shot and a cry from a native.

Bill threw himself flat, and pawed grimly at his eyes. The one shot—or that fact that Bill had dropped out of sight—seemed to satisfy Cogswell. At least the yelling of the savages ceased. A warrior scrambled up onto the platform, saying something.

"One fellow dim-dim got away?" Bill rumbled, guessing the truth from the bitter tone. He was handed a wet rag, which was all he could expect, for there is little water kept in a longhouse. He swabbed his eyes, and blinked painfully.

The wounded savage gripped a bleeding arm. Three or four men were wiping their eyes, but the rest—among them Pahea—were staring at Bill. With a shaking forefinger the headman pointed at Bill's shoulder.

"Got *puri-puri* too much!" he gasped. "Hit fellow when no see fellow! He hit along you! You hit along him too much!"

"Hell, I didn't land on him!" Bill growled disgustedly. "He sure had his nerve with him! He—"

The booming growl died to a gasp. Into the padding at the shoulder of Bill's coat was thrust a three-inch sliver of bamboo, with a bit of gum on the end, so that it might be held in a clenched fist. The poison on the silver gleamed in the torchlight like molasses.

Not a muscle in Bill's face quivered. He withdrew the sliver and snapped it away into the darkness, but inwardly he thanked his stars that he had taken the aggressive instinctively and instantly. Had he stopped to paw at his eyes first Cogswell would have driven that sliver into his face, or his throat. He would be a dead man now—and with a shock he realized that he had let slip the fact that Peggy was the sole defender of the schooner. Why hadn't he been quick-witted enough to lie, to claim that there was a crew aboard?

Cogswell was gold-mad and jungle poison. That the man was brave Bill conceded—but with what a cold, snakelike courage!

"We fellows walk about along you. Watch *puri-puri. Kai-kai* Taipi!" Pahea was saying.

"You'd better!" Bill rumbled with heartfelt earnestness. "If you don't that guy will swallow us all!"

CHAPTER IV

THE KAPIRAVI

FROM THE SIZE of the longhouse in the cuplike valley, Bellow Bill estimated that Cogswell could rely upon the aid of at least fifty warriors. He himself advanced to the attack with less than thirty, knowing exceedingly well that he could not rely upon them if his prestige and their belief in his invincibility were shaken.

Bill had the advantage of the initiative, and that was all. As he led the way down the cliffs he was grimly amused to hear a palaver in progress in Taipi's longhouse. Even Cogswell could not force savages to act without a preliminary council.

Yet as the pearler halted at the fringe of the jungle and instructed Pahea to place his warriors in ambush around the clearing, Bill felt too much alone. Too much depended on his strength and experience, for while he had been advancing to the attack Cogswell had not been idle.

The tents at the diggings had been set afire, and still glowed in three patches of embers. What was worse, a ring of torches had been thrust in the earth all around Taipi's longhouse, about thirty feet from the thatched walls. Light flickered across the clearing, and beat up into the arched, overhanging entrance forty feet high, twenty feet wide, blackened at the bottom by a low screen of palm branches, and with bundles of leaves swinging in the gap above to frighten evil spirits.

The flickering light made the longhouse a fort. To charge across the open ground was to be a target for blow-gun darts.

"*Puri-puri* belong your work quick?" Pahea whispered doubtfully.

"Yep!" Bill growled. He couldn't wait. His allies, spread in a thin ring, would lose faith and withdraw. To-morrow Cogswell would have the initiative.

Bill slipped the can of gasoline from his shoulders and tied the rope with which it had been bound to his back to the handle. He had about ten feet of rope, and he hoped most earnestly that that would be enough. If he made too plain a target of himself, Cogswell would shoot him. He could advance to the edge of the torchlight, which was sixty or seventy feet from the gaping entrance. That was too far; but if he failed he could retreat to the sea and get Peggy away.

With a handkerchief he bound the half stick of dynamite to the can, lit the fuse, and ran forward.

At once a rifle cracked. The target was the spluttering end of the fuse, but the bullet was close. Bill reached the spot he had selected, and stopped. The second bullet was almost close enough to part his hair. Grimly he set his heels in the earth and started to swing the can around his head by the rope. All his attention was centered on the high arch of the entrance to the longhouse.

The spark of the burning fuse traced circles in the air, higher and higher from the ground, moving faster and faster. Bill no longer heard the rifle shots. He whirled the heavy can till the sinews of his enormous arms began to crack, whirled thrice, and with a sob torn from his vast chest by the prodigious effort, let go.

Flat on his face he dropped, gasping. A tiny spark arched through the air. There was a clang of tin—on the floor of the longhouse. He had done it! Breathless, he waited for the explosion.

THE CRASH of the dynamite was not loud. Within the longhouse a white man shouted, half with surprise, half with relief that the bomb was so feeble. The thatched walls of the longhouse were not even broken. The bundles of leaves in the arch, hung to keep out evil spirits, merely swayed in the blast, and hung still.

On hands and knees Bellow Bill crept back.

"*Puri-puri* only little bit!" Pahea whispered dismally.

"Wait!" Bill boomed.

For all the light which flickered on the gaping entrance no longer came from the torches. Blazing drops of gasoline, scattered far and wide by that seemingly feeble explosion, were eating into the thatch at a thousand points—setting the thatch afire on the inside, where it was dry despite the incessant rains of New Guinea. Little red eyes began to glow in the dark arch of the entrance. The start of a thousand fires, spreading high overhead, hard to reach with buckets of water, too numerous to smother with wet rags. A spark dropped to the floor—the first drop in what would be a rain of red-hot embers falling on naked skins.

"They'll be out" Bill boomed. "*I* came out, when that stunt was pulled on me!" He raised his voice. "Thanks for the torches, Cogswell!" he roared. "Come on out, mother-naked and with your fingers spread so you can't hide another sliver, and I'll try to call off my gang!"

"Ho, yuss?" came the answer. "Ter 'ell with yer and yer blyze! There's 'otter fires, and ye'll feel 'em!"

Bellow Bill grunted. That wasn't Cogswell's voice, nor manner. Fitch was not only alive, but belligerent!

In a longhouse which was filling rapidly with smoke, and under a shower of embers which increased every moment, only a strong hope of victory could be restraining Taipi's savages from panic-stricken flight. As Bill wondered what this might be, the thing appeared—and a gasp of awe from Pahea testified to its efficacy on the mind of a savage.

Over the edge of the platform in front of the entrance to the longhouse, clear in the light of the smouldering thatch, slid the crude effigy of a crocodile, the vast open jaws of which could have swallowed a man. Made of wickerwork, in length perhaps a dozen feet, and in height six, it looked grotesque rather than formidable; but around the *kapiravi* center the most terrible superstitions of the New Guinea cannibal. In those huge wicker jaws, Bill knew, long pig was placed before the feast.

For a savage to look at a *kapiravi* except after elaborate ceremonies meant death, unless a heavy payment were made to the medicine man. That crude image was at once the most sacred and the most terrible possession in the village. In its wake Taipi's warriors would charge in a superstitious frenzy, and Pahea's men would scarcely dare to face the image alone.

It dropped to the ground, rolled over and advanced slowly across the field of stunted sugar cane toward Bill. A man was walking inside it, of course, his legs hidden by the body.

The pearler drew his revolver, and crawled to meet the *kapiravi*, conscious of a grim pity for the superstitious savage in the center of that frail basket. A single, well placed bullet would finish him.

BILL FIRED. Once, and twice; then shot after shot till the hammer clicked on an exploded cartridge. His bullets drilled the effigy—but the *kapiravi*, though it shook to the impact of the slugs, came on!

A quavering howl ran around the edge of the jungle. A fierce yell burst from the longhouse where Taipi's warriors clustered, black against the firelight. Bellow Bill whipped out his knife and leaped for the gaping mouth of the thing, cursing his bad marksmanship, and knowing, as he cursed, that he had never lined sights straighter in his life.

Out of the wide jaws a bundle the size of a football was flung at him. Just in time Bill saw the spark of a burning fuse, and flung himself to the ground as the bomb exploded with a crash and concussion that all but knocked him breathless.

"Wheeeeeeee!" whined scraps of iron and stone through the air. The wickerwork of the *kapiravi* was riven. Through the gaps protruded masses of white stuff, like pale, torn flesh—but it advanced!

Bill shook his head like a punch-drunk boxer, heaved himself onto his knees. A second bomb bounced out of the open mouth of the *kapiravi* and rolled toward him. The aim was poor. Bellow Bill might have dropped to the earth again—but what could he do with his diver's knife and empty revolver against this damned thing that had stood before the blast of the first bomb?

With the thought, he hurled himself forward recklessly, scooped up the spluttering bomb, and tossed it between the gaping wicker jaws. The explosion knocked Bill down. It tore the *kapiravi* into a mass of whitish stuff like cotton, in the midst of which a body slumped, gushing blood from an arm blown off at the elbow.

Knife in hand, Bill staggered toward the man. He did not hear the yell at the longhouse change to howls, nor see savage after savage leap to the ground—weaponless, in flight, racing in terror toward the spears and darts of exultant enemies. Taipi and his warriors were being most awfully punished for their treachery to Morrison. A few would escape, but not many. Bellow Bill did not notice, did not care.

The wicker framework of the *kapiravi* had been stuffed loosely with kapok fiber, which stopped bullets and bomb fragments as effectively as a mattress. The dying man in the center was clean shaven! Fitch!

"Where's Cogswell?" Bill bellowed.

"'Arf!" Fitch muttered in delirium. "Hi never 'ad nothink, an' 'e promised me 'arf, so 'elp 'im! Wot do Hi care wot the sylor's got in 'is blinkin' oil can? Hi've never feared nothink yet, myte! Hi'll fight 'im for yer!"

"Did Cogswell run away? Damn him, did he head for the beach?" Bill thundered.

The voice, or the approach of death, roused Fitch. His eyelids fluttered, and he smiled.

"Wot-o, sylor! Hi give yer best," he muttered. "No 'ard feelin's, eh? Cogswell's my myte, an' Hi sticks to 'im, like Hi always 'as… 'e's not run far, not 'e! 'E plans the show, like always…"

The flames of the burning thatch were rising high. A pale, clear light filled the clearing. From the edge of the jungle a rifle cracked, and a bullet ripped through Bill's leg between thigh and knee.

"Bart!" cried Fitch. "I fyced 'im for yer! Now give 'im what-for!"

So died Fitch, faithful lieutenant to the end.

CHAPTER V

THE BLAST

GRIMLY AND CAREFULLY Bill reloaded the revolver. The yells of Pahea's warriors, the screaming of their victims, the pale firelight made the valley a pit of hell. Bill knew that to shout for help would be a waste of breath. Not even the cautious and comparatively level-headed Pahea would have a thought except of vengeance and long pig until the last cowering fugitive was tracked down and speared. After the massacre and the feast Bellow Bill might dominate the savages again. In the meantime he was at bay.

Yet to get at him Cogswell must crawl into the open, and the light. Bill plugged his wound with kapok, thankful that the bullet had not touched the bone, and yet aware that in an hour or two the muscles would stiffen so much as to make walking difficult or impossible.

Coolly he stuffed his cheek with fine-cut and prepared for hours of tense watchfulness. At last time fought for him. Cogswell would be a master of brush craft indeed if he could creep close enough for a successful shot. Not only must he squirm up to the muzzle of Bill's revolver, but once in the open he would be a target for the darts and spear of every blood-mad, roving savage.

Bill lay just beneath the body of Fitch. He felt around, hoping to locate another bomb, and touched instead the uninjured arm of the dead prospector. The hand was bandaged, and from the shape of the bandage Bill guessed that earlier in the night Fitch had lost a couple of fingers. Cogswell had not lied entirely. Bill's bullets must have hit the rifle which Fitch had shot at him, and smashed his trigger finger. Hence in the final sally Fitch had used bombs rather than firearms. Apparently the second bomb had also been his last, for the pearler failed to locate a third. A brave man, Fitch. Simple and loyal; not treacherous, not calculating.

Beneath Bill the ground shook. The cuplike valley echoed to the boom of a heavy blast of dynamite—at least a quarter of a mile away, and higher up the course of the stream. For a moment Bill was puzzled. What was Cogswell up to?

Then through the hellish yells his ears caught the grinding thunder of oncoming water.

Cogswell had blown up Morrison's dam.

Bill had visualized the dam as a small structure. Small it might be, but from the sound of the flood the engineer had impounded a lake behind it. The first onrush was knee deep, rolling Bill over and over in the midst of a mass of kapok that covered Bill's head and hampered his movements. He pawed clear and leaped up in time to face the main wave.

But not to avoid it. Waist deep and steep as a breaker, the wave swept into the valley, loaded with the logs and broken branches torn loose in its passage through the jungle. Bellow Bill could only cover his head with his arms. He was knocked off his feet, pounded to the bottom, thrust along in a grinding mass of flotsam. A log struck him. He wrapped himself around it, clinging with arms and legs, holding his breath as only a pearler can; waiting, as the flood battered him, for the merciful shock that would bring unconsciousness.

THE CREST of the flood left him behind. He was rolled to the surface. He snatched a lungful of air. Broken jungle vines tangled around his legs like thin cords. He was content to cling to the log, great shoulders hunched, while the flood washed him along and thrust him firmly against a barrier of driftwood that had jammed in the narrow cleft where the stream left the valley.

Driftwood, the bodies of the dead, the bodies of Pahea's warriors, overwhelmed by the flood in the midst of victory, crowded inexorably against him, packing more and more firmly in the grip of the current. The burning longhouse tilted drunkenly on its foundation piles. The valley was silent. Those men who had not been caught by the water were in gasping, panting flight for higher ground.

Desperately Bill struggled to free himself from the pressure of the drift, and the tangle of vines. Already the water was receding. He could have touched bottom if he had wished to force his legs down through the mass. Thirty feet away was the high water mark of the flood, solid ground, bushes that would conceal him, but to reach them he could neither wade nor swim.

He was forced to lie on his face, spreading his arms and legs as wide as possible, and squirm ahead inch by inch. The least haste, a single careless movement, and his hand or his knee might slip through the drift and become entangled beneath.

That would be the end of him. His revolver was gone. His knife had slipped from the sheath, and he knew that Cogswell would come back into the valley in the wake of the flood. For a little while the depth of the water would prevent the jungle prospector from reaching the clearing. But the water was draining away.

So despite desperate, frantic haste Bellow Bill crawled to the high water mark like a snail. The dynamiting of the dam had been a master stroke. Even though Bill was in the bush, and could conceal himself—how long could he keep hidden? And for what result? He could hide. And Cogswell, failing to find him, could tramp to the beach, could lurk in ambush, could shoot down Peggy the first time she showed herself on deck.

No. Not that. Nor was Bill at all certain that he could get to the beach first. He could walk, though his leg was stiffening, but he would leave a trail of blood that no bushman would overlook, and the chances that Cogswell would overtake him on the trail were too strong.

Again, no. Cogswell must find him, here. In this valley, where each had won a victory, the struggle between them must be decided. Cogswell's rifle against a pair of mighty hands that could snap the neck of an enemy. Jungle craft against jungle craft, with the pale flare of the burning thatch to light the battle.

Bellow Bill was concealed in the bushes only for a moment. Only long enough to drag a long thin piece of vine from the litter which the flood had deposited at the high water mark. Despite desperate haste, the big tattooed hands arranged the vine carefully, skilfully among the bushes and the flood litter.

A FEW yards farther along the shore a big log had been washed up. Bellow Bill lay down behind it, his feet toward high water mark, his head and shoulders as far down into the drift as he could force them. With a few broken branches he covered himself—but not so carefully that a keen eye could fail to make him out. A bit of his trousers showed, and a bit of his arm. His posture was as much that of a drowned corpse entangled in the drift wood as he could manage.

Motionless he lay while the slow minutes passed. The water drained from beneath his shoulders. Cogswell must have reached the valley by now. He must have seen Bill, must be creeping along the edge of the bush at the high water mark, rifle at the ready.

Cogswell was the sort who would put a bullet into Bill before he touched him, even though satisfied that the pearler was drowned. But Cogswell was also the sort who would wish to plant that bullet in a vital spot. To do that he must walk past the log.

In the bush leaves rustled. The mud along high water mark squelched under Cogswell's feet. He had approached silently as a snake until careful scrutiny of Bill's attitude convinced him that he had nothing more to fear. What can the strongest man do whose feet point toward the shore, and whose head and shoulders are lower down, half buried in mud and broken litter?

The end of the vine which Bill held in his fist twitched as

Cogswell walked into the broad noose that the pearler had arranged across high water mark, one side of the noose flat to the ground, the other side, where the vine was hidden by foliage, waist high.

Bill flattened against the log, and hauled in hand over hand. A bullet smacked into the wood. A second tore off a sliver of bark and burned across his forearm. But the noose of vine had tightened around—something. Bill gave a mighty heave.

Cogswell shouted. His body thudded to the wet earth as his feet were jerked from beneath him. Like a bear Bellow Bill rolled over the log, scrambled up on that one bit of firm footing, and dove headlong. Cogswell had been lucky enough to be thrown onto his back. He was swinging the rifle into line, but the barrel only struck Bill's head. Tattooed fingers closed on the bearded throat. Bill rolled upon the rifle, grinding it into the mud.

For a minute Cogswell's heels churned the mud with spasmodic kicks. More and more weakly his fists beat against Bill's face and chest. Just as the blows were about to cease the pearler relaxed his grip. With one hand and a knee he held Cogswell in the mud while he took a hitch with the vine around the kicking feet.

Then at his leisure, he caught and bound the beating hands with Cogswell's belt.

"You blighter!" Cogswell choked through black lips. "Not—long pig! Damn you—they'll just—knock me on the head—with a stone ax—and eat me!"

Bellow Bill stared, incredulous.

"Blue hell, I'm saving you for a British judge, not Pahea!" he exploded. "So you'd have done that if you'd got me? Jungle style!"

Cogswell's eyes gleamed in the light of the burning thatch. He lay in the mud, gasping.

"To a judge and the law," Bill rumbled, very low, but with an inexorable purpose that made Cogswell shrink. "And do you know why? Oh, I'll show you to Pahea too, so that he'll know what the real white man magic is! The Morrisons will need labor to rebuild that dam, but it's to court you go in the end, so that other jungle prospectors like you can hear what happens to bush rats that try jungle tricks on people like the Morrisons!

"Jungle master? You? Why, you've got no heart! You let your partner face me, and he wounded, to save yourself trouble in getting a little gold out of the dirt. If you'd dynamited that dam before Fitch came at me, instead of after, I'd never have been able to snare two men. Not you. The jungle's in your blood till you're a part of it! Give nothing! Risk nothing. Grab it all."

"When I dug the foundations for the dam I found another gold pocket," Cogswell choked. "I covered it over. I thought Morrison would get discouraged, but he didn't. I had to get that gold—and with the dam washed away any new-chum can pick nuggets up with his fingers!"

"So?" Bill rumbled. "And that's what hurts you, isn't it? I'll bet you didn't care much if Fitch did get killed. You were afraid he'd blackmail you into giving him a share of the claim for keeping his mouth shut. I know you planned the murder of the Morrisons—though you'd probably be sentenced for driving that poison splinter into my coat. Murderous assault is easier to prove. I wish," Bill rumbled, "that you could see what this jungle will be like in a few years, after the Morrisons let in the sun!

"They need that gold you've washed up for them."

The pearler raised his voice.

"Pahea!" he thundered. *"Sambio! Sambio!* Peace! Peace!"

The echoes rolled through the jungle, self assured, inspiring confidence, masterful.

BLOOD PAYMENT

*Natives were running amuck, his best friend
had vanished—and Bellow Bill Williams
had to maintain the law of the Solomons*

CHAPTER I

RUMAKOTU

BELLOW BILL WILLIAMS, the tattooed pearling skipper, liked to handle his schooner alone; which is all right if a man is big enough to hoist the mainsail in a gale. Bill was big enough. Six feet three, weighing two hundred and forty pounds of hard muscle, he could easily do the work of three average sailors.

He also liked to sail to the remoter and wilder sections of the South Seas; which was all right, too, since he had plenty of self-confidence and rather enjoyed a tight corner. An immensely powerful and utterly fearless man doesn't get much chance to use his full strength in the ordinary course of the pearling trade.

Nevertheless, to play a lone hand exacts its penalties. Running southward from Christmas Island after a successful pearling season, with the hold of the schooner full of shell and the steady trade wind on the port quarter, Bill snagged his right thumb on a fish hook while trolling.

The injury was trifling. He forgot about it until two days later. Then the hand and forearm commenced to be sore. Under the tanned, tattooed skin thin red lines were visible, running from the little gash, which had refused to heal, up his right arm to and beyond the elbow. Those thin red lines were the symptoms of blood poisoning; and all around Bill was a warm, blue, empty sea.

Bone setting was the limit of Bill's knowledge of surgery. He couldn't operate on his own right arm, anyway; and the nearest hospital was at Tahiti, distant by eight days' sailing. At the rate the infection was spreading, in eight days his arm would be in such shape that the French sawbones in Tahiti would want to cut it off at the elbow, or the shoulder, in order to save his life.

Bellow Bill sat at the steering wheel in the warm sun, and filled his cheek with fine cut chewing tobacco, which he carried loose in his hip pocket. He'd be damned if he was going to lose an arm; nor was he such a fool as to fail to realize that an attempt to save his arm, in Tahiti, might kill him. He needed to see a doctor within forty-eight hours at most, not after a hundred and ninety-two.

And that meant that he must change his course and sail to the atoll of Rumakotu, only a hundred and fifty miles away across the warm, empty sea. Fat, easy-going Phil McGuire had been a doctor once—a ship's physician who had fallen in love with the South Seas, thrown up his job, and established a copra plantation with Dennis Shea, putting up the money in return for the planting experience of the older, more taciturn Irishman. Bellow Bill knew that the partners had done well. Twenty-five thousand coco palms were just beginning to bear, and though McGuire hadn't practiced medicine during the seven years that the trees were reaching maturity, except to cure the recruited laborers, he hadn't fogged his mind by laziness or booze, either.

Phil McGuire was a good egg, plenty capable of fixing Bill up. A day lost in reaching Rumakotu was a good gamble; and Bellow Bill, as he put the wheel over and trimmed sheets on the new course, was grimly thankful that his mind was a chart of the South Seas. Most sailors, lacking his far-flung and detailed acquaintance with the islands, would have held course for Tahiti. To rot in a hospital for weeks or months at best. Possibly to rot under the coral sand in the end. Whereas Bill, sailing into Rumakotu after twenty hours on the new course, anticipated a speedy cure with the two partners.

A native drum was booming wildly as he anchored in the shallow lagoon. The recruited laborers who did the work on the plantation were dancing, and by the hoarseness of the voices and the steadiness of the shouting Bellow Bill guessed that the dance had progressed beyond the stage of individual displays to

*With a mighty heave, Bellow
Bill hurled the savage
into the blazing fire*

the orgiastic mass hysteria which is always reached when natives amuse themselves, but which was rarely arrived at so early in the afternoon as this.

No one, white or native, came down to the beach to see what schooner had arrived; and though the coco palms which were planted on every foot of the island except the actual beach sands concealed the buildings ashore from Bill, and also kept his schooner from being seen, the roar of the anchor chain must have been audible at McGuire's bungalow.

"Ahoy!" Bill bellowed in the great voice that had the booming crack of a mainsail in a gale. "McGuire! Shea!"

Boom! Boom! Boom! went the drum, like a fevered pulse. No other answer to that stentorian hail for an instant, and then, from behind the waving screen of palm leaves, the crack of a repeating rifle, half a dozen shots fired as fast as the cartridges could be levered into the barrel.

"Keep a-way-y!" shrilled a woman's voice. "Don't—land—alone! The natives—are running amuck!"

Bellow Bill smiled grimly. Something else was running amuck in his right arm. Don't land alone, eh? That was a laugh, under the circumstances. He wondered, briefly, what a white woman was doing on this island of bachelor partners, and why she should answer his hail. Possibly because the people in the bungalow knew that a woman's voice would cut through the hoarse yelling of the recruits better than the deeper tones of a man.

"This is Bellow Bill!" the pearler thundered. "Callin' McGuire and Shea! Do you want me to land and give you a hand, or would you rather come aboard till the recruits quiet down?"

"I'm alone!" came the shrill answer. "Shea's been lost at sea! Phil went out to quiet the recruits. Half an hour ago! Don't—land—alone!"

Boom! Boom! Boom! went the drum, fierce and angry like the pulse that beat in Bill's arm. And McGuire had gone to stop that dance? Half an hour ago? A fat, jolly little man, who knew little of the South Seas except what he'd seen from the deck of a liner, or learned on Rumakotu. A half hour is a long, long time for a white man who tries to stop a native orgy to be away.

Bill's huge tattooed hands tightened on the rail.

"I'm landing!" he roared. "Will you be all right there in the bungalow for the next twenty minutes?"

"Yes!" came the answer. "I've got—the rifles. I'm keeping—the law of the Solomons."

The law of the Solomons is that any native who enters the clearing of a white man unclothed, or carrying a weapon, may be shot. This girl, whoever she was, was no new-chum to know that law.

Bellow Bill decided to go after McGuire first.

CHAPTER II

THE RIFLE

HE ROWED ASHORE with a revolver and half a dozen sticks of dynamite, capped and fused to explode in five seconds, stuck in his belt. A cigar was clamped in his jaw, and he was stripped to the waist. Bill's forty-eight-inch chest was tattooed with a full-rigged ship. His back, ribbed with muscles like the trunk of an oak tree, was decorated by a Chinese dragon and a snake that coiled around the hips. Every inch of skin from the neck down not occupied by these designs had its own picture pricked in colored inks, and since in the South Seas the rank of a native chief can be judged by the amount of tattooing on his body, Bellow Bill's painted skin marked him as no common man—a fact as useful as his height and weight when he had savages to overawe.

He pulled the dinghy above the high-tide mark with a single sweep of his left arm, and marched into the shade of the coco palms toward the drumming and the hoarse shouts as though he were a regiment.

The first natives he encountered were wandering through the palms one by one while they rested from their exertions in the dance. They were black and kinky-haired New Hebrides Islanders, wearing G-strings of pandamus which emphasized rather than concealed their sex. At home they were cannibals to a man. They were the most surly, the most ignorant, and the most treacherous savages from whom plantation labor is recruited; and though they were resting, their ugly black jaws were still streaked with foam from the mad excitement of the dance. Natives in their condition were as dangerous and as unstable mentally as a drunkard on the verge of delirium tremens.

Bellow Bill eyed each savage with a level, unspoken threat and strode straight at him. Each circled away a few yards to permit the pearler to pass, but once Bill was by each savage circled still farther and followed him. He entered the clearing where the fire blazed, trailed by more than a dozen men.

Fully a score of dancers circled the fire, foaming at the mouth, howling in a frenzy that made them oblivious to everything save the beat of the drum. These would dance till they dropped from exhaustion, or were knocked down and if one were knocked down the others would rush insanely at any number of white men, armed in any way whatsoever.

Yet as long as they were not interfered with, the very frenzy of the dancers was in Bill's favor. They did not see him, nor care at all because he was an alien and an enemy. Not so the mob of forty or fifty islanders who milled around the dancers in a loose, slow-moving ring.

There were men who were neither exhausted by frenzy, nor completely dance-mad. Many carried the short, heavy knives used for splitting coconuts. They scowled at the cigar in Bill's teeth and the yellow sticks of dynamite thrust between the waistband of his trousers and his tattooed skin. Momentarily the ring of islanders stiffened, attempting to bar him from the dancers and the fire.

Bill pulled out a revolver and a stick of dynamite, and strode ahead. The ring broke—widened out, and reformed with Bill inside. A knife buzzed past his head. He whirled, revolver raised. Any one of a dozen men might have thrown the knife. At his back the dancers leaped and howled. The outer ring faced him, eyes rolling in black faces, some mouths foam-streaked. Bill pushed the revolver back into his waistband. Bullets against such numbers were useless. The outer ring commenced to move toward him, and in a flash he guessed what had happened to McGuire.

The mob had surrounded him, tightened upon him, and at last gripped him, much as a python tightens on its prey. Whether the doctor had emptied his gun into the mob had no bearing on the outcome. If he had, these savages had torn him limb from limb, which would explain their frenzy.

While if he had not—they might merely have seized and bound him, saving him for the climax of the orgy. Such a dance ends, if possible, in cannibalism. Swiftly, Bellow Bill glanced around. There were no bodies near the fire, or close to the drummers. Nor were there stains of blood on the trampled sands. McGuire, who was by nature a gentleman, must have yielded to the inevitable without a shot. There was still a chance that he was alive, which altered Bill's decision to blow his way through the outer ring with dynamite.

Suddenly, while the mob was gathering courage to close in upon him, he leaped like a tiger on the drummers. One was knocked senseless by a swing of Bill's fist. The other, leaping up, was seized by the neck and G-string. With a mighty heave the pearler hurled the drummer over the heads of the dancers into the blazing fire.

The scream of the savage was less startling than the cessation of the drum beat. The dancers paused in mid stride as the drummer rolled from the embers, frenzied eyes staring around for the cause of the interruption. In that split second Bill tossed a stick of dynamite into the fire, and flattened the two dancers nearest him with swings of his left fist.

THE EXPLOSION showered him with embers and sand. The concussion was staggering, though he had whirled and hunched his huge shoulders to protect his face. Recovering himself, he sprang toward the gaping hole where the fire had been and tossed the dynamite that was left in all directions as fast as he could push the cigar against the fuses. Even so, one of the dancers rushed him and had to be knocked kicking. The others ran past or away from him and joined the flying mob.

While the dust was still flying, Bill charged after the savages. He needed a prisoner. At the edge of the clearing he overtook a young native whose leg had been injured. He flung the man to the sand and crouched over him, with the revolver against the black throat.

"Where one fella McGuire? Where boss doctor fella?" he boomed.

"Ghost take one doctor fella!" gulped the savage.

"Take him where? You come along me seven bells, savvy?" Bill rumbled. The savages hadn't run as far as he would have liked. Through the long, straight aisles through the coco palms he could see them beginning to collect into groups. He lifted the prisoner in his arms.

"You fellas *kai-kai* McGuire," he accused.

"No *kai-kai*. No kill," the prisoner gulped. "McGuire throw down gun belong him. Vaeho say ghost belong him say no kill. Vaeho take McGuire. Give McGuire ghost belong him."

This wasn't particularly clear. From his experience, rather than from the halting pidgin English, Bill guessed that Vaeho, who was a medicine man, had claimed McGuire as a prisoner to give to the familiar spirit, which is the ace of any medicine man's bag of tricks.

"Where?" he rumbled.

The native pointed across the clearing, to a thicket of pandamus which grew on a light hummock in the coral sand of the atoll. Bill went to the spot as fast as he could walk. Through the stems of the pandamus the earth was visible everywhere. There was neither body nor bloodstains nor enough cover to hide a dog.

"If you're giving me a song and dance I'll wring your neck!" Bill boomed. He felt the native tremble in his arms in terror.

"Vaeho hit head belong him with spirit club!" the savage howled. "No kill. Spirit club too much little! Put McGuire on ground. We fella turn around. Ghost take one fella McGuire. We fellas look. He gone!"

The savage was telling what he thought to be the truth. He—and Bellow Bill with him—were tricked because of the medicine man's hocuspocus. It is not hard to remove an unconscious body when an audience fears to look until the magician tells them to do so.

"Show me Vaeho!" Bill rumbled grimly. "He'll know more about the ghost than you, I guess."

Carrying his prisoner, the pearler started back toward the islanders, who had collected into a compact crowd. A skinny man as tall or taller than Bill capered and jumped in front of the blacks, shrieking imprecations. Charms as large as a soup bowl, carved from mother of pearl, clashed around his chest.

"Vaeho!" gulped the prisoner.

"Aye!" Bill rumbled.

The skinny individual was evidently a medicine man, and as plainly, to judge from the speed with which he had rallied his tribe, a leader with unusual personality.

Bill set his prisoner down. To cut Vaeho out of that mob he might have to shoot quick and straight, and he had never been much of a marksman.

"What name ghost belong him?" he growled.

"Shea name ghost belong him," gulped the released prisoner. "Ghost belong him boss Shea ghost!"

Bellow Bill started. For the medicine man of a crowd of recruits to take the ghost of a dead plantation owner as a familiar spirit was new to his experience. But he was within seventy yards of his adversary. Vaeho could explain his choice of a ghost later, if Bill could get him.

"You fella Vaeho!" he roared. "Walk along me quick too much, or I shoot you one fella plenty dead, savvee?"

Bill raised the revolver, steadying the barrel with his left hand.

The savages around Vaeho swirled and drew apart—to reveal a huge black who knelt on that sand, taking careful aim at Bill with a rifle. *A rifle*—and recruits are never allowed to have fire-arms.

Sheer amazement cost Bill his chance to fire first. Lead hissed around him. Five—ten—fifteen—more shots than he could count, or a repeating rifle hold!

He was not hit. Savages do not understand the use of sights, but the drum-fire astounded him. This was an automatic rifle, such as only soldiers and gunboats possess!

The huge black slipped another clip of cartridges into the breech with a skill that made Bill think, for an instant, that he was faced by a white man disguised as a native. But no! The matted, kinky hair, the jutting jaw, and the savage bestiality of the black face were genuine.

Bill sprang behind a palm, using the trunk as a rest, since it was far too slender to shield his body. He shot the best he could—but he missed all six shots. Bullets sang around him. The savage, also missing, slipped a third clip into the breech. His ammunition seemed to be unlimited.

In obedience to Vaeho's howls, the savages were spreading out to get behind the pearler. Bill turned and ran. With a concerted yell, the whole crowd gave chase.

CHAPTER III

THE WORTHLESS OLD MAN

FOR A BIG man Bill was fast on his feet. He maintained his lead over the savages all the way back to the bungalow, and with a thundering shout that he was white—for the tattooing on his body might deceive the woman, despite his coppery red hair—he hurdled the fence of the compound and sprang up the bungalow steps.

A rifle barked inside, and the foremost savage, who had reached the fence, uttered the choking cry of a man mortally hit. Bill pulled open the door, which was unlocked. Crouched at the window with a rifle projecting across the sill was a girl wearing shorts and a white silk shirt. Plump arms and legs were tanned a rich cream. She glanced at Bill with a quick flash of blue eyes and dazzling teeth, and pushed a rifle lying on the floor toward him with a sneakered foot.

"Where's the dynamite?" Bill boomed. "That's all I'm fit to use. I'm sore at myself."

"They're taking their fight out in yelling," retorted the girl. "We'll be all right until sunset." She relaxed, squatting cross-legged on the floor, and brushed a wisp of dark hair out of her eyes. Firm red lips were trembling.

"You didn't find Phil?" she asked. "I'm Nell Fiske. I was going to marry him."

"Neither McGuire nor his body," Bill rumbled gravely. "A native thought that Vaeho made him disappear, which wants lookin' into. You don't happen to be a missionary?"

"An anthropologist," Nell answered. "I came to this atoll to study the language before I did field work in the New Hebrides. It's the best method, now that labor is recruited from the wildest tribes. But why do you ask?"

"Most missionaries know medicine these days," Bill rumbled. "You couldn't do an operation to clear up a case of blood poisoning?"

"I'm afraid not, but why—"

The vast, tattooed shoulders shrugged. "Why, in a week at most I'm liable to be delirious," Bill explained. "Wouldn't think I was sick, to look at me, would you? I don't feel sick yet. But I've either got to find out what happened to McGuire quick or blast a way to my schooner and get you off this island. You couldn't hold out against these savages long alone, and I'll be more of a hindrance than a help pretty soon. That's something that wants thinking over."

"I shan't leave without Phil," Nell decided.

"Nor I," Bill rumbled. "Come nightfall, I'll go out and see if I can get my hands on Vaeho. I ought to. The natives ought to sleep like logs after the dance, and I ain't unhandy—except with firearms."

The blue eyes of the pearler twinkled.

"Why did the recruits run amuck?" he asked.

"Because their two years were up and they wanted their pay."

"And why didn't they get it?"

"Because the trade goods we sent for never got here. Mr. Shea went out with our season's take of copra to buy the goods. Instead of shipping the stuff by steamer, he wrote us that he had picked up a schooner at a bargain in Tahiti, and was sailing back." Nell shrugged. "A boat marked with the name of that schooner was washed up on the beach here after a storm. We inferred that Mr. Shea was drowned at sea."

"Schooners bought at a bargain often have rotten planking," Bill rumbled dryly. He reached for fine-cut. "You say Phil—and Mr. Shea," he suggested.

The girl flushed. "Mr. Shea wanted to marry me, too."

"Oh!" Bill boomed. "And how long has Mr. Shea been over-due?"

"Two months. And you see we had no schooner, and the steamers that usually stopped passed us because they must have thought we had one. And the recruits refused to wait any longer—"

"Sure!" Bill growled, deep in his chest. "Though savages aren't usually so particular about dates, and they don't usually riot. Every tribe has been shot over by gunboats at some time. You were glad to see Mr. Shea go? Both you and McGuire were glad?"

"Yes. It was difficult—"

"Difficult for Shea, too, I guess. He's spent seven years watching the palms grow, and having a swell time with McGuire."

"Just what do you mean?" demanded the girl coldly.

"Nothing. I'm just thinking out loud," Bill rumbled. "Why did you tell me you had all the rifles?"

"But I had!" snapped Nell angrily. "I heard the firing, but I can't understand it at all. The first thing Phil and I did when we saw signs of trouble was to check over the firearms. None were missing."

"An automatic rifle was missing."

"There never was an automatic rifle on the atoll. You're mistaken!"

"The target," Bill rumbled, "is never mistaken. My God, girl, the flashes from that gun were like the sparks from a pinwheel!" He shifted his quid thoughtfully. "Two partners disappear, and an automatic rifle—deadly even with a savage who doesn't understand the use of sights firing it—appears. What's your comment on all that?"

"As an anthropologist, I never heard of a medicine man who caused a prisoner to disappear," the girl began slowly.

"Nor I," Bill rumbled, "and I've fought as many savages as you've read books. It could be done, of course. Gifts to the spirits disappear. But the natural thing for Vaeho to have done with McGuire was to tie him up by the fire until the time came to turn him into long pig."

Nell shuddered.

"But if a man and a girl wanted to get rid of a third man—for the sake of his share in a valuable plantation—and a wandering pearling skipper happened to drop anchor just at the wrong time," Bill purred, "then the body would have to disappear. Murder can't be prosecuted without a *corpus delicti*."

FOR A second or two Nell did not understand the diabolical plot of which Bellow Bill was accusing her. Then her face paled with horror, only to blaze in an instant with anger.

"Shea and I—plot to murder Phil?" she gasped. "Why—why, you damned hound! Why, if that had been the scheme I'd have shot you down when you crossed the compound!"

"Steady, girl!" Bill rumbled. "Remember I'm betting my right arm—or my life—that I can get to the bottom of a complicated mess quickly. I had to find out whether I could trust what you said or not. I'm satisfied now. You wouldn't have shot me as I crossed the compound, because you wouldn't have known whether or not I was alone on my schooner. But the idea that it might be Shea you were in love with hit you harder than an accusation of murder. Are you still mad?"

"Yes!" Nell blazed.

"Then suppose," said Bill evenly, "that Shea plotted to get rid of Phil and you. For the sake of the plantation, and because he was jealous. Suppose he set a boat adrift to fool you into the belief that he was wrecked. Suppose he hid the schooner in the lagoon of some lonely atoll, or—which would be smarter—actually ran it aground in such a way that it would take him months to work it back into deep water.

"In the meantime, you and McGuire are killed by the natives. Shea is shipwrecked miles away at the time, as he can prove by the ship's log, which is evidence in any court. What's your comment on that?"

"Shea couldn't be positive that the recruits would make trouble," said Nell slowly.

"Some one came to the atoll to make certain. With an automatic rifle," Bill rumbled.

"No one could have come. There's no place a stranger could hide!"

"McGuire was hidden somewhere," Bill insisted. "Remember that before McGuire left this bungalow to stop the dance the topsails of my schooner were in sight. It is easier for me to believe that some white man realized it was too dangerous to kill McGuire at that moment, as had been planned, and instead ordered the leaders of the natives to kidnap him and hide him until the errand of the schooner was known, than it is to assume that a crowd of natives, dance mad, would do anything to anyone who interfered except knock him on the head and keep him for long pig.

"When I blew up the dance I had to be driven off, even though that involved revealing the automatic rifle. One white man driving a crowd of natives to kill another needs a weapon that's better than ordinary to protect himself. And finally, my prisoner told me that McGuire had been carried off by Shea's ghost."

"Recruits running amuck would be easier to deal with," commented Nell grimly.

"Much easier," Bill agreed. "Provided they hadn't killed McGuire before I arrived. I've got to decide how and why that automatic rifle got on Rumakotu before I can plan what to do next."

"Shea was a taciturn, embittered man," Nell replied thoughtfully. "It's true that he considered the increase in the value of the plantation was due wholly to his work. That without Phil's money he wouldn't have had the chance to work never seemed to occur to him. And it's true that when I refused him and accepted Phil he was so angry that he wouldn't speak to either of us for days. He walked around with a twist to his mouth. He was silent, but he frightened me. I half expected that at any second he'd scream and go for us with the first weapon he could snatch. We were both very glad when he left the atoll."

NELL FISKE shrugged plump shoulders. "You're not very encouraging," she remarked. "However— Look! There's a native coming into the compound! But he's an old man—and dressed—and unarmed!"

"Then let him come!" the pearler boomed.

For a savage, the man was very old, emaciated, and feeble. His knees shook as he climbed the steps of the veranda, though more from fright than from weakness.

"No shoot! Me good fella!" he quavered. "Got book belong you!"

From his loin cloth he pulled two scraps of white duck, such as might have been torn from a white man's jacket.

Bellow Bill flung the door open and jerked the old native inside. Both scraps were covered with writing in a dark fluid which was probably blood. The uppermost piece read:

Nell, dear,

I'm unhurt, except for a few bruises. Vaeho and Gorai are holding me as a hostage for the payment of the wages, and I'm sure they won't harm me unless Bellow Bill Williams attacks them again. If he does, they'll kill me in sheer funk.

For God's sake persuade Bellow Bill to sail at once. Go with him, and bring back a schooner load of trade goods. I'm sending a power of attorney so that you can raise money on the plantation for this purpose. Two years' labor for a hundred men at fifteen pounds a year comes to nearly fifteen thousand dollars, so a loan will be necessary.

Don't worry about me. Vaeho's civilized enough to realize I'm only useful to him alive.

Love.

Phil.

The second scrap of duck was the power of attorney, in regular form, but limited to the purpose of raising a loan to satisfy the wage claims of the recruits. The document was signed, Philip McGuire.

"That's Phil's writing," Nell breathed over Bill's shoulder. "He's alive! Unhurt! Oh, thank God! I never realized Vaeho was quite as civilized as this, but it's a logical explanation of what's happened, don't you think? Don't you agree that we should obey Phil's instructions?"

"You are asking me because you are doubtful yourself," the pearler rumbled. Beneath the sea tan his face was bloodless. "Vaeho must be mighty intelligent. Gorai, I take it, is the ugly black who had the rifle." Bill paused. "Neither of the savages can read?"

"Of course not!"

"Phil must have been pretty eloquent to persuade them to let him write and to make him a pen. He was bound, and just recovering from a knock on the head. He knows who I am, but he might have recognized my topsails, or heard my voice. He doesn't say where he's being held, as he could have done—and yet it's just such a letter as he might write of his own free will. He gets you off the atoll. Saves you."

"Yes, he'd want to do that," Nell breathed. "But the only reason I'd go is to save him. I'm not considering myself."

"I'm not considering my arm, either," Bill rumbled in his deepest chest tones. "I've fought these recruits, and they've licked me. The letter's logical. If McGuire wrote it of his own free will we ought to go. But I can't help wondering whether he was forced to write it at the dictation of a third person."

"It only names Vaeho and Gorai."

"That's it. We have to show the letter to a banker to raise a loan. You swear the signature is genuine—and that lays the guilt of anything that happens to McGuire absolutely upon a pair of savages. McGuire is murdered while we're gone. Vaeho and Gorai vanish. And with that letter authenticated, Shea would be safe in appearing with his yarn of shipwreck and claiming the island.

"If Shea is hidden on Rumakotu, that letter is the most devil-ishly clever note that was ever dictated to a prisoner. It even puts the onus of McGuire's death upon you and me unless we set sail instantly."

"But we can't possibly tell whether the letter was dictated or not! This worthless old man won't know!" Nell cried. "We can only guess, and if we guess wrong—"

"Yes, it's a tough choice," said Bill gently.

CHAPTER IV

MURDERER'S WAGES

"**WHERE DID VAEHO** give you one fella book?" he boomed at the old native.

"At clearing belong fire. Belong dance!"

"All right! Tell Vaeho I go. White Mary goes. We go right away too much on schooner—but—" Bellow Bill's huge tattooed hand closed on the skinny shoulder. With his right hand he took a chamois bag from his pocket and shook a pearl as big as a pea into his palm.

"Tell Vaeho I pay wages. Pay wages with pearls. White fella money for black fella! Many, many fella pearls like that fella pearl! You give that fella pearl along Vaeho!"

He opened the door, pushed the old native out, and whirled, beads of sweat on his forehead.

"What are you doing?" Nell gasped. "You haven't as many pearls as that on your schooner!"

"Every pearl I have is in that little bag," Bill snapped. "There's nothing on my schooner except some stinking pearl shell that no bush savage will accept for money. But I intend to find out whether there's a third white man on this atoll before I sail. You know and any white man knows that no pearling schooner carries fifteen thousand dollars' worth of pearls. But bush natives from the interior of the New Hebrides don't! Savages are human! Why won't they take what pay they can get? Vaeho ought to be civilized enough to realize that pearl I sent him is worth triple his wages." He leaned grimly over the girl.

"You'll run some risk rather than abandon Phil? You don't want to sail away wondering whether you were tricked?"

Nell's eyes flashed.

Bill nodded, and sprang through the door onto the veranda. The yelling of the natives had died down somewhat, but his appearance elicited a concerted roar.

"Don't shoot—even if I'm shot at!" Bill said over his shoulder to the girl. "Gorai!" he thundered in a bellow which silenced the clamor of the savages.

There was no answer, and no shot. The old native scrambled over the fence of the compound, the pearl held aloft in skinny fingers.

"Gorai, do you want a gun that will always kill?" Bill roared. "A good gun, not like the one you have, which only makes noise? How many you fellas want guns? How many you fellas want pearls? I pay with white man's guns and white men's money!"

The huge tattooed body leaned forward. Bill swept the fringe of green with his eyes. "What man of your tribe," he called persuasively, "ever brought a white man's gun which would shoot many times back to the village? Which of you wants to be that man? A gun that shoots many times will make the weakest of you a chief!"

A naked savage leaped from his place of concealment into the compound.

"Not yet!" Bill boomed, flinging up his hand. "Gorai gets his gun—which always kills—first!"

The pearler turned slowly, and reentered the bungalow. In the coconut grove the drum commenced to beat softly. *Boom— boom—boom.* The rhythm was broken, and staccato. A code, or a summons.

"Arm the recruits! Are you mad?" Nell snapped. "They'll fire at us, if only to make sure the guns we give them will shoot!"

"I shouldn't wonder if they'd fire at something—as soon as they get cartridges," Bill rumbled. A reckless little smile twisted his lips. He stepped to the gun case and selected a ten-gauge repeating rifle. "Though not at us. Not instantly, unless they are egged on. Savages are mighty human, except when they're dancing. If some one said to you, 'Here's that million dollars you've always wanted, and I'll sail away and bring you another million in a couple of weeks,' would you kill him? Savages want guns more than anything in the world, but if Shea is on the atoll I don't doubt he'll prefer the recruits unarmed."

BILL TOOK three shotguns shells from a box, and started to dig out the wadding with a jackknife. "Unload the rest of these guns and lock the cartridges away somewhere," he ordered. "Work fast. We've got to move before they do. Where does McGuire keep his dynamite and his surgical instruments?"

Nell pointed to the bottom of the gun cabinet. Bill dropped half a dozen sticks of explosive into the little black doctor's bag, snapped the bag shut, and with his jackknife started to shave dynamite from a seven stick. Nell caught her breath—and then continued to unload the rifles. Bill grunted with approval. Into the shotgun shell which he had opened he crammed as much dynamite as the case would hold, crimped it tight with powerful fingers, and worked it into the magazine. Behind it he loaded two ordinary shells, loaded with buckshot.

"That was risky," he rumbled. "If the knife blade happens to strike a spot where the nitroglycerine in the dynamite is concentrated, you blow yourself up. Got the rifles unloaded? Can you carry them all? Good! Let's go!"

He strode through the door, the shotgun over his arm and the little black bag in his left hand. Nell walked behind toward the beach, laden with weapons. Below the dragon on Bill's back a snake was tattooed, coiled around his hips like a belt. She could not take her eyes from the snake.

The drum had ceased to beat. She could hear the savages around the compound talking excitedly. Bellow Bill helped her over the compound fence. He grunted, and she looked up. The quick twilight of the tropics was at hand, and the coco grove was dark. Through the tapering trunks she caught a glimpse of the lagoon, and in that direction no natives were visible. On each side, however, were scores of men, moving slowly.

"No sign of Gorai. Nor the auto rifle," Bill reassured her in a bass rumble. "Walk in front. These fellas don't love me, but they've seen me fight. They won't rush me, and we're moving faster than their leaders."

He was right. Nell and he reached the boat which Bill had left drawn up on the beach. He lifted the girl in, and turned to face the recruits.

"I go to get rifles belong you. Pearls belong you," he said slowly. "Rifles like this!" He took a gun from Nell and tossed it into the midst of the crowd.

As they scrambled for the weapon, he gave the boat a mighty shove and leaped in, seizing the oars. He rowed with strokes that lifted the little dinghy.

"That was well done!" Nell exulted. "But I thought you weren't going to sail until—"

"I'm not," Bill grunted over his shoulder. "Can you swim?"

"Yes."

"Few bush natives can. That's why I'm going to the schooner, and I'm in a hurry because I've half been expecting a clip from that damned auto rifle to be fired at me ever since I left the bungalow. Walking across the compound was a worse risk than the dynamite. You're safe now, by comparison."

"Then you have an idea? Loading that shell with dynamite—"

Bellow Bill turned and grinned. "I got a hunch. Have you ever noticed that a really avaricious man doesn't expect others to be as eager for wealth? If Shea did start a native revolt for the sake of a plantation and revenge, he wouldn't be likely to think that his natives might want something else just as badly. I can't fight, but he can't bribe, except with the stuff I own."

"Even so, I don't see why you shaved that dynamite—"

"For an anthropologist, you've got lots to learn about primitive men!" Bill grinned. The dinghy bumped the schooner. He swung Nell and the rifles to the deck—and then sent the dinghy adrift with a thrust of his foot. The hatches of the schooner were already locked. He unlocked the cabin companionway, put the padlock on the inside, and stared for an instant, frowning, at the pile of rifles, which were by the port rail, fifteen feet or so from the companionway.

With a shrug he passed the end of the main sheet into the cabin through a porthole on the starboard side.

"Take this kit of doctor's tools below," he instructed Nell. "Then close all the other portholes and pick out a rifle of mine that you like. You may have to do some sniping."

THE SAILS of the schooner were already hoisted. Bill slipped the cable, and running to the wheel, steered toward the beach where the recruits were gathered.

"I'm going to beach the schooner so they can come aboard," he explained. The twilight was too dense for Nell to see him, but she could feel that a mocking, reckless smile was on his face. "This is risky, too," he purred. "But if they'll just come aboard we'll soon find out if a white man is at large on Rumakotu!"

The schooner barely moved through the water. It touched the beach gently, and at once Bill let the sheets go with a run, lashed the wheel, and leaped onto the slide of the companionway. His heels dangled in the doorway in front of Nell's face. She could just make out the shotgun poised across his arm.

"Does Gorai want the gun that always kills, and Vaeho the pearls?" Bill called mockingly into the dusk. "First I pay the chiefs! Then I give the guns that make you all chiefs at home!"

From the savages on the beach arose a murmur, but for five long seconds there was no movement. They were suspicious. Nell could sense it. Bellow Bill stooped until he was almost flat on the companionway.

"Why does the gun always kill?" growled a surly voice.

"Because it shoots many bullets at once, Gorai!" Bill boomed softly. "Watch the sail and see what this gun does."

Bill fired twice. The echoes rolled around the lagoon, and the crowd whispered sibilantly. Suddenly, all at once, a score of men ran into the water. Savage after savage climbed the bowsprit and leaped down onto the deck.

In the lead was a tall, amazingly thin figure with a charm clashing at the chest, and a heavier, thick-set man almost as tall.

"Here is the gun, Gorai!" Bill boomed. He held the weapon out by the muzzle. Nell saw it snatched from his hands. "And the pearls!" Bill added. But Vaeho hung back. Behind him were a dozen savages, shoulder to shoulder. More were climbing over the bow.

"Here!" Bill boomed, lifting the chamois bag.

As he spoke, Gorai pushed the shotgun forward until the muzzle almost touched Bill's side, and pulled the trigger.

THE SHOTGUN burst at the breech. Gorai screamed. One hand was ripped to shreds. Bill bellowed with pain, for his side was seared by the jet of flame which had streaked from the muzzle, but he leaped—for Vaeho! His left fist crashed into the face of the skinny man. Catching him by the throat, Bill swung him to the companionway, hurled him down, and leaped after him, closing and locking the door as the savages flung themselves pell-mell down the narrow stairs.

"All right, Nell!" boomed the pearler. "Hammer this fella with the butt of your gun if he comes to!" Bill crossed the cabin and hauled on the sheet stuck through the porthole. The schooner trembled as he hauled the sail aback, shivered, and slid off into deep water. Knives were hacking at the companionway door, but on deck a savage yelled as he saw the beach receding. "I'll take care of him as soon as the schooner's in deep water!"

"But the knives! The men on the deck!" Nell cried.

"Why, we got all the rifles that have ammunition below!" A reckless lilt sang in the rumbling voice. "This is my *schooner*, and I can sweep the decks with buckshot from the fo'c's'le hatchway, or clear them with a capstan bar!" Bill laughed aloud. "I'll choke the truth out of Vaeho!" he exulted. "And Phil won't be hurt while the two he named in the letter are in my hands!"

From the beach came a burst of rifle shots—the brief drum-fire of an automatic rifle.

"Gorai!" screamed the voice of a white man. "Cut every rope you see! Cut—"

The rattling thunder of the falling mainsail drowned the rest of the order. Gorai might be incapacitated, but the other natives were quick to accept any guidance.

"Shea thinks like a sailorman in a pinch," Bill boomed in a reckless, lilting singsong. The cabin was pitch dark. He heard Nell groping toward him. Her hand closed on his arm.

"Next he'll set the schooner afire," she whispered. "It's too bad. And yet—I don't see how you could have done any better."

"Why, he may try to burn us," said Bill calmly. "First he's got to get these boys of his off, without a boat. You might get a shot at him. From the fo'c's'le hatch, or through a porthole."

"Oh!"

"Oh is the word. You're steady as a rock when you know what you're up against," Bill rumbled approvingly. "The fact is, I figured after I got that letter, that Shea probably couldn't keep me from getting some of the natives on board who knew enough of the truth to hang him, and that I probably couldn't get the schooner out of the lagoon afterward. We swapped the bungalow for the cabin. Do you think you can defend it as well?"

"I?" Nell whispered, and despite her courage her voice shook.

"I'd like to open the lumber port forward and swim ashore," Bill admitted. "Get behind Shea, and find Phil, if I can. I'll need Vaeho, and one person is as many as I can handle in the water.

"You can come with me if you swim like a fish. Hell! You can come with me anyhow!" the pearler broke off. "To have you stay here is asking too much!"

"Not if my staying would help Phil," Nell answered. "Still—I'm glad you don't ask it!"

CHAPTER V

IN THE LAGOON

BELLOW BILL HAD changed his mind because the schooner, though still afloat, was liable to drift back to the beach and go aground again in time. Shea might and probably would prefer to wait for that to happen, for then he could set the hull afire and force his enemies into the open—force them to charge across a beach lighted by the fire, while he lurked under cover and was supported by his savage allies.

That would be suicide for Bill. A retreat, even burdened by Nell and his prisoner, was possible, though risky. The savages had no firearms. The hull of the schooner, and the darkness, would afford some protection from Shea's rifle.

With the speed and thoroughness of a sailor, Bill bound Vaeho hand and foot and gagged him with a strip of cloth torn from Nell's skirt. The little black bag with its load of instruments and dynamite he slung over his back by a string. For weapons he took a heavy diver's knife, and told Nell to lay rifle and pistol aside. If he failed she would be captured, then or later.

Whispering to Nell to dive deep, and swim underwater as far as she could, he opened the lumber port. The noise that he made was heard. As Nell's white body flashed in the air the savages massed at the rail and yelled. From the beach Shea shouted to them to throw their knives, and as Bill rose from his dive with Vaeho in his arms a knife or two did splash into the water.

"Make a light! Set fire to the sail! Quick, damn you!" Shea was screaming. At random he fired a clip across the dark water.

"Lucky for us savages don't carry matches," Bill growled. "He'll have to board the schooner himself to set her afire. Swim like hell, girl, for the opposite side of the lagoon!"

"The—opposite side?" Nell panted. She was a fair swimmer. Good enough to use a scissors kick, and not a laborious and noisy breast stroke.

"Too far?" The distance was about a quarter of a mile.

"No—but—can't Shea—overtake us in a boat?"

"I hope he tries it! I'll capsize it and knife him!" Bill growled. "But—blue hell! Speaking of matches, the ones I have in the bag are soaked! How'm I going to set off my dynamite, if I need to?"

He swam in silence, with Vaeho's head tucked in the crook of his left elbow, face above water, as though the savage were a helpless man whom Bill was saving from drowning.

From the schooner came the sound of ax-blows, and the splintering of a door. Across the water Shea was exhorting the recruits to run around the beach and kill Bill as he landed. He was promising a big long pig that night and when that feast was over—more long pig.

"I'll drown myself first!" Nell panted. "He'll give me to them—after he's—"

"Yep!" Bill rumbled. "Swim like hell. He's smarter to break into the cabin than set fire to the schooner. He's damn smart. It's a race to shore!"

Race with what? Nell wanted to ask. She learned as she stumbled up the beach. Behind them suddenly leaped up the vivid blue flare of a Coston light. It was stuck on the rail of the schooner, and it illuminated the whole lagoon, even the knot of savages who were trotting, rather slowly, around the beach.

BILL PUSHED the girl into the shadow of the coco palms as bullets came skipping across the water. Though Shea missed, he could have corrected his aim, had they still been swimming in that; vivid blue glare. In grim silence the pearler dropped Vaeho on the sand and loosened the gag.

"Where did Shea hide when he was ghost fella?" he demanded. "Where did you hide McGuire?"

The savage clenched his teeth. Bill set the knife on the big tendon just above Vaeho's heel.

"Once more I ask along you," he rumbled. "Your tribe coming seven bells. Find you with tendons cut. No can heal along you. You no good to tribe. They bury you alive, like any old man that's no good."

Not so much threat, as fact, rang in the deep voice. And it was a fact. A slash of the knife, and Vaeho, medicine man and chief, would be buried alive by his own tribe because of the customs he had helped to establish. Nell knew it; he knew it.

"One fella Shea, one fella McGuire, crawl in hole in pandamus thicket by dance fire," he gulped. "Live under sand."

"I've seen that thicket. There's no such hole," Bill rumbled coldly.

"Lift one fella pandamus! Ground come up! Then see hole belong Shea!" Vaeho howled.

"Which pandamus? It's a thicket?"

"One fella pandamus!" Vaeho howled. He could be little more specific.

"A masked entrance to a cave in the coral? Hollowed out by water seepage?" said Bill to Nell. "There are such things. If Shea found such a thing and decided to conceal the entrance by transplanting a palm, it may have been the start of his whole scheme. Where boat belong Shea?" Bill growled suddenly.

"Bury boat belong him in beach sand all same eggs belong turtle!" Vaeho gasped.

"Aren't those recruits getting close?" Nell demanded nervously.

"Let 'em. They don"t want to meet me," rumbled the pearler. "I think this fella's telling the truth. His story fits pretty well."

The blue flare, beating across the water, gave just enough light for Nell to see the hard set of the pearler's jaw.

He loosened the cords on Vaeho's ankles enough to permit the savage to walk, and drew a jackknife which he passed to her.

"Make Vaeho show you that boat," he said. "It'll be buried somewhere along the outer beach. Make him launch it for you, and put to sea. Stay close to the island until dawn, and after that—get as far to sea as you can.

"You've a chance to be picked up, and if you're not, thirst and sun will be kinder than what will be waiting for you here. Think of that, if Vaeho balks and you've any hesitation in using the knife on him."

"I do what I must," Nell snapped. "Yet if the savages coming along the beach find me—"

"They won't look," Bill promised. "Use your ears. You can tell how I'm getting along with Shea by the sounds. Don't jump to conclusions, though, before dawn."

The pearler rose, slung the little black bag over his shoulder, and strode purposely away under the coco palms, angling to arrive at the inner beach slightly in advance of the scouting party of savages. With a shock Nell remembered that he had no matches to ignite the dynamite. Nothing but a knife. She forced Vaeho to rise and withdrew, slowly and hopelessly, toward the outer beach.

CHAPTER VI

UNDER THE SAND

BELLOW BILL, ON the contrary, was not seeking to conceal, but to reveal himself. The inner and outer beaches were separated at that point by three hundred yards or more. The distance around the doughnut-shaped atoll was more than a mile. Deliberately he walked into the glare of the flare upon the inner beach.

At the sight of his huge figure the savages halted. Bill was crimping a dynamite cap into a piece of fuse with his teeth. The diving knife glimmered close to his face, and though the savages numbered more than a dozen, they had encountered Bill once before when he held dynamite in his fists. One man ready to die if he can take a sufficient number of enemies with him, and who reveals that determination by the grim swing of his shoulders as he moves to the attack, can scatter a mob every member of which is most anxious of all to keep a whole skin.

The savages broke. Across the lagoon Shea fired, but Bill merely withdrew, a little, into the shadow of the palms. The savages could see him. He was crimping another cap—into the other end of the same fuse, had they known it. While they watched, his vast, shadowy figure moved farther under the palms until it became invisible.

On the beach the savages turned and ran! Toward the protection of Shea's rifle, toward their fellows. They had no stomach to go poking into the gloom where Bellow Bill lurked.

The pearler grunted with satisfaction. Until he was incapacitated there would be no hunt for Nell. He set out swiftly toward the clearing where the dance had been held, keeping to the middle of the atoll, where the darkness was densest.

To approach the clearing took Bill twenty minutes. The Coston light burned out, and a new one was not kindled.

While that aided the pearler somewhat, the almost complete absence of underbrush beneath the palms precluded any possibility of getting into contact with his enemies without alarming some of them.

Bill was moving stealthily from palm to palm, pausing behind each. Though he got close to the pandamus thicket unchallenged, he was not surprised when a native leaped up in the darkness and ran toward the clearing, yelling that Bill was coming. He merely paused, listening intent for the sound of a mob in movement. In the midst of that mob he meant to locate, and to kill, Shea. Even if he were overwhelmed by superior numbers afterward, the savages might release McGuire if they lost their white leader.

Nothing moved in the gloom after the shouts of the sentry ceased. Yet Bill could feel the presence of men near by. Men who waited for him to crawl farther into the trap? He could not retreat.

From his bag he took all the dynamite—six sticks—and bound them tightly around the stick he had capped with bandage. Still his enemies waited. He groped among the instruments, seeking a pair of forceps, or a knife with a metal handle. He found the latter, and bound the loose end of the fuse, with its cap in place, to the steel. The instruments had clicked—like castanets, it seemed to Bill—and still Shea and the savages were content to wait!

The sandy soil under the palms was light in color. In the gloom Bill figured that he could see anything that moved two palms beyond the one behind which he crouched. Palms are set from twenty-five to thirty feet apart. If he advanced thirty feet—

He did so, rapidly. As he leaped up he glimpsed a dark mass of underbrush ahead! The pandamus thicket, which was his goal! He was running on when a rifle blazed in the heart of the thicket and a bullet sang inches above his head.

He dove for the base of a palm tree with a leap that carried him fifteen feet, the capped fuse hugged against his chest. He landed heavily. A spasm of pain ran through the swollen, feverish right arm. The bullets were thumping into the trunk of the palm, and around it, showering Bill with sand.

"Lights! Back there! Light the flares!" Shea screamed.

Bill swung the surgical knife against the trunk of the palm by the fuse. The cap exploded sharply, the fuse hissed. That Shea had laid the ambush in the thicket corroborated Vaeho. But what six sticks of dynamite, exploded above a cave gouged in soft coral, were going to do to a man within Bill dared not think. No chance to hesitate.

AT TWO points behind him Coston lights flared. Bill hurled the spluttering package of dynamite, glimpsing Shea in the heart of the thicket, sighting carefully. The planter must have tried to escape as the bomb rolled over the sand. At least, he never fired. Bill, crouching behind the base of a palm barely wide enough to hide his shoulders, never saw.

With the bombing thud of the explosion he leaped up and charged into a cloud of sand that was blue in the glare. The ground crumpled beneath his feet. He fell, blinded by dust, half buried in sliding sand, a gush of foul, smoke-laden air rising around him. A body holding a rifle tumbled against him.

Bill clutched the throat, which was limp as a rag, and drew the knife back for a thrust.

The sand stopped sliding. The whole fall, as he looked upward through the dust, was hardly more than eight feet. The cave was a mere fox hole, hardly ten feet square. A corner of the roof had broken in and the sand loosened by the blast half filled the space. Far away a pan of charcoal smoldered. Beside it, bound hand and foot, lay McGuire.

Shea was unconscious, his clothes partly ripped from his body by the explosion.

"This fella belong me!" Bill roared. Catching Shea by the neck and knees, he heaved him up to the edge of the pit. The recruits could see. Bill picked up the rifle, which seemed to be all right, and crawled toward the far corner of the cave. The air was like a hand on his throat. His head swam as he dragged McGuire into the open. The fat little man was barely conscious.

"But I'll sign—bill of sale—if you'll let her go. But I'll sign—bill of sale!" he was muttering drunkenly, over and over.

Bill pushed him up to the rim of the pit and scrambled after him, slipping in the sand.

"Ahoy!" he thundered. "This is McGuire fella! Your boss fella.'"

The echoes rolled across the atoll. There was not a native in sight, no answer to that booming shout. The flares cast a hard blue light, and the dust settled slowly under the rustling coco palms.

Then from far away came the faint, shrill cry of a girl, and from the darkness beyond the flares the faint, quavering voice of an old man.

"Me good fella! You no cross along me?"

"Me no cross along anybody any more. Go tell 'em all to be good fella. Keep quiet to-night; get pay quick pretty soon!" Bill rumbled.

"Bill?" gasped McGuire. "Is that Bill?" Though his eyes were open, he seemed half asleep.

"You all right?" rumbled the pearler with a stab of anxiety.

"Coming around," McGuire muttered. "It's that charcoal. It burned up the air. Dennis lighted it. He said he didn't want to kill me quickly, but he wanted to be damn sure I'd die. Why'd he hate me so?"

"We'll ask him," said Bill grimly. "We'll ask him where that schooner of his is, too. That'll quiet the natives. Nell's all right, I'm sure, and I'd let the deputy commissioner worry about Shea. At the trial."

The pearler had loosened McGuire's bonds. By an effort

the little man sat up, smiling weakly. He was the sort who will always try to smile.

"I've been thinking I was going to die so long it's almost queer to expect to live," he muttered. "You're sure Nell's all right?"

"Positive. That was a healthy screech of hers. When that gal's got a definite job to do, she does it!"

"She can do anything," said McGuire simply. "Of course I can't thank you, Bill—"

"No?" boomed the pearler. He thrust his right arm forward in the blue glare of the flares, and traced the little red lines running under the skin.

The eyes of the little doctor widened.

"Why, that's in bad shape," he said. "A couple more days, and that would have had to come off at the shoulder."

"You can save it?"

"Why, when I'm able to stand," McGuire smiled. "I know my profession, I think."

"I think I know mine!" Bill grinned. "The thanks are fifty-fifty, Phil. You didn't need a roughneck any worse than I needed a doctor. No chance is too long to take when you're fighting to keep your right arm!"

THE RATS OF MAHIA

*A necklace of superb sapphires was the South
Sea stake which led to murder—until Bellow
Bill Williams faced the murderers*

CHAPTER I

DEATH STALKS A DINNER

THE TAIL END of a hurricane was lashing Papeete when the guests of the French Consul General took their seats at the gala dinner given to Colonel and Lady Bailey-Nickerson. The curtains swayed in the gusts that blew through the cracks around the windows. The bamboo jalousies clashed outside, and on the long table the candles guttered.

Yet neither wind nor gusts of rain had prevented the guests from dressing in honor of the occasion. Around that long table was the cream of the society and wealth of the South Seas. Men who possessed orders wore them on ribands slanting across white shirt fronts. Women gleamed with gems or glowed with the softer luster of pearls, but the acme of the display glittered around the throat of Lady Bailey-Nickerson, at the right of the host.

For pearls are almost a commonplace in the South Seas, and by comparison with the visiting English yachtsman and his wife none of the guests was rich. Where they possessed francs or dollars, she owned pounds. The necklace of sapphires around her throat was like bits of starlit winter sky against her milk white skin. Twenty inches at least in length, fashioned of gems none of which was smaller than two carats, and cut from the superb sapphires which are more valuable weight for weight than diamonds, the necklace represented a fortune which made women jealous and the eyes of men narrow.

For a short time—a very short time—they were dazzled. The

*The other rats
crawled closer*

soup was still on the table when a window burst inward with a
clash of breaking glass and a gust of wind extinguished half the
candles. Through the aperture leaped a frizzy haired Melanesian,
naked save for a *lava-lava*, black as soot. He carried one of the
terrible half-moon knives that are used for splitting coconuts.
Before a man could rise he was behind Lady Bailey-Nickerson's chair.

One black hand tore the necklace from her throat. As she
screamed, the half-moon knife chopped down upon her blond
head, cutting through scalp and skull. The consul snatched for
the murderer, and staggered back, one hand almost severed from
the wrist by a flash of the reddened steel. With a single leap
the black plunged through the broken window. He was gone
while women still screamed, while men were kicking clear of
their chairs.

Yet pursuit was delayed only during the brief, vital seconds
while the quickwitted were impeded by the slow, and the young
men thrusting themselves clear of the old. Man after man
followed the Melanesian through the window. Outside were
gendarmes, whose concern up to that moment had been to keep

out of the rain. The foremost glimpsed a dark figure sprinting away into the night. As the chase fanned out the savage had obtained a clear lead of perhaps fifty yards.

That was enough to make shooting guesswork, but not sufficient to let the target vanish. Darkness aided him, yet he was not running through a wilderness, but through cultivated gardens where to hide meant eventual discovery. The black must have realized that, for he ran straight as an arrow toward the water front, trusting to his speed of foot.

Yelling and shouting, lancing the night with revolver shots, the chase swept by a sailor's café, picking up the seamen who poured out of the door to join the hue and cry. At once a bulllike roar rose above the clamor. Past panting men sprinted a giant in white ducks who ran at a pace almost incredible considering his height and breadth of shoulder. The bellowing roars that commenced to urge on the pursuit had a snap and a command that made men forget weariness.

Ahead was a low cliff which marked the water front, and a wide stretch of sloping, sandy ground. Across it flitted a dark figure, with a taller shape in white plunging behind. Straight over the cliff edge into the tossing sea dove the black. Without hesitation the white figure followed.

THE REST of the pursuers stopped at the cliff, and stood panting and peering. An occasional drop of flying spray wet them. They could see nothing, except dark shapes on the foam streaked water called up by their imagination.

"Who was that—big man?" gasped a dinner guest.

"Bellow Bill Williams, the pearlin' skipper," panted a Cockney. "Gord, didn't yer 'ear 'im 'oller? Hain't two kin yell like that south of the Hequator! 'E's a good man, Bill is. 'E'll get the bloody black swine, 'e will."

Minutes passed. The boom of the surf washed out all other sounds, but suddenly a huge hand appeared at the edge of the cliff. A curly head and shoulder that could have blocked a door followed. Bellow Bill Williams drew himself up and shook the water out of his white ducks like a huge, angry dog.

"Boats!" he commanded in a rumbling growl. "The motor police launch will do. Come on. That black had an outrigger canoe waiting to pick him up. What'd he do?"

Half a dozen voices told him. He nodded and made a stride toward the harbor.

A gendarme caught his sleeve. "But m'sieur, you 'ave done enough!" he protested. "Eet ees now ze affaire for ze police."

"It's a job," Bellow Bill retorted in a thunderous growl, "for a sailor." He towered above the crowd, a huge figure, dimly seen. "There were two more men waiting in that canoe. Both natives. Could three black fellows sell a necklace—except to the white man who made murdering cat-paws of them?"

"But one cannot find a canoe in ze dark, ze storm! Eet ees folly!"

"For cops," Bill rumbled. "That's why I'm going along." He paused, and into the deep voice came a lilt that was almost laughter. "If we can't find a boat, can they? Use your head, gendarme! The wind's offshore, and they can't sail a canoe against it. Are they steering out into the South Pacific? On the tail end of a hurricane? That would be folly, right!"

"Zey seek ze shelter? Ze rendezvous at ze harbor?"

"I would," Bill purred. "And if they don't, either they'll drown or we'll pick them up to-morrow by cruising around at sea. Folly, eh? This thing was meant to look like a piece of savage madness. A black runs amuck, and when he's chased he commits suicide by diving into the sea. Only I got close enough to see that canoe... and I know of an island that's down-wind and close enough for three black fellows to find on a stormy night."

"Mahia!" shouted a voice from the crowd. "The plantation on Mahia's been abandoned for years."

"There's some devil of a white man on it to-night, waiting for a necklace," Bill rumbled.

With long strides he set off toward the harbor. The gendarme trotted at his elbow like a dog that has found its master.

CHAPTER II

OLD KNIFE-HAND

BELLOW BILL WILLIAMS stood six feet three and weighed two hundred and forty, all muscle. From the waist to the neck and wrists tattooing made his skin a pictorial record of travels from China to the South Pacific, and north to Bering Sea. He had never met a stronger man and he enjoyed danger.

To dive off a cliff in the dark, to swim after an armed murderer and a canoe full of accomplices, was characteristic of the pearling skipper. To be cocksure that he had outguessed a criminal and certain that he had made a difficult case almost absurdly simple, was not.

He was still a proud man at dawn when the police launch, held back by persistent engine trouble and the heavy seas, crawled at last within sight of the low atoll of Mahia and its tossing coco palms. For about three miles from the island a schooner was close hauled on a course to Papeete. A patch of reddish brown canvas in the mainsail identified the vessel.

"That'll be Knife-hand Foster, the blackbirder," Bill rumbled. Complacently he filled his cheek with fine cut chewing tobacco from a hip pocket. "It would be... there's a guy that can make savages take orders, and with the guts to do dirt most men wouldn't tackle."

"*C'est vrai*—true, true, m'sieur," muttered the gendarme.

Bill enjoyed the look of admiration, in which the other two gendarmes who formed the crew of the launch joined. It was the pearler's last complacent moment.

For the schooner, instead of veering off to escape, suddenly hoisted the police flag. More, it turned toward the launch—not only summoning assistance, but seemingly eager to obtain it at the earliest instant possible. As the two boats drew together the schooner heaved-to, but still no one was visible on her deck.

"Lend me a gun. Keep off, and keep your heads down," Bill rumbled to the gendarmes. Light as a huge cat, despite his bulk, he caught the rail of the schooner and swung himself aboard as the vessel rose on a big wave. Swung aboard—and checked himself, the revolver swinging level with a movement wholly involuntary.

For he had jumped upon the shattered wreck of an outrigger canoe, lying on the deck behind the rail. Beyond that, propped against the low side of the cabin farther aft, were three Melanesians.

Dead. Very dead. The throat of one was cut through jugular and windpipe. Blood had gushed over the dirty, hairy body, and had not yet dried. The two others were shot. Bullet holes showed black against black skin. Here was the murderer of Lady Bailey-Nickerson. Here were the two accomplices;. They had met a more sudden, more deadly killer.

"Know 'em, Bill?" rasped a voice. "I hope so. Damned if I ever craved to see a police launch before. Take a reef in your jaw and shove that gun back in your pants."

Out of the companionway poked a bald head, sun tanned to the color of a saddle. Two jutting, pointed ears; a thin face with pale blue eyes. Knife-hand Foster was over sixty. He was not large. No one ever thought of him as large, or small. How big is a cobra? Who knows, or cares? It is deadly. So was Foster.

He was mounting the companion steps slowly. His left hand was hooked in his belt, near a holstered gun. His right hand lacked all four fingers and half the thumb. The injury was old, years old; but the maimed stub was smeared with fresh blood.

To the inner side of his right forearm was strapped a metal tube, Within that, as Bellow Bill knew, was a ten inch knife blade, two edged and needle pointed. With a jerk, Foster could snap the knife forward. A catch in the tube would lock the blade fast, projecting behind Foster's fingerless hand like a bayonet. Some said that Foster could throw the knife as well as snap it into position for use, but Bellow Bill had never believed that. The metal tube was a scabbard for a knife-hand, nothing more.

"Where's the necklace, Foster?" Bill boomed. "Killing those three black tools to shut them up ain't going to do you any good."

Foster's left hand moved to the buckle of his belt. The gun at his hip dropped to the deck, holster and all. He advanced a few steps, far enough away from the companionway to be unable to snatch a hidden weapon.

"Why, Bill," he said, "you ain't a new-chum. You ain't a damned frog gendarme, without brains. Take another look at those blacks. I killed them more than an hour ago, and considerable time before I sighted your launch. You'll find the blood on them is starting to dry, even though the sun ain't up yet."

"**THE NECKLACE?**" Bill boomed, though a quick second look at the bodies revealed that Foster was speaking the truth. Even to get the wrecked outrigger canoe aboard would have taken one man more than an hour, for it was a block-and-tackle job.

"I wish to hell I had it," Foster said. "Likely there'd be a reward for returning it. Here's the facts, Bill: I sailed from Moorea to Papeete, and in spite of the hurricane I'm pretty well on my course, as you can see. Just at the false dawn I make out an outrigger canoe, cracking on sail and driving themselves half under with every sea. That don't look right. You know natives don't put to sea too soon after a hurricane."

"Yes, I know that," Bill rumbled.

"I yell to them to come aboard. I want them, because I'm short-handed. I lost my deck hand in the blow. They're not anxious for help, but I show a gun. Of course, their canoe gets battered up some against the side of the schooner, but what's that to me? I got to have deck hands. The leader of the three is scrambling aboard. The schooner is pitching, and so is the canoe. His G-string slips, and I saw something flash against his black hide. Bill, it was like a gleam of blue fire! My eyes must have popped like a calf's—and he damn near got me while I was realizing it was gems he had.

"He swung at me with a coco knife, Bill. I just ducked. Then—" Foster jerked his right arm, and bloodstained steel snapped beyond his maimed hand swift as a snake's tongue. He made a sweeping slash at the air. "Then—I got *him*. He tumbled back into the canoe, and one of his chums snatched a necklace out of his G-string. Both of them jumped for the rail with knives, Bill.

"I had to shoot. I got them both, but the black with the necklace dropped it when my bullet hit. It fell into the sea, Bill. I could see it sink. Down, down into blue water. Forty, fifty fathoms of water, Bill. I didn't even bother to buoy the spot. It was too deep for a diver, and I wanted to kill that black all over again. Instead I damned near broke my back getting them and the canoe aboard. I figured I'd better, because questions was going to be asked. I could guess they'd come from Papeete. They'd have to, with the wind as it was."

Foster paused, pressed the catch of the knife with his left hand, and shook the weapon back into the tube.

"And you expect me to believe that?" Bill boomed.

"I don't give a damn whether you believe it or not," Foster rasped. For an instant a line of white showed beneath the iris of his pale eyes, as the eyes of a horse show white before it kicks. "It's the truth. If you don't believe it you can search me and the ship."

"Where?" Bill rumbled.

His eyes wandered to the wind-tossed coco palms of Mahia. A complicated problem of time was in his mind. By how many minutes had the canoe beaten the launch to the island? How long would dead bodies last under a tropic sun? Had Foster intercepted the canoe, as he claimed, or had the blacks helped him to hoist it after it had been battered in the surf around Mahia? Had the blacks attacked Foster, or had he suddenly set upon them with knife and gun, after learning that Bellow Bill had seen their canoe in Papeete?

The offer to search the ship was safe to make. To be thorough, a search would require a dozen men, and the schooner would have to be hauled out of water to make certain that the necklace had not been stuffed into an open seam and held in place with a handful of tar.

Foster's story was just possible, but Bellow Bill believed there had been quick thinking and quicker knife-play there in a gray dawn. Foster had moved his pawns over the sea. At the first hint of a counter-move he had swept the pieces from the board. Who in Papeete would blame him for killing the black who had chopped open Lady Bailey-Nickerson's skull? No one.

"You're a good man in a fight," said Bellow Bill calmly. "It takes us old-timers to savvy some things. I'll bet it was hell watching that necklace sinking in deep water. Some will say that you'd have followed gems like those to hell, Foster. But you and me are sailors, eh?"

IN THE half-smile that creased the face of the blackbirder Bill read defeat. The necklace wasn't on the schooner. Foster had submitted to arrest too tamely. Bellow Bill grinned back—and with a sudden inspiration let the grin stay on his face, a twinkle creep into his eye. With the utmost deliberation he signaled for the gendarmes to come aboard.

"Put Mr. Foster in handcuffs," he ordered. "You'll know why when he's told you his story. Not for all the blue blazes of hell would I interfere… with the law."

Bill was grinning. The gendarmes stared goggle-eyed at the corpses.

"And right now," the pearler rumbled, "make a very careful search for the necklace—in the dinghy."

"Ze dinghy—ze smallest boat alone, m'sieur? We search the whole ship!"

"Later—if the police desire," Bill purred. "Right now the dinghy will be enough for *me*." He had his reward. The half-smile was gone from Foster's face. A rim of white showed beneath the pale eyes.

Still grinning, Bill strolled below. He found nothing, though he picked up a heavy diver's knife and added it to the revolver in his belt. Yet when he came on deck again the gleam was still in his eye.

"I've been looking at your deck hand's bunk." He purred—and reexamined the beaker of water and the can of hardtack in the dinghy, though the gendarmes had already probed these, as they had searched every cranny and seam of the tiny craft.

"What the devil are you getting at?" Foster rasped.

Bellow Bill bent slowly and grasped the dinghy by the two gunwales, amidships. With a quick heave he lifted it into the air and tossed it over the rail of the schooner, jumping after it and alighting into the little boat with dry feet.

Two ordinary men would have strained to duplicate that launching. Not one sailor in twenty could have made the jump without capsizing the little craft.

"Why, the necklace isn't in the dinghy—is it?" Bill boomed at the gendarme. "I'm just rowing ashore to search the island. It's my—duty." He was grinning.

"Eet ees to search ze needle in ze haystack!" howled the gendarme, uncertain of what to do.

"Well, if I do it does that interfere with the police, then?" Bill boomed in reply. "Don't sail till you hear from me again, though!" Mighty strokes at the oars were opening a gap between the dinghy and the schooner. The bald head and pointed ears of Foster stuck far out over the rail. To shout to the blackbirder to take a reef in his jaw was in Bill's mind. He refrained. He didn't hope to find the necklace ashore. In the tangled underbrush that covered twenty acres beneath the neglected coco palms such an effort would be folly indeed. No plan lay back of Bill's grin. His inspiration had been merely to take all the pleasure and assurance out of Foster's victory—to prove that another old-timer who saw that he had been outwitted could do the unexpected.

The dinghy was in shallow water now. A commotion in the water caused by fish rising to the surface, an unusual thing after a storm, caught Bill's eye.

He let the dinghy drift, and peered over the side for what must have seemed endless minutes to those on the schooner.

Down below dogfish and sandsharks were tearing at a mass of flesh, already shapeless. Smaller fish, attracted by the blood which spread in a reddish cloud over the sandy bottom, were constantly being chased away by the snapping jaws of the smaller scavengers.

Was that six-foot mass of flesh a fish injured by the gale? Perhaps—though there is little blood in fish. With his diver's knife Bill could have plunged to the bottom safely and discovered whether or not he had found Foster's missing deck hand. He was content to stare, to pick up his oars at last and row ashore.

For the body was already so mutilated that the cause of death could never be known. The shark-gnawed bones of a brown deck hand would never pin the murder of Lady Bailey-Nickerson upon Foster. Only the recovery of the necklace could do that.

And for this same reason Bellow Bill did not even attempt to enter the tangled thickets of Mahia. Instead he kept to the beach. He walked entirely around the island on the rain-beaten sand.

He was not looking for hidden men, but for any sign that a boat had been brought ashore and concealed. That task the very thickness of the vegetation, which grew to the edge of the beach, made simple.

There was no boat. Half an hour later Bellow Bill was back at his starting point. The gendarme meanwhile had sailed the schooner close to the shore, and secured the police launch astern, ready to be towed.

"No one's here," Bill thundered across the water. "Go on back and report to the prefect of police before the sun gets at those bodies!"

"But m'sieur!" wailed the harassed gendarme.

"I'm all right. Plenty of hardtack and water!" Bill roared decisively.

"But m'sieur, you stop! You look in ze water—"

"Did I? Hell, I was just resting after chucking the dinghy overboard," Bill roared. "Go on back to Papeete, Jean. They'll make a sergeant of you for catching that murdering—Melanesian. This island is swell for an—old-timer!"

CHAPTER III

THE FANGS OF THE ISLAND

BELLOW BILL BELIEVED in the dying gambler's advice: never play the other man's game. Because Knife-hand wanted him away from Mahia he was determined to stay. As far as he had a theory, it was that the necklace must be hidden either on the island or in the waters around it. If the latter, the necklace would be marked by a buoy held under water temporarily by a bag of salt, which would come to the surface when the salt melted. Bill could get the cache when the buoy rose. If an accomplice of Knife-hand's landed, Bill figured he could get him; but the pearler did not anticipate anything save the boredom of a lonely vigil with hardtack and water for rations during the remainder of that day at least.

His first care was to hide the dinghy by carrying it across the beach and concealing it in the brush beside an overgrown trail which led to an abandoned and rotting bungalow. He had not staggered into the shade of the coco palms, bent double beneath his unwieldy burden, before he observed that Mahia was cursed with far more than its proper share of rats.

All coco plantations are plagued by rats more or less. Rats live on the nuts that fall, and will even climb any palm with a slanting trunk. Tin rat-guards placed around the trees are as much a part of a planter's equipment as hoes to keep the weeds down, and rats and weeds had both swarmed on Mahia unchecked for years. There were obscene squeaks behind the leaves along the trail. A rat stepped into the path ten feet ahead, rose on its haunches to flash beady eyes at Bill—and vanished. He set the boat down in the path.

At once the squealing ceased. From foliage still damp from the night rain he breathed an odor of decay. Close to the ground a sharp nose poked out; a pair of beady eyes. As he remained still he glimpsed another rat, and another. Watching him. So fearless or so desperate from hunger that they dared to watch. Within a yard of his feet, in broad daylight…

The thought of sleeping on the ground in such a place made Bill's toes curl. He could imagine the beady-eyed, brown-furred army bellying closer and closer as he lay unconscious. At last the boldest rat would bite… Bill would thrash in the darkness… the rats would scatter…

On impulse he took two thwarts from the dinghy and improvised a deadfall, using the boat to weight the trap, and the painter as a trigger-line. A piece of hardtack served at bait. He had hardly moved away the length of the painter before a rat was gliding toward the biscuit. Bill jerked the line.

The deadfall was slow in action. The thwart, thudding against the earth, barely caught the haunches of the rat as it leaped to escape. The animal's back was broken just above the hips. For an instant it writhed in the path—then brown streaks flashed from beneath the leaves. Half a dozen rats were biting and worrying the wounded victim. It lifted its head to squeal, and sharp teeth closed in the light colored fur under the throat.

Bill snatched the diver's knife and hurled it into the mass. The blade, quivering in the ground, scattered the rats. He kicked the bloody body as far as he could into the underbrush, and stood with clenched fists while it was torn to pieces to an accompaniment of shrill squeals. That was a matter of minutes only.

Bill thought of sleeping on the beach. On sand that was clean. Yet he might have to remain on Mahia for days. No one knew better than he how silently a boat can steal in to shore. On the sand his body would be no better than a target, even at night. No. He would have to sleep among these vermin. Repugnance twisted Bill's mouth. He concealed the dinghy, kicking out savagely when he stepped into the weeds, though that necessitated some careful work to rearrange the broken stems and the tangle of vines which he had disturbed.

He picked up his knife and walked toward the ruined bungalow. He was watching the path for tracks, though the recent rain had blotted out all traces—if, indeed, Knife-hand had followed the path at all. The necklace was no longer uppermost in Bill's thoughts. After a glance he decided that the bungalow was so rotten and tumbledown that it was liable to be more rat-infested than the open ground. The sagging posts of the veranda did afford, however, material for building a sleeping platform raised above the ground, such as natives use.

Bill commenced to cut down a patch of weeds with his knife. He selected a spot close to the path and the bungalow, where four palms grew close together, with vines passing between them that would serve to lash his platform in place. One large vine was dead, but that would give him firewood.

THE WORK went slowly, for the knife was too short and light for the task. The best Bill could do was to hack down the tallest of the weeds. He stopped to eat at noon with only four beams of his platform lashed into place. The sun was close to the horizon when he finished. He went down to the beach and circled the island to see if any ships were in sight, or if a buoy had risen to the surface. The ocean was a complete blank. Bill took a swim to cool himself, tied two vines across the path, ankle high, and returned to his platform. It looked as welcome to him as the hotel at Papeete to a tired man. He was rather surprised at the extent of the clearing he had made—but he hadn't cleared too much! He could hear the rats squeaking in the weeds. With a grunt he climbed off the ground, ate hardtack and drank tepid water, and settled himself for the night.

Darkness fell. He was dozing when he caught the sound for which his ears were subconsciously attuned—the creak of a block as a schooner shifted sail to run in to land. He slipped from the platform and stole down the path, kicking his trip-wines out of the way.

Already the schooner had launched a boat. Two men were crossing the beach in the starlight. They passed so close to Bellow Bill that he might have touched them as he crouched in the underbrush. He let them go—to rise, silent as a huge shadow, to step back into the path, to follow them, perhaps twenty feet in the rear.

He knew them both. The white man was Babson, the black-birder. Behind his squat, long-armed figure strode Uri, Babson's giant negro mate. The pair were rivals of Knife-hand in the recruiting of labor—and almost never, so far as Bill could remember, did their schooner touch at Papeete.

The pearler cursed Knife-hand's cunning. Collusion with Babson was the last thing he had suspected, yet it was obvious that while Knife-hand engineered the crime, Babson had lain-to to run to the island and secure the loot in case of a slip-up.

At the edge of Bill's clearing Babson halted—suddenly. There was a gleam in the starlight as he jerked out a revolver.

"By God, Knife-hand's been double crossed!" he whispered. "There must have been a settler here."

"A settler would have store lying around. Can't be no *settler*, boss," Uri muttered.

"That's true! Some beach comber, then. And he's got it! Knife-hand didn't meet us. He must have cached it." Babson paused. "Get the crew ashore," he commanded. "We'll search the island first for a man, and then—"

He checked himself. "—for a man that may not have known what he was doing when the cleared that tangle," he added slowly.

Bellow Bill thought fast. The crew of a blackbirder rarely consisted of more than two or three men. If the skipper and the mate didn't come back the natural thing for the crew to do was to come ashore one by one to see what the matter was. To overpower one man in that brush-grown path would be easy—absurdly easy.

"Drop that gun!" Bill rumbled.

Both men swung toward the sound of his voice. The ambush was perfect. Slowly the revolver slipped through Babson's fingers into the weeds.

"Reach high!" Bill rumbled.

They started to obey. The sudden push which Babson gave Uri, hurling him toward Bill, was as unexpected to the pearler as to the mate.

"Rush him!" Babson screamed—and threw himself face down in the weeds.

Uri charged as Bill fired. The bullet smacked into the big negro's chest. He swayed—but from the weeds flame leaped to answer the flash of Bill's gun.

Babson's shot ripped Bill's arm from wrist to elbow. He gave a roar of pain. His gun slipped from his hand.

BABSON LEAPED up. A bound carried him into the thicket. He crashed through the bush, firing as he went. Wild shots that missed Bill, who picked up his gun with his left hand and fired as wildly. Uri had fallen backward. He was dead. Sacrificed.

Bill discovered that, and twisted his shirt around his bleeding arm. Grimly he strode down the path and stepped aside in the brush near the beach. For the second time he had been outgeneraled by cold blooded murder. For to push Uri toward him had been murder. Babson had not even tried to fight after the first shot. He had fled, had dashed into the sea without pausing to launch his boat. Bill could hear him calling to his crew to hoist him aboard. A moment later the schooner's sails were trimmed. She moved toward the shore in grim silence till her bow grated on the sand.

"A hundred pounds for the man that gets him!" Babson screamed. "Jump, you black devils!"

Four men leaped from the schooner. They carried rifles. The manhunt was on.

For Bellow Bill the temptation to blaze away with his few remaining cartridges as the four crossed the beach was almost irresistible. But many fights had taught him the bitter lesson that he was a poor shot. His huge body tensed in the underbrush like a coiled spring. The four blacks realized that they were advancing into darkness against an armed and ambushed enemy. They drew together, shoulder to shoulder, the rifle barrels jerking in nervous hands. Step by step they advanced.

With a bound Bellow Bill was among them. He dove beneath the rifles as a halfback dives at interference. One shot from his revolver sped before him, one black toppled with lead crashing through a naked chest. Then Bill's shoulders struck black knees. His huge arms, outspread, holding gun and knife, gathered in legs as he brought the natives down in a screaming heap.

Beneath the mass his knife slashed. His gun jabbed and swung in six-inch, crippling blows. He did not pause to kill. Thirty seconds of wild work that left him drenched with blood that he had shed, thirty seconds punctuated by agonized screams, and he jumped erect in a circle of writhing figures.

Feet were pounding forward on the deck of the schooner.

"Hold him! Hold him! I'll shoot him!" Babson was howling.

A leap took Bellow Bill beneath the schooner's bowsprit, which projected over the beach. He paused to jerk once upon the martingale—a pull that was transmitted to the jib, and made the head-sails shake as though he were climbing aboard over the bow. But with a splash Bill dove into the shallow water. For an instant or two he was exposed as he crawled rather than swam aft, his shoulder scraping the side of the schooner.

Then he was swimming beneath the surface through water that grew ever deeper—swimming aft, with the hull at his shoulder to guide him. His hand touched the rudder. He reached up, caught the rudder chains. He had boarded a schooner against an armed man in that way before. He gripped his knife in his teeth, shook the water from the barrel of his gun. One huge, tattooed hand gripped the edge of the deck at the stern. One foot was on the rudder chains.

With a swift lunge he flung himself over the taffrail, dropping on hands and knees, crouched, ready, the knife gleaming in his teeth.

BABSON WAS forward. He fired. The bullet whanged through the brass of the binnacle. Bill fired back, missed, scrambled behind the wheel, fired again, and heard the hammer click on a cartridge spoiled by water. The wheel shook as a bullet from Babson smacked into the oak.

"Ha!" Bill roared, deep-toned, voice fierce with battle-lust. Out from the shelter of the wheel he charged, bent double, low to the ground as a charging lion, keeping the mainmast between Babson's gun and himself. The knife gleamed in his right hand. The gun he did not mean to use again until its muzzle touched flesh was shifted to the left.

Babson's shot was wide. He still might have shot it out. Twenty feet still separated the two as Bill charged past the mainmast. Twenty feet—a brace of seconds—the certainty of a knife in the guts if a bullet failed to stop that huge onrushing figure. To kill was not enough. Bill might drop dead—on Babson's disemboweled corpse. In the face of cold steel Babson faltered. A gunman to the core, he wanted space, time to take sure aim. With a wild scream he leaped down the fo'c's'le hatch. With an angry roar Bill leaped after him, lashing out with knife and gun in the thick darkness below decks.

The blows were wasted on empty air. In the darkness a steel door clanged shut. Bill hurled himself at the sound, and recoiled, half stunned, as his forehead struck a metal barrier bolted and immovable as the side of the schooner. Behind him, at the hatch, sound the rumble of a sliding door, a second clang of metal. The faint glimmer of the stars was blotted out.

Bill jumped for the hatch. His groping fingers found the spring which had pushed a steel plate across the hatch when

Babson tripped the catch, probably by electricity, from a push-button amidships. A dry cell and an electro-magnet working like a trigger would have done the trick. The schooner was a blackbirder. Steel door that could be slammed shut in an instant from far off were useful to keep kidnaped, maddened natives below decks.

For there was no lock on the under side of the hatchway. The steel plate was held shut by a spring catch on the upper side.

Bellow Bill exerted all his strength, and stepped back, panting.

He thrust knife and gun in the waistband of his trousers; filled his cheek with fine-cat chewing tobacco soaked by the sea.

"You win, Babson," he boomed. "And you're a damned sneaking coward."

Through the steel door Bill knew that Babson could hear.

CHAPTER IV

THE PRICE OF A NECKLACE

THE BLACKBIRDER DID not answer. Indeed, the silence was so absolute and so prolonged that at last Bill groped for matches, and lighted a hurricane lantern which swung from the deck beams overhead. Light only emphasized the hopelessness of his predicament.

The fo'c's'le was equipped with deadlights, not portholes, and the bunks and mess-table were built of thin pine boards, much too light to be of any help in battering down the doors.

There was a peep-hole about an eighth of an inch in diameter in the after-door, and below this a three-quarter-inch hole, closed by what seemed to be a flat steel bolt, or bar. This, however, was immovable. Bill broke more than one finger nail proving the fact.

Babson must have had sufficient-confidence in the fo'c's'le as a jail to go ashore, for although Bill heard the wounded natives drag themselves onto the deck, and lie tossing and groaning on the planks over his head, an hour or more passed with no sign from the white man. Bill had stopped swearing; had begun to wonder if one of his shots had taken effect, if a mortally wounded man had slammed the steel doors around him…when for the second time he heard a rattle of blacks as a schooner approached the island.

Fiercely hope flared up—to die at rasping words in the voice of Knife-hand Foster:

"Well, then, damned if you ain't a better man than I thought,

Babson! I figured Bellow Bill would eat ye! *Kai kai* all the same one fella, *poi*, like mush. I *had* to get back!"

The answer was inaudible. With nasty self-confidence Knife-hand continued:

"Him? Why, of course he has! You leave him to *me!*"

The trader rapped on the deck to attract Bill's attention.

"Know you can't get out, Bill, eh?"

"I'm waiting for you to get in," boomed the pearler.

"You would be." Knife-hand's tone was worse than nasty. "Well, I ain't comin'. Figure I've got to get rid of a schooner. Might as well burn this one. An' how'll you like *that*—old-timer?"

Bill shifted a quid which had suddenly become tasteless.

"How'd you get rid of the gendarmes?" he rumbled.

"They forgot that a hand with the knuckles gone slips through handcuffs. They were nothin' but landlubbers, Bill. Two of them were asleep below. I knocked them on the head, because I figured that was what you would have done if you wanted to get shut of them; and the third come below to see what the noise was about. He's driftin' around now in the launch with the other two. The Consul General will think you done it, Bill. I used a hammer on them."

"And you waste time talking to me?" growled the pearler. "The hell you would! Ain't you got matches? You'd burn this schooner for the fun of it."

Slow seconds ticked by in silence. "Aye," rasped Knife-hand softly. "I would. We ain't new-chums, Bill. I ain't goin' to talk bilge to you. I've got to kill you, but I won't hurt you, Bill—not if you're reasonable."

"Reasonable?" Bill boomed.

"Aye. Back up slow against that after-door until your shoulders touch it. That's bein' reasonable. Otherwise—you roast."

"I'm backing," Bill boomed. Like a flash he blew out the lantern, and whipped out knife and gun. He strode to the door, but though his flesh crawled at the touch of the cold metal, it was his chest he thrust against it, not his back. Muscles braced, he waited the slightest movement of the steel.

THERE WAS none—only a clicks and in the same split second the jab of a revolver barrel through the lower hole against his chest.

"Got him!" Babson screamed.

"Shoot if he moves!" yelled Knife-hand from the deck. He threw the hatchway back and leaped into the fo'c's'le, slamming the steel hatch shut as he jumped. The certainty that the least movement meant death held Bill rigid. Knife-hand swore in the darkness. A match flared, and simultaneously the point of the knife, fastened bayonetwise to the maimed arm, pricked Bill's back.

"You would try something!" Knife-hand snarled. "Now— where's that necklace, Bill? By God, the papers said it was worth sixty thousand pounds. I'm sick of stealin' stinkin' natives for a few shillings a head. I'm going to have it!"

Bill thought like lightning. "I buried it in the beach sand," he growled. The knowledge that death was to be delayed at least was like a blaze within him. Babson must have double-crossed Knife-hand. That must be it—and Babson, at the first opportunity, would have to kill his leader. Bellow Bill meant to give that opportunity. He dropped the knife and gun to the deck, relaxed his straining muscles.

"I damn near got away with it, at that," he growled.

"Hold him, Babson," Knife-hand rasped. He stepped back, lighted the lantern, and picked up a length of rope. Bellow Bill reached back his hands to be tied. He winced and his heart sank as Knife-hand passed turn after turn of rope around his wrists, too many for his strength, and with utter disregard for his wounded forearm. If Babson had double-crossed Knife-hand, why had he delayed so long at the island? Because his crew was wounded? Or because, with Bill in the fo'c's'le, he had a bear by the tail? Neither explanation was wholly satisfactory.

As die knife-point prodded him up the fo'c's'le ladder and onto the deck, where Babson joined them, it was some relief to see the two surviving deck hands huddled by the rail. They shrank aside as Bill passed. The fight was out of them. They were apprehensive of the pearler even though his hands were bound behind his huge tattooed back. So, for that matter, was Foster. He kept the knife so close that Bill was cut again and again. Blood trickled down his back in tiny streams. His wrists grew sticky.

At Knife-hand's command Babson jumped from the bow of the schooner first. He waited on the sand, hand on gun, while Bill jumped. Knife-hand swung himself down, watchfully, taking no chances. As they passed the two dead natives near the water's edge, a dark, squeaking mass that hid the outline of the bodies broke apart and fled with louder squeaks of rage—obscene, gibbering shadows which ran no farther than the brush. Bill shuddered.

"Damn!" Knife-hand grunted. "Shove those stiffs in the water, Babson. Sharks and dogfish have got teeth that are clean, anyway. The tide's goin' out. They won't be found."

The blackbirder obeyed. He paused to rinse his hands when he finished—and to the delight of Bellow Bill he remained a few yards away from the trader. Was it the instinct of the gunman? The desire to have space to draw and shoot? Knife-hand hesitated—only momentarily, yet perceptibly enough to force Babson to step out slightly ahead of the other two.

"I won't stand for being run around too long," Knife-hand warned.

"You won't need to," Bill rumbled. He stepped out with long strides, hoping to pass Babson, but the blackbirder kept ahead. Bill swore under his breath—but after all, even with the starlight reflected from the sea and the sand, the beach was dark...

ABRUPTLY BILL halted where a frangi-pani, in bloom and scenting the night with its perfume, afforded a recognizable landmark which he might have used.

"About here," he rumbled, kicking at the sand with his toe. "And about six inches down."

"Dig, Babson," Knife-hand grated. The prick of the knife moved Bill aside two paces. Babson fell on his knees and clawed at the sand. In the darkness the sweat broke out on Bill's forehead. In imagination he could feel the white-hot burn of a knife slipping between his ribs, but his only movement was a very slight, a perfectly controlled inclination of his body forward, as though he were watching Babson. His real movement, when he made it, was quicker than the thrust of a knife.

Sidewise and forward he flung himself, diving at the sand at Knife-hand's feet, twisting as he fell, pivoting on a left leg suddenly doubled, landing on his back and the point of his shoulder with an impact that knocked him breathless—but with his right heel flying waist-high, kicking out as he fell.

His heel caught Knife-hand in the stomach. It was the terrible half-turn and kick known to *savate* as *le coup au ventre ou diable*—the kick to the stomach or the devil, which cripples if it succeeds and leaves the man who dares to use it lying helpless on his back. Knife-hand doubled up and went down.

Babson leaped back. The starlight flashed on his gun. In the same split second Bill saw that Knife-hand was unconscious, that Babson was not going to shoot, was leaping, not at Knife-hand, but at him. Then the revolver barrel smacked down on Bill's head…

Slowly he came to, conscious first of feet that kicked sand in his face. Dimly he became aware that Babson was wrestling with the trader, preventing him from driving the knife into Bill's chest.

"Snap out of it!" Babson was panting; "Of course he's hidden it somewhere! My God, you were unconscious ten minutes! Why'd I lie to you *now?*"

Knife-hand said nothing. Like a demon he struggled to get free.

The breath whistled through his nose, and though Babson calmed him at last, he continued to breathe like a madman.

"Where—where—is it?" he panted, glaring at Bill.

"I don't know," the pearler rumbled in a bitter growl. "I thought Babson had it, and had guts to take it all when I gave him a safe chance."

CHAPTER V

THE BLOOD

HE MADE A motion that commanded Bellow Bill to rise. He pointed back toward the schooner. In silence the three men tramped over the sand, Bill first. With a touch of the knife-point Bill was halted while Babson got a rope from the schooner, then was prodded up the path through the brush and halted again by his sleeping-platform. The knife pricked his shoulder at the base of the neck, forcing him down until he was sitting with his back against the trunk of a palm. The rope was passed round and round, and knotted. All in silence.

"You looked for the necklace?" Knife-hand demanded. Of Babson, not Bill.

"Sure! But it was already dark. I only had a ship's lantern—"

"Yes, we need light. Pull that contraption down. Pile the timbers around him."

The thump of the first beam that dropped by Bill's feet made the rats in the underbrush scamper and squeal.

"Look here," Babson objected. "When you get in a dumb rage like this, all you think about's killin'. A fire is a signal of distress. It'll bring any ship that happens to be passing quicker than anything."

Knife-hand said nothing.

"Maybe he didn't find the necklace. Maybe he just lost it," Babson persisted. "You put it where you said?"

In the gleam of the starlight Knife-hand's bald head moved in a curt, savage nod.

"There was a dead vine between these palms," said Babson to Bill. "Hollow, and split. He twisted a joint open and slipped the necklace inside. It was hanging in mid air, savvy, and any tracks that he might have left would seem to be goin' right by. People look in the ground for things that are hid. That's why he picked the vine, but the necklace could have slipped out, easy, when you pulled the vine down. It was pretty rotten. I found lots of pieces of it, scattered around. I searched the ground all around, too. But maybe you can remember seein' something, Bill. Out of the tail of your eye, like."

"I don't," Bill rumbled. Most fervently he wished that he had.

In silence Knife-hand dragged a pole off the platform and cast it down.

"Don't be in such a damn hurry!" Babson swore. "We got all night. You knocked those gendarmes on the head so the consul would look for Bill, didn't you? You weren't dumb-mad when you thought of that. How's it goin' to help us to have his scorched guts found here? Give him time to do a little remem-berin'!"

Knife-hand broke a dry stick in half.

"How about the rats that were chewing Napavi and Tolo?" Babson ejaculated. "Hell, there's worse things than fire! Bill's bleedin'! They'll get to him! Wait, Knife-hand, wait!"

The palm tree quivered as Bill lunged frantically against his bonds. The ropes gouged his chest, but did not slacken. No hope. No hope. In the starlight the bald head jerked upward like that of a thirsty horse which scents sweet water. Softly, caressingly, Knife-hand spoke.

"Once in a while you really get an idea. But we'd have to leave Bill alone. I won't."

"Why must we? Here's his platform! We can climb up there and lie comfortable," Babson urged. "Hell, we can lean over and see his legs! Let's try it an hour anyway!"

"Right!" Knife-hand agreed.

The palm tree quivered to Bill's lunges as the two climbed

over his head. He had a mad, a frenzied idea that by movement he could keep the rats away. The very violence of his efforts revealed the futility of that. He could move—a few inches, twist his body toward and away from the trunk, kick his legs. And a few minutes of violent effort left him panting. Break loose he could not.

"Better start remembering—old-timer!" drawled Knife-hand.

That mockery restored Bellow Bill to sanity. The sweat on his face turned cold, but—but he remained still. Though muscles jerked uncontrollably under his tattooed skin, limbs and body did not shift. Still. So still that from the weeds a rat lifted its head.

A big rat. An old rat, incredibly thin, that moved forward a foot like a flash and stopped like a shadow, sniffing. Behind the big rat were others, ready to sneak forward but afraid. The big rat was afraid. It circled behind Bill, circled until he could no longer watch it, though he turned his head till the neck tendons ached. Still it was creeping forward. Bill could sense that. The advance, inch by inch, belly to the earth, dirty teeth bared. Starving, desperate, still not sure he was helpless. The other rats were nearer, too. A yell would scatter them. Bellow Bill's throat swelled—and relaxed. Sweat runneled down his cheeks and dripped from his chin. Bill did not move.

EVEN WHEN a scaly paw touched his back he did not flinch. He felt the rat's fur against him. He heard its teeth come together—but—but he did not feel a bite! Eyes bulging, jaw locked, determined to endure the bites without outcry, Bill could not understand. Seconds passed. The rat was gnawing—*on the bloody ropes twisted about his wrists!* Desperate with hunger though it was, the rat was too cunning to attack living flesh while there was other food. Yet the taste of blood would embolden it once the smears on the rope were gone.

Bellow Bill's head twisted. His bared teeth closed on the flesh of his own shoulder, and bit deep. Agony made his legs jerk, but a trickle of blood started down his arm toward his bound wrists. His body remained rigid.

"A rat bit him then!" Knife-hand gloated.

"Sh!" Babson warned.

The big rat had retreated. Yet only an inch or two. It was back, gnawing, gnawing at the body rope. Its teeth made short work of the outermost strand. Bill felt the cords slacken, but the rope that bound him to the tree remained. He could untie that knot, given a second or two. Though not—not with the blackbirds within a few feet of him.

"Good God!" he bellowed. The rats scampered. "I've remembered something!" Bill went on in a hoarse rumble. He had no need to simulate mental agony and desperation. "I didn't find the necklace myself, but I think—I'm sure—I know what became of it. The rats carried it off!"

"Keep on thinking. Maybe you'll remember something I'll believe," retorted Knife-hand with savage sarcasm.

"Don't be a damned fool!" Bill raged. "You knifed the man that was carrying the necklace, didn't you? I'll bet there was blood on the stones when you hid it, and when it dropped to the ground the rats carried it off because it had the smell of something they could eat. For God's sake, give me a break! Why should I be burned or eaten alive? The rats wouldn't take it far, but they'd drag it away from the spot where Babson expected to find it."

There was silence for two, three, four seconds. Abruptly Babson slid off the platform, moved to the edge of the space Bill had cleared and leaning over, struck a match.

"Bill may be right, at that," he urged. "Shall I get a lantern?"

More slowly Knife-hand climbed to the ground.

"No," he contradicted. "Rats could not drag a necklace as long as that far without its tangling on something. Matches will do." He struck a light and bent forward, searching.

As match after match flared, the light of each temporarily blinding the eyes of the two blackbirds to an object in the darkness, Bellow Bill shook the cords off his wrists and untied the knot of the rope. The turns passed around his body gave him more trouble. Each turn was a quick, breathless task synchronized with a flare of light. At last he was free. He remained seated. Arms held close to his body kept the rope across his chest. His feet, however, were drawn beneath him.

Knife-hand uttered a yell of triumph. He pawed at the earth. When he rose something dangled from his hand.

"Blue babies!" he gloated, and let the necklace swing against his cheek. "A house in Sydney, that's what you are! And wenches—white wenches and whisky! No more trade gin!"

Babson snatched at the string. "Hi! They feel slippery and cold!" he cried out. "No wonder people call 'em ice. God, look at them shine in the stars!"

"Aye," Knife-hand rasped. He thrust the gems into his pocket. The brief outburst satisfied him. His tone stopped Babson's exultation like a douse of cold water. "Let's get underway. We can use both schooners now. Safer. Won't start tongues rattling. I'll attend to Bill."

WITH A *click* the knife snapped out of its metal sheath. He walked across the little clearing, neither fast nor slowly. He had business to do. He did not need to taunt his victim to enjoy it. He caught Bill by the hair, jerked his head back to expose the throat.

A huge hand flashed upward. Iron fingers buried themselves in Knife-hand's neck. A fist closed like a trap on the maimed knife-arm. It was done so suddenly that the blackbirder did not cry out. Only the agonized writhing of his thin legs as Bellow Bill rose, lifting him into the air, made Babson cry out, sent a hand streaking to a gun.

"Drop him!" Babson yelled. He sprang backward, hesitating to shoot.

The lean, bald-headed figure spun in Bellow Bill's arms. Perhaps Babson thought that Bill was dropping his partner. The movement was too quick, the night too dark to see that Bill had only whirled him around, that his back was now against Bill's chest, that the hand which had gripped the wrist was now hugging the skinny waist, that the hand which had been at the throat now held the skinny forearm to which the knife was strapped.

But at the flash of steel in the starlight, at Bill's leap forward, Babson understood. With his partner hugged in a huge arm to stop the lead, with his partner's knife pointed forward like a spear, Bellow Bill was charging him. In the brush he could not run. Babson cried out, and fired. He got in two shots. Then Bill dove headlong. The knife drove through Babson's body as they fell.

A fist like a mallet smacked down on Knife-hand's head. Bellow Bill struck Babson, and then got slowly to his feet. Across one huge, tattooed forearm was a painful bullet gouge. That slug had gone on through Knife-hand's heart. The knife had caught Babson under the breast bone and, pointing downward, had ripped him to the belt. He had not been dead when Bill punched him. But he would never recover consciousness now.

The huge pearler shuddered, and reached for fine-cut. His mouth was too dry to moisten the tobacco. He blew it from his lips, bent, and with a grimace of distaste, took the necklace from Knife-hand's pocket. A little later he picked up Babson's gun, stuck it in the waistband of his trousers, and, sure at last that Babson had died, picked up both men, a hand in the belt of each, and carried them back to the schooner.

One after the other he tumbled then; over the rail and climbed aboard himself. At the sight of the bodies the wounded blacks had groaned. They shrank back against the bulwarks as Bill's great shoulders rose over the rail.

They were too frightened, too certain he had come to kill them, to plead for mercy.

"Be easy, lads," Bill rumbled. "You ain't sailing with Knife-hand any more. I'm taking you back to talk to the Consul General at Papeete, that's all."

He walked aft, leaving the sentence unfinished, and swung the main boom to back the sail so that the wind might draw the schooner off the sand as soon as the tide served. Even in Papeete Bellow Bill never told the details of what had happened on Mahia.

FANGS OF THE FETISH

Where that mysterious South Seas trail led,
Bellow Bill Williams didn't know—but he
guessed at death and treachery ahead

CHAPTER I

BLOODY BEACH

TATTOOED IN A triple circle around Bellow Bill Williams' hips was a snake, tail uppermost, its head invisible. Therefore the knowledge that a serpent travels in an indirect and sinuous course had been jabbed into Bill's hide by thousands of painful needle-pricks. And he certainly knew, as every survivor of the tough old times knows, that the safest place in the South Seas to hide anything from a white man is the spirit house of a Solomon village.

Persuade a hundred cannibals whose amusement is hunting heads that anything is a fetish, and it will be guarded with a fanatic and murderous zeal from white men, while at the same time the savages who worship it will be afraid to lay a finger on it, lest the devil blast them.

Bellow Bill knew that. Nevertheless Namu Pierce fooled him completely. There was a good reason. Pierce was subtle. He was daring. He wanted desperately to put a certain proposition up to Bill. Yet it was not his cunning, but a chance encounter, which gave Bill a wrong slant on the whole affair.

It happened this way:

Bill anchored his pearling schooner in the harbor of Malitia and disposed of his season's take of shell that same night to Charley Wong, the wizened and honest old Chink trader.

Never were two men more unlike. Wong didn't weigh a hundred pounds. Bellow Bill Williams tipped the scales at two hundred and forty—and every pound of it was hard muscle. He

Bill stood over the fallen Pierce, whirling the chain

stood six feet three, a blue-eyed giant with curly, coppery-red hair who knew the South Seas from Hawaii to New Zealand, and who was known wherever there was a tight corner that only an exceptional man could escape from with a whole skin, or a job that required a man with double the average man's strength, and a cool head to boot, to bring off.

Bill ran a pearling schooner. But he had been into the New Guinea jungles after gold, brought virgin diamonds from fields no white man before him had seen, mastered a round half dozen of the South Seas' more violent ruffians, and at least once, solved a mystery that opened a big section of Northern Australia for settlement. It was his boast that he went where other men wouldn't, and never demanded his profit in advance.

Even so, he wasn't renowned chiefly for his exploits, or feats of strength. Bellow Bill's notoriety sprang from his tattooing, and his voice. From waist to neck and from wrist to shoulders every square inch of his skin was covered in designs in many colored inks. Anchors, stars, daggers and butterflies filled the space between the full-rigged ship pricked on his chest, the Chinese dragon and the triply-coiled serpent on his hips.

His voice had the deep reverberating roar of distant thunder, or ground swell booming on a reef. It was impossible for him to whisper; and when he shouted he raised echoes a mile away. He was a strange friend for wizened little Wong, and yet the two were good friends.

During the bargaining over the pearls they drank a quart of *kan shao chin* each. That is triple-distilled rice wine with the bite of liquid fire and the power of an angry elephant. Wong liked it flavored with Chinese herbs which tasted something like caraway seed. He claimed it made the liquor medicinal as well as pleasant.

He had no idea of getting Bill drunk during the bargaining. He had tried that years before. Along with Bill's tattooed six feet and three inches of bone and muscle went an iron head. Even so, *kan shao chiu* consumed by the quart is mean stuff. Bill wandered out at dawn for a dip in the sea—just to get the lingering taste of the medicinal herbs off his tongue.

HE WAS coming out of the breakers, naked and dripping, when five kinky-headed Papuans marched out of the brush onto the beach and started single-file toward a detached hut. Close to the open door they paused. Over the oiled, soot-colored bodies ran a ripple of tightening muscles—that quick, unmistakable tension that hardens the body of a cat about to spring. One of them whipped out a knife; made a stride toward the open door.

"Ahoy in the hut! Shoot fast!" Bill bellowed. The boom of his roaring voices started echoes a mile away. By the sheer tremendous sound he gained the occupant of the hut one precious second. For the Papuans half turned to make sure that Bill was too far away to interfere—and though they rushed the hut, in that lost instant a white man sprang to the open door.

His Colt roared. The bullet doubled the leading Papuan up like a jack-knife. Over his tumbling body leaped the white man, between the knives that flashed at him, so close that the bared steel seemed to touch his bare ribs. Twenty feet he ran, then whirled. The four blacks were charging him. The Colt swept up at the end of a long, lean arm, rigid as a ramrod. He fired twice.

At each shot the recoil made the Colt jerk upward, as high as his head—to drop instantly back into line. At each shot a black figure plunged face first into the sand. One. Two. Quick as a pulse-beat.

And for the third time that unerring Colt dropped into line, gripped at the end of a long, rigid arm like a pointing finger of Death.

Perhaps there was an infinitesimal pause. Bellow Bill was sprinting to get into the fight. Perhaps he only caught one vivid picture out of the midst of action that was uninterrupted, but thereafter that was the picture that came into his mind when he thought of Namu Pierce. A lean old man, stark naked, with white hair cropped close to his skull. Jet-black eyes, set close together, that gleamed over a revolver barrel. He faced the flashing knives that would rip open his naked belly in a pair of seconds as though he had all the time in the world. Coolly as an executioner he selected his next target. He was squeezing the trigger with a caressing gentleness.

His cold deadliness, the certainty that he would not miss, was too much for the blacks. With a howl of terror they sprang right and left. They threw their knives away, turned, and ran for the brush. The long arm that held the Colt swung slowly to follow one of them, but though seconds passed, there was no shot. The blacks dove into the brush. Bellow Bill, panting, reached the white man—who coolly lowered the Colt and faced him. In the close-set black eyes a red glare slowly faded. Otherwise not a muscle in the lean, saturnine face changed.

BELLOW BILL turned over the three bodies on the sand. The first was shot an inch under the breast bone. The second two were drilled cleanly through the forehead.

"Damned fine shooting," Bill rumbled. He was a poor shot himself. "And you're lucky at that."

"Luckier than you think," said the stranger. He flipped open the loading-gate of the old-fashioned, single-action six-gun, and began to eject the shells. One by one six empty cartridge cases dropped to the sand. "Do you ordinarily mix into a knife-brawl barehanded?"

Bill eyed the empty shells. He answered dryly. Something about that lean, dark face seemed to demand clipped speech. "As often as you bluff a pair of butchers without a bullet left in your gun."

"I only bought this gun yesterday. When I got out of jail. I used three shells to learn the balance of it, and didn't have spare ammunition to reload. But the blacks didn't know that."

"No," Bill rumbled. He added:

"Most men would have run."

"Most men would have been knifed in the back, too." Lean lips twitched. "Twenty years ago, if they'd been in my shoes. If you hadn't shouted, though—"

He shrugged. The sound of the shots had brought a crowd running along the beach. Foremost among them was a man wearing a constable's coat, and no other clothing. He was about to ask questions. A lot of questions. A British policeman is thorough when he starts to investigate a crime, but before the constable could speak the man with the close-cropped white hair flipped a thumb at Bill.

"My name's Namu Pierce," he said. "This big chap with the ship tattooed on his chest and the snake coiled three times around his hips will testify I shot in self-defense."

"Yes," said Bill.

The constable shut his mouth, opened it, and shut it again. Something about Pierce silenced routine questions.

"Oh!" the constable said. "Oh—all right. But I say! Do you know who you shot?"

"For twenty years I've been where I didn't see any strangers to know," Namu Pierce answered coolly. "I'm just out after serving my time for manslaughter. You're bound to find that out, so

I'm telling you now. I've never laid eyes on these blacks before. But—I'm guessing that I *do* know who they are. In a general way. As they were coming to knife me while I was asleep, they ought to be some of Wallaby Marsden's blacks."

A MURMUR ran through the crowd as he mentioned the name of the millionaire trader. A good third of them were in debt to Marsden. The rest bought most of their supplies and sold most of their copra or shell in the Marsden godowns. His was not a name to associate lightly with an attempted assassination. Emphatically not. As the murmur died, every eye—including Bellow Bill's—shifted to a sun-dried little man whose up-slanting eyebrows gave an expression of saturnine surprise to an otherwise grim face. Pointed black mustaches gave his face a Gallic touch. The high cheek bones and light gray-green eyes also indicated French descent.

He stared a little harder at Namu Pierce.

"John Wellington Marsden, you mean?" rasped the constable.

"Wallaby, to me," Pierce retorted unabashed. "He was the skipper, and I was the mate. Our cargo was square-face gin and Winchesters, goin' out, and black recruits comin' back." Pierce caught Bill's eye, and grinned. "That was twenty years ago, when skippers would take chances."

"How about it, Rameau?" the constable asked the Frenchman.

"Oh, it is possible," said the latter indifferently. He stirred one of the bodies on the sand with the toe of a pointed shoe, white with pipe-clay. "Zees' man I know." The accent was barely discernible. "It ees one of Marsden's blacks, *oui*. The othaires?" He shrugged, and the gray-green eyes bored into Pierce's face. "You say the boss sent zem?"

"Me? No!" Pierce answered contemptuously. "I just said they were probably from Wallaby's plantation. Why they left I got no idea. None at all. And you haven't, and Wallaby hasn't. No. Of course not!"

"Well, I'm holding you for an inquest or trial. And anything you say will be used against you," the constable interrupted belligerently.

"Sure," said Pierce coolly. "And in the due course of your damn' colonial law I'll be acquitted. You'll see." He handed his empty revolver to the constable, and grinned at Bill.

"By your tattooing and your size you'll be Bellow Bill Williams," he went on. "News filters into a jail, and it brought me here hoping I'd find you. I've heard"—the tone was tinged with mockery, and yet in the face of that hostile crowd it carried a challenge that a bold man could not disregard—"that Bellow Bill was as handy in the jungle as on the deck of a pearlin' schooner, and that he never asked to see his profit in advance."

"And if so?" Bill rumbled in growling chest-tones.

"Then you're the man I want for a pardner. I got a damn good proposition that needs *two* men. Something that dates back to the days of Bully Hayes." Close-set, glittering black eyes looked disdainfully over the circle. "Bully Hayes, the pirate," said Pierce. "There's ten thousand quid in it for you, Bill—if you figure I'll be a good pardner in a tight pinch. It'll be tight, all right."

The cool impudence of that speech tickled Bill. An ex-convict, under arrest, going to jail… who had the gall to hint that the most powerful personage in the Islands had ordered his murder. And the sheer brass to dangle a fifty-thousand-dollar secret before a money-hungry gang!

It was a daring play; yet Bellow Bill, quick-witted himself, recognized it for a stroke of genius. Marsden had influence enough to railroad an ex-convict back into jail. But to do so after that remark would set a very ugly rumor afloat.

"You got your nerve," Bill rumbled.

"Oh, quite. See me this evening, then. At the jail," Pierce answered coolly.

Bellow Bill nodded. It was a mistake. He misjudged the man completely. And yet Bill can hardly be blamed. He loved a reckless adventure as an Irishman loves a fight, for its own sake. Namu Pierce was a snake, as the future proved; yet he possessed two virtues: courage and audacity. On that bloody beach chance had enabled him to show Bill his best side. Recklessness appealed to recklessness.

There are few living things that possess courage enough to stalk and attack an armed man. And because a lion is one, men are prone to forget that a second is the king cobra.

CHAPTER II

THE MAN WHO WAS
TOO STRONG

THE CONSTABLE REFUSED pointblank to let Bill into the jail. The shooting called for discussion, which in turn called for gin. It was the most exciting event of the season, and it was after sunset when Bellow Bill rowed back to his schooner. The liquor was warm in his belly, but he was disgruntled. All day men who drank with him had looked at him sidewise. They hadn't quite dared to be frank or friendly, and their glances inferred that they thought him a fool. That was annoying.

As he made the dinghy fast and swung himself over the rail, Charley Wong rose from a hidden seat at the head of the companionway. Bill uttered an angry grunt.

"A miserable worm begs your distinguished pardon—nephew," whispered the old man. The slender fingers were shaking in the wide sleeves, and his eyelids fluttered over the sloe-black eyes. Wong was nervous, which was amazing; and though the honorifics meant nothing, to be addressed as "nephew" did. In a Chinese family an uncle is given more respect and has more authority than a father.

"My poor boat is yours," Bill rumbled. He grinned, and yet he meant it. "Even though our business is done."

"It is easy to go on the mountains and fight tigers. But to open the mouth and out with a thing, that is hard," Wong muttered. "Nephew, there is a pearling concession where no divers have been for ten years. You may fish it for nothing if you start for the grounds tonight."

The bribe was colossal. The shell alone from such a concession would amount to two thousand pounds; the pearls to no one could say what. But Wong was a trader, who leased no oyster beds.

"Uncle," Bill boomed, "what do you know?"

"Nothing except that one birds'-nest in the soup is worth two hundred high on the walls of the cave," said the old man emphatically. "I was not in these islands twenty years ago. Something buried then is stirring. It will be thrust back into the grave with money, or with blood. And that is all I know—except that the offer is good. The pearl shell is there waiting for your fingers."

"Marsden's shell."

Slender yellow fingers trembled in the wide sleeves. There was no other answer.

"Charley," Bill rumbled, "I came to the South Seas nearly twenty years ago. Not quite, but I was just a kid when I crossed the equator last to serve on an American transport in the war. I was a pearler at the beginning, and I'm only a pearling skipper now. Yet there's been more than one fortune pass through my hands. In virgin diamonds. In gold. In men that I've pulled out of trouble, who were willing and able to set me up in business, either here or elsewhere.

"Here I sit, in a fifty-cent cotton singlet and a pair of duck pants, on the deck of a schooner worth six thousand at the most. Do you know why? Because I'd rather rip a pearl out of deep water with my own hands than sit between four walls and make ten times the profit. So you go back and tell Marsden he's tried to bribe me with the wrong coin."

"*Rih chiu chien ren hsin,*" Wong muttered. "In the course of time men's motives may be seen." He rose with dignity.

"Marsden wouldn't make that offer unless he had a damn good reason for stopping this fella Pierce," Bill growled.

"Would he make it to keep Bully Hayes' loot from being found?" Wong retorted. "Muddy water, unwisely stirred, grows darker still. Left alone it clears itself." He paused, but Bellow

Bill only shook his big head of coppery-blond hair. With a little sigh the old Chinese slid over the rail into his own dinghy, tied close under the overhang of the stern.

HIS LAST remark, however, had made Bill thoughtful. For a moment he watched Wong row toward the beach, which was about a hundred yards away. Then, with a scowl, the pearler went below. The liquor was dying within him. He wanted a long drink of water from the scuttle butt.

The water had a queerly bitter taste, but Bill had filled the cask himself, and that recently. He drained the dipper. In his ears a low roaring commenced. The deck of the cabin suddenly seemed to heave and spin under his feet. He staggered, hurling the dipper away, and lurched up the companionway to the deck. He was drugged. The treachery sickened him. The extravagance that drugged a whole barrel of water to make absolutely certain that a dipperful would go down his throat meant—his spinning head couldn't tell what. Defeat, surely.

He swayed toward the rail. Out from the shadows of the bow a lean figure glided toward him, catlike. The starlight gleamed on blued steel. The high cheek bones… The mustache… It was Rameau…

Bellow Bill made one step forward with doubled fists. He couldn't even feel his arms, couldn't tell if he were lifting them. He fought to fill his lungs, shouted:

"Ahoy! You on the beach—"

And before Rameau could reach him, he threw himself over the low rail into the sea. He struck with a terrific splash. The drugged brain clung to the grim thought that now Rameau would have to shoot him in the open, before witnesses, in case he shot. Desperately Bill struck out for the shore. The water revived him, somewhat. But he knew before he made a half dozen strokes that he would never last a hundred yards. He fought ahead, whirling darkness in his brain, little waves slapping at his gasping mouth like soft fingers.

He did not hear the dinghy that rowed to him. He hardly

felt the slender yellow fingers that twisted in his singlet. His own huge tattooed hands caught instinctively at the gunwale of Wong's boat; his eyes, with pupils hugely enlarged, stared unseeing at the little Chinese.

"He called the beach for help, not me," Wong muttered.... "Only an idiot builds a trap for a tiger out of reeds." The wizened old man glanced once at Bill's schooner. He saw no one aboard, but nevertheless he began to scull with one oar for the beach, making the best speed he could. The necessity of holding Bill's lolling head out of the water handicapped him terribly.

Men were coming—and foremost among them was a burly figure that loomed against the whiter sand, all massive head and heavy shoulders with no neck between. Wizened little Wong stopped sculling. From the beach roared a voice arrogant with authority:

"What goes on there, eh?"

"My fliend Bellow Bill dlunk," Wong quavered. "I take him home velly quick."

"What're you headin' for shore for then, eh?" roared the voice. "That's his schooner out there. What's a stinkin' Chink doing, looking out for a white man, eh? Hell, I'll look after him myself! Drag that boat in, Otua!"

A BIG Melanesian dashed into the sea as far as his shoulders and caught the bow of the dinghy. Wong muttered under his breath in Chinese.

"What's that, eh?" roared the voice. A heavy hand tightened in Wong's jacket and jerked him onto the sand. "You get for home very quick yourself or I'll knock seven bells out of you, eh?"

"Allee light, Miste' Malsden," old Wong quavered. But he did not go. Not far. Only to the edge of the crowd, where he lingered while Marsden and his big black climbed into the dinghy and rowed Bill out to his schooner. They remained aboard only a moment—barely long enough to carry the pearler to his bunk. Then they rowed back.

"He was just drunk and fell overboard," Marsden announced

arrogantly to the crowd. "That's all. Come along, all of you, and have a drink with me, eh?"

Still Wong lingered in the rear. Five minutes later the anchor was raised on Bill's schooner. Ghostlike, never showing a light on her deck, she slipped out to sea. Neither anchor nor sails had been raised as Bellow Bill raised them—hand over hand, with a strength that mocked their weight.

Wong shuddered and turned slowly to go home.

"To be aged and weak in one's own village is an honor," he muttered, "but to be weak and aged in the country of the foreign devils is bitterer than gall! Honorable nephew—your uncle tried twice to save you."

Bellow Bill Williams recovered consciousness with his head splitting in the particularly vicious headache induced by knock-out drops. He was on land. With his first movement a chain clanked. He rolled over and discovered that he lay in a shed so dilapidated that the stars gleamed through the huge holes that rust had eaten in the sheet iron roof. By the stars he judged that the time was not yet midnight—which meant that he could be no more than ten miles at most from the town. For the wind had gone down with the sun.

That he had been taken no farther surprised him. It argued that his captors were confident that no one was going to look for him very hard. So did the fact that he had been left chained up with no one to guard him. The handcuff on his left wrist was a clumsy iron contraption. About three feet of chain ran from it to a heavy bar set near the ground, and extending the length of the shed. He felt beside him, and found, as he expected, another length of chain, a similar cuff.

He grunted. He was in a bacarroon—one of the sheds where unruly contract laborers used to be imprisoned in those early days when blackbirders flourished and contract labor was thinly disguised slavery. A stronger British government had stamped out such things. Even though these iron cuffs undoubtedly came from one of the British ships that had carried convicts to

Australia, nearly a century earlier. He could feel the ridges that long exposure to the damp sea air had eaten in the wrought iron. Governments were funny. They enslaved whites, used their chains for blacks, and finally freed the blacks. The three great chapters of South Sea history were epitomized in that length of ancient blacksmith work.

Bill gave another grunt. He fingered the old chain, link by link, and found—as is so often the case—that rust had worked beneath one weld that had been carelessly hammered when the iron had been red-hot. Some blacksmith had paused to wipe the sweat from his face, nearly a century ago. The diameter of the links was still nearly three-sixteenths of an inch, but the metal was wrought iron, not steel. It would bend.

HE SET his feet against the bar, and wrapped both hands in the chain. Anyone who had been watching him would have seen his immense back broaden, his waist draw thin. The dragon tattooed between his shoulder blades swelled and writhed—and suddenly he was flat on his back. The free end of the two feet of chain that was still locked to his wrist flew back and struck him in the face. The straightened link clanked against the rusty sheet iron walls.

Bill jumped to his feet, his enormous chest heaving. Savagely he kicked the shed door open, and stepped out into dense undergrowth. With a growl he pushed through interlaced branches and vines which seemed to have been disturbed only once in years. He was guided by the booming of surf, and came out at last on an empty beach.

On shore there was not a light, not a sign of mankind, but anchored about two hundred yards beyond the surf was his own schooner. No riding light swung in the rigging. By night the vessel would be invisible from the sea; by day any passing ship would have suspected only that Bill had anchored to prospect for a new bed of pearl shell.

"Chained in a deserted station to starve, huh?" Bill rumbled. "Only—how in hell did Rameau have a key to those irons?"

He dove through the surf and swam out without stopping

to figure that out. The question that really bothered him was whether the schooner had been sailed north or south after leaving the town. There was no way that he could tell without sailing along the coast until he recognized a landmark.

He paused on deck to listen before he swung himself down the companionway. He heard nothing. His feet hit the lower deck as lightly as a cat's, but the chain dangling from his wrist gave a loud clank. In the darkness a man gasped.

Bill leaped at the sound—and from his own bunk the flash of a shot leaped to meet him. The bullet *zupped* by, so close that the powder burned his cheek. Left handed he swung for the gun—and the chain flailing from his wrist smacked on bone with a hollow crunch. The gun hit the deck—just as there was a rush of bare feet toward Bill from behind. The impact of a big body staggered him. For an instant he wrestled in the grip of an immensely powerful man.

Then he twisted, tore an arm free, and struck—the vicious rabbit punch for the neck that is delivered with the edge of the hand. The man he gripped seemed to turn to water. He slipped through Bill's arms, and lay without a sound. A blackjack could have been no more effective.

Bellow Bill jumped for the arms-rack and snatched down his favorite weapon—a sawed-off ten gauge shotgun loaded with buckshot. He covered the cabin. After a moment he swore softly with relief and lighted a match. A huge Melanesian lay on the deck. In his bunk was Rameau, with one side of the head a gory horror. The skull beneath was so badly fractured that one eyebrow was far out of line with the other.

"You shot at the first sound—and yet you used knockout drops instead of poison. And waited around to pick me up again," Bill rumbled at the dead white man. "That means that if I could just be kept away from town a little while... it would be enough. Wong's right. There's a damned sight more than any South Sea pirate's loot behind this."

Bill bound and gagged the Melanesian, doused him with

water and hoisted anchor and sail while he was coming to. When he had learned where the town lay—it was to the south—Bill set sail. Grimly he wondered while the schooner slipped slowly through a calm sea what he would find there. Namu Pierce had been in jail, without a friend, all night.

It was the dark hour before dawn when he anchored in the harbor again. The town was quiet. That was to be expected, but he was armed for vengeance as well as rescue when he rowed ashore. The shotgun if the constable tried to arrest him; dynamite, capped and fitted with one-inch fuses in case he was mobbed—and one other bit of preparation. He carried the Melanesian ashore and left him lying like a bound pig above high-tide mark, but as Bill advanced toward the jail the body of Rameau was over his shoulder.

ALMOST TO his surprise he moved forward unchallenged through a sleeping town. He reached the one room jail, stepped to the barred window, hissed softly. Instantly Pierce's face was at the bars.

"You, pardner? Praise the devil!" he grated. His eyes were rolling in his head. His lips were drawn back from locked teeth. He was as frantic as a caged wolf. "They gave me no water till supper," Pierce whispered. "Then I got a dipperful, but before I drunk a fly lit on it—and died. Poisoned, pardner!"

"Aye?" Bill rumbled. "Steady, now."

All South Sea buildings are flimsy. Bellow Bill found a beam, thrust it under one corner of the jail, and heaved. The sheet iron structure rose six inches. The space didn't seem to be enough to permit a man to pass, yet Pierce was out—in one swift wiggle that made Bill start.

"Open your jackknife and lemme have it!" he panted as he caught sight of Rameau, face down on the sand. He held out handcuffed hands to Bill. "Damn them, I'll cut that blighter's throat!"

"Steady!" Bill boomed. He didn't like the cold-blooded

murderousness of that demand. "None of that—and anyway, he's dead. Shove him under the jail while I hold it up."

"What for?"

"Because I'm asking it, stranger," Bill growled. "When he's inside you can strike a match and look at his forehead. I'm betting the constable is miles away from here, and there's a handful of buckshot waiting for him if he ain't. You can strike a light."

In the darkness Pierce scowled. There was a perceptible pause. Then he did exactly what he was told. A lithe wriggle took him under the jail. A match flared—and he swore aloud, far too surprised to hold down his voice.

On Rameau's forehead Bill had written in blood-red letters:

> *Returned with thanks*
> *To Wallaby Marsden*
> *from Bellow Bill*

Pierce squirmed out. "That's going far, pardner," he said dryly. "There will be constables trailing both of us now."

"I'm sore," Bill rumbled. "Damn all dirty fighters." The jail dropped gently back on its foundations. Bill tossed the beam away. "You lied to me about that pirate loot stuff," he accused grimly.

"Oh, quite," said Pierce, perfectly cool. "Too many fellas standing about then to tell the truth, what? The fact is, I'm Wallaby Marsden's partner, and I can prove it. Half of everything he's got is mine. That's why he's trying to kill me. The stake isn't hundreds of thousands. It's millions."

CHAPTER III

THE TICKET TO HELL

THREE DAYS LATER Namu Pierce and Bellow Bill stood at the edge of a jungle clearing in the wild hills of Malitia, far from the sea. It was half a hour after dawn. Less than fifty yards away a big native village was beginning to stir, yet they could not see it. The morning mist still covered everything, as thick as the thickest fog.

They could hear the wheezing breath of an old woman blowing the embers of a fire into flame, the thud of an empty pannikin on a pole floor, the yelp of a puppy being strangled for breakfast. They could guess that a village which had boasted a hundred warriors twenty years before had grown still larger; wonder how many guns the village possessed, in addition to wooden war-clubs that could cut flesh like an ax and the multiple barbed spears which every warrior would possess. There were sure to be some guns. They might be modern repeating rifles, taken from recruiters murdered during the past year. They might be flint-locks a hundred years old. There might be plenty of ammunition, or almost none.

The clubs and spears were certainties. So was the fact that the instant upwards of a hundred fuzzy-headed cannibals discovered that two white men had been so exceedingly foolish as to walk into the village, there would be an instant, concerted, and gleeful attack. Namu and Bill were armed to the teeth, with dynamite as well as firearms. No matter. They were outnumbered fifty to one, and the Solomon Islander is a fighting man by inclination, training, and religion. They would look on Namu and Bill as so much meat on the hoof, and two prime heads to be smoke-cured in the spirit house.

The rising sun was a red ball that slowly sucked the mist away. Already the white men could make out the thatched roof of the spirit house. Somewhere within that huge structure was a clay plaque about a foot in diameter, crudely modeled in the form of a devil's face. In the center of the clay was a sheet of paper that was worth a million dollars to Namu Pierce. But until the sun sucked away the mist, and the interior of the spirit house got light enough for a stranger to see and find a small object, Bill and Namu could only wait and finger their weapons. In five or ten minutes more they could attack. Meanwhile they stood in the dripping foliage, and wished the mist wasn't so damned cold.

To come as far as they had, they had risked their lives more than once. First there had been a race along the coast, with six hours' start from Bill's schooner against a swarm of launches that had left Malitia as soon as Rameau's body had been discovered. Bill wasn't sure he had shaken off that pursuit, but he thought he had. He had let his schooner go sailing on with no one aboard while he and Namu swam ashore.

Then there had been a long march up a trail guarded with man-traps, with only Namu's memory of twenty years before to guide them. Finally, here they were.

THE STORY Pierce had told during those three days had been plausible to an old-timer like Bellow Bill, who remembered the tough times. As a matter of fact, except for one lie, Namu Pierce had told the unvarnished, literal truth.

Wallaby Marsden had been the skipper of a blackbirder, and Namu the mate, but British gunboats were rapidly taking the profit out of blackbirding, and they both knew it. They decided to pool their money, and set themselves up as traders. Almost to their own amazement, the venture succeeded from the start.

Each partner knew that the other was a tricky, murderous scoundrel. Pierce was clever enough to make no bones about that. The money was rolling in. He wanted it all. So did Wallaby. Each was safe as long as the other was unable to lay hands on the partnership agreement.

"Wallaby put his in his safe," Pierce explained. "I was planning to crack it. Oh, quite. I figured I was smarter. I gave it out that I was carrying my agreement in my money belt. But the agreement in my belt was a forgery I'd made myself. The real one was in this clay plaque all the time. I'd given it to a witch doctor, a friend of mine. I knew he'd keep it."

"Why?" Bill had asked.

"Because it was a boss-devil fetish. I dipped the plaque in thin glue, and powdered it thick with potassium cyanide. I told the witch doctor that any man who licked that plaque would die. They would, too. Get enough cyanide on their tongue to kill 'em on the spot. No village would let anything happen to a devil-fetish like that, what?"

"No," Bill had rumbled. For a second or two he hadn't trusted himself to speak. Only a devil would give such a thing to a savage. Bill wondered how many blacks had died writhing in front of that fetish in the last twenty years. Plenty. No doubt of that.

"I still don't savvy your scheme, though," Bill had said at last. "Why the forgery in your money belt?"

"Because I hoped Wallaby would try to kill me to get it," Pierce had explained coolly. "I'm the better shot. I'd kill him—in self-defense, savvy. Then I'd blow his safe."

"That was taking a chance."

"I'm not timid," Pierce had said dryly. "But Wallaby was too smart, damn him! While I was thinking of hot lead he was thinking of knockout drops. I took a drink with him one night and keeled over. He took the agreement out of my belt and tore it up in front of my face. I couldn't lift a hand. Couldn't hardly keep my eyes open. When I did come to, there were handcuffs on me, and a constable waiting to read me a warrant for my arrest on a manslaughter charge. I'd killed the man, all right. But only

Wallaby could prove it. He got the thanks of the court for help-ing to arrest a dangerous criminal."

A red glare had come into the close-set black eyes.

"After I was safe in jail, where he couldn't get at me, I was so mad that I told him that the agreement he'd torn up was a forgery, and that when I got out I'd have half of every dollar he had. I wanted the poisonin' devil to suffer. It was a damn fool thing to do, but when you've got twenty years to wait it seems like a lifetime."

"Did he know you'd made that fetish?" Bill had asked.

"No-o, though he knew I'd bought cyanide. He's smart, and he might have put two and two together in the course of years. Rumors of a boss-devil fetish like that are bound to drift back to the ports. But even if they did, what could Wallaby do about it?

"He'd have to sneak into the village to steal it. Even I'll have to do that now. The witch doctor I gave it to is dead long ago. An old savage don't live twenty years."

Bellow Bill had nodded. "Suppose Wallaby had located the village and gone after the fetish with a big armed party?" he suggested.

"The blacks would skip out and take the fetish with them," Pierce retorted. "You know that. It's a job for a thief. For one man, or two at most. I'll admit a good pardner is worth half a million to me. That's why I wanted you. But nothing in the South Seas is so safe from white men as the boss-devil fetish of a Solomon spirit house."

AND THAT was true. In the cold morning mists it was more than true. It was grimly self-evident. Safe, even from the owner. As the two men waited, Pierce's saturnine face was so expres-sionless that it might have been carved from hard brown wood. To Bellow Bill, on the contrary, danger was intoxicating. There was a little grin at the corners of his lips, and golden flecks were beginning to dance slowly in his eyes. The mist was thinning out fast. The roofs of the huts in the village were becoming visible, like rocks rising out of a gray-white, swirling sea. Bellow Bill

pointed with a huge, tattooed arm, and leaned close to Namu
to speak in a rumbling whisper:

"That roof there is sheet iron! What do you make of that?"

"Nothing!" Namu whispered. His eyes were on the spirit
house, and he hardly turned his head. "Chief's hut, maybe. To
hell with that! The boss-devil fetishes are usually at the little
room at the back end of the spirit houses, aren't they?"

"Usually," Bill rumbled, scowling at the straight, sharp line of
a white man's roof that didn't belong at all in a cannibal village.
Savages preferred watertight sheet iron to thatch when they
could afford it, but...

"I swore to Wallaby I'd go through hell to smash him," Pierce
was whispering with cold ferocity. "Got that dynamite ready,
Bill? Let's go!"

Shoulder to shoulder they walked forward. The mist was
thinning out and disappearing like a dissolving curtain. Behind
them a woman screamed in alarm, on a rising note that went up
and up until it broke in a shrill falsetto. The spirit house stood
on a forest of piles higher than Bill's shoulder. Its walls were of
closely woven thatch. He snatched a stick of dynamite from
his belt, lit the match tied in the short, split fuse, and thrust it
under the thatch wall. He had barely time to leap back before
the explosion ripped a gaping hole in the wall.

Pierce leaped on Bill's shoulders and scrambled through
the gap. A .45 was blazing in each hand. The room had been
crowded with warriors. Some were stunned by the explosion.
Others wilted before the spiteful deadly fire in which each slug
sped into a target coolly selected. Bellow Bill, vaulting into the
house at Pierce's heels, found him ringed by writhing black
bodies. Beyond the wounded and dead, warriors were snatching
at spears that were too long to handle in that crowded space.

"Ahoy!" Bill roared in his thundering bass. Headlong he
rushed that wavering crowd, swinging a weapon that was peculiarly his own—a three foot length of ship's anchor chain that
smashed skulls and caved in ribs. There were ten wild seconds,

punctuated by yells and shrieks. Then such warriors as could move scuttled on hands and knees to escape the huge, tattooed devil who swung a dripping chain that dropped a man at every blow.

BILL WHIRLED. They had broken into a room lined with shelves, from which scores of skulls, some fleshless, some still covered with withered, smoke blackened flesh, grinned down at them. The treasure room of the village.

"It ain't here," Pierce snapped. Swiftly and coolly he was shoving shells into his smoking guns. From the main room of the spirit house a growling noise was growing louder and louder. The savages had seen their wounded. They knew now that they were attacked by only two men. Bill tossed a spluttering stick of dynamite through the door, but the *boom!* of the explosion was followed by a wild yell. Some deep chested savage began to scream.

"*Kai kai! Kai kai!*—Meat! Meat!"

"Then it must be in the main hall. Come on!" Bill rumbled. He walked through an opening in a rattan partition into the view of the savages. There were dozens of them. Because of the explosion they had rallied in the center of a huge room. It was at least fifty feet square. The thatched roof arched fully thirty feet overhead. And on the right hand side, a little closer to Bill and Pierce than to the blacks, was the fetish.

But nothing ever spawned of hell had a more diabolical shrine. Even in that split second before the charge Bellow Bill halted and stared, his mouth open. Behind him Pierce swore with the vicious hiss of a baffled snake.

The fetish lay in the center of the flat top of a kind of devil's altar, built of the trunks of palm, trees in the form of a cylinder about three feet in diameter and four feet high. The whole surface, both top and sides, was carved in an intricate design of open snake mouths, with holes bored deep into the altar, so that the representation of a snake's yawning gullet as it opened its mouth to swallow its prey was startlingly vivid. The palm wood was blackened with blood, and the devil's face of the fetish, still glistening white here and there with the crystals of poison that adhered to it, seemed to grin.

At the base of the altar lay three skeletons, as though three men had reached for the fetish, and died, and been allowed to remain where they had fallen. Nor was that the worst of the sight for two white men who must snatch their prize and run. In a ten-foot circle around skeletons and altar had been built a double fence of bamboo butts, the upper ends of which had been pounded into splinters, and the splinters bent outward and lashed in place so that each bamboo butt resembled a huge feather duster.

The edges of splintered bamboo cut like the sharpest razor. The inner circle was set upright; the outer inclined at an angle. That fence was one bristling mass of sharp-edged splinters, too high and too deep for a man to jump over; formed of bamboo too tough for a man to cut a path through without many, many minutes of labor.

Bellow Bill saw the diabolical ingenuity of that devil's shrine with a glance. Obviously attempts had been made before to steal that fetish. The witch doctor was taking no chance of losing the thing that made him all-powerful. None whatsoever. A rope, looped along the arched roof, indicated how he got over the fence when necessary.

A SUDDEN thrust from behind staggered Bill. Pierce pushed past him. A mad glare was in the black eyes. He was going to try to jump the fence. The attempt was utter madness.

"Steady!" Bill thundered. A huge paw clamped on the lean man's shoulder and swept him back. "Here's the key for that lock! Hell, it's like the Western Front!"

Bill stuck the fuse on a stick of dynamite, tossed it into the midst of the bamboo. A second followed; a third was in the air as the first exploded. The triple crash of the dynamite filled the air with flying yellow splinters. A gap, of a kind, was blown through the barrier, but the dynamite also knocked a hole in the pole floor. Where a man could pass bamboo splinters still waved like knives, but in dozens, not hundreds; like a thicket instead of an interlaced hedge.

It all happened with a speed that mocks the telling. From Bill's first glance at the fetish to the triple explosion only a few seconds elapsed, and splinters were still flying when Pierce whirled and leaped back toward the room they had left. The mad glare in his eyes told Bill that he was not running away. He was back almost instantly, carrying the savage with the shattered spine in his arms. Desperation and hatred gave him the strength to carry the warrior before him like a shield. He rushed at the barrier, protecting his own body with the naked black flesh of the wounded man.

The savage screamed horribly as the slivers slashed him, but Pierce broke through. The black body was jammed against the altar of carven, open-mouthed serpents. Over a black shoulder that suddenly streamed blood Pierce reached a long arm toward the fetish. It was all very quick. From the savages massed for a rush came a long-drawn "Ah!" of fierce exultation uttered by a score of men simultaneously.

Pierce lifted the fetish. The weight of the plaque must have acted like a spring that holds out a trigger. As he moved it there was a booming thud. The whole altar quivered with the shock of wooden springs released inside it, and out of the carved snake mouth flashed a shower of arrows. The savage in Pierce's arm was drilled from breast to back, and through his body a barbed arrow-point gouged deeply into Namu's shoulder.

CHAPTER IV

THE MELÉE

HE STAGGERED BACK. The bamboo slivers cut him cruelly, but despite the shock and the pain of the wounds he still gripped the clay fetish. A concerted yell came from the savages. The instant they saw that the devil's altar had failed to trap the white man, they rushed.

A volley of clubs and spears, aimed mostly at Pierce, preceded the charge. He tried to dodge, but pain and injury sapped his speed. In side-stepping a seven foot spear barbed with sharks' teeth he moved his head into the path of a club that hurtled like a bullet. Without a sound he pitched forward on his face. The fetish fell from his hands and split in fragments.

Bellow Bill fired both barrels of a sawed-off shotgun into the mob, and followed the buckshot with a stick of dynamite. The explosion caved in the front rank, but the charge only divided into two parts and came on. Bill leaped for the bamboo barrier, and stood over Pierce, whirling the chain around his head. The savages could not get off the barrier at his back—but it was not high enough to stop a spear.

As the leading warrior leaped in, and dropped before the crushing sweep of the chain, as Bill tossed dynamite almost at his feet, the mob divided again. They retreated, diving out of the way as the crash of the explosion blew a gaping hole in the floor where they had stood—and a spear hissed past Bill's ear. He crouched to protect himself, and in a flash realized the only possibility of escape.

The heavy chain went flying at the mob. With one arm he lifted Pierce and tossed him upon a broad shoulder. The movement caused him to lean over the fragments of the fetish. It had split where the paper in the center had weakened the clay. The yellow-stained paper lay directly under his eyes, right side up, legible.

Bill snatched it up. As he whirled, as he jumped through the hole he had blown in the floor, carrying Pierce over his shoulder, his eyes seized on the words of the document that were printed in the largest type.

He landed in the soft earth under the spirit house. He dodged through the forest of piles, while over his head the baffled savages howled like devils. He was running for his life—and he was swearing with astonishment and cold, bitter rage. Namu Pierce had lied. Partnership agreement? Partnership agreement, hell!

The most prominent words on that earth-stained paper were:

JOINED IN THE BONDS OF HOLY MATRIMONY

And filled in on the printed form in ink was the name:

Rufus Marsden

That was Wallaby Marsden. The paper was a wedding certificate. Bellow Bill wondered who Marsden had married, how Pierce had gotten the certificate, why he had risked his life so freely to recover it. Bill had a right to wonder.

By leaping through the floor he had gained a few seconds' lead on the savages, but they were pouring after him now as fast as they could jump through the hole. And the village was just about roused. Between the piles he could see blacks running toward the spirit house to get into the fight, and others who had run through the big door at the large end leaping from the veranda to the ground to head him off.

ONLY THE very natural dread of the Melanesian savage for dynamite would enable Bill to get through the comparatively open ground around the village. They wouldn't be too anxious to rush a man certain to toss explosive under their feet. Once in the jungle, however, compelled to follow the narrow, twisting trails because he couldn't possibly carry an unconscious man through the tangle of vines with any speed, Bill would have no chance. Absolutely none.

He could feel Pierce's heart beat. He wished the hard-bitten old convict was dead—grimly, as a man does wish for a bit of luck that he really has no right to expect. Bill didn't consider abandoning him. Calmly, quickly, he considered making a last stand among the piling under the spirit house, and decided against it. The piles would be more cover for the natives than protection to him. To reduce the odds against him was essential.

Bill did that by pausing to throw dynamite behind him, and then by setting fire to some litter that had collected at the top of a pile under the pole floor. With luck, that little flickering blaze would involve the whole spirit house. If so, a good many of the warriors would be drawn away to rescue their bloodstained gods and their treasures of skulls and heads. It was very like setting fire to the bank in a small town. It would draw off the older men, who had most to lose. Bill tossed dynamite into the thickest cluster of warriors who were waiting for him to show himself. They scattered, and he strode into the open. He was not running. He walked, with a rolling sailor's gait, a yellow stick of dynamite gripped in one huge, tattooed hand.

His objective was the sheet iron hut. If it was the house of the village headman, and the headman and a bunch of his picked warriors were inside, that hut was still Bellow Bill's only hope. Dynamite would drive them out. Even if he wrecked the hut he would live longer in the wreckage, barricaded behind sheet metal that would turn a spear. Spears were beginning to fly. Bellow Bill weaved in his walk like a boxer. He moved just enough to let the barbed shafts fly hissing past his body, encouraging another throw. Despite his size and strength he was as quick as a lion.

Guns were what he was afraid of. As he approached the hut the *crack* of a high powered rifle made him flinch. A tiny white curl of smokeless powder floated away from the hut door. He didn't connect a scream from the mob of warriors behind him with the bullet. Because he didn't hear the bullet, Bellow Bill merely decided that some native was a rotten shot. Most of them were. Because ammunition is precious and guns are never cleaned, most of the savages in the Malitia jungles don't pull trigger until the muzzle actually touches the thing they want to kill.

Bill advanced toward the unseen marksman at the same slow, weaving pace. Above him the rifle spat. Another miss, he thought—until he was hailed, in English!

"I say! For God's sake, can't you *run?*" A white man's voice, shrill with excitement.

BILL RAN. He scrambled up the ladder, kicking it down behind him. The door opened. Papers scattered on a floor covered with sheet metal, and the devil-masks, skulls, tools, pottery and art objects of a Melanesian village that covered the interior walls explained this bit of phenomenal luck. The hut belonged to an archæologist. One of the many white men who live for months in villages where no trader would dare to show his face, who win the confidence of savages slowly, who are accepted because they are considered harmless. Nevertheless, this hut with its iron floor was a fort. Bill grasped the fact while he was lowering Pierce to the floor and turning to help his rescuer repel the attack.

Two men were standing at loopholes with repeating rifles. One was white, thickset, blond, and amazingly young for an archæologist. Hardly more than a boy. The other was a native—a Polynesian to judge from his handsome features and light-colored skin. He was very little older than his boss.

"Watch the village, Eroro," snapped the archæologist. He whirled on Bellow Bill, the rifle at his hip. His jaw was set, and his narrowed eyes probed the big, tattooed man from top to toe. "I hand it to you," he said. "Some jobs take a pair of dirty, double-crossing thugs, I guess. Or maybe only the old-timers were really tough, after all."

Bill reached mechanically for the fine-cut chewing tobacco that he carried loose in his hip pocket. Every muscle tingled at the call of a danger instant and deadly. The rifle in the young man's hands was lined with his belt buckle. The narrowed eyes were implacable.

The Polynesian named Eroro turned slightly away from the loophole. Bill rolled the fresh quid over his tongue.

"I don't get you," he lied.

"Don't stall. I speak the language of these blacks. I can hear what they're yelling. You snatched the boss-devil fetish,"

"He did," Bill purred. "Only the arrows in the altar got him, and he dropped it. And that was that."

For an instant the narrowed eyes widened with a bitter, secret knowledge.

"So? Don't stall, sailor. That wasn't that. This is." He jabbed Bill with the rifle, and drew back. "Five years I tried for it—and you get it in less than ten minutes," he snarled. "Four years in a college, learning about the damned basket-work and art of stinking cannibals. Art!" He packed the word with hate and contempt. "Then a year in this crawling, heat-cursed, insect-cursed jungle rubbing noses with a pack of human wolves. And still I didn't dare to do what you did. But you couldn't have gotten away with it without me! So hand it over. Don't say you haven't got it, or I'll drill you. By God, I ought to drill you anyhow—both of you. My name is Terry Marsden. So d'ye believe I'll shoot?"

The Polynesian had turned completely around. His lips were retracted over clenched teeth. He took one catlike step forward.

"Sure," Bill rumbled. He reached for the piece of paper in his pocket, slowly.

IT WAS the Polynesian who was quick. His bare foot, flashing upward, kicked Marsden's rifle away from Bellow Bill. The butt of his rifle smacked against the archæologist's bare head. Eroro sprang back, whirling the rifle around to cover Bellow Bill. The whole movement was deftly executed. Marsden went down like a log—but Eroro was not the first man to make the mistake of judging Bellow Bill's speed by his size.

A huge hand shot out and clamped on the rifle barrel, twisting it aside. Eroro fired. The bullet only clanged through the sheet iron wall. Bill jerked on the rifle, pulling Eroro into the path of a tattooed fist that plunged forward like a piston. The punch hit the native in the forehead, but it dropped him, dazed, onto hands and knees. He tried desperately to rise. He couldn't make it. He lifted himself an inch or two, but only to fall back on the floor and roll limply onto his back.

He was fighting against unconsciousness. "No good… I'm no good," he muttered. "Waited… years for my chance… too… my name's Marsden… too… His… isn't… It's *my* mother's name… on that license…"

His eyes closed. Bellow Bill leaned over him, uncertain whether Eroro was unconscious or shamming. At that instant, from the direction of the trail that led toward the sea, someone fired a repeating rifle three times, in rapid succession. No outburst of yelling such as heralds an attack by savages had preceded the shots. Indeed, for the time being most of the savages were engaged in attempting to save the treasures in the spirit house. Only a few warriors had been left to besiege the fortified hut.

Bellow Bill crossed swiftly to a loophole. Three of these besiegers were writhing on the ground. The shots had been fired by a white man who was leading another attack upon the village!

CHAPTER V

THE FIRES OF HELL

OF ONE THING Bellow Bill was certain: the leader of that force was no friend of his. Either a British Resident had arrived with the constabulary, or he had failed to throw the pursuers from Malitia off his trail. In one case rescue meant jail for an unprovoked attack upon a "peaceful" village. In the other, he would be forced to give up the marriage license or be shot. Probably to give it up and then be shot, to judge from previous encounters with the trader.

And therefore he whipped the license out of his pocket. Eroro had told the truth. A marriage had been solemnized between Marsden and a certain Hurana. Obviously a native name. Probably herself a half-caste, since the color of Eroro's skin was very light indeed.

In an instant he saw the whole situation. One that was typical of the South Seas, possibly scarcely anywhere else in the world. For a tough black-birding skipper such as Marsden had been once to marry a half-caste was shrewd. But a trader whose operations run into the millions needs a wife whom Residents and Commissioners will entertain. Undoubtedly Marsden had thought that he had gotten rid of Hurana. Somehow he had blundered in making the transition, and Pierce, knowing the facts, able to prove them, was in a position to blackmail Marsden out of his last dollar.

For that earth-colored paper that had been wrapped for twenty years in poisoned clay made Eroro, and not Terry Marsden, the trader's legal heir. The child of a drunken frolic on some coral beach would inherit his millions; the boy he had reared to bear his name would be disgraced.

Bill's jaw set. It was lucky for Namu Pierce that he was unconscious. Bill would have broken his neck. That devil had told Marsden the revenge he was planning. For twenty years Marsden had lived, waiting for him to get out of jail and strike. What thoughts had been in Marsden's mind every time he took a baby boy on his knee? What fears had poisoned his pride as he watched his second son broaden, grow strong, and become a man. Waiting... waiting for a day, years hence, when a man with close-set eyes that glittered like a snake's should step from jail.

And yet that was only the half of it. The license tightened between Bill's iron fingers—but he did not tear it. Both Marsden's sons lay on the floor, unconscious. At some time Marsden had told Terry the truth. Terry had devoted his life to the recovery of this poisoned bit of paper. Trained himself in archæology, gone into the jungle, located the fetish, camped near by, hoping to seize it.

Bill did not wonder that he had failed. Pierce had tried to steal the thing by force, and Pierce would have failed.... If Terry had set fire to the spirit house the natives would have carried off their boss-devil before the thatch burned. Nothing—nothing in all the South Seas—is so well guarded from white men as the fetish of a cannibal village. Terry had played a man's game.

AND WHAT of Eroro? He had played the harder game. He was twice the man. For Bill was certain that Eroro would admit his true name only at the last gasp. Certainly Terry had been unaware of the identity of his native assistant. The holdup of Bill proved that. And Eroro hadn't been backed by a rich father. Marsden was tough. The easiest out for him would have been to kill his eldest son and the half-caste he had legally married. Maybe he wasn't tough enough to do that, but he could have easily transported them to another island, thousands of miles away; made natives of them.

A woman whose name was Hurana had been too brave and too shrewd. She must have hidden herself and her son, trained a boy to recover his heritage for himself and for her. When the proper time came Eroro had come back…. A handsome boy, barefooted, naked except for a *lava-lava*, asking another boy for a job. Getting it, sharing every risk, keeping a secret—and at the last, failing because a big, tattooed sailor could swing a fist with the speed of lightning.

"You dirty—you damned snake!" Bill rumbled at Pierce.

But—what to do? Bellow Bill thought fast. Here he was, in a hut with three unconscious men. Maybe none of them would be alive by sundown. Maybe in ten minutes more the constabulary would clear the village. Momentarily the case was in his hands, but how—how could he keep control? It was no case to be settled by a snap judgment. The matter of race was balanced by Eroro's better claim.

Bellow Bill had his own code. He wanted Marsden's fortune to go to the son who deserved it most. To the better man, to put it crudely. And not once, not once since the beginning of the whole hellish affair, had either of the sons received fair play. What feud existed between Pierce and Marsden Bellow Bill didn't care to know. He was thinking like lightning, Not more than a minute had elapsed since the three rifle shots.

What to do? Hide that earth-stained paper? Where?

Gold lights danced suddenly in his eyes. From the wall he snatched a bow and arrow. With a thread pulled from his singlet he bound the license tightly around the shaft of the arrow behind the barbed point. He alone would know where that arrow went. On the other hand, a man who was brave, and smart, might find it.

He drew the bow until the tough wood creaked. His target was a warrior standing on the bare ground in front of the spirit house, up the side of which the pale flames of burning thatch were beginning to flicker. The distance was greater than a man of ordinary strength could send an arrow. Bill missed. The shaft stuck quivering in the earth, some twenty feet from the veranda of the spirit house.

Bill smiled grimly, unstrung the bow, and replaced it on the wall. Only a smart man would notice that an arrow was missing from the iron hut. Only a brave man would learn from that yelling warrior, and the other savages who had noticed the shot, what had become of that arrow.

STILL GRINNING, Bellow Bill sloshed water in the faces of three unconscious men. As he did so a savage and triumphant yell arose from the direction of the trail that led to the sea. The sound gathered in volume as black after black took up the cry. Despite its bloodcurdling timbre it was a cheer, which ran from the guards at the trail, along the line of warriors besieging the hut and ended in a full-throated bellow from the warriors clustered around the blazing spirit house.

The cruel derision in the yelling puzzled Bill. He stepped to a loophole—snatched up a rifle with an oath, and emptied the magazine. He missed. He usually missed at long range. And along the outskirts of the village two blacks were bearing the limp body of a white man. They carried him by the feet and shoulders toward the spirit house.

A seven-foot spear transfixed his chest. The barbed point and the butt touched the ground alternately as the limp body shifted in the grip of the howling blacks. In the rear a third warrior danced, waving a captured repeating rifle over his head. The dead man was red-faced, bull-necked. It was Marsden. But where were the other men, or the constables that Marsden had led to capture Pierce and Bill?

With a flash of insight Bellow Bill guessed that there were— that there could be—no others! For if a stranger or a constable saw that certificate Marsden would be plunged into the hell that Namu Pierce had prepared for him. He would not even have the alternative of buying himself free. He had been forced to take the trail alone. Single-handed he had charged into that aroused village to aid his son. The blacks had jumped him. Three shots, and then that long spear had ripped through his chest.

He had drugged Bill treacherously. Possibly he had planned to leave Bill to starve in chains in a bacarroon. Marsden was an old-timer, tough and hard. As tough and hard as his courage. Bill clenched his fists as he watched what the blacks were doing with Marsden's body. The trader was dead. Cruelty couldn't hurt him any longer. Nothing would be gained by shooting into the yelling mob that worked and danced in front of the spirit house, but the reason for the derision in the yells was now grimly clear.

Bellow Bill sloshed more water on three men who were struggling back to consciousness. He helped to revive Pierce, who had received the hardest blow, with the toe of his boot. His sawed-off shotgun covered Eroro until the other two were able to sit up.

"Every damned one of you is a double crosser," Bill rumbled. "All right. Sit still. I'm not done."

In silence they stared back at him. Eroro was fierce. Terry Marsden was wondering if he could knock the shotgun aside. Pierce's close-set eyes glittered in coldly murderous fury.

"First point: I've hidden that marriage certificate. Try a double cross again on me and none of you'll get it."

No one spoke. They believed him. They must have wondered if he meant to shoot. Bill was angry enough.

"Second point," he growled, glaring at Terry, "Eroro there is your half brother. Mr. Marsden, meet Mr. Marsden."

The two young men exchanged a look.

"As for you, Pierce, your game's finished. As you'll see. So tell these boys why Marsden married Hurana. The rest they know, and I can guess at. And by God, come clean!"

PIERCE'S EYES glittered. He was without shame, or fear.

"Oh, quite," he said coolly. "As for double crossing, Bill, you can see that both of these lads have got to be alive if the license is to be worth a cent to me. I did have to be a bit devious with you, but I'm not mean. I remember feeling the fetish fall. You've earned your cut, pardner."

"Belay that!" Bill boomed.

"Quite," snapped Pierce, unmoved. "Going back, Hurana was the prettiest girl that ever made men wet-lipped. I wanted her. So did Marsden. So did everybody. But the missionaries brought her up. You had to marry her. I was going to do it. That's how pretty she was.

"Marsden found a missionary named Kellog and beat me to it. Kellog was a hellion, and Marsden thought he'd been kicked out of the church. Kellog said so, because he was trailing with blackbirders then. But I knew his synod hadn't acted. Marsden thought he was making a fake marriage, but he wasn't." Pierce's eyes glittered. "I killed Kellog a week later to keep him from finding out," he said. "That's the killing I served time for. I stole the certificate from Hurana, and hid it while Marsden was chasing me through the bush. That part of my story was one hundred per cent true, Bill."

"Go on," the big man growled.

"There ain't any more," said Pierce coolly. "Marsden saw a chance to marry a white girl with money, and he got rid of Hurana by telling her her marriage was a fake. She never believed it. She was an educated girl, but she didn't have the license, so she couldn't bring suit, what? It was easy enough for Marsden to drive her out in the islands, and he did. That's the whole truth, and what of it? What you think you're going to do about it—now?"

Eroro and Terry would have done something about it. From each side they lunged at Pierce. With hand and foot Bill swept them back.

"Sit still!" he growled over his leveled gun, and addressed Pierce—who had not moved, even when four hands reached for his throat. "I'm straightening out one hell of a mistake," he rumbled. "For once Bellow Bill *isn't* going places that other men *are*, and he *does* see his profit in advance, while they don't. I'm going to do nothing whatever at all. And if you want to know about what, take a look toward the spirit house. All three of you, together."

Bill stepped back and motioned toward the loopholes. He had seen what they saw. He was prepared for the exclamations of rage and horror that burst simultaneously from three pairs of lips.

About fifty feet in front of the spirit house stood a tall, slanting pole. The reason it had been erected was obscure, but the cruel brain of a maddened savage had adapted it to a grisly use. From the pole dangled the body of Marsden. It had been stripped of clothing, but the long spear still transfixed the chest. From the end of the spear long ropes ran to the hands of savages hidden beneath the nearest huts.

By pulling on these ropes they twisted the naked body, back and forth, back and forth. The spirit house was blazing more fiercely every instant. Fifty feet away the heat was still not intense, but it soon would be. In full view of the besieged men whom the savages believed to be Marsden's companions his body was being roasted on a hanging spit for a cannibal feast.

"What's your answer to *that?* You three that have spent your lives fighting for another man's money!" Bill challenged.

CHAPTER VI

THE BOSS-DEVIL

"**GETTING HIM IS** my job!" said Pierce instantly in his clipped, cold speech. That either of the younger men heard him was doubtful. Terry and Eroro were both snatching long, pointed, oval South Sea shields from the walls. Eroro selected a war club; Terry a revolver. Pierce put his back against the door.

"My job!" he repeated. "Think what you like, and damn you all three! Sorry for yourselves, what? What about me? Twenty years I spent looking through the bars, dreaming what I'd do when I got—here." His lips twisted in the coldest of mirthless grins. "We're waiting, the lot of us, to be starved out, roasted out, and *kai kai'd*. But if I get you away I ought to be paid a fortune for doin' it, what? I haven't given up yet."

"Get out of my way!" yelled Terry furiously.

It was really a gesture of Bellow Bill's sawed-off gun that made Pierce step aside with a grim shrug.

"Support them with a rifle," Bill rumbled. "And shoot straight or I'll shoot you."

Pierce snatched up a repeater as Terry and Eroro jumped to the earth, side by side. A howl arose from the savages. The first few steps of their charge was a race. They had a comparatively short distance to go. The village was laid out like a wide street, with the spirit house at the end. The smoke from the burning thatch was rolling thickly toward the hut, and though a bunch of savages rushed from the nearest shelter to cut them down, the party withered under Pierce's deadly rifle-fire—leaving six

181

black bodies sprawled in line, the head of each one close to the feet of the next to fall.

After that exhibition of marksmanship Bellow Bill loaded the rifles for Pierce—and there was no other concerted rush. But from beneath every hut, from every bush that the two must pass, a storm of missiles were hurled at Marsden's two sons.

Half the distance to the naked, slowly revolving body they ran—and then a spear, hurled from a hut they had passed, sped toward Terry's unguarded back. Eroro made a frantic leap and turned it aside with his shield. Terry twisted a white face over his shoulder at the death that had been parried. His stride faltered. Though no word was exchanged between the two they adopted the only possible tactics. Terry, crouching behind his shield, *walked* ahead. Eroro, with his shoulders close to those of his half brother, walked backward, warding off missiles flung from the rear.

They made another ten yards before a war club, whirling along close to the ground, cut Eroro's legs from under him. He fell. Terry made a step forward—and came back, standing over the other until he could rise.

"He can't walk! They'll never make it!" Bellow Bill thundered.

A lunge of his shoulder flung back the door. He snatched two shields from the walls. When he leaped to the ground he struck the match heads in two sticks of dynamite on the posts of the hut; howled his thundering war cry that seemed to boom through the smoky air, and charged.

"Ahoy!" A sailor's hail? Not as Bellow Bill roared it out. It was to that war cry that the Saxons charged behind the blind Harold at Senlac, and all but broke the armed ranks of the Normans. It was the lion's roar of a man gone berserk—a huge man, tattooed, looming more enormous through the smoke, who waved two shields around his head and gripped two spluttering sticks of dynamite.

SPEARS WERE flung, but with uncertain aim—and not at the two young men covering one another with their shields. As he passed them Bellow Bill hurled the dynamite at the nearest huts. The sticks seemed to explode as they left his hands. He reached the naked, dangling, twisting body while the explosions still shook the air, while a hut, blown from its foundation, was falling in splinters and fragments of thatch. One terrific jerk snapped the rope that held Marsden's body.

"The fire!" Terry yelled. "Throw him in the fire—a clean grave!"

Bellow Bill obeyed. Cool-headed in the thick of fight himself, he recognized coolness. He whirled on his heels like a hammer-thrower. Marsden's body arched through the air and disappeared into leaping fire that would consume it utterly.

"Ahoy!" thundered Bill. He raced back, but Terry had already swung Eroro onto his back. Bill's task was only to cover the pair of them with his shields, and few were flung. The savages had not rallied from that charge.

It was when Eroro was swung to the platform of the iron hut and Terry was scrambling after him that Bellow Bill looked up—into the muzzle of Pierce's rifle. Bared teeth gleamed above it. For an instant a cold finger seemed to touch Bill's spine. His jaw squared. With the briefest interval, Pierce lowered the rifle.

"Damn you," he said in his chilly, clipped voice. "You'll keep your secret, what?"

"Secret?" Terry echoed. He was dragging Eroro into the hut. Already Bellow Bill had vaulted to the platform and was shoul-dering through the door. "Secret? To hell with you both! D'you think I carried him in to rob him."

With a defiant glare at the two old-timers he snatched up one of the sheets of archæological notes that had been scattered on the floor, tore a blank strip off the margin, and wrote rapidly with a pencil. He thrust the sheet at Eroro.

"Keep it!" he snapped. "We've worked together for two years. God knows we were friends—or I thought so! That's a note for fifty thousand pounds, given in consideration for saving my life, just to make it more legal.

"And if you want more from me and I've got it, you'll get it!"

Furiously Terry whirled on Bellow Bill. "And what's your answer to *that*, you tattooed, murdering blackmailer?" he howled at him.

Bellow Bill grinned—slowly. Amid the intense excitement that grin sobered them all, like a bucket of water flung on snarling dogs.

"Answer?" Bill rumbled. He leaned toward a loophole, and peered through the smoke. "Why, I've got one. If things stand that way. Provided you can still see it. And—yes—you can. Take a look toward the spirit house. All three of you. Especially you, in fact, Pierce. There's lots of spears and arrows scattered around, but the one I want you to look at is closest to the fire."

They obeyed his orders.

"See it?" Bill rumbled. They nodded. "Pretty hot there. See that little curl of smoke rising from the shaft, just in front of the feathers. There! It took fire. See that little blaze? Up it goes, and out."

"Why—the shaft of the arrow isn't burning any more!" said Pierce in his cold, clipped voice.

"No," Bellow agreed. "Wood wouldn't burn yet. That bit of flame was Hurana's wedding certificate. Gone. That's my answer."

IT TOOK them a second to get it. The crackle of burning thatch was loud in the hut. Terry coughed in the smoke.

"Gone!" Pierce whispered in a low, strange tone. He looked steadily at Bellow Bill. "We could have used it, old-timer," he accused.

"Maybe you could have," Bill rumbled. "This was my first chance to express myself, partner."

"That makes me nothing but an old ex-jailbird," said Pierce. "Old—damn it, I'm sixty. The things I knew and liked are gone. Like that."

"Aye," Bellow Bill rumbled. Though he had been mistaken

in Pierce once, he knew men. He said but the one word; Terry and Eroro, staring at the pair, did not in the least understand.

Pierce shrugged coldly. He ran his eyes around the walls of the hut and selected, from the dozens of archæological treasures, a flat, carved idol of wood. Its shape was something like that of the clay plaque. He dipped it into the water bucket, took a handful of sugar from the stores, and powdered it thickly.

"The sugar glitters just like the poison did on the one I gave Murongi," he said grimly. "Murongi's dead, but he'll have sons here. I'll get their attention—for a few minutes."

"It's your own idea," said Bill very quietly.

"Sure. That's understood," Pierce nodded.

And still the two younger men didn't get it. Pierce examined the cartridges in his Colt. Bellow Bill picked up a loaded rifle.

Both were waiting—but when a puff of breeze brought smoke from the spirit house swirling around the hut both moved without exchanging a word.

Pierce leaped to the ground and ran into the open. He was holding the fetish above his head as he plunged through the smoke.

Bill pushed the two younger men from the hut, but as they jumped to the ground his big hands caught them by the shoulder and prevented them from following Pierce. Terry threw an arm around Eroro to help him along.

"Sons of Murongi! Sons of Murongi!" Pierce was shouting. "One fella boss-devil fetish! One fella new fetish!" He couldn't be seen through the smoke.

Bellow Bill gave the two younger men a push. "Run for the trail to the sea. Run like hell!" he growled. As they started running, he leaped past them. Despite his size few men could run as fast.

There was still one sentinel guarding the trail to the sea. He rose from the brush. Before he could cry out the butt of the rifle Bill carried thudded on his skull. He dropped without a sound. Bellow Bill ran on, and the two younger men followed him—

down a trail that now stretched unguarded to the sea. With the start the three had, they could now outdistance pursuit. Bill was strong enough to carry Eroro on his back if the need arose.

Terry and Eroro must have thought still that it was part of a stratagem—some old-timer's trick recalled from the tough old days. The *boom* of a revolver shot undeceived them. They stopped. So did Bill, but only Bill counted the shots. Shots that came as swift as a trigger can he squeezed with deadly aim. Two—three—four—five… An infinitesimal pause… *six*… The savage yells which had accompanied the shots ended in a howl of frustration.

"But—shouldn't we go back?" gasped Terry. "They'll kill him—"

"They didn't," Bill rumbled. "He killed five of them, and saved his sixth bullet for himself. Go on, son. He was a good pardner—in a pinch. Don't spoil the only good point he had for him."

Bellow Bill pushed the two younger men down the trail. They would never be old-timers. Not in the old sense, even though they lived in the South Seas until they were eighty. After all, Bill had only been half mistaken. A lion will charge undaunted into the face of overwhelming odds. But—so will a king cobra.

THE GOLDEN OYSTER

Bellow Bill Williams, South Seas pearler,
dives for a $5,000,000 prize

CHAPTER I

DEATH HARBOR

"**BELLOW BILL! BELLOW** Bill Williams!" Through the dull splash of the anchor in the purple-black of the South Seas lagoon and the echoing rattle of the anchor chain the tense, excited whisper barely reached the ears of the big tattooed pearling skipper who was addressed. The speaker was invisible. The voice seemed to come from the concealment afforded by the overhang of the stern of the pearling schooner—but Bellow Bill was grimly aware that neither boat nor swimmer had been moving in the harbor of Moluna a minute ago when he had swung his schooner into the wind and hurried forward from the steering wheel to drop anchor.

As always, he was handling his vessel alone. In the few moments required to drop anchor, then, someone had stolen out to hail him. Ashore the coco palms waved like silhouettes in black ink, a hundred yards away. From the village of Moluna there was not a glimmer of light. It was that black-dark hour before the dawn, and in the whole South Seas only two people knew that he was coming to Moluna.

Why shouldn't Norman-Pierce, the Resident and Governor of the island, or his protégé Professor Griswold, carry a lantern? Why shouldn't they wait for him ashore, and get their sleep?

"Aye, aye," Bellow Bill answered in a whisper that was like the growl of a mastiff. His booming, reverberant voice made whispering hard. Easier, much easier for him to utter a shout that would awaken men sleeping half a mile away.

Bill plunged in with his knife

"Come here! Quickly! It's Griswold. Don't make a sound. My—er—discovery has been blabbed. We've got to slip out of here before dawn."

No mistaking the desperate urgency of that whispered appeal. The important lines in the letter from Norman-Pierce which had summoned him to Moluna flashed through Bill's mind:

> An American professor named Alvin Griswold has made one of those amazing discoveries possible only to a scholar or a scientist. All I'll tell you is that treasure worth *at least* a million pounds is involved. $5,000,000 to you, you tattooed Yankee.
>
> He's convinced me the treasure is where he claims, and he's here with his daughter and her fiancé, calmly proposing to charter a schooner, sail to the fringes of the South Seas, dig the treasure up and carry it back. That's the kind of a chappie he is, and his future son-in-law is the sort of new-chum that believes any white man with a revolver can lick the South Seas singlehanded.
>
> It's murder to let them sail, and yet they have money and

equipment and I have no legal grounds for holding them. I've warned them, however, that I'll refuse to countersign the charter of any schooner except yours. That will hold them for three weeks or so, but eventually they'll appeal to a higher official and be sustained.

For old times' sake, hurry and help out this hard-pressed British official! You're an American, and I know a million pounds isn't enough to bribe you... you'll probably have to take a charter at freight rates, but you never did ask to see your profit in advance.

Bill, the treasure is there! Griswold actually bored into it with a diamond drill, and carried the mixture of gold dust and coral dust back to the States. He had to raise money before he could dig a shaft, but he is so naïve that he actually mentioned his discovery to illustrate a lecture on philology Philology, Bill, with *at least* a million pounds at stake. But he seems to have lectured to a bunch of dry-as-dust chappies like himself, and I think the secret has been kept. What has saved Griswold is the fact that practical men think he is a dreamer... just another crazy professor with a crazy theory in—God help us—philology.

Get here quick before I go mad myself.

And now, Bellow Bill thought grimly, a five million dollar secret had been blabbed. No wonder no lanterns were lighted, or that Griswold and Norman-Pierce had scarcely given him time to drop anchor. He walked aft, and leaned over the stern.

In the darkness he could make out the white blur of a face, and a shapeless figure balancing precariously in a small native dugout. His visitor had thrown a blanket, or a dark cloak, over his white ducks. That precaution must be due to Norman-Pierce, for the man was handling his paddle like a new-chum—a greenhorn.

"Give me your hand," he whispered. "If I try to stand up I'll fall over—"

BELLOW BILL reached out. Fingers that possessed amazing strength closed around his own huge tattooed paw. No professor ever had a grip like that. No pr—

The sky fell on Bellow Bill. He did not even feel the impact of the sock loaded with beach sand that thudded on his bare head. Fingers that were much too strong were gripping his own—and next, his head was aching, water was gurgling against the planking of the schooner close to his ear, and a light was shining into his eyes. He had been carried below decks and laid in his own bunk.

Now Bellow Bill Williams was six feet and three inches of bone and muscle. He weighed two hundred and forty pounds. If his voice was known through the South Seas, so was the amazing display of tattooing that covered every inch of his skin from hips to neck and shoulders to wrists. There was a full-rigged ship on his chest, a Chinese dragon on his back, bracelets of rope tattooed in pale blue ink around each wrist, and a snake coiled three times around his hips.

Pearling skipper he called himself. But a strength equal to that of two ordinary men, an unsurpassed knowledge of natives, and a calculating recklessness that made him seek danger and chuckle when he found it had turned him into an adventurer whose position in the South Pacific was peculiarly his own. Bellow Bill liked to go where other men wouldn't. And as a consequence he was frequently summoned—as in the present case—for affairs that other men steered shy of.

Now to get a two hundred and forty pound man down a narrow companionway is a feat of strength. Ordinarily it is a two-man job. But through slitted eyes Bill saw one man only.

He was as big as Bill himself; blond, like the pearler, though the color of his hair was tow rather than Bill's coppery-yellow. He was young, muscled like a wrestler—and he stood stripped to the waist, a mirror in one hand and a small brush in the other, painting a rough imitation of Bill's tattooing on his own body.

He worked with fierce and desperate haste, but he wasn't doing a bad job. The masts of the full-rigged ship and the blue rope bracelets were well imitated. He was wearing a pair of

Bill's duck pants, and one of Bill's singlets was tossed on the cabin table.

The pearler gave a tentative wiggle—and grimaced with pain. His hands were lashed together by the thumbs, and his feet by the big toes. A leather belt strapped his arms to his body. Bill opened his eyes wide and grinned.

"You've tied up men before, eh, lad?" he rumbled. "I dislocate my thumbs if I pull, and I can't untie knots with my fingers alone, eh? But that tattooing won't wash. I don't get the idea."

"Shut up!" was the answering growl. The brush worked frantically. The big man snatched up Bill's singlet and drew it over his head. Across the harbor sounded a guarded hail:

"Ahoy! Bellow Bill!" It was Norman-Pierce's voice.

The big man picked up a revolver and jabbed the muzzle against Bill's teeth. "Answer that, 'Ahoy! Come on aboard!'" he growled. "Not a word more or less. And yell it loud. Yell it like only Bellow Bill can yell it, savvy?"

BILL DID get the idea then. That hail would identify any big man who appeared on the deck of the schooner as himself. His voice could not be copied. Dancing flecks of gold came into his eyes, but his obedience to the command was instant. His chest strained against the tight belt.

"Ahoy! Come aboard!" he roared. The cabin rang with the sound. Instantly the big man clapped a square of adhesive tape over Bill's mouth, effectively gagging him. He blew out the hurricane lantern in the cabin, and leaped up the companionway.

Bill listened. He caught the faint *thump* of a paddle against the side of a dugout. Norman-Pierce was pushing off. Bill had the minute or two the Resident would take to paddle a hundred yards. No more. His chest strained against the belt. He thrust outward with both elbows. The belt snapped, and he swung both legs over the edge of his bunk to the deck.

A twinge of agony shot up his legs from his bound toes as he stood upright. He wondered why the big man hadn't knocked him out.… Evidently because his voice would be needed, later, for another identification. Norman-Pierce would be brought into the cabin, and forced to answer, too. A simple, daring scheme....

A slight motion of the deck made Bill fall. Bound as he was, he couldn't stand. But he could crawl. Like an inch-worm, on elbows and knees, he crossed the deck, clawing the adhesive from his mouth as he went. In his own cabin he needed no light. The arms-rack was against the after bulkhead. Bill rose, swaying, and lifted down a Winchester.

With his thumbs bound, the rifle was awkward to hold. He would never be able to aim it. Never be able to carry it up the companionway, either, without making a noise that would warn the man on deck. A shout or a shot would warn Norman-Pierce—now close to the schooner, and a perfect target if the man on deck cared to shoot.

Most men would have shouted or shot because they could think of nothing else to do. In that split second Bellow Bill weighed the chances, and used other tactics. He rolled to the deck and squirmed, feet first, to the bottom of the steep companionway stairs.

"Bill!" Norman-Pierce's whisper sounded urgently across the water. He wasn't ten yards away. "Hoist anchor, Bill! We're leaving tonight. Griswold's secret has been blabbed!"

"Aye, aye," growled the big man on deck in a muffled tone. The only light on deck came from the binnacle. He was standing well behind it, so that only the bulk of his head and his body against the stars would be visible to the Resident. But the binnacle light revealed one bare foot, resting on the seat behind the wheel.

Bellow Bill rested his heels high up on the companionway stairs and dropped the rifle barrel into the notch of his toes. His bound hands fumbled with the trigger. He could see the front sight, though not the rear one. He centered the bead on a white ankle, and waited, hoping the big man would move.... He didn't. The dugout bumped softly against the schooner.

Bill fired. "Go overboard, Pierce!" he bellowed. "Under the counter!"

THE CRACK of the rifle and the shout blended with a scream of pain. A bullet smashed into the side of the companionway, showering Bill with splinters. Over the side there was a splash, a man's shrill shout and a cry from a girl. As Bill jerked the loading lever the big man leaped across the companionway and dove over the rail.

"On deck, Pierce!" Bill roared. It took seconds to swing his legs around. He dropped the rifle. As he crawled up the companionway Norman-Pierce was swinging over the rail. Bill shoved the rifle toward him.

"Get him!" he roared.

"The constabulary will get him tomorrow. It's a small island, what?" the Resident retorted snappily. "The professor can't swim." He reached far over the taffrail, and bent as he lifted a weight. "I say, Bill! I saw you, and I heard you, and the two didn't register. When the rifle went off I jumped as high as—er—one of you did. Startling, what? I capsized the bally dugout without orders, 'pon my word."

Norman-Pierce grinned over his shoulder, and pulled into view a thin little man whose gray head and pointed beard, dripping wet, made Bill think of a half-drowned and indignant billy-goat. Two slim hands caught the rail. Bill got a glimpse of a figure slender and trim as that of an aerial acrobat, every curve accentuated by the thin, wet dress. Then a blond girl of twenty was sitting on the taffrail, wringing water from the hem of her garment. Her face was triangular and piquant, grave except for eyes that sparkled with excitement.

"Miss Susan Griswold—and the real Bill Williams. His roar is worse than his bite," said Norman-Pierce, without seeming to turn. He was peering at the shore. "The other tattooed gentleman seems to have vanished, temporarily. Too bad you missed him, Bill."

There was a splash of blood near the wheel. Bill leaned down and picked a small object from the waterways, holding it in his huge hand so that Norman-Pierce could see it, and the girl could not.

"I didn't—altogether," he growled. The thing in his palm was a toe, shot clean off. "He won't run far, I guess. And since this is a small island—who is he?"

"I don't know," retorted Norman-Pierce. "In fact, I'd have been willing to swear not only that there wasn't a man as big as that on Moluna, but that there weren't two in the South Seas." He spoke snappily, but Bellow Bill, who knew British officials and who was acquainted with the tradition that makes the true-blue Briton jest at a crisis, detected the consternation that Norman-Pierce sought to conceal by crisp speech.

CHAPTER II

CORAL KIND AND GOLD CORE

"**ALL I DO** know," the Resident added, "is that every kinky-headed Melanesian savage on the beach, down to the very sago gatherers, than which there's nothing more stupid, is talking about the gold that the professor here is going to bring back from the Lieuana Islands. And the Lieuana Islands is right. I've tried to trace the leak. You can be damn sure how far I got."

"Aye," Bill rumbled. " 'One fella Mary belong cousin along me gammon one fella Mary belong me, my word, yes!'" The deep voice of the pearler slid into a sarcastic imitation of the sing-song of a savage being cross-examined. "Great language for concealing information, *beche de mer*. But what are the facts, Pierce?"

"You be hoisting anchor. Run as near my bungalow as you can get. I've all the engineering supplies ready to rush aboard, with Paul Carson—that's Susan's fiancé—guarding them with a gun, and your clearance papers are in my pocket. I planned to rush you out on an hour's notice, and keep anyone from following you."

"And the lad without a toe figured he'd short-circuit the scheme," Bill rumbled.

"Quite, quite. I'll attend to him come sunrise," Norman-Pierce snapped. "But up anchor, Bill. The professor will explain while we're working."

"I wonder if either of you could give me a cigarette, too?" Susan Griswold asked in a husky contralto. She sat on the taffrail perfectly at ease, though her father was tramping the deck like a wet hen. The ducking and the blood on the deck didn't bother her at all. The request, as she made it, seemed to say: Now, after all, why get excited?

"I've got nothing but chewing tobacco," said Bill gravely. In the light of the binnacle her eyes flashed. A sense of humor, in a small party out to fight long odds, is worth more than a gun. In that second a partnership was born between Susan Griswold and Bellow Bill. "Fine-cut," he added solemnly.

"I'll try it—provided it will burn," Susan answered. Bill extended a huge fistful of the tobacco he carried loose in his hip pocket. The professor made a strangled sound of protest as the three men moved forward. He didn't speak to his daughter, however. Which was illuminating.

"You understand, Mr.—ah—Williams, that the Basque language is related to no other," he began as the pearler slipped a handspike into the anchor windlass. "I am a professor of Spanish language and literature. Verifying the independence of the Basque tongue has been my life's work."

BELLOW BILL raised an eyebrow at Norman-Pierce.

"This," said the Resident drily, "is the manner in which a scholar arrives at a five million dollar discovery. Better listen."

"Imagine the shock to me," Griswold continued indignantly, "when a colleague called my attention to the fact that the dialect of the natives of the Lieuana Islands contained a dozen words the roots of which were unquestionably Basque. My life's work was destroyed—unless I could prove that at some time a Basque had been shipwrecked on those islands. Naturally that would account for the incorporation of a few words in the dialect."

"Naturally," Bellow Bill rumbled. The anchor was away. He walked aft, with the professor's pointed beard wagging at his elbow.

"I plunged into research—and discovered no record that a Basque had ever been within five hundred miles of the place. Even in the archives of Madrid—nothing."

"Tough," Bill rumbled.

"Disastrous," Griswold corrected. "But in an old manuscript I found a record of an old plate ship that left Panama bound for the Philippines in the year 1590. It carried so many thousand arrobas of gold, and miscellaneous treasure amounting to five million dollars or so. Not an unusual cargo at that time. What was unusual was that news of its fate came back to Spain through the sole survivor of the shipwreck. That survivor was a Basque cabin boy.

"His story was that a violent gale had carried the ship entirely over the coral ring, as he called it, of a small island. The ship was hopelessly wrecked, and the natives of that group of islands were numerous and hostile. Cannon drove them back for a time, but in the end the result was certain.

"The Spanish captain, Jaime Mendoza by name, was a man of resolution. At night, secretly, he lowered all the gold in the shallow water beside the ship, and covered it with earth and stones from the ship's ballast. To every man still alive he announced the latitude and longitude, and reminded them that under Spanish law one-fifth of that vast treasure belonged to whoever enabled the King of Spain to recover it. His purpose," Professor Griswold explained, "was to insure that a punitive expedition would destroy the savages who were about to murder him.

"But it happened that every man was killed except my Basque. He escaped, after many years, and spent nearly fifteen years getting back to Spain. His story was believed, but when a ship was sent to the latitude and longitude he gave, no islands were discovered at all."

BELLOW BILL hauled in the main sheet. The schooner began to move through the blue-black water. "And that was that," he rumbled.

"To gold-greedy fools!" contradicted the professor testily. "But to a scholar who must prove the independence of the Basque language or see his life-work crumble, the deduction was inevitable. Here was an island the dialect of which proved that a Basque once lived there. And here was an account which claimed that a Basque lived on such an island. Why should a poor Basque lie? His story would be certain to disgrace him. That Mendoza's reckoning was in error seemed much more probable to me. It was a logical certainty that that Basque had been shipwrecked on that island. To prove it to the world I had to recover the gold—"

"And so," Norman-Pierce cut in, "Professor Griswold goes to Lieuana. He finds that one island in the group is a circular atoll, and that there is an old native tradition of a shipwreck. So he examines the bottom of the lagoon and sees an odd, conical-shaped mound. In the course of centuries, coral has covered it, but he explains to the local trader that he is making a study of coral formations—astonishin' flash of insight, that—bores into the mound with a drill, and brings up gold-dust."

"How does the gold lie?" rumbled Bill.

"In less than three fathoms of water, and under less than two feet of coral. For the takin', you might say," snapped Norman-Pierce. "And yet, there it would have lain till the end of time if two—er—old scholars hadn't got to quarrelin' about a funny language only a handful of people speak. But once the trader at Lieuana—Vansteen, his name is—gets wind of the rumor that's driftin' around among my blacks…"

"How many holes did you bore, professor?" Bill asked.

"Dozens," said Susan slowly. "Hundreds… I was with father, you see."

The bow of the schooner touched lightly on the beach. Out of the shadows of the coco-palms rushed the figure of a man clad in white duck. He was brandishing a revolver.

"That's Carson—bein' impressive," said Norman-Pierce drily.

Bellow Bill noticed that Susan bit her lip with embarrassment.

"Don't be hard on a new-chum," the pearler grumbled. "He ain't tied up, or sandbagged, is he? It's him that should be laughing at me."

Paul Carson grasped the chains under the bowsprit and swung aboard the schooner dryshod, with the ease of an athlete. He was a tall, loose-jointed man, certainly not older than twenty-three, with a short, straight nose and a wide, good-natured mouth. A likeable cuss, but lacking, Bellow Bill decided instantly, in the core of hardness essential to an adventurer.

"What was the shooting? Who did you hit? I'm rushing the natives down with the gear!" It was all uttered in a breath.

"Oh, a lad about your age and my build," drawled Bellow Bill. "You ain't seen a fella that size lurking around?"

"Why—no."

"Sound like you had," the pearler rumbled. Carson had an open face. A queer expression—chiefly incredulous amazement—had flashed across it. And his left hand had unconsciously closed into a fist. That sign of a lie is a thing for which men who deal with savages watch.

"Needn't be ashamed to admit it," Bill drawled. "He was a blond, too, and he had a red birthmark on the left side of his belly. A damn stout fella."

"No. Never saw anybody like that," denied Carson, all in a breath.

NORMAN-PIERCE AND Bill exchanged a glance. There was a queer look on Susan's face, as though she were trying to remember something. Bill's great shoulders shrugged.

"Give me my clearance papers and rush the gear aboard, Mr. Resident, and I'll get underway," he decided. "What's one man more or less, in a five million dollar gamble?"

Bill had assumed the responsibility. And yet, in the breathless haste of that lading in the starlight, he made certain dispositions that Norman-Pierce watched with narrowed eyes. Griswold's gear consisted of a diving suit, an air pump, and six cases of forty percent dynamite. Bill stowed all these in the cabin, and assigned the professor and Susan quarters there.

Carson he sent to the fo'csle, with a hammock to sleep in. And as a favor to the new-chum, Bellow Bill slung the hammock himself—in good sea-going style, as tightly stretched as his big hands could pull it, and a good five feet above the deck. It would be hard for a greenhorn to get in, and harder to leave without landing on the deck with a thump.

He warned the loose-jointed youngster that at dawn he would have to roll out to sail the schooner, so that he'd better get his sleep. Norman-Pierce grinned at that command. When everything was ready for sailing the two old-timers clasped hands.

"What do you make of it?" the Resident whispered under his breath.

"Why, the big fella got on your island without your knowing, so I guess he'll leave the same way," Bill rejoined. "Carson knows who he is, all right, though the professor and the girl don't."

"A double cross?"

"Can happen, though Susan seems like too smart a gal to fall in love with a rat. I'll find out, before dawn."

Norman-Pierce dropped over the bowsprit onto the beach. Bellow Bill backed the mainsail. The schooner gathered sternway and slid off into the blue-black water.

CHAPTER III

THE NAME ON THE BULLET

THROUGH THE JUNGLE a blond man was staggering. One foot left a crimson blot at each stride. He was whimpering with pain and rage. Vines clutched at him like fingers; leaves wet with the night dew slapped at his face; the faint trail, hard to follow by day, made the mile he must cover seem endless.

At last he heard the beat of surf on the outer reef. Before him rose the stiltlike roots of a pandamus palm, covered with a thick growth of parasitic plants into which he dived with a sob of relief. Hands caught him.

"My foot!" he snarled. "God, I'm bleeding like a pig!"

Under the pandamus it was dark as a pit. Men stirred. There was a curse in Dutch as someone fell over a native dugout, which had been lifted from the water and concealed.

"Damn it, strike a light, Vansteen!" snarled the blond man. "We'll have to lam out of here. They'll sail now, as Tari warned us!"

"*Ja?* It was your plan, Meinherr Dolin." Calm and implacable, that voice. A match spurted, and set an oil-nut alight. In the smoky, yellowish flare a round head whose hair had been shaved off bent over the wounded man. To the suffering and death of others Jan Vansteen was indifferent. "Maybe you bleed too much? Perhaps you tell all about the gold now, *ja?*"

"Think I'm a mug? You'd cut my throat!" Dolin snarled. "You'll never get that out of me!"

"You don't know," Vansteen grunted, but from the dugout

he lifted a handful of kapok, which he clapped on the wound and bound in place with his handkerchief. The oil-nut, blazing higher, revealed two natives in the background. One of these was a fat and greasy black who wore around his neck for an amulet the top of a human skull strung on a string. He had a man's finger bone thrust through the septum of a nose. The other native was a young boy whose eyeballs rolled in terror.

"You say there is a shipload of gold on my island because your uncle, who is a professor, heard another professor say so," Vansteen went on in cold and heavy irony. "You say we must come here and spy on the Griswolds, and now you say run! Bah, you take too much on yourself, my American friend. I tell you what to do, and you come back whining because you have cut your toe. You must do better, or I *will* cut your throat."

"Is that so?" They glared at one another in the smoky light. It was the Dutchman's eyes that fell. Dolin's big fingers, that were hooked into talons, relaxed. "You don't fool me, you Dutch pig. I need you and you need me, now. Afterwards we'll settle. You can divide or shoot it out and I'll meet you half way in either, get me? But don't you call me yellow! *You* wouldn't go and slug that tattooed sailor. *You* told me not to kill him! Bellow Bill! Hell, with that name I thought he must be a big bag of wind. Damn his soul, I'll put a bullet through his gut the next time I see him. I tied him up so a snake couldn't get loose, and the next thing I knew he shot off my foot!"

"To kidnap Bill was a good idea," retorted the Dutchman. "Unless he was alive to hail the Resident, the Englishman would never set foot on the schooner. So that also was a good idea. Think, *meinherr*, and do not snarl at me like a dog until there is a bone. I am the trader of Lieuana! Will I stick my head in a noose because a strange American comes to me with a tale of gold that someone else has heard of?

"To come here and lie hidden was to do much. Already my natives have robbed my godowns. To send my witch-doctor Nauma to find Tari here, and to warn him that unless he spies on the Englishman Nauma will put a spell on his father and mother back in Lieuana—that is simple. But why should I commit a crime until I am sure there is gold? Now that I do believe there may be... perhaps it would be a good idea if you did shoot Bellow Bill... in Lieuana.... We will see. A dugout with two paddlers is faster than a schooner. We will be back at my islands first."

"Why me?"

"Because if I turned you over to Bellow Bill, and told him, 'Here is a stranger I found hiding in the bush on my islands,' Bill might trust me," grunted Vansteen. "Enough to drink a glass of schnapps... once. I would take the antidote to the poison in the glasses before I drank. Then it would be very simple, and I should not need you at all."

Again the glances of the two men locked, and this time Dolin licked his lips nervously.

"You're a cold devil," he said.

"Ja," Vansteen agreed complacently. "I am a trader, and I risk nothing until I must. I will give you advice, but I tell you now, *meinherr*—you are a new-chum who has nothing but the gun I loaned you, and I am the trader of Lieuana, with every native in my debt and Nauma to put ideas in their thick heads. All you can carry out is a murder—and we will not be equal partners until you bring me Bellow Bill dead."

Dolin nodded briefly. "That won't be long," he said. "What'll we do with Tari? He can't go back to the Resident again."

"No, but why kill him?" Vansteen answered calmly. "He can come with us. We shall need him to paddle."

He motioned to the natives to pick up the dugout. They were through the surf, squared away before the trade wind and speeding with two paddles to help the sail, long before the bowsprit of Bellow Bill's schooner poked through the channel in the reef, and headed for Lieuana under plain sail.

IN THE moderate breeze Bellow Bill could easily have carried topsails. He might have set a more direct course for the island group two hundred odd miles away. The fact was that he wanted the schooner to sail herself. The wheel was in the becket, and Bellow Bill was not even aft, but forward—belly down on the deck near the open fo'csle hatch, his ear against the planking directly above Carson's hammock.

An explanation of the confusion that had appeared on the young man's face seemed to the pearler a matter far more important than speed. That he was engaged in a race he had no idea. He listened to the faint squeak of the hammock ring-bolts, which were not a foot from his ear.

Carson was restless. Any landlubber in a sailor's hammock for the first time would be that. But Carson's restlessness continued long, long after a man who had been up half the night should be asleep, and at last came the sound that Bellow Bill half expected—the thud of Carson's body on the deck below, and an oath, instantly stifled. Carson had tried to get up quietly, and had ended, as was almost inevitable for a landlubber, by falling.

Like a snake Bill's huge body crawled to the hatchway. There was a long silence, then a sigh of relief from Carson, followed by a *click* of a snap-lock on a suitcase. Another silence—and then the sound of paper being torn.

Bill vaulted down the hatchway. Carson had just time to cry out, once, before huge arms gripped him, squeezing the breath from his lungs. From his hand something dropped with a thud.

"Steady, lad," Bill rumbled. "Make a move and I'll smack your teeth down your throat."

"I—I... a drink of water..."

"Belay that," Bill growled. He stepped back and put a match to the lantern hanging from the beams. On the deck lay a thick mechanical engineer's handbook. Clenched in Carson's fist was the fly-leaf from the volume. He didn't want to give it up, but Bill opened his fist with an almost contemptuous push with a thumb, and smoothed the paper out. It was inscribed:

Floyd Dolin, '34

Above the signature was an amateurish but unmistakable

sketch of the heavily muscled blond giant who had sandbagged Bill.

"You damned double crossing rat," Bill purred like a cat that has caught a mouse. "So—you didn't see anybody? You mess of sheep guts! Murder would have been aboveboard, anyhow."

"I saw—nobody," Carson gulped. Bill struck him in the mouth with the back of his hand. He staggered, but he did not cringe. Blood ran down his lips. He gathered himself, and leaped at Bill's throat, swinging a wild blow. Bill snapped a fist to the unguarded chin. Carson dropped like a sack, and the pearler stood over him, breathing hard through his nostrils.

Treachery maddened the pearler. He picked up Carson's gun, shoved it into his own pocket, searched the suitcase swiftly without finding anything incriminating. The younger man was beginning to stir. Bill gagged him with a sock, and tied him hand and foot with the rope of the hammock lashing.

"I haven't been in the States since the war," he rumbled. His lips barely moved. "But I've heard that up there they are getting tough pretty young. Tough! I'm going to show you what being tough is like."

HE PICKED Carson up and set his back against a deck stanchion, reaching around him so that one great tattooed arm was around his chest. He hooked his foot around Carson's legs, holding them immovable, and pulled. Carson's back bent like a U against the stanchion. He struggled, eyes wild above the gag. Inexorably Bellow Bill bent him back another inch.

"I'm going to snap your back… girl-killer," he purred. "Feel it? Hear your bones creak…"

At the last instant Bill relaxed the pressure. With his free hand he snatched off the gag.

"Talk!" he growled.

Carson couldn't talk. His mouth made vague movements and uttered incoherent sounds. Then the words came, faintly:

"Didn't see him… Didn't know…

"Tougher than I figured you were," Bill rumbled. His grip tightened on the limp body.

"Damned gorilla! Go to hell!" It was a gasp—feeble, tortured, but defiant. Could a man who was a rat take it? Doubt nagged Bellow Bill—but implacably he twisted Carson's back over the stanchion.

"Well?" he growled.

"Knew you'd see that book and think so," Carson gasped. "Didn't know—Dolin followed. Did see him—here—tonight— for first time—in years. Never told him—anything."

"How'd you come to have that book? Why didn't you admit you knew Dolin?"

Pain racked Carson's face. Bill eased off the pressure—a little.

"Couldn't. You and that Englishman would have kept me at Moluna. I'm class of '36—college, if you understand that, you big ape!" Fury was in that racked, gasping voice. "Dolin was '34. Two years ahead of me. Taking the same engineering course. I bought his books because they were cheaper."

"You knew him, though!" Bill rumbled. He was merely holding Carson against the stanchion now. The certainty that he had made a ghastly blunder hammered at him. He'd dealt with tricky and desperate beachcombers on the make too long, and too often. Carson was just a new-chum…

"I met him." Carson was helpless as a child, but in his eyes gleamed undying hate. "God, I met a thousand men! He's the son of a prof in another university, and that's all I know about him. I never knew he was following us. Never knew he'd left the States until tonight. Take it or leave it, you—you punk!"

BELLOW BILL swung Carson away from the stanchion. The new-chum instantly collapsed onto the deck. The pearler scowled down at him, so intent that only the sudden red flare in the eyes of the younger man warned him. At that instant a pistol was jammed against his back. Bill didn't move. That saved his life. He could feel the cold muzzle against his spine shaking because of the fury of the person who held it.

"Has he—has he hurt you much, Paul?" Susan raged.

"Hold it! Yes. And I'll settle that with the tattooed punk," Carson gasped. "Tell him where I bought my books, damn him!"

"At the second hand store—"

"Hear that?"

"Aye," Bill rumbled. Not a muscle moved.

He didn't blame these kids. He had lived too long among treacherous savages. Gotten too used to acting first.

"Was he trying to kill you, Paul? I heard you cry out, and then when I came on deck there was no one at the wheel."

"Leave that to me, Sue. Was there a Professor Dolin around when your father gave his lecture? He showed them the gold dust in that coral borings. *They* talked."

"I don't know, Paul."

"That'll be it, though. Give me that gun."

He took the pistol. Bellow Bill met his eyes over the barrel, which was aimed at the tattooed ship in the center of the broad chest.

The kid wanted to shoot. But he'd never killed a man. That isn't easy, the first time, in cold blood.

Carson's eyes fell. "I can't sail a schooner, Sue," he temporized. "Norman-Pierce said he was honest, but—you're a damned stupid brute!"

"Aye," Bellow Bill agreed.

"Get out of here! From now on you take my orders. *We* don't know anything about you. By God, I'd like to kill you."

"Sure," Bellow Rill rumbled. "I was wrong. I'm sorry. But in the South Seas a man has got to be sudden. We're gambling four lives against five million dollars."

"So what?"

"In the South Seas a life ain't worth much. That's all. It's a double cross we've got to worry about, not Dolin. He's somewhere in the brush at Moluna, nursing a crippled foot."

He had the new-chum there. The red eyes shifted.

"You'd like the five million," Carson snapped.

"Sure. Figure it out, kid, while we're sailing to Lieuana. Figure this, too: can you get that gold out of eighteen feet of water alone? Can you keep a bunch of black cannibals from rushing you while *they* do it? Salt-water blacks know what gold's worth. And there's a few white men on every island."

"I can look after myself. Get on deck!" Carson ordered hoarsely.

Bellow Bill turned on his heel, caught the hatch coaming, and was out of the fo'csle in one lithe upward leap... An impractical scholar, a girl, and a stubborn, over-confident new-chum who itched to shoot him. Bad, rotten bad... and it was the biggest stake he'd ever played for.

The vast, tattooed shoulders shrugged.

"Wish I was alone, though," Bellow Bill rumbled to the blue-black sea.

CHAPTER IV

HANGMAN'S KNOT

IT IS AN unusual man who can forego the pleasure of explaining and apologizing for his own mistakes. Bill possessed that gift. He had blundered. With good reasons. But to hell with the reasons. What remained was the fact, and the consequences. He admitted the fact; he calculated the consequences, and everything else he forgot.

Throughout the long sail to Lieuana no word was addressed to him save in command. Invariably his answer was, "Aye, aye—sir." With a dead pan, and eyes in which the twinkle was so deeply buried that it was invisible. Griswold and Carson and Susan sat around the deck, mostly in a silence that gradually became embittered. Bellow Bill sat at the wheel and chewed fine-cut, calmly; and spat imperturbably to leeward. Let 'em give orders while there wasn't a stranger in sight. The time would come when they wouldn't know what to do.

It came, with emphasis, when the schooner raised Paleu, the island in the Lieuana group within the lagoon of which the gold lay covered with coral. Sailing directly to Paleu, instead of the larger island where the godowns of Vansteen the trader were located, was Griswold's order. It was good sense. But Griswold had explained that Paleu was a very small circular atoll, with only a shallow break in the reef. Except when copra was to be collected, it was so small that no natives lived there. This wasn't the season when coconuts were ripe. Therefore Paleu would be uninhabited.

It wasn't. Not by a good fifty lean, black, hard-muscled young savages it wasn't. They eased out of the dense underbrush that grew to the edge of the beach as Bill dropped anchor. They carried ten-foot, slender spears. Fishing spears, as Bill knew. But he couldn't see any fish, and a fishing spear in the hands of a husky savage is just as nasty as a pitchfork to meet end-on.

There wasn't a woman or a child in sight. Bill wondered if Griswold and Carson would realize that that meant trouble. The men seemed to range in age from sixteen to about twenty. Bill couldn't figure what that meant himself. The bachelor's club house and the young unmarried male are the two most important social fixtures in any South Seas community, but bachelors usually hang around near the women, in the South Seas as elsewhere.

To the age of that group there was one exception—a scarred, greasily fat, middle-aged native who was obviously a devil-devil doctor, and who hailed them in English:

"Ahoy! We fella belong good black fella, my word, yes! You land pretty quick too much!"

"He seems a trifle eager to get us ashore. As if he were waiting for us," Professor Griswold chattered. "Better not show any suspicion, I suppose—"

HE GLANCED at Carson, who was fingering a gun, and at Bill. Bill crammed a fistful of fine-cut into his mouth.

"There's too damn many of them," Carson growled. He looked at Bill. He was young, and his girl was watching him. He hated to admit he didn't know what to do. Bellow Bill shifted his quid, and saved Carson's face.

"The custom is to invite the chief aboard," he rumbled. "The chief *only*. Give the witch doctor three sticks of trade tobacco."

"Suppose they all come?"

"Then the custom is to start shooting when they shove off, and toss a stick of dynamite into the canoes when they come alongside," remarked Bill conversationally. "Men get *kai-kaied*

in these waters for errors of etiquette—or judgment. Knowin'
the etiquette, they *won't* all shove off together."

"Then tell that fat chief to come aboard," Carson ordered
sullenly.

"Aye, aye," Bill rumbled. The "sir" was omitted, but he kept a
perfectly dead pan. They didn't trust him. That was just a fact, to
be taken into account. He rose, and gave the invitation to come
aboard in a bellow that made the group of blacks jump, so that
the long spears stirred like a nest of snakes.

"Can you slip an anchor cable, Carson?" he muttered as a
dugout bearing the witch doctor put out from the beach. It was
about a hundred and fifty yards away. Easy rifle shot.

"Yes. Why?"

"Because I'll have to go ashore, later. A return call, savvy?" Bill
muttered. "In case of doubt kick the compressor off, and let the
chain run. The bitter end isn't shackled."

Carson didn't know that the bitter end was simply the end
of the anchor chain. *He'd* never anchored off a lee shore in a
gale and paid out chain fathom by fathom to keep the anchor
from dragging, until the bitter end was reached, and nothing
remained for a sailor to do. Carson didn't know too many things.
No time to tell him. The dugout was alongside, and the witch
doctor was climbing aboard.

"You trader fella stop along here today. No stop along here
tomorrow, my word, no," be announced authoritatively. "Big
feast tomorrow. Plenty young Marys walk about too much. Take
husbands, my word yes. You go along Lieuana belong trade. This
island tabu. My word, yes!"

"What's all that mean?" Carson grumbled.

"Some kind of annual marriage festival—if it ain't a stall,"
Bellow Bill rumbled quickly, under his breath. "A witch doctor
can make an island tabu for a year, if he likes."

Bill didn't like the greasy native. There was a leer in the bloodshot eyes, an impudence far greater than normal… If Paleu

was tabu, the party would be driven to Vansteen, the trader at Lieuana.

"What name belong you?" Bill boomed.

"Nauma name belong me."

"What young Marys walk about?"

"Young Marys never know man fella walk about."

Bellow Bill's eyes narrowed. A parade of virgins, scheduled for the morrow. Hence all the young and marriageable young men were on Paleu. An explosive situation, even if the witch doctor was telling the truth. Which he probably wasn't, completely, since witch doctors as a class are sinister and congenital liars.

"Give him three sticks of trade tobacco," Bill ordered Carson curtly, and went below.

IN THE cabin the pearler picked a Winchester from the rack and made sure the magazine was full. He stuck a twelve-inch diver's knife in his belt, scowled for a moment, and then, from a secret hiding place in a deck beam, reached down a chamois bag of pearls—the cream of a season's fishing. Witch doctors are the racketeers of the South Seas, and pearls are cash.... A bribe alone, however, might not work. Bellow Bill thought fast, and picked up a ten foot length of hard-braided fish line.

He was grinning when he returned to the deck and squatted in front of Nauma. His big, tattooed fingers began to tie a hangman's noose in the end of the fish line. Bloodshot eyes watched him uneasily.

"Plenty fella pearls belong you—no tabu belong here," Bill rumbled. "You make young Mary walk about next week? My word, yes!"

He opened the chamois bag to reveal the pearls, and suddenly tossed it against the dirty legs of the witch doctor. Nauma snatched at the bag. As he bent forward Bill slipped the noose around his throat, drawing the hangman's knot snugly against the brown Adam's apple. It was swiftly done. Nauma made an involuntary effort to leap up, but Bill's hands on his throat repressed the movement—which would have buried the thin cord deep in the fat of his throat and garroted the native before his fumbling fingers could have found the knot.

Nauma realized that. He stared wild-eyed in Bill's grim face.

"You good fella," the pearler purred. "You move slow now. My word, yes. You tell black fellas one big tabu on Paleu. No black fella walk about. No black Mary walk about. Not this week."

Nauma got the idea. He clutched the pearls more tightly, but sweat squeezed out of his greasy skin in big drops. One hard pull on the fish line would finish him.

He nodded.

"But—you've lost his friendship. It's treachery! The blacks will hate us!" Professor Griswold bleated. Carson scowled, and Susan, quicker-witted, stared at Bellow Bill with a mixture of admiration and distrust.

"Friendship? We never had it. Fear is all these devils ever understand," Bill rumbled. "I know what I'm doing." He flashed a smile. " 'Cast not your pearls before swine,'" he quoted.

"But it's an unprovoked assault!" Griswold chattered.

"Sure," Bill agreed. "You're here to loot this guy's patrimony, ain't you? And his great-great-grandpappies got the gold by killing and eating a shipload of sailors. It's a rough business all round."

He rose, and at the light pull on the cord Nauma rose too, and stood trembling. His face was the grayish-green of a black in abject terror. Sweat runneled down the tribal scars that ridged his forehead and chest.

"But why must you go ashore?" Susan asked.

"To show them I ain't afraid of the whole gang, and to show you that I'm on the up-and-up," Bellow Bill answered frankly. "You aren't sure of me up to now, and I don't blame you. I'll show you a good job of handling natives—and I'll do it in the open on that beach, where you can watch every move and hear every word. But remember about that cable, Carson."

BELLOW BILL wrapped the cord around his left hand, and

dropped the Winchester into the crook of his left arm. The stan-
dard tactics in dealing with natives—worked out by the blackbirders who used to land on lonely beaches to persuade a mob
of murderous cannibals to sell themselves into slavery—is for
one boat to go ashore with an unarmed crew. Unarmed because
savages have rushed a boat for a gun. A second boat, or the crew
of the schooner, covers the first boat with rifles.

That way savages gain nothing by a rush. They only make
themselves targets. Bill couldn't use this scheme, for he trusted
neither the marksmanship nor the judgment of Carson and the
Griswolds. Nevertheless the noose around Nauma's neck repro-
duced the essential point of blackbirder tactics; a rush would be
the witch doctor's finish, and would not endanger the schooner.
Bellow Bill figured that he had hit upon a pretty smart scheme,
under the circumstances.

The young natives came to their feet as be paddled toward the
beach. He motioned them to stand aside. Nauma called out the
same order, hoarsely, and it was obeyed. The long spears swayed
as the crowd divided into two groups about fifty yards apart—
theoretically, but not actually, beyond earshot of the coming
palaver. Savage etiquette is strict, but savages possess an entirely
human and civilized amount of curiosity. The tide was low, so
that the beach was about forty feet wide—white sand glaring in
the late afternoon sun, sloping toward underbrush that looked
solid as a green wall. As Bellow Bill and Nauma stepped from
the dugout they were as exposed as two flies on a white wall.

"Steady, fella! Fright along you too much," the pearler soothed.

Terror was making Nauma's legs incapable of bearing his fat
body. Animal noises gurgled in his throat. He plucked vainly at
the thin cord, trying to slip a finger beneath it. The beauty of a
hangman's knot is that it will tighten, but never loosen. Bill had
utilized it before.

"Tell them," he muttered with grim humor, "that a big devil
has put a tabu on Paleu. Tell them they must go back to Lieuana

and hold the marriage parade there." The big voice boomed out. "What the devil's the fright along you?"

For Nauma was in such a state that he couldn't have uttered a coherent word to save his life. He slumped against Bill's chest, making slavering, gasping sounds. Wild eyes stared across the beach.

Bill pushed him away and stepped from behind him, striding onward so that Nauma must also walk ahead, or strangle. To the pearler such abject fear was incomprehensible. And would have remained so, permanently, except for the sun, dipping toward the sea at Bill's back. Those fierce, level rays were reflected with a gleam, even by blued steel.

Otherwise Bellow Bill would never have seen the tip of a rifle poking slowly through the densest of tropical thickets. There was nowhere to run. There was but one outcome possible to a duel between a rifleman in a thicket and a six-foot, three-inch pearler out on the open sand. Bill had a flash of bitter sympathy for Nauma—who'd paddled out to lure him into an ambush, only to be forced to accompany him with a garrote around his neck.

The rifle barrel steadied in line for Bill's forehead.

CHAPTER V

TWO-LEGGED FISH

EVERY MUSCLE HARDENED to meet the shock of a slug. To the eye that looked over the rifle sights Bellow Bill's movements must have been disconcertingly swift, but to Bill they were slow. Every watch-tick was an eon. He dropped flat on his face. Sand filled his mouth and nose.

He pulled on the cord—pulled hard enough to jerk the staggering witch doctor off balance, to drop him, with eyeballs starting from their sockets and wide open mouth that would never breathe air again, flat on Bill's back. A huge, tattooed arm that was tensed against the impact of a slug that did not come reached backward and wrapped around Nauma's neck.

An eternal second—then, with a leap, Bill was on his feet, Nauma's black body pinwheeling over his shoulder to be clasped in huge arms and hugged to his chest. Behind that shield of flesh that was dying or dead Bill rushed at the rifle. He didn't look. He was trying to shrink his own body behind that of a smaller man.

It was all so quick that Susan's scream of alarm still rang in the air. Not one of the natives of either side was up. Yet Bill was conscious only that the soft sand was slowing down his rush. Why—why didn't the rifle blaze. Why didn't the guy shoot?

Bill crashed into underbrush that was like a wall. He hurled Nauma aside, snapped his own rifle to his hip. There was nothing to shoot at. The branches through which he had burst snapped back across his face. He dove for the base of the nearest palm tree, squirmed belly down behind the spreading root.

He wasn't—couldn't be—five yards from the point from which that rifle barrel had been thrust. Had the guy gotten buck fever? That was possible.

The damned undergrowth was like a green blindfold. He couldn't see farther than the end of his gun. The natives were yelling, starting to rush him. They knew he'd killed the witch doctor. They'd get him for that. They'd be on him, twenty together, in a dozen seconds. But right now there wasn't a sound, not the stir of a leaf in the undergrowth around him.

Bill squirmed forward. He could stalk as well as any man. He'd shoot this out—

A rifle cracked, once. He didn't see the flash. No bullet came tearing through the leaves. Out on the water Susan screamed piercingly:

"Bill!"

"Ahoy!" he thundered his war-cry in answer, and fired at random in the direction of the shot. There was a stir in the bush—a noise suddenly multiplied twenty-fold to right and left as the natives plunged into the undergrowth like a cavalry charge.

HE FIRED. That shot hit, for a native screamed. That would slow them up. Bill turned and lunged through the thicket like a bull, trusting to the noise behind him to cover the noise he made, and to his greater strength to make the faster time through vines that tightened across legs and chest and had to be snapped, through huge serrated leaves that ripped at his clothes and slapped him damply across the face.

He was panting, sweating, desperate. They were on his heels, and if they got him he would go down under a black, squirming mass and never get up. He ran blindly as a charging bull, but not as a bull runs, in a straight line. He kept his head…. Two new-chums and a girl, on a schooner that would be rushed. *They* didn't know how to use dynamite, and it takes dynamite to halt a crowd of blacks that swim like sharks, that come tumbling over the rail on the port side while you are putting a bullet through a kinky head that is swimming toward you from the starboard.

Bill had to get back. So he circled, even though that meant skirting the front of the mob that was crashing behind him. They were getting braver with every foot he ran. He knew that by the deeper-throated, snarling yells. The underbrush thinned out. They saw him, and yelped like hounds that are closing him. But his circle was completed, and his face again toward the sea. He kept ahead, smashing, whirling, twisting; beating a path with the butt of the rifle, slashing with his knife when a vine caught him that was too thick to break.

A native that followed the trail he broke could have caught him. And caught a bullet or a foot of steel. They knew that. They kept in groups—four or five men together, but as the chase turned back toward the sea those who had lagged behind now tried to cut him off. They had as far to go as he. He kept his lead, hacked through a thickening mass of undergrowth, and burst out on the beach.

A spear flashed by him as he bounded across the sand, but only a few natives had stayed by the water, and they were clustered near the spot where he had disappeared, almost beyond spear-throw. He fired, with one hand, swinging the rifle like a pistol. He missed, but his targets ducked for cover, and with a booming yell he plunged into the sea and swam like an otter for the schooner.

The rifle was useless once the barrel filled with water. He dropped it. Carson, the damned fool, hadn't slipped the chain yet. His head and the muzzle of his gun were visible behind the rail of the fo'csle. Trying to stand off forty blacks, like a hero, instead of obeying orders. Bill cursed him—and cursed again as the natives seized their opportunity.

Five blacks rushed for the dugout, sprinted with it until they were waist deep, and sprang aboard. As one they seized paddles and the dugout jumped ahead under the push of the spade-shaped blades. Bellow Bill could swim. Few men faster. But he wasn't going to beat that dugout to the schooner. And Carson—with some damn fool notion of holding his fire till he could see the whites of their eyes, probably—was covering the dugout instead of slinging lead as fast as he could pump a Winchester.

The anchor chain did let go with a rattle and roar. Susan, likely, or the professor. The cooler heads. But the dugout was angling toward Bill, determined to cut off the helpless swimmer before they tried conclusions with the schooner. The bow paddler was standing up, spear poised.

BELLOW BILL stopped swimming. Head and shoulders out of water, he filled his lungs to their utmost capacity, taking the quick, deep breaths of a pearl diver before the plunge. He gripped his knife. The dugout was between him and the schooner. That was why Carson still didn't fire… afraid he'd hit Bill. That was a grim joke—and like a new-chum. All theory.… The dugout came on, faster; the paddler yelling with every stroke. They thought the tattooed white man had given up. They knew they had him. Bill gripped his knife, and measured the speed of the boat with the care of a matador who stands in the path of a charging bull, aware that the least miscalculation will spell life or death. He waited, coolly treading water—and suddenly, with a flash of feet, dove straight down. Deep. Deep enough to get beyond the thrust of a ten-foot spear, counting seconds, turning at the bottom of the dive and letting the air in his lungs lift him. Sunset filled the water with yellowish light. He waited till he glimpsed the black shadow of the boat racing toward him and swam upward—not to intercept the boat, but to meet the slim black shadow of the outrigger that raced parallel with the larger shadow.

The natives saw him rising, but his timing was perfect. As he rose the outrigger was between him and the harpooner, spoiling a good shot. The black waited for Bill's head and throat to break the surface—but Bill's head never did emerge! Only his hands—one tattooed paw that gripped the outrigger, one fist gripping a foot of steel ground to a razor edge which slashed at the cords of coconut fiber that bound the float to the poles of the outrigger.

A spear gashed Bill's thigh. A second flew above him as he severed the forward lashing, let go so that that dugout forged ahead, and cut the after lashing. The dugout capsized as the outrigger floated clear and five blacks were struggling in the water, with ten-foot spears and wooden paddles that were too long and awkward to fight with. Bill dove in with his knife. He drove it into one leg to pay for the wound he had taken himself. He could have disemboweled the savage as easily, but that would have been wanton murder. The cry of pain the man uttered was enough.

Spears and paddles floated free as five blacks swam for the beach—each expecting Bill's knife in his back at every stroke. Bellow Bill was swimming just as hard in the opposite direction, keeping under water except when he had to rise to snatch air. That sniper ashore must be waiting now for another perfect shot—even if he was as slow on the trigger, almost, as Carson.

Bill swam until he was in the shadow of the schooner's stern, shielded from the beach by the hull, and rose with a loud "Whoosh!" of pent-up breath and relief. He felt he'd done damn well for a man without a partner. The whole thing had taken how long? Less than five minutes, likely. He swam for the schooner's taffrail, easily, a broad grin on his big face.

Susan was aft, crouching close to the deck with a Winchester. She was staring at him with eyes as big as saucers. Bill didn't wonder. He rated it. Carson appeared beside her. The new-chum stared. His teeth bared in a murderous grimace. He snapped his gun to his shoulder and fired.

The bullet burned red-hot across Bill's side. Carson levered in another cartridge, grinning with a joy in the kill that was devilish.

The water closed over Bill's head.

CHAPTER VI

THE TATTOOED SNAKE

INSTINCT MADE BELLOW Bill duck. He was under water before he knew he had moved hand or foot. His only thought was of the malevolent delight stamped on Carson's face. The kid had wanted to kill him—and might have done it. The first shock of the bullet kept Bill from knowing how badly he was hurt. His hands groped along the slimy hull of the schooner, and closed on the rudder. The salt water smarted in the wound. The pain was a good sign. He wouldn't feel that if he had been hit hard.

Gently he let himself rise, hidden by the overhang of the stern. Carson had shot at him as though he were a mad dog. Because of the breathless hurly-burly of the past five minutes Bellow Bill couldn't figure why, but he was aware that Carson would shoot again.

The pearler made no sound. He braced one foot against the rudder and waited, while the water around him slowly tinted with red. Carson would lean over the taffrail to watch the body of the man he had shot sinking slowly through the water. A killer could never restrain curiosity; the trick had never failed.

And did not. Carson's head came into view. Bellow Bill lunged upward, gripped him by the slack of the shirt, and pulled him over the rail so suddenly that the rifle flew from the new-chum's grip. The water would have made it useless anyhow, and once in the sea the young man was easy to handle. Bill choked him, gripped him in one arm so that the point of the knife was under

Carson's chin, and thrust himself backward from beneath the overhanging stern.

The movement made him look upward into the muzzle of Susan's gun. Bill grinned. He was on his back, half submerged, with Carson clasped to his chest. The least movement of the knife would cut Carson's throat.

"Chuck that gun overboard, sister," Bill growled.

She hesitated. Hatred made her face dead-white and rigid as a tortured mask. Her neck knotted as she swallowed the lump in her throat. Then, with a shrug, she dropped the rifle into the sea.

He was careful that the knife menaced Carson while he lifted him over the taffrail. To swing two men from the water with one arm hardly taxed Bill's strength. A glance showed the beach black with natives, but the loss of the dugout had dampened their fury, and the schooner was drifting slowly away.

"Well?" Bill rumbled.

Susan's mouth twisted with bitter loathing.

"You win. As you said, life is cheap," she answered. She turned, rigidly, and pointed to the foredeck. Bill had to step aside to see Professor Griswold, partially sheltered behind the main mast. He was flat on his back, and the front of his shirt was red.

"Your shot went through his lung," she said. "Though he isn't dead—yet."

"My shot?"

SUSAN'S RESERVE broke. Her face flamed. "Yours, damn your rotten soul!" she shrilled. "I saw your tattooed forearms when you fired from the bush. For God's sake, don't try to lie. That's almost worse than—than murder. You killed that poor black just—just to fool us, I guess. God knows why—why didn't you kill us decently? You could have! Were you too slimy-crooked to face us, or does it amuse you to play with us like a cat with a mouse?"

"My forearms? But that wasn't me. There was someone in the bush—"

"Dolin, I suppose? Painted up like you? Dolin, that's left behind us at Moluna. I saw *you*, you tattooed murderer! Kill us—steal our gold!"

It was hysterics, and it was madness—and it was a fact, too. Her father lay with a bullet through his lungs, and Bill's knife was pricking the throat of her fiancé. In that second of silence Bellow Bill cursed the cold and calculating trickery of Dolin—and wondered how he had got to Lieuana first. It had taken guts to roll aside in the brush and shoot at Griswold, with confidence that Bill could be killed later.

Bill gripped Carson more firmly, and crouched—behind the schooner's rail.

"Did you hear those blacks yelling?" he asked slowly.

"Yes, I heard them!"

"And you saw me wreck that dugout—and think that was a stall?"

"Yes!"

"Then… then—okay," Bill rumbled. He was grim. He could talk himself blue in the face and get nowhere. He made his decision. "Have it your own way," he said. He reached out, cut a length of rope from the main sheet, bound Carson's hands behind his back, and flung him to the deck.

"Turn around," he growled to the girl, and bound her, too. Not roughly, but firmly enough to hold. He pushed her down until she was sitting on the deck.

"What are you doing—now?" she panted.

"I'm bleeding, sister," Bill told her. He trimmed the sail and put the wheel in the becket, so that the schooner stood away from the island, gaining speed as the wind filled the sail. The sun dipped under the horizon, and darkness reached like a black hand across the sea. Bill went below and got bandages, but it was to Professor Griswold that he went first.

There was bloody froth on his lips, but the bullet had only touched the lung. It had drilled clean through the lean body. A clean wound. Bill put on a compress, moving the professor as little as possible. He would live, with luck. The best surgeon could have done little more for him, under the circumstances. Susan and Carson had squirmed to the rail where they could lift themselves, and were watching him.

"What are you doing?" the girl called.

"You believe your eyes, sister. Use them," he growled.

BILL BOUND his own wounds, using tape to make the bandages firm and water tight. He was creased across the ribs. The wound had begun to hurt like hell, and he had lost a lot of blood. But it wasn't bad enough to stop him. He went below and brought up a box of dynamite. He lashed the sticks to a lead line, two feet apart, using instant fuse. Twenty-five sticks. At the end, another lead weight, and a long length of slow-burning miner's fuse. He inserted a cap where the fuses joined, and bound the joint carefully with tape.

Susan and Carson watched every move. He let them wonder. He did not say a word. His lips were set. He hated them—as badly as they hated him. He put the schooner about so that it headed toward Paleu, and as the boom swung across the deck he hooked a lantern in it. They would be puzzled to know what that was for—and so would forty-odd black men, and one white one, watching him from the island.

"To save time," Bill rumbled, "you might tell me whereabouts in the lagoon that cone-shaped mound of coral that covers the gold is. I can find it, of course. Or make you talk."

They could understand that. To make new-chums believe a lie was always easier than to convince them of the truth. In a dull and despairing monotone Susan informed him that the coral mound was in the southwest quarter of the lagoon.

Bill grunted. Would they believe, for example, that to sail the schooner through a tortuous channel in an unbuoyed reef was the trickiest and most dangerous operation that confronted him. No. And yet his big shoulders hunched as he came within rifle shot of the island. The rail protected him from a bullet, and yet he should have been forward with the light, conning the schooner with his voice. To work without a partner was hard.

As the water shoaled the lantern light was reflected from the light-colored coral on the bottom where the depth was not more than a fathom or two. Reefs were revealed as gray shadows against black, and by the depths alongside he had to guess at the coral formations ahead. If he went aground he'd be sunk, burned, and eaten. His lips twitched. They'd wonder what he was grinning at. Yet it was a grim joke that he had decided upon. To work a double cross, with reverse English. To enlist a formidable ally, though the hand of every man was against him.

Twenty years of South Seas experience were drawn upon as the schooner tacked through that crooked channel. Bellow Bill handled the wheel with a mastery that made the passage seem easy. On the inner beach a fire was burning, but there was neither a shout nor a shot. Forty-odd savages and a single white man, watching a lantern move slowly toward the southwest quarter of the lagoon. A circle of light on water that was faintly phosphorescent, a dark hull, a sail partly lighted, partly shadowy.

"About here, sister?" Bill rumbled.

"Yes, about." She was nervous.

He saw the cone-shaped peak as she spoke. To find it so soon was luck, though he would have tacked until dawn if necessary. He slipped the wheel in the becket, and lit the fuse. The lead line with its dynamite beads flew through the air, falling beyond the mound. Bill paid out the line, slowly, as the schooner forged ahead. He flipped the fuse into the water and took the wheel, sailing straight onward. Thirty seconds passed.... A minute....

THE EXPLOSION was like a thunderclap—one ear-splitting boom, echoed from ashore by amazed yells. A sheet of water leaped high, and fell in a gleaming, ghostly shower of phosphorescence. The radiance seemed to boil and spread in a widening circle. Ashore the savages were silent, surprised to find themselves unharmed after that blast. The lantern gave just enough light to gleam on the eyeballs of Carson and the girl.

Bill put the helm down, and sent the schooner back through the center of the white, shimmering pool. All three craned their necks.

"By God, gold! Damn you, I can *see* it!" Carson snarled.

"Aye. Dynamite exploded that way will dig a trench as neat as a hundred men with shovels. I've opened up a golden oyster, eh? Coral for shell, and gold for meat. Rich pickings."

He sailed on for the passage through the reef.

"You grinning, tattooed ape—" Carson began.

"Yeah," Bellow Bill agreed. "It's plenty funny from where I sit." He was thinking of Dolin. One white man, ashore. "Look aft. What do you see?"

"By the phosphorescence about a dozen men are swimming out."

"There'll be forty or more swimming out in five minutes," Bill prophesied. "Salt water savages know what gold is worth. Bush savages wouldn't, now. Those blacks are swimming out to find what all the noise was about."

Bill stepped abruptly, for the schooner was in the channel. When the schooner was again in the open sea he set a new course, and put the wheel in the becket. In the steady trade wind the boat would sail herself for miles, nearly as straight as though a hand were on the helm. Bill's voice hardened.

"Your old man will live if he gets careful nursing. Otherwise not," he told Susan. "So you've got to go to Lieuana. Sail the course I've set, and, run the schooner on the beach if you can't stop it any other way. Slip a blanket under the professor, carry him ashore, and get some old grandmother to fan away the flies. A grandmother or an old man is all you'll be able to get."

"But—" Susan interrupted.

"But nothing!" the pearler boomed. "When a village has a marriage ceremony once a year, nothing but a witch doctor and fear of his devils can keep the Marys and the bucks apart when the day comes. Nauma's dead, so all of Lieuana will be here tomorrow—for a *golden* wedding." In the faint light of the lantern on the boom Bellow Bill's lips twitched. "Vansteen must be there. A smart, tricky trader Vansteen must be. Well—trade with him. A share of the gold for his help, eh? And if you lie back to back those ropes won't be too hard to untie."

Susan leaned forward. "What do you gain by sending us off?" she asked. "I can't believe you didn't shoot—and yet—no, you're not afraid, either…. It's some scheme…. What shall I tell Vansteen?"

"Anything you like," Bill boomed. "What you saw, what you thought you saw, or any lie you can cook up. When he sees my schooner, without me, he'll come like seven bells whatever you saw. Lieuana is five miles wide, and less than ten miles away. Even new-chums can't miss that—and if you *don't* go there your father will die. So don't try to be smart."

Bill tightened his knife in the sheath, and vaulted over the taffrail into the sea.

CHAPTER VII

THE GOLDEN OYSTER

HIS WOUNDS BOTHERED him. He swam slowly. He alone, of all the people on the islands, had time to spare. Ten or eleven hours intervened till dawn. A desperate enterprise confronted him but he was heartened by the fact that his situation was no worse than the threefold dilemma into which he had plunged others by the blast that opened the golden oyster. If he was alone and handicapped he had dragged the rest into the same pit.

With the warm sea buoying him up, paddling along on his back, his anger at Carson and Susan changed to sympathy. It was a tough traverse he had made them steer. But Vansteen… who must have helped Dolin from the first, or Dolin would never have beaten him to Paleu, and been waiting with the fighting men of the island.… Bill had never seen Vansteen's face, but he would like to see it when the trader became aware that someone had shot Griswold, that Bill himself was at large, and Dolin unaccounted for.

Come to Paleu the trader must. The marriage festival and the treasure both compelled it; but miles away, with only Carson's perplexing story—or lies—to guide him, Vansteen must guess who had fired that shot, what had happened in that chase through the brush, and what was to happen during the coming night. Vansteen could be sure of just one thing: if he guessed wrong, or if he blundered when he arrived at Paleu at dawn, he would be on a spot.

And Dolin? Bellow Bill had a grim account to settle with

that big blond youngster. Dolin was too cold-bloodedly smart and tricky. But Dolin was already in a predicament that would turn the hair of the most experienced old-timer gray. Already faint echoes of the shrieking pandemonium in the lagoon were drifted out to sea. Wildly excited natives can no more be silent than a pack of dogs. Dolin would be fingering a rifle, counting seven cartridges in the magazine, trying to watch forty-odd gold-crazed savages with one pair of eyes. Dolin would be sweating blood already. Let him sweat!

Bellow Bill walked out on the beach. He found and cut a length of thin and flexible vine, as strong as linen thread. Dolin hadn't fired, yet. Stout lad, Dolin. The shouting of the blacks had changed to a succession of short, high-pitched yelps.

"Aie!" Another voice. "Aie.... Aie!" Expletives torn from corded, straining chests by ungovernable excitement.

Bellow Bill squirmed into the underbrush and worked his way across the atoll, calmly and noiselessly, until he could peer through the brush onto the inner lagoon. He could have made more noise than a cow, and no natives would have cared. Dolin wouldn't have dared to turn.

Against black water and the black mass of cocopalms, mad, purposeful activity was lighted by the silver flash of phosphorescence and the ruddy glare of a leaping bonfire. Through the water seemed to squirm two lines of huge black snakes, swimming out, ducking under, black body after black body outlined in pale silver fire, rising with a gasp, swimming back to rush up the beach—naked devils, black against the firelight, hugging ingots and bars to their chests. Naked devils, each of whom dropped the gold in a pile of its own, screamed, "Aie!" and turned to dash madly back into the water for more.

IN FORTY-ODD places the flames gleamed dully on piles of golden bars. Piles that grew, like—like the piles of coconuts in a South Seas harvest, when a whole village goes into a grove, and each man gets as many as he can carry to his own pile. Dark fingers clawing for golden spoil only a few fathoms down, raking and reraking every inch of the shattered coral, each diver guided by flashing, silver gleams stirred by the man who preceded him. More than forty blacks were making short work, even of tons of gold. Each of those bars, Bill judged grimly, weighed a couple of *arrobas*—about fifty pounds. And yet there were bars enough, but the moment would come, soon, when a diver would return empty-handed. When a savage who had piled up two would glare at the neighbor who had amassed three. Already some of the divers were returning with handfuls of coin....

And Dolin? He stood behind the fire, with his rifle across his arm. The light gleamed on the paint that still tattooed his forearms. He was standing like an overseer, but he had been cool and smart enough not to attempt to interfere.

"That's right! Pile it up!" he kept shouting. "Every guy in his own pile! The more you get the more I pay!"

Sweat was streaking down his face. He was telling the wind to blow, and he knew it. It was smart, to order them to do what they were going to do anyway. But—the fire, untended, was gradually dying down. The natives were too busy to bring fuel, and Dolin did not dare. Even his hollow claim to power was dying with the light. It would be dark soon, and he would be alone with forty-odd men who knew he would cheat them of their labors if he could. Once the gold was salvaged one idea would pop into forty kinky black heads: Kill the white man, and hide as much of this gold as I can where no one but myself can find it.

Dolin was smart and cool. He foresaw the inevitable, A sweat-streaked face kept turning right and left, seeking a refuge. In front, the water, behind, the jungle that would be full of men crawling toward him, jabbing into his hiding place with long spears, as soldiers jab bayonets into hay when they suspect an enemy is hidden beneath it.

He kept wiping his forehead and shaking the sweat from his fingers.

"That's right! Pile it up, you guys! Every man for himself!" His voice was hoarser, more hollow, and as the bonfire died he backed toward the jungle, reluctantly, foot by foot, aware that nothing awaited him in the darkness but a delayed, and probably more painful death.

WHILE THE search for the gold was still furious Bellow Bill squirmed through the undergrowth parallel to the shore. He had planned differently. He had prepared a doubled length of vine like a garroter's cord, but now he marked the tallest, thickest palm that grew near the fire. Dolin marked it too, by instinct; backed toward it.

As his shoulders touched the brush a huge, tattooed arm crooked around his throat. Bill's knife-point pricked his back. Dolin could not cry out. Beyond a single convulsive leap he hardly struggled. The rifle dropped from his hands as Bill drew him out of sight. A few blacks paused for an instant and plunged back into the lagoon for more gold. As Bill relaxed the pressure Dolin panted like an animal.

"They'll cook you and eat you if you make a sound," Bill growled in his ear. It wasn't a threat, but a plain statement of fact. The panting ceased. Bill reached out and secured the rifle.

"I can outrun and outswim these devils," he purred. "You say, 'Uncle,' or I'll heave you out on that beach—without a gun—for them to play with."

He felt Dolin shudder.

"Going to be a good boy?"

"For God's sake, lay off the razzberries!" came the desperate whisper.

"Okay. I'll give you a break," Bill purred. "Take off your shoes, and your pants." Dolin started. "Damn you, crawl over to the base of this palm and take off your shoes and pants," Bill repeated in a purring snarl. It was hard for him to whisper. "Quiet, if you don't want to be long-pig.... So.... That's better." The knife continued to prick Dolin's back. "Pass your pants around the trunk, and tie one leg to each wrist. They new?"

"Yes," Dolin breathed.

"Better hope they are. A new-chum's would be," Bill purred.

"You've seen a lineman climb a telegraph pole? Well, that's the idea." He felt the knots on the pant legs, and pulled them tighter. "The idea is to lean way back. Coco bark is rough, and your bare feet will stick like a lineman's spurs. If you slip *I'll* knife you, and they'll find you hitched to the tree with your own pants. Get it? Okay—up with you!"

Bill climbed at Dolin's heels, but about ten feet up Dolin hesitated, leaned back, and whispered desperately:

"They'll see me! I'm getting above the underbrush!"

"Sure. I want them to see you," Bill prowled. "Get this, buddy: when they see you, sing out that if any native leaves the beach the man next to him can have his pile. Then climb down where they can't see you—but keep above reach from the ground, or *I'll* cut you open. Get it?"

"Will—will that work?" Dolin whispered.

"Naw, it won't work. Savages ain't that simple," Bill purred with deep-chested contempt. "But you say that, and nothing more, or I'll settle with you. And you stick to your tree. They'll spear you if you go high, and I'll cut you if you come down. Get it?"

"And you said you'd give me a break," Dolin whispered. In that instant Bellow Bill almost admired him. Cold-blooded, but a fighter.

"*I* am," the pearler answered with menacing emphasis. Dolin went on up. Bill stopped when his head was above the screen of leaves. The embers of the fire still gave some light, but against the background of the palms the savages could not be sure that Dolin was not carrying a rifle. Anyway Bill hoped so.

A few natives had ceased to hunt treasure. These turned as Dolin shouted the order Bill had put in his mouth. His voice didn't quiver much, considering.

THE RESULT, as Bill had anticipated, was to bring every man swimming in to protect his pile. For a little while they paused, the reddish light flickering over their black bodies. Then from savage to savage a low-toned whisper began to pass. The flaw in Dolin's tactics was obvious. South Seas natives are divided into clans. Bill, clinging to his observation post until the last second, could watch the clans organize. Men changed places. In a moment or two a long line became four loosely organized groups. Clan watched clan still but half a dozen men snatched up spears and ducked into the bush. Bill could hear Dolin's sharp intake of breath.

"Stay up, lad. I'll take 'em," he whispered, and dropped noiselessly to the earth. At the base of the tree he caught up the rifle, and squirmed into the heart of a thicket. In a tight corner a man must have a partner, or make one. Dolin, in the tree, was an ally or a sacrificial goat. Which he was depended on whether or not he kept his mouth shut.

The natives closed in with a barely perceptible rustling of leaves. Close to the earth there was not a glimmer of light, but above, the thinner leaves let the firelight through even to reveal the blurred shape of a naked white body twelve feet from the ground. Bellow Bill didn't want Dolin speared. He was well back from the tree. By smell rather than sight—the smell of rancid coconut oil on crawling bodies—he judged when the natives were in position for a rush.

Into the darkness, low to the ground, he fired three shots as fast as he could pump the lever. Not to hit, but to make men startled by the noise leap to their feet. Into the midst of them he lunged, slashing right and left. A foot of razor-edged steel, and the butt of a gun, both backed with two hundred and forty pounds. Three shots, a yell and a scream—then the crash of four men running headlong for the beach, and behind them the horrible choked coughing of a man dying from a stomach wound. The gun butt had crashed against a head. Bellow Bill lifted the body by arm and leg, pushed forward, and slung it through the bush onto the sand. The dying man followed, to sprawl on his dead neighbor.

Dolin had dropped to the ground, and was tearing frantically at his wrist. Bill let him feel the knife-point.

"It's me," he purred—and covered Dolin's mouth with his hand.

"Tell them, 'Give the gold of the two fools I killed to the man on the right, and the man on the left,'" Bill whispered.

Gulping and faltering, Dolin obeyed.

"Talk up," Bill purred. "Now tell them, 'Each man sit down by his own gold.'... That's better."

"Will—will they do it?" Dolin whispered.

"Wouldn't you?" Bill purred. "Sure, they've made their play now."

He cut one of Dolin's wrists free, twisted his arms suddenly behind his back, and pushed him on his face, using the knife to make him lie still.

"Not a word till dawn," Bill warned. That was a long time off, and his wounded side hurt like hell. He could smell the blood of the man he had stabbed. He couldn't move. Less than thirty feet away a line of savages squatted, each by his little pile of gold, shivering, listening for the slightest sound. It would be weary waiting until dawn. It was, but the sky was barely gray when his schooner nosed through the channel into the lagoon.

CHAPTER VIII

THE MARRIAGE PARADE

BY THE SOUNDS Bellow Bill kept track of Vansteen's approach. First an exclamation of one of the young men on the beach, then the creak of the boom as Vansteen tackled, then the gabble of natives' voices across the water—the voices of women and girls who gazed at such wedding preparations as they had never hoped to witness.

Their young men—not all of them—two stiff bodies on the beach here—but the others—young men they expected to marry with a few yards of calico, perhaps, if the young man were very wealthy, with the coveted bockis-with-bell—the box which rings when a thief opens it and which is,' next to a phonograph, the chiefest of South Seas treasures—these young men rose to greet them, wan, sleepy-looking, with bodies scratched by the brush instead of oiled and painted—but with bars of gold at their feet.

Ten thousand parrots could not have equalled the noise made by the marriageable girls and their female relations. With one glance, marriage compacts that had taken years to arrange were upset. Overboard they went, mothers and girls, to touch the gold, to handle and smell, to claim a suitor or deny him.

Under cover of the shrieks Bellow Bill prodded Dolin close enough to the beach to see out beneath the thick bushes. Bill knelt on his back.

"One word out of you and you get it, savvy?" he rumbled, peering to locate Vansteen. The trader sailed the schooner directly to the shore, running the boat aground so that the bowsprit projected over the beach midway in that line of piled gold. Cautiously Vansteen moved forward.

By the round, shaved head and the flat, hard face Bellow Bill sized the trader up. No mercy there. Vansteen was flint. Carson stood beside him, pop-eyed. Susan wasn't to be seen. Undoubtedly she was taking care of her father. That pleased Bill.

"So? So?" Vansteen was saying to Carson. "I apologize, *meinherr!* It is truth you tell." His small eyes glinted up and down the beach, seeking signs of a white man, striving to guess which white man had killed the two bodies close at hand. Knife-thrust, and gun-butt blow. Farther up the beach, Nauma's strangled corpse. Vansteen wet his lips.

"You do not blame me?" he asked. He could not look away from the treasure. He hitched his gun belt forward; the fat face turned red and white, as though with fever.

"Damn screaming women!" he snarled. "This would be today, of all the year." He beckoned to a young man, and leaned over the rail as the black walked waist deep into the sea. Bellow Bill could not hear that low-voiced colloquy in native dialect, but the pantomime made him able to follow it. The native pointed at the bush and the bodies, drew his shoulders together like a man who shivers in the dawn, and then, in answer to a question, spoke one word that made Vansteen's head jerk up and his small eyes flash triumphantly.

"So!" he said.

"Bill killed them, eh? But where is he?" Carson asked.

"Bill? Yes, Bill. Of course," Vansteen answered—but absently. Ashore Dolin squirmed under Bill's weight. The pearler stilled him with a jab of the knife.

"Bill comes later," Vansteen was saying. "First… it is wrong that so much gold should belong to simple souls? Not so? Watch me then, *meinherr,* and learn trading." He filled his lungs.

"Pigs!" he roared, so that for an instant even the chattering women on the beach were silenced. In dialect he shouted, "Each man bring his gold aboard, and I will give him credit for its value in my books. Hurry, for it is time for the feast!"

MEN AND women stared at him, sullenly; knowing they were cheated, but not understanding how. Gloomy looks, from beneath lowered brows. Credit they understood. He took their copra and shell in the season, and gave them goods through the year. This sounded the same, though they knew somehow that it was not. He waited, thick fist on hips, handy to his gun. He did it well, with sheer brazen effrontery. A native stooped and lifted three gold bars, walked toward the ship staggering beneath their weight. He was the first of a flock of sheep. Vansteen whipped a notebook from his pocket. In ten minutes it was all over.

The men remained in a compact group by the schooner. The women withdrew, farther up the beach.

"So!" said Vansteen explosively—though his eyes flicked uneasily toward the bush. "After work, play, eh, *meinherr?* You have not seen a South Seas marriage festival, no? It is worth seeing, even if you must come half around the world, but a man must sit with the other bachelors to see it." He laughed. "Where else do the prettiest girls of the village parade with only a necklace and a belt of beads before the eyes of their prospective husbands?"

Vansteen nudged Carson in the ribs. "I have a wife already, but you will jump down and sit with the others, eh?"

Carson jumped to the beach. Instantly two natives seized him by the elbows. He tried to throw them off, but a dozen hands fastened on him. On the fo'csle Vansteen grinned. "It is not good to give too much treasure to the simple," he leered. "You are a young fool, *meinherr,* and Bellow Bill is another, for he gave you his schooner instead of cutting your throats. Or perhaps he would not let you know that your bullet was mortal. That would be like him. A man, *meinherr,* too proud of his strength to admit he is dying—from the bullet of a fool! He never got back to this island."

Vansteen raised his voice. "You can come out now, Meinherr

Dolin!" he shouted with grim joviality. "To stay hidden was well done! If you had shown yourself on the beach I would have had to kill this fool, and now you and I can trade with him—five million and immunity for us, against three lives, eh?"

The trader's lips smiled, but his eyes were slits and his face a flaming red. In the bush Bellow Bill cut the trousers that bound Dolin's hands.

"Go on—walk out," he purred. "He's your partner—but if you open your mouth before you are on the schooner I'll put a bullet through your back."

DOLIN ROSE stiffly. As he stepped forward, Bill picked up the gun. He covered, not Dolin, but Vansteen. The blond man was hardly out of the brush when Vansteen whipped out his revolver and fired. The bullet caught Dolin under the heart. He pitched forward, arms out-flung. The paint on the forearms was vivid in the level rays of the rising sun. Red, and blue, and green, crudely imitating tattooing. In the cry that Carson uttered was as much surprise as horror—but the boom of the revolver was echoed by the crack of Bellow Bill's rifle. He aimed at Vansteen's treacherous heart, but he was not a good shot. He missed, a little. The bullet only drilled through Vansteen's lung, but it knocked him down, and Bellow Bill charged across the beach and swung aboard the schooner before he could rise.

Bill kicked the revolver away from a hand too weak to reach for it. The gray pallor of death was in the trader's fat face, for Bill's bullet had not missed the heart by two inches. Bubbles of blood broke on lips that tried to ask a question that was mirrored in eyes.

"How—how?" Vansteen was asking.

"I sank your dugout!" Bill thundered at the natives. "I killed your witch doctor. I knocked your heads together while that man"—a huge arm stabbed at Dolin—"hid in a tree. Do I come ashore with my knife, or do I pay you two years' wages for my gold that you brought ashore? Answer, you!"

The long arm swung at the blacks who held Carson. They couldn't answer. Not so quickly.

"Let go my friend and I not be cross along you!" Bellow Bill thundered in English.

They obeyed. He grinned at them, and at Carson, who stared at him as incredulously as any black, and began to stammer:

"But—but—"

"But nothing! Don't be a new-chum all your life," Bill boomed. "It's a fact, ain't it? I agreed to raise your gold for you and get it on my schooner, and I've done it. I let a pair of double crossers judge each other, and they did that, too. What chance did Dolin give the professor, or me?"

"But the gold!" Carson said.

"We'll let Norman-Pierce decide how we'll divide that when we get Susan and her father back to Moluna," Bill boomed. "Come aboard, lad, and watch the marriage parade. For if you think this will stop it you haven't even learned anything about the South Seas!"

THE ATOLL OF FLAMING MEN

*A pearling lugger drifts aimlessly in the South
Seas, with five dead men in the cabin—carrying
a strange mystery to Bellow Bill Williams*

CHAPTER I

THE CABIN OF GREEN FIRE

BELLOW BILL WILLIAMS used every sailor's trick he knew to reach the derelict before sunset. But he could not make a breeze, and the sun was low when he sighted the pearling lugger—hove-to, as though there was a hand at the wheel, drifting slowly to leeward with a diver's life line and air hose angling over the side, as though the lugger was on the pearling grounds and the diver was walking along the bottom snatching up shell with both hands.

But this was not the pearling grounds. It was the open sea. If that diver was on the bottom he was five hundred fathoms down. He wasn't, of course. He was twisting round and round at the end of that life line, drowned and dead, with a blue face and popping eyes.

Something had made his shipmates abandon him—suddenly. Even the most callous and brutal murderer would have hauled up that dangling body that was twisting slowly round and round— to dispose of its mute accusation, if for no other reason. And no partner will desert an air pump while he can move a finger.

Yet that something had not damaged the ship. She sailed on, though her bow was pointed toward no port in the South Seas. Behind her the sun, setting through cirrus clouds, streaked the sky with bright red knives and patches of scarlet. Jet-black against the sunset that revealed every rope and spar, the lugger drifted along alone.

Bellow Bill was alone. He was a big man, with a voice that

*Bill was dragged
helplessly*

boomed like surf. A curly-headed, blue-eyed pearling skipper; six foot three and broad as a door, tattooed from wrists to shoulders and waist to chin with designs that did not leave a square inch of him undecorated. He could say, as a simple matter of fact, that he had never met a stronger man. He could boast— which he did rarely, and only when he was very drunk—that he liked going where other men wouldn't. He knew the South Seas from New Guinea to Papeete, and there were many scars in his tattooed hide, from bushmen's spears as well as white men's bullets.

But he did not want to board that lugger in the dark if he could help it. However, the sun dipped below the sea before he could bring his own schooner alongside, and the prompt darkness of the tropics left him no choice. A few stars were out when he hauled in the life line—finding, as he had expected, a man at the end of it. Bill did not unscrew the face plate. Time enough for that. He moved, with a reluctance that was pure instinct, toward the open companionway.

Though it was dark, he heard flies still buzzing below decks.

"Not storm, or the ship would be smashed up. Not pirates, or the crew would have died on deck," Bill rumbled in the booming voice, like the low notes of an organ or the mutter of distant surf, which had given him his nickname. He wanted at that moment to hear himself speak, for most clearly he realized what any sensible sailorman ought to do.

Slide the hatch on that companionway and lock it. Tow the lugger back to the nearest port, and turn her over as she was to the authorities for investigation. Runaloro, a small atoll that was a pearler's rendezvous, was within three hours' sail. Why stick a nose into an ugly business that was no concern of his?

"Since when did that bother you? Get down there, you tattooed ape!" Bill growled at himself, and swung down the companionway—landing, for all his bulk, as lightly as a cat, with bent knees and doubled fists. He was expecting something out of the common. But nevertheless—

"Hell's *fire!*" he roared.

AT FIRST glance it seemed exactly that. In the pitch darkness

of the cabin, scattered on the deck close to his feet, floating in mid-air as high as his waist, unearthly greenish lights glowed and waned; as breath comes and goes upon a window pane. Those points of chill green flame outlined faces in the dark—the faces of three dead men.

Bill reached down. His groping fingers touched a naked shoulder, oily and cold. He started as though he had touched a snake, stepped carefully over the prone body, and with fingers that shook, lighted the hurricane lantern that swung over the table in the center of the cabin.

As the wick spluttered and caught, it revealed, not three corpses, but five. Seated in a chair facing Bill across the table was a young white man with blue eyes and sun-bleached hair. He was handsome, and not over twenty-five.

The other four were all sprawled on the deck, and were natives. But—what made the muscles along Bill's back crawl— of the five, only one bore a visible wound. That it should be a relief to look at a man shot twice through the chest seemed strange, but it was a fact.

That was at least comprehensible—the rest was not.

Bellow Bill Williams reached for the fine-cut chewing tobacco that he carried loose in his hip pocket and filled his cheek. He could reconstruct the scene, up to a point. Beyond that even his vast knowledge of the *devil-devil* societies of Melanesian villages, which are founded and supported by murder and grisly superstitions, offered no parallel. Something here was new, and neither civilized nor savage, but the worst of both.

For the blond white man was bound in his chair. His right shoe had been ripped off. Scorched skin between his big and first toe, and the charred mark of a cigarette on the deck, was evidence of torture that had succeeded in its purpose.

For his last act had been to open a secret drawer cleverly concealed in the cabin table. Near his hand was a cloth bag in which pearls—big pearls and an astonishing number of them— nestled in a packing of kapok.

So far so good. Pearl pirates and torture. Ugly, but simple.

The native who had been shot had evidently been manning the air pump. He lay there where the impact of the bullets had knocked him, close to the foot of the companion way. That he had heard the noise when his skipper was attacked and rushed below, trusting to the reserve pressure in the pump to sustain the diver for a few minutes, was a simple guess.

Everything else was a headache. Three powerful and ugly-looking pearl pirates had been in complete control of the lugger after those shots were fired. Then they had died, suddenly. It was as though a giant hand had flung them in three different directions away from the table. And there wasn't so much as a pin scratch on any of them, for Bellow Bill looked with grim care.

PUZZLE NUMBER two was that the pirates had smeared their faces with some queer stuff that glowed greenishly in the dark. It had been wet at the time, for it was curling away from their skin now in strips.

The deck was littered with broken bits of the stuff. It was translucent and curled up at the edges like a thin sheet of dried gelatine. They hadn't come aboard with that stuff on their faces. The greenest pearling skipper would not have let such visitors on his lugger. And where was the boat they'd come in, anyhow?

Bellow Bill gave that one up, too. He put the bag of pearls in his pocket, and searched for the lugger's log. There wasn't any. There wasn't even a letter or ship's clearance papers to identify the dead skipper, and there wasn't anything in his pockets except a package of cigarettes and the broken half of a sixpence with a hole drilled through it so that it could be worn around the neck. English sailors frequently break a sixpence and give the other half to a girl.

The murdered deck hand wore a crescent-shaped piece of green glass—probably the bottom of a beer bottle with the edges smoothed by being tumbled about by the waves on some beach—thrust into the elongated lobe of his right ear. Which wasn't much of a means of identification, either.

The men with smeared faces wore nothing but *lava-lavas,* and a Melanesian doesn't remove his amulet unless he's under the protection of some boss devil. He believes too implicitly in too many evil spirits. Of the three, one had a skull that came almost to a point under the frizzled, kinky hair. Some one at Runaloro might know who Pointed Skull was.

Or might not, or might be afraid to say. There would be no British Resident on so small an atoll. Probably no official at all; and the lack of a log book—which could hardly have been destroyed by the pirates—was as startling to a sailor like Bellow Bill as the cold green light that had illuminated the faces of the corpses.

Pearlers were careless, but not that careless.

Bill shifted his quid. The face of the blond young Englishman, staring at him rigidly from across the narrow table, had a mute and desperate appeal. It was a decent, likable face. "I held out as long as I could, white man," it seemed to say. "They were a slimy gang, and they jumped me so suddenly I didn't know what to expect."

"Lad, you got nothing on me," Bill rumbled aloud. "I don't know what to expect, either, but I'm carrying on." He grinned, and into his blue eyes came dancing golden flecks. He smelled battle, and long odds, and a wily, diabolical enemy.

The prospect appealed to him. "But I think, fella," he remarked in the straightforward tone that he might have used to a living man, "that I'd better not work along normal lines, either. There's so many queer slants in this that I'm going to put in a few more."

CHAPTER II

THE SHIP FROM NOWHERE

HE BEGAN BY closing the secret compartment in the table and putting the bag of pearls in their kapok packing in his pocket. Next he cut the lashings that bound the dead Englishman, but left him sitting in his chair.

Finally he went on deck, threw the lashings overboard, disconnected and coiled the life line and air line, and carried the diver down to the cabin. Bill left the corpse, still in its suit, sitting on the deck with its back against the forward bulkhead. When he left the cabin he closed but did not lock the companionway slide.

On deck, after this was done, the lugger looked normal in every respect. Below decks—Bill's neck crawled at the memory of what the first person to go below would see. He planned, moreover, that that person would be utterly unprepared for the sight; and he had removed everything that gave a reasonable explanation of those glowing, scabrous corpses.

What in hell made that cold green fire, anyhow? Why were the faces smeared with such stuff? Bill chewed over that all through the night, while he sailed toward Runaloro with the lugger in tow.

The distance was not great. In the dark hour before dawn, when sleep is deepest and men suddenly awakened are least likely to have their wits about them, he made out the white line of the surf on the reef of the atoll. It was a half mile or so ahead. The land itself he could not see, and even in the starlight his schooner and the lugger behind it would be invisible to the keenest eyes ashore. Bellow Bill Williams grinned like a small boy about to play a particularly startling practical joke.

He hove-to, boarded the lugger again, and trimmed the sails and lashed the wheel so that the lugger moved slowly ahead. As it gathered way he dove overboard and swam back to his own schooner, but the lugger sailed on in the gentle breeze.

No hand on the helm… a crew of corpses in the cabin, three of them with faces that flamed… he could still call to mind a vivid picture of the face of the native with the pointed skull. The lugger would crash on the reef, of course, and the population of the atoll would come to examine the wreck. If those who had guilty knowledge could keep a poker face in that cabin they were superhuman.

Grinning, Bill swung over the rail and picked a pair of binoculars from the rack. They were the best glasses in the South Seas. Their previous owner had waited at the top of a shaft, with a gun and a pack of dingoes, for Bill to climb to the surface. That had been a narrow squeak, but those glasses gathered every faint glimmer of light, and seemed to bring the line of surf within a hundred yards.

Bill watched the logger sailing on, saw it strike with a crash that must be audible on shore, which was to leeward, though he could not hear it. He waited for a lantern or torch to appear on the inner beach.

Waited… and waited. After a half hour the sky commenced to pale. The lugger, pounding gently on the coral, had only swung broadside to the reef. The thing was unnatural. Those men ashore were nine-tenths of them sailors. The crash of a hull against the reef would certainly have awakened some of them. Could they *all* be in a drunken stupor?

No—*for suddenly the lugger began to move!* Suddenly the bow turned into the wind, which was a job for a powerful boat's crew. Ghostlike, the sails shifted and the lugger moved again toward the open sea. Not a pin point of light had shown until then, but suddenly there was a red glow. Not on the lugger's deck, but in the cabin. A curl of flame that licked through a seam, caught on a tarred rope and twisted up the rigging.

WITH AN oath Bill dropped his glasses and got his schooner under way, but the fire had been set far too well for him to have any chance of getting alongside and extinguishing it. Within minutes that twist of flame became a column that roared upward through an *open* companionway. Sails blazed and fell in a shower of sparks, lighting the sea so that Bill's schooner was revealed.

He sailed as close to the lugger as he dared, as though he were trying to give aid or effect a rescue, but even he did not care to board. Grim-faced, swearing under his breath, he hove-to until fire was gushing from every hatch and porthole, until it was obvious that the lugger was going to burn to the water's edge and then sink to the bottom because of the weight of her ballast. The water off the reef was deep—too deep to recover even a charred body.

"Some one was damned wide awake, and able to get plenty of help," Bill rumbled. "Well—what made you think this was going to be simple, you damned fool?"

He steered his schooner toward the entrance to the harbor. There were lanterns and torches moving along the beach now—plenty of them. As he entered the lagoon he noted that there were many of the dugouts and outriggers used by native skin-divers in pearl fishing, but no luggers or schooners that would presumably belong to white men.

He dropped anchor. "Ahoy!" he sung out in his enormous voice. Far away a bird, roused by that stentorian hail, squawked an answer. "Did the crew of that lugger swim ashore all right? I was cruising by, and no one left her at sea."

On the beach there was a long pause. Lanterns and torches drew together.

"What crew?" a man's voice shouted back in English that was slightly but curiously and definitely accented. It was as deep a bass voice as Bill's own, and he could not place the singsong accent. It was not Chinese, nor Australian, nor native.

"The crew of that burning lugger, of course," Bill boomed. "What ship was that, and who owned her?"

"How do we know? Didn't you see the name on her stern?"

"Painted out," roared Bill. "Hell, man, didn't you recognize her? She sailed from your lagoon, didn't she?"

A pause. A very brief pause while the owner of that bass voice filled his lungs.

"Why, no. She was skirting the reef when we caught sight of the fire," he lied. "We thought you'd pick them all up, or we'd have been out in outriggers. Didn't even one of 'em get clear?"

"Nary man. Blind drunk, I guess," Bill shouted cheerfully. In the dark his big head, with its thatch of curly-blond hair, canted to one side. Oh, yeah? Skirting the reef, hey? That guy ashore had the gall of a Liverpool monkey.

And—not one voice on the crowded beach was raised to protest that amazingly brazen lie! Did they take Bill for a simple sailor who happened to be cruising past Runaloro? Or did they guess pretty accurately at what he was? They must have seen that some one had carried that diver in his suit down into the cabin after the strange massacre....

BELLOW BILL WILLIAMS grinned in the darkness. Any sensible sailor in his position would slip his anchor chain and get out of that harbor as fast as the wind would carry him. Better to lose your anchor than take a chance on your schooner and your life. Instead Bill prepared to go ashore. His only preparations were to slip a revolver into his right hip pocket and put on a belt.

The gun, though loaded and in perfect order, was a decoy. Bellow Bill was a rotten shot, perfectly capable of missing a man with all six bullets at any range greater than fifteen feet. Of course, most practical revolver shooting is done at less than fifteen-foot ranges, and when a man carries a gun that is the weapon which strangers watch. Bellow Bill actually relied upon his strength and his startling and unexpected speed.

A two-hundred-and-forty-pound man ought to be slow, and by the same token a lion ought to be slower than a jackal. But isn't.

And Bill's belt, though it looked merely like a wide and thick affair of leather, was specially made of flat two-inch links of steel, covered with thin kidskin. The links were studded, so that they would never tangle or kink. The studs were solid gold—part of a cargo of Spanish gold that Bill had raised from the coral where it had lain hidden for centuries. A grateful young man and his fiancée who had learned what a terrible weapon a length of chain was in Bellow Bill's hand had given him that belt. Five pounds of steel, two pounds of gold, and a heavy square-edged buckle that would cut as well as crush. Bill patted the buckle, touched the bag of pearls, the broken sixpence, and the native amulet of glass in his pockets, and paddled ashore. He was chewing tobacco slowly as he sauntered into the light of the torches and lanterns on the beach. He looked like a big, gentle, slow-witted bull chewing placidly on the cud.

"How are we going to report the loss to the authorities if we don't know the lugger's name, huh?" he complained.

He addressed the only other white man present among that crowd of nearly a score of natives merely because the man was white, and so, by South Seas etiquette, the leader. But from the first instant Bill's attention was on three other men—who were black.

Black and as alike as three black vultures. Tall, powerful statues in ebony, with muscles corded on their folded arms and naked chests, who stood in the rear of the crowd, and yet dominated it.

To encounter twins who are full-grown and cannot be told apart is rare enough. These men were triplets. The same hooked nose, the same thin lips, the same jutting, craggy eyebrows. Only in the way they wore their hair was there a difference. The men on the right and left had the drizzled topknot of Melanesian savages, but he in the center sported a shaven skull. Three vultures—one bald-headed.

Bellow Bill licked his lips. The mystery remained, but he had come face to face with his enemy.

The white man in front of him, meanwhile, was thrusting out a dirty hand. Mechanically Bill grasped it.

"I'm Owsley, the trader," the man was mouthing in a slurred tenor voice. "Titus Owsley—Titus by name, and tightes' by nature." He laughed shrilly at his own pun. "The drunkes' trader south of the equator. Neve' been north of the equator. Can't say about that, but bet I'm the tightes'. Come have a drink. Lugger burned… forget lugger, eh? 'Ave drink…"

HE WAS shaking like jelly, and he was drunk, very drunk, no doubt of that. His eyes swam in the flickering torchlight. He breathed hard, so that his cotton singlet, soaked with sweat, clung tight to his sagging belly. Yet it was not liquor that made him quiver, but fear too abject for alcohol to drown.

In the blurred and swimming eyes Bellow Bill read the panic-stricken realization that they were two white men surrounded by a score who were pressing closer.

"Drink?" boomed Bellow Bill. "Say, that's the word I want to hear!" He slapped the trader mightily on a soft, sweat-soaked shoulder, and as Owsley staggered back he cleared elbow room for Bill in that pressing crowd.

"Have you got a bottle?" Bill rumbled. He saw the neck of one sticking from Owsley's pocket. "No man can say he's the best in the South Seas till he's drunk with me."

He took the bottle, which was a good three-quarters full of gin, and gripped the neck in his teeth. For the first few swallows he steadied the bottle with his hand. Then, still biting on the bottle neck, he hooked both thumbs in his belt near the buckle. Slowly his head went back. Swallow by swallow, steadily, the gin disappeared. With a twist of his head Bill flipped an empty bottle onto the sand.

"Can you match that?" he rumbled.

His eyes were on the face of the vulture with the bald head. The crowd murmured. They eased back, waiting for Bill to stagger… they would wait without seeing it… but not a muscle of that black, powerful face changed. He was wondering whether Bill would be easier to seize when that prodigious drink had time to take effect. Only that, and Bill knew it.

"Gotta have another bottle," Bill growled. "Got it at your godown, I suppose?"

"Y-yes," chattered Owsley.

He started to turn away, but Bill gave him a powerful, seemingly negligent shove toward the three silent men. At that moment neither white man could have turned his back on the crowd and lived to walk ten yards.

"Wait—we got to have a light!" Bill roared.

He thrust himself forward and snatched the torch nearest the three, but it was not the flaming stick of wood that he wanted.

On the dark and muscular arm of the man with the shaven head was a fleck of something that gleamed coldly, even when the torchlight did not fall upon it.

Deliberately Bellow Bill picked it from the dark skin. His knuckles, as he held it, were less than a foot below the big man's jaw.

"What's this?" he roared drunkenly—and waited. If it was to be a fight for his life he could knock out the triplets before the crowd closed in.

"A fish scale, isn't it?" replied a bass voice in English. The folded arms never stirred.

"Of course! Sure it's a fish scale!" Bill whooped. He snapped the little fleck of gleaming stuff away with a contemptuous thumb. It was not a fish scale, and he knew it as well as that staring, uncertain crowd. "Well—good fishing. Come on, Owsley, let's get that drink!"

He seized the trader's arm and strode away, swinging the torch over his head. Gage of battle had been offered, and declined. For a moment or two it was safe for a white man on Runaloro to turn his back.

CHAPTER III

ARANO, BUNO, AND COARO

OWSLEY GUIDED HIM past a deserted bungalow to a shed of sheet iron, and unfastened the padlock on the door. The heat of the air inside the place made Bill gasp. It was wet and hot as a steam-pit. Behind him a bar was slid to bolt the door. Owsley lit a candle, and crossed the room like a panting dog to paw for a bottle of gin.

Bill reached for the water jar and drank deep to stop his head from spinning. Three-quarters of a bottle had been a terrific dose even for his huge frame and iron head. He wiped his lips and moved to unfasten a shutter to get air.

"For God's sake, no!" Owsley squealed. "They've followed us. They are outside now—with spears, arrows, bullets! I haven't dared open a window after dark for weeks!"

"Have they got any way to kill a man without leaving a mark?" Bill rumbled.

The watery, terrified eyes of the trader rolled in bewilderment.

"No?" Bill purred. "Now, that's interesting. Who's 'they'?"

"Arano, Buno, and Coaro!" It was a chant of despair.

"The Black Alphabet, eh?" Bill purred. "Those are Melanesian names, but a savage mama doesn't know her A B C's, mister. There's a white man's brain behind that."

"No!" Owsley denied, and gulped raw trade spirits. "I—I didn't name them. I swear it. I've been sweating here for weeks waiting to be speared. They—*they've taken my guns away!* What did you come ashore for? Were you crazy? Couldn't you see that you were going to get us both speared? I tell you they're waiting outside for either of us to show our faces!"

"Sure," Bellow Bill agreed emphatically. "About twenty of them, aren't there? That makes Runaloro ninety-five per cent black, and five per cent pure yellow. Ain't there any Dutch courage in that gin you swill?"

Owsley flushed.

"He can still get mad," Bill rumbled in a tone of wonder, as though he were speaking to himself. "Maybe he ain't the biggest coward south of the equator." And in a harder voice, "Well, mister? *I've* seen—too much since sunset. What do *you* know about tonight?"

"I—I heard the lugger strike. But I didn't unlock the door. Till Arano came and ordered me to come out. You were sailing into the lagoon—"

"Why didn't you unlock the door?"

"Because I knew the Flaming Men must be at work!" Owsley yammered in despair. "God, don't look at me like that! What can one unarmed man do against twenty? They paint their faces with some kind of devilish stuff that burns cold and green—"

"That stuff is phosphorus from the heads of common kitchen matches, I've figured," Bellow Bill remarked calmly. "Only it's mixed with some kind of seaweed jelly—agar-agar, for a guess—that keeps it moist and makes it last. It's the *devil-devil* magic of a Melanesian secret society. Witch doctors are getting up-to-date these days. But—damn your yellow soul—can't you see that the jelly stuff is beyond a savage's brain?"

"Arano was educated by missionaries," Owsley explained sullenly. "He comes from Malitia. The island that's so savage it's never been thoroughly explored."

BELLOW BILL had been farther into the interior of Malitia than any exploring party. He remembered a tribe dancing around a headless corpse, roasting slowly before the embers of vast fires. He had run for his life down the bed of a jungle creek. No doubt at all that Malitia was savage.... He kept a poker face.

"The idea was that Arano could do missionary work where a white preacher couldn't stay alive," Owsley droned, pitifully eager to explain his own surrender. "But he said there was no money in that. He's the one with the shaved skull. He came here and offered me ten pounds sterling a week for a partnership in my trading station. He was going to do all the work, too. I—I could just sit on my veranda and drink, and go to Sydney once a year to buy the supplies. Ten pounds was twice what I was clearing myself. It looked to me like a jolly deal, all round. Runaloro is a small atoll, and isolated. There's practically no copra. But why shouldn't I take his money while it lasted?"

There was a hint of aggressiveness and defiance in the swimming, drunken eyes. Bellow Bill nodded. What he thought to himself was, You besotted fool… couldn't you see that all Arano wanted was a white man as a front?

"He paid the ten pounds every week," the slurred, drunken voice droned on. "But he never even tried to gather copra. His two brothers arrived, Buno and Coaro. Plain, uneducated, unwashed savages. He didn't fish hard for pearls, either. The lagoon here was fished out long before my time, of course, but he said he'd found a new, rich, untouched virgin bed off the reef. He's paid my ten pounds every week, so I guess he did—"

"You lie! You dirty murdering coward, you *lie!*" snarled Bellow Bill under his breath. "I can see the whole scheme now, by God! Guess, do you? *The rumor of the richness of the new pearl beds at Runaloro has gone all over the South Seas!* What do you think brought me sailing here? What will bring every other pearler that's a free agent and not tied to one spot by fishing grounds he's leased? What but the hope of a pearl bed that *isn't* fished out—grounds where a man can bring up a hundred pounds in an afternoon, like in the old days. Why, all the free-lance pearlers—all the little fellows that are broke and ready to take a chance—are sailing to this out-of-the-way, God-forsaken atoll. One by one they come, as the rumor reaches them and they act on it! Guess, do you? *How many luggers have come to Runaloro this season?*"

Bellow Bill was too strong a man to lose his temper often, but at the look on his face, the sudden taloning of his tattooed hands, Owsley squealed and twisted into the farthest corner of that shed, with both fat arms thrown up to protect his throat.

"Ten, so far! You make eleven," he gasped. "But God help me, I didn't dare warn them. I tried to drink myself unconscious as soon as I sighted their topsails, for if I warned them the three black men would have painted their faces with fire and come for me! They'd have eaten me, Captain. It isn't just death—it's knowing I'd be *eaten*. I'd sit here without a gun, and in the dark they'd hammer down the door. Those green, flaming faces would peer in, and then—"

SHUDDERING, SHRINKING from Bill, Owsley started to crawl across the floor on hands and knees. His objective was the bottle. "You're right. *There's no new pearl bed been found at all,*" he whispered. "Arano and Buno and Coaro are pearl pirates without a ship, and every man on this island but me is in cahoots with them. They paddle up to the pearlers that come into the harbor and make friends with them like any other natives, and then they turn on them suddenly.

"Every lugger that comes has a partial load of shell that's been fished elsewhere, and a few pearls tucked away in a bag somewhere. I knew what was going on, but I never heard them at work and saw them burn a lugger before. Now they'll eat us, I tell you! We're both as good as dead men!"

"Shut up!" Bill growled.

Pirates—without a ship! It was a scheme appallingly novel. It was no wonder he had been baffled by the queer slant it gave everything on that lugger of dead men.

The pirates had painted their faces after they had boarded and captured the lugger, for instance.

And yet in spite of its novelty, it was a scheme as old as tribal murder in the South Seas. It was the overlay of an education on a savage mentality, the transfer of the customs of the deep jungle to salt water, that made the scheme so deadly. For in the jungle human heads are wealth. Every village builds man-traps on its paths and roads to slay the unwary stranger.

Arano had merely arranged a trap to catch ships and white men, and terrorized the natives of the atoll into acting as his executioners with painted faces of cold green flame.

Regretfully Bellow Bill thought of the rifles and the dynamite aboard his schooner. They might as well be in the moon. Yet he could not blame himself for failing to imagine that an atoll might be transformed into a pirate ship.

"Arano won't trust me any more, now that I've talked to you alone," Owsley was moaning. "You bluffed him on the beach, but he'll settle with both of us now."

Owsley, Bill thought contemptuously, was nothing but a lump of quivering fat, useless for any purpose. Not guilty of any crime himself. Merely totally lacking in courage. The pearler reached for fine-cut, shrugged, and strode to a shuttered window. He peered out through a crack in the boards.

Arano had certainly decided to sweep the atoll of white men. At the edge of a small clearing that surrounded the godown, close to the ground, were six severed heads.

Though they were painted with phosphorus, the features were indistinguishable. But one of the heads had a pointed skull that was unmistakable. Here was what was left of the crew of the lugger, and the pirates who had attempted to capture it.

Attempted, and failed—which was queer. A white man bound in his chair had killed them instantly, leaving no mark upon them.

"Who was the skipper of the lugger that was burned tonight?" Bill rumbled.

"Fella named Shaunessy. Claimed to be a pearler, but he talked too educated," Owsley muttered. "His sister wouldn't even let me speak to her."

"Sister?" roared Bill. "Where is she?" He crossed to the cowering trader and kicked him viciously. "D'ye mean to say there's a white girl on this atoll and you've kept your slobbering trap shut about her?"

OWSLEY'S FACE was covered with his arms, but the head nodded. "Left a sister and a houseboy when he sailed for the pearl bed," he muttered. "They're holed up, like us, in a bungalow a couple of hundred yards farther down the beach. What was the use of talking?" he ended with a whine. "We'll never get out of here alive ourselves."

"I'd never get a girl aboard my schooner alive, and that's a fact."

The sudden disappearance of anger from his voice surprised the trader into lifting a face from the protection of his arms. This huge, tattooed pearler spoke calmly, almost as though he were amused. He stood with his thumbs hooked in the square steel buckle of his belt, staring into space with eyes that seemed to dance and gleam in the candlelight. Anyone who knew Bellow Bill would have recognized that look as the prelude to an act utterly reckless, but to the trader the expression seemed to be one of hope.

"You think—you and I could—"

"Why, sure." Bill was forced to rely upon a drunken coward for help. As he stood there he was planning tactics in which drunkenness and cowardice would be helpful. "Surely," he rumbled. "Or at least, you can. That is, you can if you've got some of that native cord that's twisted out of coconut fiber in the store. Rope won't do. It's too strong."

"I've got some coir!" Owsley replied eagerly. He went swaying and staggering in search of it. While his back was turned, Bellow Bill pulled out his revolver, snapped all the cartridges from the cylinder, and put back one, returning the other five to his pocket. He turned the cylinder so that the trigger had to be pulled five times before the gun would fire.

Owsley, pawing in a box, never looked up until he straightened with a length of coir in his hand—half-inch, strong-looking rope, but actually only a quarter as strong as manila. Bellow Bill drew his revolver again, and laid it on the table.

"Right now Arano figures to cook you, all right, and why not?" he remarked coolly. "All you've ever done for him is keep your mouth shut—because you was scared to open it. That ain't enough. But if you were to walk me out of here, bound, and at the point of my own gun, you'd prove yourself the kind of Judas he admires. And you'd be saving him a lot of trouble. While he was dealing with me you could slip off to my schooner. Slip the anchor and trim the sheets—and none of the dugouts can catch you."

BILL'S EYES twinkled as he watched the idea sink slowly into the drink-sodden mind.

"You mean—you want me to pretend to tie you, so you can run for it, too?" Owsley whispered.

"No," Bill contradicted. He extended his elbows behind his back. "You tie me up good and tight. Nothing phony about the knots at all. The girl and I are as good as cooked anyway, understand? But you sail to Sydney and tell them what you know, and the British will send a gunboat. That will square my account with Arano."

"The murderin' devil!" breathed Owsley piously.

He advanced with the cord, and drew Bill's, elbows behind his back—as tightly as Bill would let him. Which looked as tight as possible, though it left the pearler a precious half-inch of slack.

Bill grinned as Owsley tied the knots—carefully and well. Those rough brown cords looked too thick for human strength to part. Actually, if you were abnormally strong and knew the trick of arching your back and adding the expansion of your ribs to the jerk of your arms, they could be broken in a second.

Bellow Bill meant to wait until Arano was within arm's reach. Natives who have seen their leader killed before their eyes never fight well.

Owsley picked up the revolver.

"Damn you! You double-crossing—" Bill roared suddenly in his enormous voice.

"I'll shoot!" Owsley squealed with a convincingness far beyond Bill's hopes. "Lie down, you big hellion!"

The pearler dropped heavily to his knees. They waited, holding their breath, until he nodded at the door. Owsley threw back the wooden bolt and flung the door wide open. The candle flickered, and a shaft of light leaped out into the darkness. Bill was slowly rising to his knees. Owsley, in his excitement, was jabbing him with the gun.

"I've got him—I got him!" he shrilled.

"Good!" said a deep voice from the shadows. "You'll be a man yet. Bring him out."

Bellow Bill stepped through the doorway. Instantly something tightened around his ankles and jerked both feet from under him. He was being hauled along the ground by half a dozen men before he realized that a noose had caught him. It was so sudden that Owsley did not even click the revolver. The pearler was dragged across the clearing and through a fringe of bush toward a tall figure that loomed huge in the darkness.

"Avast hauling!" Arano shouted. "Keep that line tight! Don't let him get up! Buno—Coaro—see if he has those pearls!"

As his brothers walked toward Bill, who was squirming helplessly on the ground, Arano laughed aloud. He had not moved. He was still in the fringe of bushes from which he had kept watch on the shed.

"I told you all he would have to come out of that door!" he gloated aloud. "Though I expected him on the run, shooting. Tie his feet when you get the pearls, Buno, and then we will all paint our faces!"

CHAPTER IV

THE SACRIFICE

THE DISASTER WAS so sudden and complete that Owsley failed to react. Bellow Bill, peering upward, saw him still standing in the lighted doorway, with the wobbling revolver pointed at nothing in particular. Which was lucky, for if he had fired and the gun had clicked harmlessly, Arano seemed to be a leader quick enough of wit to shoot Bill as he lay.

The pearler roared like a hobbled bull. He seemed to struggle desperately to get to his feet—with the result that the natives still holding the rope dragged him a yard or two farther toward the two big men who came swaggering toward him with drawn knives. He *seemed* to struggle—but did not.

Even in that horrible instant when his feet were jerked from beneath him, Bill had restrained the impulse to snap his bonds. He lay on his back, kicking and roaring profanity—and actually waiting, with cold and grim detachment, for *both* of the advancing brothers to get within arm's reach. He might be able to take the two to hell with him.

That was all he hoped for—and that, apparently, was too much. Even in triumph the brothers were wary. Buno walked up, kicked Bill in the ribs, and squatted beside him. Coaro remained standing and leaned over his brother's back. A hand thrust roughly into Bill's trouser pocket grasped the bag of pearls and jerked. The pocket ripped as the big black fist came out with the loot, and—

Buno uttered a coughing, strangled gasp. He swayed on his

heels and clutched at his throat with both hands, the bag of pearls slipping through his fingers. Bill caught a whiff of a sharp and bitter odor. Low as his head was, the effect was as though a huge rotten peach were jammed over his mouth and nose and pressed there by the hand of a giant. He could not breathe, and with senses that suddenly reeled he fought to keep from breathing.

His nostrils were low. But that pungent, biting, deadly gas burst from the pearl bag close to Buno's face, and as Buno toppled forward Coaro leaned down to discover what the matter was. He must have drawn one deep breath of the gas. That was more than enough. He fell across his brother's body.

Bill snapped his bonds with a surge of strength born of the terror of a death that would come with a single breath. He snatched at the knife Coaro had dropped, and slashed blindly at the rope as he rolled over and over along the ground—anything to get even a foot farther away from that bag of pearls.

The natives were dragging him. That helped. Arano was shooting as fast as he could pull trigger. Sand showered Bill as the bullets whacked the earth all around him. He didn't care. He'd take a bullet rather than raise his head—yet. That damned stuff seemed to rise, and even in the open air a circle of death was spreading around the two big black bodies whose collapse must have seemed like magic to Arano. Once he whiffed that peach-like odor he would recognize hydrocyanic acid gas, and run. Bill's knife cut the last strand of the rope, but he kept on rolling.

"Back!" Arano screamed—at natives who wanted to do nothing so much as run. A huge tattooed giant was rolling at them with a knife that glimmered in the faint light from the open door. An enormous, fearless enemy who had left two corpses behind him that he had not touched with his hands.

"Run for the beach!" Arano yelled. "Don't let him get to his ship!"

BILL CURSED the missionaries, who had trained the brain under that shaven skull. That order saved him, for the moment;

but had the positions been reversed he would have given it himself. It would keep Arano master of the atoll in the end—and never was an order obeyed more enthusiastically. With howls of fright the natives bolted for the beach.

"Owsley!" Bill bellowed.

No answer. The trader had also taken to his heels. Bill rolled through the fringe of brush, thrust his face against the good clean earth, and dared to draw a breath. The air was fresh. He leaped up and ran toward the interior of the atoll. The Shaunessy girl was in a bungalow a couple of hundred yards farther down the beach, Owsley had said.

Bill pounded along in the darkness under the palm trees until he found it Not a gleam of light showed, but after the yelling and the shooting a girl and a houseboy must be awake inside, alert for a glimpse of an enemy. And they would be armed.

"Ahoy! I'm a friend!" Bill rumbled. He walked forward, acutely aware that his white ducks would make him visible. If the girl didn't believe him it would be just too bad, but he had no time to waste in identifying himself. The night must be nearly gone. Dawn in the tropics is as abrupt as sunset. At dawn Arano, with rifles and dynamite and over a dozen men, could easily mop him up.

The door of the bungalow swung open. Not a sound, not a word—only an oblong patch of deeper darkness. For Bellow Bill to step through it was to put his head in the lion's mouth, but the boards of the veranda creaked under his weight as he strode on with unfaltering steps.

"Good tactics!" he rumbled approvingly—and, as he entered, he stopped short. He was expecting the touch of cold steel. The revolver muzzle that was jabbed against his side was almost a relief—but at that instant there was a rustle of leaves and a hiccough from the clearing behind him.

Close to Bill two people caught their breath. That sound hinted at treachery. For all those two knew he had come ahead to clear the way for a charge, and the gun that touched him quivered as the hand that held it shook, uncertain whether to pull the trigger or not.

"Come in here, Owsley—damn your yellow soul!" Bill said. He was calm—the least show of excitement and he'd be a dead man. "He's nothing but a tool of Arano's, I think, Miss Shaunessy," Bill added. "Not quite innocent, but altogether innocuous, eh? I think so. Me, I'm different. I got a bit of bottle glass and a broken sixpence in my pocket."

The gun trembled. Across the room the unseen girl caught her breath.

"You—know what became of my brother?" she said.

There are voices that give a clear picture of the speaker. Hers was one. It was clear, imperious, and unafraid. She would be a tall girl, self-confident, a girl brought up in a big family of boys, who knew men and liked them. Bellow Bill thanked his lucky stars, for this was no time for a clinging vine or hysterics.

"Yes. He was a brave man," he answered, and let that simple statement announce Shaunessy's death. "He saved my life."

"I saw the flames—and guessed." She spoke quietly. Only a tremor in the tone told of grief, like a harp string plucked and instantly muted. "When? B-before he died?"

"Afterward. With those pearls he carried."

"There was nothing strange about those pearls."

"You're wrong," Bill rumbled. "Among them were some little bulbs of compressed hydrocyanic gas that could be broken with the fingers—or a careless fist—if necessary. Did he tell you the case was as dangerous as that?"

"He asked me not to come. But I'd gone with him everywhere before. I insisted. It was just a routine trip. The Commissioner at Thursday Island sent us to officiate at the new pearling beds. A white girl is safe anywhere—"

"With black men or white. This atoll's neither," Bill contradicted. "When did you arrive?"

"Yesterday. He told me to be careful and watch the trader. We couldn't conceive how a sot like Owsley—"

"That's still outside, afraid to go ahead or back," Bill grunted. "Say, tell your boy to take this gun out of my ribs, will you? We're wasting time."

"His name is Evishi. I'm Oreen Shaunessy."

"Thanks. Bill Williams—Bellow Bill—talking. And if we ain't off the atoll by dawn we're all long pig. How much time have I got?"

ACROSS THE room the radium dial of a wrist watch flashed as Oreen twisted her arm.

"It's twenty after five."

"That leaves thirty-five minutes, about," Bill estimated swiftly. "And what weapons have you got—outside of the peashooter Evishi is still jabbing me in the side with?"

"Another revolver that I *was* pointing at you. You can put yours down, Evishi," Oreen ordered crisply. "They are both .32s."

"I'm an American, so nothing under a .45 seems to me like a gun," Bill rumbled. His voice had a taut, gay lilt to match the reckless gleam in his eyes. "It doesn't much matter. I'm a rotten shot, and I was hoping for dynamite…"

He dropped his voice to a low growl that was not exactly a whisper, yet which did not carry outside the four walls. "Owsley is afraid to go, or stay. He's useless—understand? And a real man in his shoes would have died days ago."

"I—"

"Listen!" Bill purred. His mind was racing. "I'm a good man in a fight, and I ain't bragging.… But—thirty-four minutes now to get rid of nearly twenty men? It can't be done with .32s.… That Arano hasn't lost a trick yet. He thinks like a whip, and because the man who holds my schooner is master of the island, that's where he'll be now. I'm not underestimating him again. He is waiting for dawn—and he's so right I can feel my head lifting off my shoulders."

"Are you trying to frighten me?"

"You aren't that kind.… I'm thinking out loud and counting

on your nerve, girl. I'm hoping you'll see the answer as I see it. We can wait here and put up a swell scrap. In about—er—fifty minutes from now we get dynamited out with my own powder, damn it! If we're still livin' we watch Arano paint his face with green fire and settle down to enjoy himself with us.

"Or else inside of thirty-three minutes I've got to cut a quick-thinking black devil out from among his men. If I can get Arano I can handle the rest, *I've got to get him alone on the schooner*—and he's too smart to be alone. That is, unless—"

Bellow Bill stopped short. In the perfect silence he could hear Oreen's wrist watch tick.

"I—see," she whispered. "You—you do rely on my courage, don't you? But—if I succeeded, could you? You and Evishi—he's only a boy—against twenty?

"And Owsley," Bill purred with grim relish. "I aim to use Owsley, and how. Yeah, I can try. What's an extra half hour of livin' while you wait for the butcher? My way we both take the greatest gamble there is!"

"I want to see your face," said Oreen suddenly. She struck a match, and with the same motion snapped it out. Bill glimpsed a face with the clean-cut line that marks the thoroughbred. She was pretty. An English blonde who is pretty stops a man's breath. In darkness she crossed the bungalow floor. A slim hand groped for his own and pressed it firmly.

"You like the idea of fight," she whispered. "That's what I wanted to see! And so do I—so do I, Bill! You're on."

"Let's go," he said, and shouldered toward the door. She checked him.

"Have you any of the pearls my brother prepared for a desperate gamble like this?" she asked quietly.

"Not in my pocket, but I reckon the bag's still lying on a dead man's chest," Bill purred. "Think you could look at your brother's face again? It's there."

She caught her breath. She knew that Bill had avoided saying, "Your brother's head."

"I know I can," she answered. "I'd feel safer, later, if I had one of his special pearls in my mouth."

"Aye, aye," Bill admitted. "A quick poison is an antidote against Arano's devilment, sure enough. We've a half hour. We'll stop at the clearing and pick some up. But first—"

He strode out of the door and across the veranda.

"Hey—Owsley!" he called sharply. The trader came shambling forward in the dark, and Bellow Bill swung back his right fist. The blow landed on the button, its force nicely calculated. Owsley dropped as though he were pole-axed. Bill swung his limp figure over one huge shoulder.

"*He* won't know nothing for at least ten minutes," he rumbled with a reckless zest. "And that's the point of my whole scheme. Step along, Oreen. We'll gamble with split seconds for a chance to make a real fight."

CHAPTER V

DEATH RIDES THE BOOM

IN THE EAST the stars had lost their brilliancy, and though the night seemed as dark as ever, dawn was not a quarter-hour away. On the beach near the harbor entrance a huge fire had been lit, and its yellow glare sparkled on the little waves that roughened the surface of the lagoon save when a huge black shadow leaped from shore to shore as one of Arano's sentinels walked in front of the blaze.

The shaven-headed pirate had planned shrewdly. Every dugout on the atoll capable of facing the sea had been shifted close to the fire, with a dozen men to guard them, and over the rail of Bill's schooner an occasional green glimmer, like the flash of a distant firefly, marked other lookouts whose faces were already painted in preparation for an early, easy triumph.

The tide was on the ebb. The schooner's bowsprit pointed inland, and in the stillness Bellow Bill could hear the thump and rattle of the main sheet blocks as a puff of breeze caught the after sail, which he had left hoisted, but free to swing. He was alone, and unarmed unless his belt be counted arms. His chest heaved from a sprint under the coco palms that had brought him half way around the lagoon. He bellied across the beach, his eyes on the paling stars, and crawled into the water unheard, and unseen.

An instant later a large mass of seaweed started drifting away from the beach at the point where he had disappeared. It moved with the tide, yet all but imperceptibly faster than the tide. It headed for the point where the anchor chain of the schooner angled sharply from the water. It had, in its center, a bulge where Bellow Bill's forehead and nose floated above the surface, plastered thickly with seaweed.

At dawn keen eyes would notice that bulge, and the gleam of wet white skin beneath the brown-green weed. But dawn was fourteen minutes off, and the distance from shore to schooner was only a little more than two hundred yards. Save for the unavoidable guess at the exact moment of sunrise, Bellow Bill's attack was timed to the second and judged to the foot.

Half way around the lagoon, under a thick bush, Oreen was crouching. A pearl that was not a pearl, but Death, bulged her cheek. Her glance shifted between the second hand of a wrist watch and the patches of weed that drifted toward the harbor entrance with the tide. Less than twenty feet in front of her, at high-tide mark on the beach, lay two of the tiny dugouts that children use in the South Seas—the frailest apologies for boats. At her elbow Evishi was working frantically with a wet cloth to bring Owsley back to consciousness.

Courage and cowardice, split seconds and luck must join hands in Bill's attack.

"He groaned then," Evishi whispered. "He moved a little—"

"Then carry him out, as Bill told you," Oreen ordered tensely. "Don't let them see you, and don't forget his gun—"

"But I do not see the big tattooed man," quavered the houseboy.

"You fool, he said that he hoped we wouldn't!" Oreen snapped. "We've only a minute or two more... Go!"

The houseboy clasped Owsley's limp arms around his neck and crawled across the beach, dragging the half-conscious trader. Evishi's teeth were chattering with fright. He could see the savages whose faces were painted with green fire so clearly that he forgot it was the water of the lagoon that collected the light, that to them the beach was a gray black stripe beneath dead-black foliage. With a desperate effort he pushed the light dugout before him and dragged the heavy trader after him. Only ten feet to go, down grade, over sand packed by the tide.

OWSLEY GROANED and stirred as the dugout slid into the water. Panting, Evishi dragged him over the gunwale, which was only inches high, made sure that the gun, fully loaded now, was in his pocket—and gave the dugout with its semiconscious passenger a mighty push out into the lagoon!

Instantly there was a savage shout both from the fire and the schooner. Arano's deep-toned voice brayed orders to launch a big dugout—to spread out along the beach to prevent a landing. But Evishi lay flat on the sand at the water's edge. Unseen, he crept backward. Panting, trembling, he huddled against Oreen.

"Well done!" she whispered, never looking at him, but at the second hand of her watch. "Now hide, lad. God be with you!" She pushed a .32 into his hands. His teeth chattered as he squirmed away.

Out on the lagoon a big patch of seaweed warped itself around the schooner's anchor chain. The bulge in the center rested against the chain itself, and remained there. Near the fire a big dugout was being launched with savage yells—and suddenly, from the tiny, drifting dugout came a scream of terror that rose to falsetto and broke as Owsley's breath failed.

Oreen pitied him. His silence had sent better men than he to their death. Her brother had been one—and yet she shuddered to think of what the return of Owsley's senses must have been like. He must have thought it a hallucination from the dugout's bottom. The fire—the dancing shadows, the heads of green flame along the schooner's rail, the bigger boat, shoving toward him with a yelling crew. He had screamed with realization that the scene was real.

Then he fled. He had a gun. It was a paddle he caught up. He might have shot his way past the dugout and made the open sea. But he whirled his little craft, anxious only to keep the greatest possible distance between himself and the boat that dashed for him, black against the firelight. Whirled toward the far side of the lagoon and paddled with the crazed strength of terror.

Instantly Oreen rose, walked across the beach, and launched the second dugout. She paddled straight for the schooner and the harbor entrance, which was a course at right angles to Owsley's line of flight. She was seen. Her heart hammered too hard to distinguish the orders Arano was braying. They didn't matter. She heard a deep voice that dominated and directed the howling savages, but the memory of other orders in the rumbling whisper of Bellow Bill filled her consciousness.

"… drive straight for the schooner… don't let yourself be caught too easily… shoot *at* them, but don't hit anyone. Arano'll order them not to kill you when he sees you are alone. And they won't, unless you madden them by drawing blood.…"

Wouldn't they? She knelt, plying the paddle, the .32 lying ready in the bottom of the dugout. The first crew, after hesitating, had gone on after Owsley, lashed by Arano's roars. Another dugout was shoving off by the fire. But—the shaven-headed devil thought of everything—it turned away from her, blocking escape from the lagoon. It was with the cooler, more trustworthy men who were with him on the schooner that Arano was going to capture her. They were swinging out a dinghy.

They would intercept her if she drove straight on. They couldn't hurt her—not with what she had in her cheek—but within another minute she'd be dead. A longer life—a little longer—if she whirled her frail craft and paddled back as she had come.

She gritted her teeth, and drove straight ahead. In the mass of seaweed by the anchor chain the bulge had disappeared. She didn't see that. She'd never even seen Bill, save for an instant. Thick, curly reddish hair, a square jaw; blue eyes…

"Drive on!" he'd said.

TWO OARSMEN whose faces flamed rowed the dinghy at her. She caught up the .32 and emptied it high in the air. She heard their savage, mocking yells. She wanted to scream that she'd have killed them both if Bellow Bill had not ordered her not to.

Then the prow of the dinghy struck and smashed her frail craft. She was flung in the water. A hand reached down and twisted brutally in her hair. She was dragged to the surface and held there, her outstretching chin against the dinghy's stern. A face of green fire bent down and leered at her.

"Good!" growled Arano. "Bring her to the schooner, and then go help them catch that other fool. I told you—they had no chance to escape at all."

He laughed. The sky had suddenly turned to gray, and as Oreen rolled her eyes to see the schooner she realized with despair that even now Arano had not blundered. Even now he had not stripped himself of guards. Behind his shaven head were the gleaming faces of two other savages. For an instant she believed they were his brothers. But they were dead. Like her brother. Like herself, in another minute....

Bellow Bill Williams pulled himself hand over hand down the anchor chain to the anchor itself. He had waited only until the dinghy was launched without stopping Oreen's progress. By their voices he had counted the number of the savages on the schooner; he had never really hoped that Arano would send all his men away. The big savage was a flawless tactician. Too flawless, since his orders became predictable.

A fierce pleasure in Oreen's nerve warmed Bill's heart. She and Evishi had carried out their assignments. It was his turn now. He stripped off his belt. With its steel tongue he unscrewed the shackle that held the anchor chain to the anchor. Six or eight turns only—thirty seconds' work. Oreen, thank God, had driven her dugout almost to the schooner's side. They were carrying her aboard, now. Arano would order her carried below—and then like a flawless tactician, he would order his men on deck again to guide the chase after Owsley and keep watch for Evishi and Bill.

The chain jerked clear of the anchor as the shackle dropped and the tide caught the schooner. Bill was holding it with one hand. He was borne along. He worked himself upward while he waited to see which way the schooner would swing. For a boat set adrift in a tide swings broadside to the current. She fell off to starboard—and to the right, therefore, Bill swam for the surface like a shark that rushes from the depths to snatch its prize.

To Oreen, struggling feebly in the grip of the three who were carrying her down the companionway—to the savages in the dinghy and those others in the dugout, who were yelling in triumph as a well-flung spear struck Owsley's back and skewered him like a beetle—what happened next seemed magic.

It was nothing of the sort. Only a superb swimmer like Bellow Bill, only a man of vast strength and a seaman whose experience amounted to intuition could have performed the feat, yet it was the result of skill.

AS THE schooner turned broadside to the tide the main boom swung out over the water, and the slackened main sheet became tight. A huge tattooed hand shot out of the water and gripped the main sheet below the block. With one arm Bellow Bill chinned himself. His tattooed body, clear to see in the dawn, seemed to be flung by invisible hands from the lagoon to cling like some huge gorilla to the boom. A mighty pull at the sheet with his free hand started the boom swinging inboard, bearing him with it.

Over the water, over the rail, over the deck of the schooner he swung. The breeze was light. Its pressure against the sail could slow that movement, but not stop it against the mighty pull of Bill's arm. His belt, looped on a forefinger, dangled like a snake. Ponderously he swung toward three men, wedged in a narrow companionway. They dropped Oreen. They snatched at the weapons in their belts, but the swinging boom had carried Bellow Bill directly over their heads.

"Ahoy!" he roared exultantly, and flung himself down the companionway upon them.

Two hundred and forty pounds, falling a good five feet. Bill's weight knocked them down. In a tangled mass they rolled down the companionway, to tumble in a heap on the deck below. With arms and legs spread wide Bill hugged the three men to his chest. With a jerk of his wrist he wrapped the belt around his left fist. A knife, half drawn, was cutting into his thigh. Arano's head was under Bill's left arm. The savage burrowed to bite at the soft flesh of Bill's belly.

Bill's left fist smashed on the back of the shaven skull. The blow did not travel six inches, but the bone crushed beneath it, and on the shaven skin remained the deep imprint of a square belt-link, as though Bill had struck putty. The next blow snapped the back of the savage straining to draw the knife. Bill rolled clear. The third savage leaped up—and the flying belt caught him across the forehead. The gleaming paint was wiped off in a black, Square-edged streak. The forehead, when Bill leaned down grimly to touch it with a forefinger, was soft.

"It's the weight of the gold studs that does it," Bill rumbled. "It's better than a chain."

He stood with the belt dangling from his left hand, listening, staring down at three dead faces painted with flame. The savages in the boats must be still wondering what had happened. They hadn't even yelled yet. The actual battle had not taken twenty seconds.

Oreen, over whom the fight had rolled, lay on her back at the foot of the companionway, unconscious. Her lips were parted. Bellow Bill shuddered, and a perspiration which the fight had been unable to cause broke out on his forehead. Very delicately he felt inside the girl's mouth with a huge forefinger, and pulled out the tiny globule that looked like a pearl, and was Death.

"God, if you'd lost your nerve and put that between your teeth too soon! But you're thoroughbred," he muttered. He snapped the pellet up the companionway, and overboard, and lifted the girl onto his bunk. Her heart was beating strongly. She would come around all right.

Outside some savage uttered the first shout—of doubt, and alarm.

Bill crossed to a porthole. "Got Owsley, didn't you, you devils?" he rumbled. "Well, that saves the hangman at Thursday Island a job.... And you saw me swing aboard and now you don't like it. Heading for the fire, eh? Waiting for orders from Arano—the chief that's never wrong, huh? Well—you'll get them!"

Very careful not to expose himself, Bellow Bill crawled up the companionway and back again, dragging a bight of the main sheet. Into the loop of the rope he tied Arano and the two savages, on whose faces the flaming paints still burned. For a moment he stood scowling, dissatisfied.

Then his face cleared. From a locker he took a can of red hull paint, dipped in his hand, and pressed his huge palm and five spreading fingers across each face. Then he hauled on the main sheet. One by one the three bodies were dragged up the companionway stairs and out to the end of the boom. Once again the boom swung, bearing with it three bodies whose bestial, flaming faces were all but obliterated by the red print of a white man's hand.

From around the schooner arose a cry of abject terror and surrender. The sound brought Oreen back to consciousness. Her eyes fluttered open.

"Bill! Bill!" she cried out in desperate appeal.

"I'm here," he rumbled. "It's all right, Oreen. Rest easy, gal. The fire on Runaloro is put out."

SHARK TRAIL

*Bellow Bill Williams was certain that somewhere
the swamp held the evidence—buried in
morass—to bring a murderer to justice*

CHAPTER I

THE BOAT-FOOTED MEN

ONLY A KEDGE anchor on a thin rope held the sloop against the thrust of the South Pacific swell. The two men aboard dared not risk the noise a rattling anchor chain would make; dared not show a gleam of light even within the hood of a binnacle, though the night was like soot.

They sat on the rail, back to back, in silence. Tonga, a native of the Society Islands, jabbed nervously at the rail with the point of a two-foot bush knife. He kept watch to seaward. He could see, far out, the scattered riding lights of a fleet of pearling luggers, none of which moved toward him; and, scarcely half a mile away along the shore, a faint glow in the darkness that marked the white man's town, Port Cooke. The palm of the hand that gripped the knife hilt was sweaty; his naked back could feel the sweat that was wetting the shirt of his white companion, for Tom Foster, the trader, was keeping watch toward the shore.

There lay the more probable source of danger; behind the reef which the sloop almost scraped was the lagoon, and the village of the boat-footed men.

These were New Guinea natives who did not set foot on dry land one day a week throughout their whole lives. Men who were born in flimsy huts built on piles over a mud flat which the lowest tide never left wholly uncovered. Who learned to keep balance in their narrow canoes when they were babies scarcely able to walk, who were as amphibious as frogs, living on the sea

and by the sea, trading its products with the bush natives for the taro they needed to eat, instead of growing it themselves.

A strange tribe, whose currency, even so close to a white man's town, in these days when white men were everywhere, was still dog's teeth. They speculated in the debts incurred in lavish tribal marriages as Americans might speculate in stocks and bonds. True, their young men had abandoned the sinister customs that had once been part of the tribal ritual. That is, the British Commissioner at Port Cooke said so.... But...

Something broke the surface of the black water, sharply, like a rising fish. Tonga started, and relaxed.

"Will he come?" he whispered.

"Bellow Bill Williams says he'll go where most men won't, and never asks for his profit in advance. God knows he'll have to do both."

"But how'll he find us?" whined the Society Islander. "We'd better show a light—"

"And bring The Shark? Damn it, Tonga, you follow orders!"

Foster was uneasy. Therefore he spoke angrily. The two were master and servant, but Tonga had been faithful to Foster's father before him. Had almost prevented the murder of his father.

"You ought to know that keeping a secret from The Shark around here is next to impossible," the trader added apologetically. "My father bought those pearls unexpectedly and under cover, yet he didn't live till dawn afterward. It's uncanny, and yet it's happened so many times—"

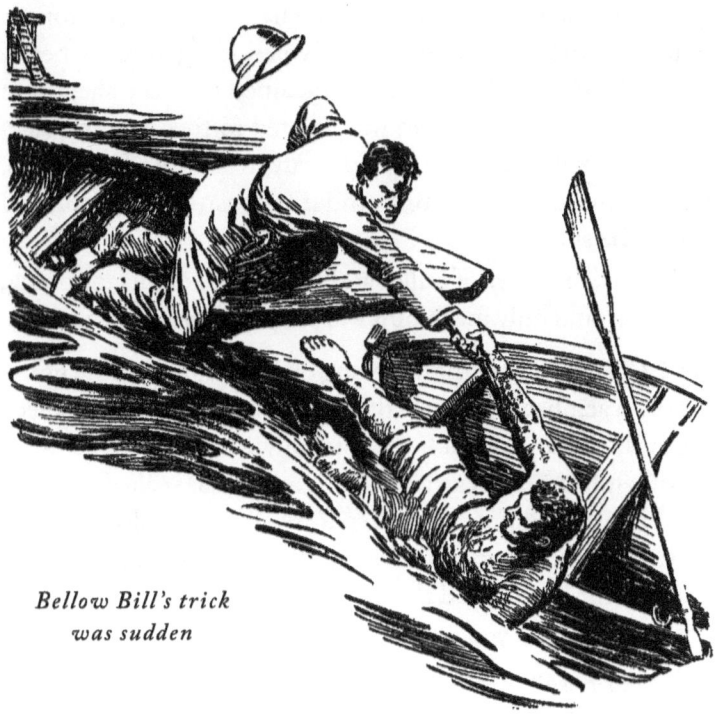

*Bellow Bill's trick
was sudden*

"Ahoy!" hailed a purring basso whisper from the darkness within a yard of Foster. With a panic-stricken oath the trader leaped up.

"Steady—it's me—Bill," warned the voice. Even in guarded tones it had the deep, powerful purr of a huge machine running at high speed. Bellow Bill couldn't really whisper, and unrestrained, that voice was a reverberant boom.

A huge hand gripped the rail beside the two who threatened him with knife and gun. Even in darkness they could sense, rather than see, the pair of enormous shoulders and the huge body that lifted out of the water. Bellow Bill stood six feet three. He weighed two hundred and thirty, and every ounce was power. Tattooing covered every inch of skin above his waist. A pearling skipper, a bush-ranger, and an adventurer always, he knew the South Seas from Papeete to New Guinea. He could say, as a simple matter of fact, that he had never met a stronger man. Huge in body, tremendous of voice, Gargantuan when it came to food and whisky, his eyes gleamed with the sheer love of excitement. When a man was wanted to trek into the bush after a lost explorer, or find a pearl pirate in a maze of coral reefs, one thought naturally of Bill. And if he wasn't thought of, and sent for, he sulked.

There were plenty of bullet and knife scars on his tattooing, but that would only make him wary and shrewd, not cautious.

DESPITE HIS weight he swung over the rail with the lightness of an acrobat, and reached into the pocket of a pair of knee-length duck pants, which was his only garment, for fine-cut chewing tobacco. Bill carried it loose, and it was soaked with salt water. He sucked out salt and spat noisily, chewed vigorously, and spat again. The tobacco was strong enough to kill even the tang of brine. He shifted the quid into his cheek, and grinned.

"But—how did you find us?" Foster demanded.

"Well, you said to come on the q.t.," Bill purred. "So I swam. There's just enough tide-current to make a bit of phosphorescence show around the hull of your sloop. Not impossible for a man to find you—if he's good."

"But you're unarmed!"

Bill shifted his quid. There was a deep-sea diver's knife in his belt, and the belt itself, under a thin covering of leather, was made of flat links of steel weighted with studs of gold. Hand to hand that belt was a formidable weapon—but if this pair thought he was unarmed, that was all right with him.

"Aye, aye. And what of it? Ain't this a conference? I'm here. I'll admit that arranging a meeting by writing me a message in water on the deck on my own schooner, so that I just had time to read it before the sun dried it up, was a smart idea. You could make sure no one else saw it, and we didn't have to exchange a word. But it did seem unnecessary when the nearest boat in the harbor was a good two hundred yards off."

"That's too close, dealing with The Shark. You know of him?"

"Of him? Sure. So does the whole coast of New Guinea. A pearler comes to Port Cooke with his season's take. Or maybe a Port Cooke trader makes a big buy. Either way, the man goes to sleep. Some time in the night he gets up, *with* his pearls, and walks straight into the bog between the town and the village of boat-footed men. Which swamp won't even hold up a dog. The Commissioner ain't even been able to recover a body. And the best native trackers swear there isn't a back trail." Bellow Bill's rumbling whisper was grimly derisive. "That's happened damn near two dozen times in the last three pearling seasons. It sounds exaggerated to me."

"It's literal truth," Foster insisted. "I've lived here three years. After my father—was picked up in his own house, sand-bagged."

"And I was sand-bagged, too," Tonga cut in. "After my brother was stabbed. But I saw The Shark. While we jumped for him, my brother and I!"

"It was the first time his scheme failed to click—you see, Bill?" Foster interrupted. "It gives you something to go on. I'll admit it's too much for me to handle. Every move I make has been watched ever since, but you've come to Port Cooke like any other pearler. You can make use of what Tonga saw—"

"Yeah," Bellow Bill purred. Back on his own schooner was a letter from the Resident who governed this whole coast asking him to go to Port Cooke and investigate those disappearances.

The last killing had made the trail of The Shark hot. The letter ended:

> *... above all, trust no one. It seems obvious from the mere number of the killings that they must be the crimes of a white man, and a regular resident. That narrows the circle to no more than six suspects, and to remain undetected so long in such a small place implies some remarkable kind of alibi.*
>
> *But I leave the details to you, Williams. You found the core in the Golden Oyster, and unmasked the Dingo Man of Cape York....*

"For after all Tonga is the only eye-witness," Foster continued.

"Yeah," said Bellow Bill. "Well, let's go down in the cabin and make a light."

"And warn The Shark?"

"Sure—I'd like to see him," Bill purred. He was thinking that even a native could lie successfully in the dark, where his face couldn't be watched. Sons have killed fathers before, and brothers, brothers. Hadn't Foster admitted that he had been a regular resident? Bill rose casually, but he managed to follow the others down the companionway into the stuffy cabin, and until the lamp flared his back was always against the wall.

YET THOUGH the two men were nervous, they made no suspicious move. They faced Bellow Bill across the little table, their backs against the foreward bulkhead and the door that opened into the next compartment. Tonga moistened his lips.

"The trail of an evil man is that of a vulture in the air, or a shark in the sea."

"I've already heard he can't be tracked," Bill growled. "Gimme facts. You saw him. What did he look like."

"I do not know."

Bill scowled.

"It was moonlight," Tonga reminded. "We leaped, my brother and I, and he struck us down. So there was not much time to see. Yet the reason I do not know him was because he had turned his skin inside out."

"Listen, damn you!" Bill rumbled—and checked his anger. The preposterous statement was made in absolute sincerity.

"It is true," Tonga insisted. "His face was bleeding flesh, without features, and his hands dripped blood. So I do not know him. That is why he has never been seen, but once. When he is The Shark, he is not human. When he is close to men—he turns his skin and becomes someone we all know, and do not suspect."

"A werewolf, eh?" Bill rumbled. He was no longer angry. Only watchful. He had been in the bush too long to laugh at the idea of black magic. He had seen strong men die, untouched, because a witch doctor looked at them and told them to die. Yet Bill did not believe in magic. In the diabolic marvels that can be accomplished by human ingenuity turned devilish he did believe.

"Yes," said Tonga. Simply, like that. "No one can know him. But I can name him. Look at this!"

Onto the table he tossed a small pocket compass coated with dried mud, and beneath the mud, stained dark-brown with what looked like blood. In a sea-going community pocket compasses are common enough, but this one did not belong to a sailor, but a landsman. It had a pivoted needle, instead of a floating dial. A man could walk with it, but scarcely steer a ship.

"I was very angry when my brother was killed," said Tonga quietly. "I thought of the boat-footed men because the trail that leads into the swamp points toward their"—he made an all but imperceptible pause—"village. But they could not trade so many pearls."

"Right," Bill agreed.

"So I looked for a white man and I looked for him by asking questions of their servants. Bungalow walls are thin, and bamboo floors creak when a man leaves his hammock in the night—"

"Are you avoiding the name because you're afraid to speak it?" Bill demanded.

"Yes," snapped Foster. "Let him tell it in his own way, Williams."

"So I asked them, 'Are you sure your master did not move on

one of the nights when The Shark used his teeth?' They all said that they *were* sure, but one of them lied. And that night I went into that white man's bungalow while he and his servant slept. In a box where nothing else was muddy I found this compass, and the mud on it was fresh. It was—Commissioner Mowberry's bungalow."

"You accuse Commissioner Mowberry's man?" boomed Bill.

"He accuses Commissioner Mowberry himself, and so do I," Foster cut in savagely. "That's why we got you out here. A whisper in town, and he'd throw us into his damn jail. Bill, The Shark knows of every big trade—and so does the Commissioner. And the rest of us come on the run when there's any excitement, but the Commissioner, damn his British dignity, waits for a report to be made to him. That gives him time. And the bungalow backs on the swamp. It all hangs together."

"Does it? You've been drinking *namu*," Bellow Bill rumbled contemptuously. He meant they were both mad. Compared to *namu*, whisky is milk. White men and natives who use it see visions, and abandon themselves to appalling orgies. "I've had my swim for nothing," he growled, and rose, jerking at his belt.

Foster flushed beet-red. "If that's your answer—" he began, when a hail came across the water.

"Ahoy! That you, Foster?"

"How'd anyone know I was here?" snapped the trader in a whisper. "You answer, Bill!"

"Like hell," purred the pearler.

Foster shrugged, and followed Tonga up the companionway.

"Have you seen Commissioner Mowberry? He said he was going to inspect the native village?" called out the voice across water.

"No. Why?" Foster growled.

"Why, his daughter has arrived from England. She wants to surprise him. I say, can you lend me a lantern? I won't go poking into that village without a good light," continued the voice.

"I'll get one," Foster agreed grudgingly.

Bellow Bill's curiosity got the better of him. The companionway creaked as he went on deck. He had scarcely turned his back when the door in the bulkhead flew open an inch or two. Through the aperture reached a hand—red, wet with blood, skinless, without fingernails. It snatched the little brass compass and disappeared. The door in the bulkhead closed.

On the table where the compass had been there remained a tiny smear of fresh blood.

CHAPTER II

WET FEET AND DRY HEAD

FOSTER WAS NOT visible on deck when Bill emerged from the cabin, but a few seconds later a glow that sprang up through an open hatch in the forepeak revealed his whereabouts, and the fact that he had lighted a lantern. Astern of the sloop a native sailing dugout was drifting along. It was a craft that was both swift in the light breezes blowing that pitch-dark night, and soundless.

A feeble lantern, lifted high, cast a dim light upon its two occupants that gave the effect of a soft focus picture, and though Bellow Bill was intensely suspicious because Foster had been hailed after all his precautions to insure secrecy, he decided instantly that the dugout itself was harmless.

The man at the tiller was a fat Polynesian—a grinning, good-natured representative of a gentle, friendly race. And the girl who gripped both gunwales of the narrow craft, as though she feared the dugout might capsize, was obviously a newcomer to the South Seas.

The dim lantern light beat down upon her, revealing the slenderness of the fingers that gripped the rough-hewn wood, the fine blond hair that lifted gently in the breeze, the beads of perspiration on the pale forehead. A flash of insight made Bill want to shout:

"Go back! The sun will be too much for you—the country will be too much! You're razor-steel, girl, in a land of bludgeons!"

She was too frail, too delicate, and too calmly and aloofly

courageous. English blond beauty is of two types: the round-cheeked, or dairy maid; and the hollow-cheeked, whose appeal is to the spirit. This girl wasn't twenty. She didn't weigh a hundred pounds, and here she was, seeking her father half way around the world, tossing away every shelter and protection amid which her face showed all too clearly that she had been reared; too impatient to wait at the commissioner's bungalow, and too brave or too innocent to fear following him amid darkness, swamps, and naked savages.

Bellow Bill was rarely at a loss, but he gaped; and though the girl startled him she seemed to stun Foster. The trader pulled himself lithely out of the hatch and came aft, carrying the lantern high. His face was also thrown into relief—young, dark, determined and hard. His lips parted. The girl threw back her head, and smiled.

That was all that Bill's eyes could see, yet he knew that in that second these two had overleaped Distance and Time. Their first word was exchanged in the tone used between old and trusted companions.

"I am Felicia Mowberry. Have you seen my father, Mr.—?"

"Foster. Tom Foster. No—unfortunately. He didn't expect you?"

"Of course not. I took a four-day steamer and a plane across the States. I'm a month early. I wanted so to surprise father. Oh, absolutely."

Bellow Bill cleared his throat. "Best to wait at the bungalow," he rumbled.

Felicia glanced at him indignantly. So did Foster.

"But really, rumors travel so fast, don't they? You see I know all about it!" she objected. "I'm determined on a *pukka* surprise. Oh, absolutely."

"He must be in the native village somewhere," Foster reflected aloud. "Here, I'll exchange lanterns. Yours *is* going out."

The Polynesian thrust the dugout alongside. The exchange was made. But Foster never looked away from the girl.

"Don't go out to the pearling fleet," he said. "You'll be safe, inshore...."

"But of course!" she said.

The Polynesian thrust off; the matting sail creaked as he trimmed it to catch the wind.

BELLOW BILL put his lips against the trader's ear. "And *why* is she safe inshore?" he growled. He was thinking grimly that British commissioners don't earn salary enough to put their daughters in the most expensive schools. A poor and ambitious official with a daughter like that had a motive for signing an alliance with the devil. *If* Mowberry were poor—you could never tell about Englishmen. So many penniless younger sons had their children educated by wealthy relatives.

Foster shrugged Bill off. "I don't know why I did say that," he answered, and it was plain enough that he wasn't really aware of what he was saying even yet. "The man's a fiend, and *that's* his daughter! Now, I don't know what to do. Let's go below, and talk it over."

Bellow Bill nodded. Foster did need to show him facts now before he would act. Wild tales and riddles would no longer serve as evidence.

He was nearest the companionway. He descended first. It was characteristic of him that he noticed instantly that the compass was gone. He saw and interpreted the smear of: blood on the table. The bulkhead door, which had been shut, was slightly ajar. Most men would have uttered an exclamation and hesitated. Not Bellow Bill.

He turned on his heel. Both hands shot out and gripped the belts of the two on the companionway. With a heave he pulled them down the stairs, flung them past him to crash in a tangle of bodies and legs against the bulkhead. Tigerlike he leaped onto the pile—holding the bulkhead door shut with the weight of three men, placing two bodies between himself and the bullet that might come crashing through the panel.

A jab of his knee into Tonga's belly stretched the Society

Islander limp. Bill clipped Foster in the jaw, but not too hard. His mind was racing ahead. He slapped Foster's pockets. No compass there. He leaned over the two unconscious men, put his ear against the door. No sound of breathing.... No trap had been prepared for him in the cabin, then.

Bill leaped up, whipped out his knife, and was up the companionway at a bound, to run forward and jump down the open forepeak hatch. He meant to catch any man hidden aboard from the rear, while his enemy struggled to push the two bodies away from the door. Swiftly, his knife stabbing before him, he crawled through the pitch darkness of the sloop—to come to the bulkhead door himself, having encountered no one.

He growled in his throat and pushed his way into the cabin. The light, shining into the hold, revealed the prints of bare, wet feet. There was a puddle by the door where a man had crouched, dripping, listening to the evidence against him while he awaited an opportunity—to steal a compass? Bill growled in his throat. More probably, to kill all three men if he learned that they possessed any evidence against him. For Foster wore shoes, and Tonga's feet were dry.

"By God! It looks as though Tonga might be telling the literal truth!" Bill muttered to himself. Swiftly he followed the trail of wet feet, back across the hold, out the mail hatch, over the side.... The shore was close by. Over a swampy ridge lay the village of boat-footed men. Bill had swum to the sloop. Had he supposed he was the only man in the South Seas who could swim?

The big pearler reached for tobacco, grinning to himself. So there was another man who could use his stuff! Another man who could prepare an ambush, and who could keep his head, crouching behind a door, when a hail in a girl's voice gave him what was undoubtedly the surprise of his life.

"He had to run," Bill muttered. "But why did he bother to take the compass, and where the hell did he get the blood?" For along the trail of wet feet there wasn't a drop. "My stuff!" Bill muttered. "If I'd been him, I'd be half way to the native village by now. And so—"

THE GRIN broadened. Bellow Bill stepped lightly across the two men, who were struggling back to consciousness, and went on deck.

"Ahoy! Miss Mowberry—come back, please!" he hailed in his enormous voice. Everyone within a mile could distinguish every word. That amused Bill. Let The Shark listen. "Tom Foster's just remembered where to find your father!" Bill roared again. "Come back, please!"

The lantern on the dugout made a circle as the craft was put about.

"Snap out of it, Tom," Bill whispered down the companionway. "And if I marked your face wipe off the blood quick. Miss Mowberry needs protection, and I'm sending you and Tonga to the village to look after her."

"Eh? Oh—quite!" mumbled the trader. "Must look after Felicia!"

Even with half formulated plans racing through his head Bill was amused at the eagerness with which the punch-drunk trader leaped to that excuse. "On deck now.... You're supposed to know where the commissioner is. He's in the village, of course," rumbled the pearler.

That fact was the one thing of which Bellow Bill was sure. The smear of blood puzzled him, and the compass was a riddle, but if *he* were in The Shark's shoes, *he* would be at the village, snugly hidden in some native's hut.

"Of course," Foster echoed.

Feverish with impatience, the big tattooed man watched the dugout sail back, gritted his teeth while Foster made excuses that were accepted. Felicia appeared glad to have the trader's company. They sailed off. Bill promised to stay at the sloop until they returned, but the instant they were far enough off for his movements to be unobserved he exploded into action.

He lifted the dinghy from its cradle, his huge tattooed hands hooked in the gunwale, the weight of the boat on his bent legs. Straining every muscle, he lowered it into the water without a sound, snatched up pieces of cloth to muffle the oars, and rowed madly for the shore.

The dugout had to sail to the inlet of the lagoon, and back to the village. It must cover nearly a mile. By crossing the reef and the muddy bar, a swimmer—a swimmer like Bellow Bill, that is—could reach the cluster of huts in far less time than it would take the dugout. That was the way The Shark must have gone, and Bill estimated that he was only fifteen minutes behind him.

It was dark—black dark. When the dinghy's keel scraped on the bar he sprang out and lifted the boat onto his back, grunting with the strain. He was as strong as three men. He needed to be. The oars, which he had been forced to place under the thwarts, rolled and rattled as the weight settled on his shoulders.

If The Shark were still hidden on the bar—as Bill might have been—he might believe that the huge figure staggering through the mud with a boat on its back would be easy to bring down. Bellow Bill hoped The Shark would make that error. To reach him he would have to come under the dinghy, and the pearler meant to let it fall on them both, like a huge candle snuffer, so that they might fight hand to hand beneath it.

But if The Shark was on the bar, he sensed the trap.

Bill staggered to the lagoon. The dinghy made a splash as he set it down; he couldn't help that. A torch or two was being kindled in the village of boat-footed men. *They'd* heard.... Half a mile away the faint glow of a lantern marked the position of the dugout. Foster and Felicia would be in the village too soon to permit Bellow Bill to stalk an enemy who left no track, either on land or water.

AND THEREFORE the tattooed pearler, made no attempt to conceal his movements. With *un*muffled oars he rowed for the village—but *not* toward any of the lights. Those torches were kindled by the more alert, more powerful natives. The chiefs and leading men—and among the boat-footed ones position and leadership comes through the possession of money. The money was only dog's teeth, the riches consisted of clay pots, shark-tooth tipped spears, and crude iron axes; nevertheless no "civilized" community ever worshipped the Great God Spot Cash more than that primitive, amphibious town.

Bellow Bill was seeking a poor man, ridden with debt for the wife he had purchased by mortgaging his labor for years ahead to richer men who bought shares in the wife's dowry as millionaires in Wall Street might speculate in the stock of a newly-organized corporation. And Bill found his poor man as he would have found him in New York—by selecting the poorest looking house, one that leaned crazily on thin, rotten piles, and knocking at the door.

Only, instead of knocking, he reached up and shook one of the flexible rafters on which the floor was built. The whole crazy structure vibrated. There is a Papitali proverb: Only the thief walks on the stout center pole.

"Me fella one good fella," Bill whispered placatingly. "Come in house belong you quick too much."

"Me no *kuskerai* (government appointed headman)—me no *luluai* (village headman)—me only Ponkob!" was the whining, timid retort.

"Ponkob no want bargain belong him?" Bill purred. That word "bargain" was magic, and he knew it. The crazy structure bent under his weight. In the darkness he glimpsed a man's white eyeballs; and behind the husband a white shape. The wife was covering herself with a long, shroudlike cotton garment, as was etiquette, but she was listening.

Bill stripped off his belt, slit the leather cover with a knife, and cut out three of the studs of gold.

"One fella fire ember, *piramatan*—woman who is the center of a feast!" he purred.

It was taken from a box of sand in the hut's center with a splinter of bamboo. For an instant the spurt of yellow flame gleamed on the gold. The man and the woman gasped simultaneously. Their money was dog-teeth, but they lived close enough to Port Cooke to know gold.

"One belong you, to answer question," Bill purred. "Three belong you to answer with single tongue. Where is the Commissioner?"

Silence. He heard them pant, man and wife alike; heard the panting change to sob. Riches and freedom from debt was spreading before those itching black fingers—*and they did not know.* They could not answer—and the disappointment was so great they could only sob, wordless.

"Take, then, *piramatan*," Bill rumbled. He pushed the gold toward fingers that clawed so eagerly that long nails drew blood from the back of his hand. Silence was an answer, after all. There is neither concealment nor secrets in a Papitali village. The Commissioner was neither hidden in the village, nor had he passed through it.

"May the skull of your father's brother bring you riches," Bill rumbled politely in the native dialect, and moved over the quivering floor to his dinghy.

At the other end of the town a dozen torches were blazing. The dugout had reached the hut of the *luluai,* and Foster was demanding news of Mowberry in the dialect, and receiving replies that he had not been seen.

Bellow Bill let the dinghy drift, watching. Suddenly the little boat rocked at his violent start. He swore aloud.

For into the ruddy glare of the torches glided a light, swift dugout. A squat, kinky-haired paddler drove it along, and in the bow sat Commissioner Mowberry.

"Were you looking for me, Foster?" he called clearly, and added excitedly. "Felicia! Why—Felicia!" He stood up excitedly, snatching off his sun helmet.

It was then that Bellow Bill swore, and reached for tobacco with fingers that fumbled for the pocket. The Commissioner's hair was perfectly dry. So was the kinky head of his paddler.

There wasn't time for hair to dry since The Shark had left the sloop. No native would have abandoned a perfect ambush, satis-fied by the mere theft of a brass compass. Mowberry must be The Shark, and yet—the torch light was strong enough to preclude possibility of error. His hair was dry. He couldn't be The Shark.

Slack-jawed, Bellow Bill Williams stared at the tail, sinewy official who clasped his daughter in his arms, her blond head close to his black one.

"Fella," the pearler rumbled under his breath," you can fly over a bottomless bog, you can turn your skin inside out, and you can swim and keep dry. And you steal my stuff! I can guess at one of the answers—but here and now I'm admitting it: fella, you're the smarter man!"

Bill lifted the oars and rowed for the torch-light.

CHAPTER III

THE SHARK BITES

AN IMMENSE AND alert curiosity filled his mind. There stood a murderer a dozen times over—who embodied the Law. There was his enemy, and Bill must row toward him, not with doubled fist, but with extended hand! The love affair between Felicia and Foster added the last bizarre touch. No tropic blossom that swells in a single night from bud to full bloom had ever flowered more quickly than that romance.

Even now, with the first greeting of her father barely finished, Felicia had edged along the narrow dugout so that she was nearer to Foster than the Commissioner. Their hands hungered for contact. Palm would touch palm the instant the big tattooed man rowing into the torch-light drew the attention of the others.

Bellow Bill noticed that. He noticed everything—that Mowberry leaned toward his bushy-headed servant and whispered without moving his lips; that tiny lights glared in Mowberry's eyes which were not reflections from the torches; that there was a revolver on the Commissioner's lean hip.

They knew the duel had begun—and they had to smile at one another politely. In that strange village of bending floors, water, and mud: there was not even a solid space to stand and shake hands.

"Oh, I say! Bill Williams? Glad to meet you no end! Heard the name so much it's a treat to see the man behind it, what?" Mowberry chattered.

"Aye…. Always glad to fit the right name to a man myself,"

Bill's deep voice rumbled back. *They* knew—the pearler boated his oars and stood up. The dinghy came drifting toward the dugout, and the gleam in Mowberry's eyes brightened as an ember glows when the wind fires it. But Bill's hand was outstretched.

Mowberry took it. He could have done nothing else—and as the boats touched Bill staggered. The dinghy seemed to shoot from beneath him, and with a mighty splash he soused into the water, still clasping Mowberry's hand, pulling him overboard by greater weight.

The others believed that Bill had been clumsy, but the two in the water knew. Mowberry doubled like an eel. His feet came against Bill's chest and he thrust to break a grip on his fingers which had become a vise. He couldn't do it. Bill sank, pulling the lighter man down. His free hand groped for the pockets of Mowberry's uniform, and as he found the first pocket empty, stiff fingers jabbed for his eyes. But Bill's head was bent. The nails only raked his scalp as they touched the muddy bottom.

Already he had learned that Mowberry could swim well. As well as he; and only his own iron grip on Mowberry's right hand enabled him to search pocket after pocket, finding nothing. Yet this man had risked discovery to steal the compass. What hiding place was safer than his own clothes. The Commissioner was no longer struggling. Bill couldn't drown him and claim an accident. The water wasn't deep enough.

In the dugout they could see the water swirl, if not the figures. Already the pearler had held his man down as long as he dared. He was letting him float upward when with a swift, sudden movement Mowberry snatched the knife from Bill's belt.

Bill tensed—but an instant passed without the hot bite of steel. Mowberry couldn't claim an accident, either. After that one quick movement he had not struggled. Bill shifted his grip, found and caught the left hand, and found it empty. Then he understood, and raked the muddy bottom for the knife. Mowberry had snatched the weapon and thrust it deep in the mud to hide it. Their struggles had roiled the water so that a long time would elapse before a diver could find it.

Their heads broke the surface. Both gasped for breath.

"Sorry—damned clumsy of me," Bill panted.

"Oh, don't apologize, old chap," Mowberry wheezed. He was smiling, genuinely, mockingly. He pulled himself into the dugout and began to scrape the mud from his ducks with sinewy fingers. Bill clambered into the dinghy.

"Oh, I say! You've lost your knife!"

"I'll find it. Or get another on my schooner," the pearler growled. That mocking smile maddened him. Mowberry was smarter than he thought, and quicker. He had gained something by disposing of that knife; thought a scheme out instantly, even though Bill had taken him by surprise. But what—unless he believed the knife was Bill's only weapon.

A faint grin twisted Bill's lips, and he felt better.

"Can I give you a lift back to your schooner, what?" Mowberry was saying.

"No," rumbled Bill. He meant to stay here and find out where Mowberry had been, if not at the village, and how an excuse had been handed to him. "That knife's worth five dollars. I'll wait till the water clears and find it.

"Cheerio! I wish you luck," said Mowberry.

BILL DIDN'T like his tone. It was too self-confident; too damned cold-bloodedly polite. Too much like that mocking smile; like everything about this shark who was triumphantly aware that water leaves no trail. Yet the bushy-headed servant was stepping into the dugout from the house of the *kuskerai*, or headman appointed by Mowberry; the party was ready to return to Port Cooke with the Commissioner. Bellow Bill didn't fear the whole village of boat-footed warriors—so what was there for The Shark to grin about? Except darkness... except the mud that hid the knife.

Bill only pretended to look for that while the dugout was

sailing toward the entrance to the lagoon. Once the whites were gone, he rowed away from the Village and its torches, seeking the place where Mowberry had reclothed and dried himself.

Even in darkness that place should not be impossible to find because of the nature of the lagoon. The enclosed waters occupied a space of perhaps a square mile, but the banks were largely mud rather than the usual South Sea coral sand.

Toward Port Cooke, indeed, the water merged into a morass utterly impassable both to a boat and a man on foot. Yet toward this Bellow Bill headed. Instinct told him that the answer to a riddle always lies in the seemingly impossible; and he sought a narrow gap in the reeds where a boat had been forced through; a cunningly hidden water trail.

It was slow work, and complete drudgery for more than an hour. Then his ears caught the faintest, seemingly most insignificant sound that ever sent the prickling thrill of danger down his spine.

The muffled *click* of a paddle blade against a dugout....

Bellow Bill whirled the dinghy around. He was skirting the morass nearest Port Cooke, so that he was caught between an enemy and the mud that would entangle him hopelessly. He took three mighty strokes with unmuffled, creaking oars which shot the dinghy out into the lagoon. Often as he had been stalked in the bush, he had never played the Red Indian game on black, open water before. Yet this was cat and mouse—and while a dugout can be paddled noiselessly save when a paddle blade slips, oars always make some noise....

As the impetus of the dinghy ceased, he leaned over the gunwale and immersed his head in the water. Now he could hear—and it wasn't one enemy, but many. A dozen dugouts, creeping toward him in a half-circle. The boat-footed men, who could handle canoes as though they were part of themselves, playing the game they knew best. Even with water to aid him all he could hear was the drops that dripped from wet, black hands, like the faintest patter of rain. Closing in… and twenty feet was as far as he could see.

He whipped off his belt and crouched in the bottom of the dinghy. Barbed, pronged fish spears make nasty weapons. In his clumsy dinghy he could neither flee nor charge, and in water and mud his strength would help him little. He could grapple one, and be speared neatly while he throttled him. Had The Shark commanded the attack, or had the display of the gold in his belt been imprudent? It might be either. Everything about this affair was elusive, like the mud that slips away from a man's feet when he wants to fight, and chokes him while he tries to come to grips with his enemy.

BELLOW BILL didn't try to come to grips. He waited till a dark shadow glided toward him, almost colliding with his dinghy, but twisting aside at the last instant with superlative skill. His belt lashed out at the full length of his arm, and the flying tip ripped flesh from the ribs of an unlucky paddler. The man's scream rang shrilly. The other paddler yelled and dipped his blades so that the dugout shot beyond Bill's reach, but as it disappeared something was flung.

Wet cords slapped Bill's face, a fish net tangled around his shoulders. "Ahoy!" he roared—a yell that was touched with laughter. Just a fish net, when he was expecting spears! One of the small nets, scarcely three by five feet, that the natives used in shallow water! They weren't warriors; they were money-loving minnow catchers. That described them better.

Bellow Bill pulled the net away from his head. With a rush and slap of paddles a dugout flashed past, eight feet away. Another net dropped over the arm that pulled the net from Bill's head. The end of it slapped his face. A third net went over his head; a fourth, poorly thrown, struck him in the waist—and another dugout was flashing past.

Again the slap of wet cords—and he had not torn the first set clear yet. Strings ripped under the convulsive jerk of his fingers. A mass of nets were twisted somehow under his left arm. A jerk of his elbow tore through the netting, but his own thrust tightened one thin cord over his adam's apple. It snapped—but the pain made him see a flash like fire, for a second his breathing was stopped.

"Ahoy!" he roared—but the mighty voice was choked. The slap of paddles and then dugout followed dugout—the slap of nets, thicker and thicker over Bill's head, tangling around his feet. Little nets, used to catch minnows. *That* was what angered him as he ripped and tore with arms whose movements were more restricted every instant.

Spears he could have flung back. On solid ground he could drive this whole village screaming before him. They weren't fighting him. Since his first blow, not a dugout had come within arm's length. They just fished for him… and they had him by the gills already. When he couldn't move an arm they'd capsize him, push him down in the mud.

And if they liked, or The Shark liked, they'd take the nets off after he was drowned, pretend that he'd capsized his own boat and drowned in the mud. *Now* he knew why Mowberry had stolen his knife.

"You damn black cowards!" Bill roared. Maybe that shout would be heard in Port Cooke. Maybe Foster would guess that at least Bill hadn't died like a stupid fool.

He was hopelessly entangled. He was panic-stricken, for the first time in his life. He kicked out and found his leg wedged under the thwart. In sheer blind anger he straightened his leg and snapped that eight-inch oaken board in two. He was strong, damn them if he would let them kill him as they pleased. He had no clearer idea than that. He could still move his feet, twist his arms.

He rolled to the side of the dinghy, capsized it. He sank, and rose under the upturned bottom. Bits of the broken seat floated up around his bare belly. One piece had a sharp point. He could feel it. But it was only a wooden point… useless.

Nevertheless that fact steadied him. There was a bit of air

trapped under the round bottom of the dinghy. He filled his lungs. He could swim without moving his arms. But—swim to what? The shore was bottomless muck. After being netted like a minnow, should he let them spear him like a turtle.

He could hear them yelling. Amphibious themselves, they suspected he might be under the boat. They were arguing which of them should dive underneath to see. The wounded man was screaming to be taken home to his wife before all his blood ran out.

That was something, Bellow Bill thought grimly. If he only had a knife....

HE TWISTED a finger through the net and found the shark oak splinter that was floating beside his face. It wouldn't cut butter—but the worst panic, with Bellow Bill, was over in a few seconds. Grimly he worked that bit of wood through the nets that enveloped him until the butt was against his chest. He had already broken out the center thwart. He worked forward until he could put the back of his head on the little shelf formed by the triangular bow thwart. Stretching out his full six feet three, he discovered that he could hook his heels in the extension of the stern thwart. He grunted. He was lying on his back, his face in the sharp angle of the dinghy's bow. The air was best there. He let one leg dangle.

The splash with which a diver struck the water warned him. He let himself go muscle-limp, like a man who has just drowned, as hands fumbled along his body. The native rose alongside him, dragging at Bill's body and attempting to lift the side of the dinghy to extricate the corpse.

Bellow Bill had known that would be done. Any swimmer would do the same. Like springing steel Bill stiffened his body, jamming the native's chest between his own chest and the side of the boat. The pointed sliver of oak twisted in Bill's fingers. The butt of it dug cruelly into his own flesh as he arched his back, pressing himself against the native, but he could feel the sharp point rip forward an inch; the tortured, spasm of the native as the splinter drove into a rib, and ground against the bone.

The dinghy rocked madly. Pain ripped like fire across Bill's back as the native knifed him. Then suddenly, but not too suddenly, the sliver of oak slipped past the round rib bone and drove into the heart. The native gave one more convulsive spasm. As his body relaxed Bellow Bill let himself sink, straight down, twisting in the water as he sank, groping with his finger tips in the mud for the knife that had slipped from a lifeless hand.

Bill found it. He was cutting at the net as he floated upward; cutting his own chest, too, but gaining greater play for his hand at every slash.

The native's body was pinned under the dinghy. Bill let it stay, but he rocked the boat to let in fresh air.

CHAPTER IV

THE BAIT FOR A MAN-EATER

"**THE WOMAN-STEALER IS** fighting the *kuskerai!* Dive to help him, Ngalen!" some native was yelling.

"You dive, Pwilep! She is not my woman—I have bought my wife!

"You, Iamet—you killed the shark!"

"No, you Ngatchumu—you are a poor man!"

The long slash in Bellow Bill's back hurt like the devil, but he grinned. No one wanted to crawl into a den after the bear. He rocked the boat again, filling his lungs, and cut away the last of the netting.

"Someone must go! Listen! The boat is rocking! They are fighting! The white man who is kind to us warned the *kuskerai* that the painted man had come to steal the woman he lets us keep—"

So *that* was it! That explained both Mowberry's hold over the village and the ease with which he had provoked an attack on Bill. Among the boat-footed men, "the woman" was a literal term. In the old days she was captured by war, and later she was purchased, but always there was just one woman, and she was the mistress of the entire village.

She was kept on some island from which escape was difficult, and her fate was so atrocious that the custom was the first one to be put down by the British. Naturally, "the woman" was the institution most dear to the bachelor warriors of the village.

Bellow Bill could foresee the next step, and for the first time he was thankful for the darkness. He filled his lungs, and swam under water very slowly, keeping close to the bottom. Someone would dare to dive beneath the dinghy soon, and when they learned he was gone someone else would light a torch. But a few more enterprising souls would hurry to see that "the woman" was still safe.

Beyond the ring of dugouts he came up for air, and skirted the rush-grown shore in the direction in which he had been searching. Almost before light sprang up behind him, a dugout passed him. Another followed, carrying the *kuskerai's* body, but even with that aid he almost missed the entrance. He could hear boats pushing into the rushes. A torch was kindled far back in the morass, yet even then he could see no break in the reeds.

He squatted in the mud like a frog, with only his nose showing. After a long time the two boats came back.

The secret of the entrance, when he came to investigate, lay in a screen of reeds growing in a wickerwork basket that could be moved back and forth. Beyond that lay a path that was adapted only to men whose feet were boats: an eighteen-inch wide trail through the rushes just wide enough to pass a dugout, with about four inches of water and below that soft and sticky mud.

It wasn't deep enough to swim in, and it was perfectly impossible for Bill to stand. He tried, and all but bogged himself. Thereafter he dragged himself along by grasping the stems of the rushes. He was going directly toward Port Cooke, as far as he could judge. Less than three hundred yards away in an air-line was Mowberry's bungalow and garden, which backed on the other side of this same morass. That was what kept Bellow Bill going.

He came to the place where the torch had been lighted at last. The butt had been stuck in the mud, and the glowing end still smoldered, giving a little light. Beyond it the ground looked more solid, but still Bill had to drag himself along like a tattooed water-snake. He wished the natives had extinguished the torch.

"Stop there!" ordered a voice in English. It was curiously muffled "Mup mere!" was really what it pronounced.

BELLOW BILL drove a foot downward on the chance of finding solid footing, and didn't. He had to lash out behind him with both legs to keep from being bogged.

The man on the solid ground behind the smoldering torch chuckled.

Above the torch appeared a face that was skinless, inhuman. Eyes, but neither hair nor visible mouth, a reddish surface on which stood drops of blood. A red, bloody hand without finger nails followed, gripping a native spear whose point was covered for three feet with barbed shark's teeth, like hundreds of knives.

Bellow Bill gripped at a rush, and pulled it from the oozy muck by the roots. Nothing near him was solid; nothing at all. The spear, however, was not long enough to reach him.

The reddish surface below the eyes puffed as The Shark spoke.

"I can throw it very well, Williams... You look like a snake dragging itself along with a broken back. You're stronger—much stronger—than I expected."

"Take off the mask, Mowberry," Bill rumbled. One hand was fumbling for his belt. "I guessed it must be something like a bathing cap when I saw that your hair was dry."

Bubbles of air slid under the tine rubber as Mowberry spoke.

"I'd lose face—the natives, you know. I'm a special devil who guards the woman, when they see me at all. Only two ever have. She, poor wretch, would give her life for anyone who was kind to her." He stood up and poised the spear.

"Well, good-by, Williams," he said. "You really did very well against the nets. Wish there was time to make you tell me how you did it, really. Romans had a gladiatorial contest that was much the same. Armored swordsman against a naked little fellow with a net. Looked like murder, but the netman always won. Only practical idea I ever learned at Oxford."

He hurled the spear viciously as he pattered on, the bubbles sliding around the mask. The point darted accurately at Bill's throat, but the pearler's fist, wrapped in his belt, knocked it aside. The shark-teeth splintered like flakes of glass against the steel links. The spear drove deep into the muck under Bill's left shoulder. Mowberry leaped to catch the haft, sinking in the muck to his knees. Bill was quicker.

He flipped an end of the belt around the jagged shark teeth that would have cut a bare hand to the bone; twisted the steel links. Mowberry's tug on the shaft only dragged Bill a yard forward through the ooze. With his elbows the pearler squirmed forward, feet churning in the muck to find solid ground.

Under the thin rubble a huge bubble of air swelled. Mowberry uttered a choked cry, let go the spear—and ran. For a gun, Bill thought, as he squirmed over the last yard of muck and leaped up on solid ground. *But Mowberry couldn't use a gun!* A shot, heard in the center of a morass deemed bottomless, would be sure to bring on an investigation.

White skin made the Commissioner visible in the darkness. He fled straight toward his own bungalow, over the narrow island of solid land in the muck, into the morass beyond. Bill growled in his throat. He had him! He knew it when Mowberry crouched, knee-deep in the ooze, turned at a sharp angle, and floundered on, still bent almost double, one hand held before him. That hand seemed to scrape the surface of the mud.

JOYOUSLY BELLOW BILL cut across the angle. He was only thirty feet from the Commissioner when he hit the morass, but thirty feet is too far to throw a spear at a target that is only a white blur. Few men could outrun Bill—especially in mud, where strength counts.

His first step sank him to the knees—but Mowberry, thirty feet farther out, was only ankle deep. Bill plunged on, and abruptly there seemed to be no bottom at all. He was waist, chest, shoulder deep in as many steps. Frantically he thrashed his arms, kicked out of the sticky grip of the bog that had all but swallowed him, bellied back to the solid ground behind.

Farther out, Mowberry had paused, as if for an instant he were tempted to turn back and attack Bill. But the pearler still held the spear. Abruptly the white blur vanished.

"Damn your cunning guts!" Bill snarled. He stood panting, conscious of the blood trickling from the gash in his back, aware that he was weaker than he should be, less alert. Mowberry had been running for his life, yet he ran doubled up, one hand swinging close to the ground. And he had zigzagged when a turn brought him closer to the spear point.

Anger rumbled audibly in Bill's chest. When Mowberry pulled a mask over his face and stripped off his duck he was The Shark. Dressed, he was His Excellency, the British Commissioner—damn him! *He* would not be caught tonight.

But the trick of crossing a bottomless morass was what had given The Shark his immunity.

Bellow Bill was growling like a wolf hound as he tramped into the morass and forced his way parallel with the solid ground, retracing the angle he had cut off in the chase. Ten feet out, when he was waist-deep, he struck it—a slippery plank, buried in the muck, but solid enough. Plank upon plank a path had been laid down. It angled at crazy zigzags, so that Bill was able to follow it only step by step.

Anger began rumbling in his chest. Mowberry had followed it at a run. The thing was safe enough from discovery by strangers unless The Shark were hotly pursued—who'd wade for yards into an impassable swamp? But why hadn't the devil drowned himself long ago by taking a wrong step?

Alone in the dark, with a wound weakening him, Bellow Bill figured it out. That was why Mowberry had risked everything to recover the compass. Bill stooped and fumbled in the mud around the plank. As he expected, his fingers closed on a wire. Here was the shark trail. Direct current was flowing through that wire from a buried battery. The needle of a compass, held above it, would always be parallel to the wire, would reveal every twist and turn of the hidden path. That was why Mowberry had run crouched, with a hand scraping the mud. The needle of the brass compass, Bill remembered, had been luminous....

He reached for his fine-cut, though the tobacco was bitter with salt water and gritty with mud.

Step by step he groped along the shark trail until he came to a spot of green, loose ooze.

Fifteen minutes later he groped his way back to the island of solid ground. Somewhere near him "the woman" was cowering—but who would believe what such a debased creature would say against an official? Bill wasted no time hunting for her. He took the boat trail through the rushes, determined to return to Port Cooke along the outer beach. Deep in his chest he was humming that grandest of all halliard chanteys:

> Give me some time
> And I'll blow the man down!

CHAPTER V

DEVIL'S BARGAIN

AT THREE A.M. Bellow Bill crept into Foster's bungalow at Port Cooke and shook the snoring Tonga out of a hammock. Bill's knees quivered when he stood still. Dried blood made a grim arabesque on his back and legs.

"Quiet!" he warned in a rumbling whisper. "And no lights.... Where's Foster?"

"Never came back from the Commissioner's."

"God help him.... Mowberry—when did he sail, and where?"

"Eh? He didn't sail, sir! He's at his bungalow—"

"Oh, is he?" Bill rumbled sarcastically. "How do you know no boat has left? You were snoring like a pig!"

"My friends, sir—"

"Aye, aye," Bill agreed. "Get me clean water—bandages—something to eat. Quick."

"There's gin, sir!"

"Damn your soul, I'm beat, I tell you! Plug a couple of coconuts and stir in all the sugar the milk will hold. I need a real pick-up, fella. Get me paper—pencil—a hurricane lantern and a blanket. Slap something on that slash in my back while I write. I've hooked The Shark—"

"Is he—?"

"Yes, he is! And what of it? He'll be gone again by dawn, if you let your tongue rattle! And quiet, Tonga! I crawled here on my belly. That's one smart fella and one poison fella, savvy?"

315

The pearler kicked off his muddy shorts, flung a blanket on the floor, lighted a lantern beneath its shelter and wrote while Tonga strapped up his back. The surgery was rough to make Bill swear in a growling bass, but he never winced. He blew the lantern out before he crawled from beneath the blanket, and thrust an envelope into Tonga's hands.

"For the British Resident himself, at Port Moresby, in case I'm not back before dawn," he ordered, gulping the sickly-sweet drink that is the quickest source of energy an exhausted man can put into his stomach. "And now, where is a shotgun? Sawed-off preferred."

"There's a Webley revolver, sir—"

"I'm a rotten shot," Bellow Bill growled truthfully.

Foster's shotgun was long-barreled. Stalking naked through the darkness, with a low growl rumbling in his chest, Bill loaded both barrels, and caught up a dark cotton *pareu,* or loin cloth, belonging to Tonga.

"Foster has clothes, sir," the native objected.

"Damn Foster's clothes! They're white aren't they?" Bill snorted. "Think I want to be a lighthouse? My tattooed hide is more blue than anything else, praise be…. All right, fella. Climb into your hammock, and give that letter to the Resident yourself, or I'll haunt you."

Bellow Bill strode to the doorway—and seemed to melt into the darkness. He crossed the veranda on his belly, as he had entered, wormed across the compound and slipped into the bush with a sigh of relief. Foster's bungalow was close to the Commissioner's, but in every dark yard lay peril of an ambush.

If Mowberry had not fled, he would be somewhere near, seeking to silence Bill.

Before dawn The Shark would put over another of his spectacular murders, or Bill would obtain what he lacked as yet: decisive and irrefutable proof of Mowberry's double life.

In bush-ranging the pearler had no master. Like a dark shadow he glided to the fence around Mowberry's compound, choosing a spot where the shadow of a pandamus palm lay like ink. Within the fence a garden grew lushly down to the morass. Bill understood the reason for that planting, now. Like a lion ambushed beside a game trail, he waited for a rustle to sound in that shrubbery. Before dawn The Shark must kill him, or pick up what loot he had been unable to dispose of and flee. Either way the Commissioner would not be in his bungalow now. Bill planned to catch him as he returned—with his mask, or his loot, on his person. To carry the war to the other man was always Bill's method.

WITHIN THE bungalow one lantern dimly burned, throwing horizontal streaks of light through the window jalousies. Odd, that; and from time to time there was an odd sound, deeper-pitched than the hum of insects. A brief murmur; a long pause, another brief murmur. Because Bill's ears were attuned for the stealthy approach of a thief and murderer, he failed to interpret that sound correctly until a match flared suddenly beneath a tent-like bush covered with profusely flowering frangipani. Foster was lighting a cigarette. On his shoulder rested Felicia's blond head. In the brief spurt of light the faces revealed a glowing tranquillity; an ineffable oblivion to time, place, to everything but a love which had been declared and accepted.

Great God, Bill thought. They've been there all night, and they'll be there till dawn! He would have infinitely preferred to discover a dozen armed men. He would look pretty ambushing Mowberry before his daughter's eyes. And he had been planning to enter the house.

He rose. "Ahoy!" he called softly.

The coal of the cigarette jerked upward. Felicia gasped audibly.

"As you were!" Bill rumbled. "It's all right, as it happens. Though I ran into The Shark. He got away, and is roaming around."

"Oh—oh, really? I say, that's top-hole!" Foster stammered.

"Is it? You wouldn't know," Bill rumbled disgustedly. "Where's the Commissioner?"

"He—he went to bed—"

"Did he?" Bill grunted. "Would you mind calling him, Miss Mowberry?"

The girl turned toward the bungalow, but before she reached the veranda steps a clipped voice spoke out of the heart of the pandamus thicket in the shadow of which Bill had lain.

"Not in bed, exactly," Mowberry called. He pushed the leaves aside and stepped close to Bill. He was dressed in ducks, and wearing a revolver with the holster flap open. "I heard the native shouting and you were—er—so oblivious, Mr. Foster, that I felt a watch should be kept." He smiled thinly at Bill, whose shotgun was lined on his waist. "Knowing Williams was there, and his reputation, I—er—rather expected him to be along."

"Lucky you didn't mistake me for a native," Bill boomed. "I came pretty quiet."

"Oh, not at all," Mowberry replied crisply. "An intelligent man can't make such mistakes."

"Smart. Devilish smart," Bill reflected. But how Mowberry must have ground his teeth because of the lovers under the frangipani when Bill crawled up. For he could have shot Bill full of holes, except that by so doing he would have lost all chance at Foster and Tonga, who must also be silenced before he could be safe. That was a point Bill had overlooked. Mowberry had not.

"I apologize for eavesdropping," he was saying. "It's quite all right, really, Felicia. No finer young man than Foster in the archæpelago."

"I'd best be getting home now, rather," answered the trader awkwardly. "Coming, Bill?"

Silence—that lengthened significantly.

"No, I've something to say to the Commissioner."

"Quite so!" Mowberry agreed instantly. "Well, it's late; but it's been an exciting day for us all. Let's have a drink all round.

A stirrup cup—or better, a loving cup, eh?" He was quick, suave. He made the offer sound casual.

"I don't think I want—" began Bill and Foster together.

"But I insist," Mowberry retorted firmly. "A health to those we love, eh? For I want you to share it, Felicia. Half a mo', please."

COOLLY HE turned his back to Bill and walked into the bungalow. Bill couldn't stop him, but with three strides he stepped between Foster and the girl. It was the only place he was safe, with Mowberry out of sight. And his shotgun might be the only protection for Felicia, daughter of The Shark though she was...

Yet when the Commissioner reappeared he bore only a tray, and four glasses.

"Three strong stengahs for the lads, and one weak for the lass," he said hospitably, handing a glass to Felicia. "You others choose, please." He offered the tray.

Foster drank deep. Bill barely touched the liquor with his lips.

"For courtesy," he explained in his rumbling voice. "I don't like to drink with a fresh wound, sir."

"As you please," Mowberry nodded. He picked up Bill's glass, drained it, and followed it with his own. Felicia returned her empty glass to the tray with a wry pucker of her mouth.

"It's bitter," she complained.

"Trade gin often seems so to newcomers," said Mowberry lightly.

But Bill knew that he had drugged his daughter's glass.

CHAPTER VI

SHARK'S BARGAIN

GOOD-BYS WERE SAID. Foster tramped off across the compound, and Felicia excused herself and retired. All that time the shotgun over Bellow Bill's arm covered Mowberry. It was done casually, and the act was not observed by the others, because Mowberry made no effort to step from in front of the twin barrels. Even when they stood alone, in the faint cross-barred light that streamed through the jalousies, he did not move, he only shrugged.

"It was just a bromide I gave her. Enough to make sure she sleeps," he said. "I take it neither you nor I want any interference?"

"No."

"They talked there for hours. As though they'd been the first in all the world who ever fell in love at sight. I—couldn't foresee that, Williams."

"Nor I."

"No. Though I did out-think you. No good to offer you what I've buried? It's considerable. Put my mask on that native you killed, and let sleeping dogs lie, eh?"

"Not while they're murdering dogs like you."

"I imagined you'd be like that—I began with robbery—till I was caught in the act and had to use a knife. Then I improved my methods. A Commissioner's salary is a pittance, Williams. I could be honest, but I had to see my daughter a clerk's wife in a Bloomsbury flat, or do what I did. Money is everything in

London today, Williams. No one cares how you get it, unless they see the blood on it. You understand, I'm explaining, not apologizing."

"I savvy," Bill rumbled. "And you savvy that if the Resident checks your remittances to your daughter, it'll indicate you were The Shark. If he takes up that plank shark trail of yours, I'll bet he'll find the balance of the loot tied to it somewhere."

"You've won," Mowberry agreed smoothly. "Williams, when I'd hidden myself in that pandamus thicket and saw them come out of the house, I chucked up the sponge. You were too damned determined and strong, and I had to kill three men to keep facts that would hang me from getting to the Resident.

"I don't care to hang, Williams, because my disgrace would ruin my daughter's future. I'm beaten, and so I'm going to be killed. Legally, or otherwise. I'd prefer it to be otherwise, for Felicia's sake. I've given her an education, and she's found a man for herself who's a decent enough Englishman. She's established in life if—*if* you're man enough to take the law into your own hands."

"I do what most men don't dare to, and I think the girl's worth taking a chance for," Bellow Bill rumbled. But in the back of his head instinct murmured warningly: he's smarter—smarter than you, Bellow Bill...

"Take my gun," said Mowberry crisply. He lifted his hands. "Hold it against my belly. That's right! Now, there's two compasses in my coat pocket. Take one. Good!"

Bellow Bill stepped back, watchfully, holding compass and revolver. During the search he had satisfied himself that Mowberry carried no concealed weapon. The Commissioner now pulled the mask from his pocket and pulled it over his head. The air-bubbles slipped and slid as he spoke on:

"I'm going to Felicia's room and shake her hammock. There's light enough for her to see The Shark's face, but she's drugged too much to see well, or think quickly. She'll scream. Then you and I will tear out of the bungalow to the morass. You'll have a gun on me all the time, Williams, and you know there's no escape.

"Somewhere on the planks, Bill, I'll turn and face you. Shoot me, and go on. Fire a shot into the *kuskerai's* chest to cover that stab wound you gave him, and pull the mask over his face. Chuck my gun in the swamp—not that there's any equipment nearer than Sydney to compare bullets, but just to leave no loose ends. Then it appears that I have been shot by a wily native while protecting my home."

"SHOOTING YOU appeals to me," Bill rumbled. "You might beat this case in court. Get off with penal servitude. How many natives are ambushed in that swamp?"

"None," Mowberry said. "Once is enough to try that, Williams."

Instinct spoke warningly: Smarter than you are—smarter!

"You're on. I'll do it," said Bellow Bill. The future of a living girl came before abstract justice with him, but stronger than that, though he would not admit it even to himself, was the determination to prove he was the better man. Of course, the village of boat-footed men would know the truth, but native testimony is not acceptable against a white man in the South Seas.

Mowberry turned on his heel. His scheme took far longer to explain than to enact. Bill covered him with the shotgun while he thrust his masked face into Felicia's. Her scream was ringing as Mowberry rushed past him, dashed across the veranda.

"The Shark! The Shark!" Mowberry yelled. "Head him off, Bill! He's running for the morass!"

Bill wasn't two yards behind. He fired a revolver shot into the air, plunging through the garden shrubbery that screened them both from the house, saw Mowberry leap into what looked like a bottomless quagmire—and wondered, as he jumped himself— if the Commissioner were leaping into quicksand that would smother them both?

But no! Mowberry struggled up. Bill, heavier and further back, had to struggle to reach the head of the planking. Mowberry gained, but never more than a few yards. His mud-splashed coat was always visible, though Bill's attention was fixed upon the compass.

That illuminated needle swung like a magic wand, keeping his feet on slippery planks that zigzagged erratically. Mowberry, lighter and more familiar with the trail, was gaining.

"Wait!" Bill warned.

"Farther on!" the answer came back. They were already three quarters the way across the morass.

Smarter than you—smarter! The whisper of instinct had become a shout. Bellow Bill stopped in his tracks. Ahead the suck and gurgle of Mowberry's feet in the muck trudged on. The sound was like a moist kiss. It ceased. Five, six seconds of silence. Then Mowberry plodded on. Had he stopped to wait for Bill, and discovered that his nerve was not equal to waiting for an executioner who trudged and floundered? He was going faster now.

"Wait for me!" Bill called softly—but he himself went slower. It was hard for a man as tall as he to hunker near the earth, but he advanced in the posture of a Russian dancer, half sitting on his heels, holding the shotgun before him like a pistol with its barrel high. That saved him—that and the length of his arms, which had a reach inches longer than those of an average man.

Mowberry the clever had foreseen the possibility of pursuit. He had simply stopped and hooked the black string attached to the trigger of a set gun across the path. It was the outstretched shotgun that tripped the trigger. The blast of buckshot knocked the gun from Bill's grip, but he was untouched.

HE CROUCHED, ears ringing from the shot—and grinned. The shotgun disappeared in the muck. Bellow Bill let it sink. The revolver was poised. He listened—to feet that had begun to splash through watery green slime, hurrying toward the island and the boat-trail, racing to return to Port Cooke and creep upon Foster and Tonga, who lay asleep. Smart. Too smart…

"God! Willi—"

Mowberry's scream, shrill in the darkness, abruptly cut off…
The needle of the compass in Bill's hand veered suddenly toward
the north. The current flowing through the buried wire had
been broken.

Bill shrugged. He hurried forward as fast as he could, feeling
his way with his feet.

At the edge of the slimy pool he stopped, and lit a match.
Of Mowberry there was no sign but a bubble that rose slowly,
and burst.

The pearler inched along a plank pathway that suddenly
ended in green slime in which a man would sink as though in
water, but never rise. Grimly, he thrust down a long arm. He
could just touch Mowberry's head. He stripped off the mask,
and thrust the revolver down beside the corpse. The Resident's
men could find that, too, when they took up the shark trail and
dredged for the body.

Bill gathered himself at the plank edge, and leaped ten feet
out. His outstretched arms caught the plank on the other side
of the gap. Those planks had been tied to stakes with withes,
which the slime had made so slippery no human fingers could
untie them. For all his cleverness, it had been inconceivable to
Mowberry that a man could stand on a slippery plank and break
those lashings.

The memory of that stupendous effort made Bellow Bill
wince. It was that which had made the wound in his back break
out afresh and bleed so freely.

He inched forward, to put the mask on the *kuskerai* and drive
the spear that he had tossed away, through the dead native's
chest. His story would be that Mowberry, chasing The Shark,
had slipped. He had overtaken the native, knocked a spear aside
with his belt, killed. On his way back he must hurl the set gun
into the morass. Only the natives would ever know the truth, and
native truth is—just one more South Sea rumor. Which is a pity.

"Aye, I was stronger," Bellow Bill mumbled to himself.

ABOUT THE AUTHOR

THE TROUBLE WITH writing an autobiography is that you begin to ask yourself, "Why?"—and no reason is discernible. I was born in Medford, Massachusetts, on the 23rd of March, 1895, and so qualify as a Yankee even among Yankees. When I was a kid I was captain of a baseball team and played third base, instead of pitching, which shows unusual restraint. The trouble was I could throw an in, but not an out, and what's a pitcher without an out? Exactly. A third baseman.

Nothing else happened until I graduated from Columbia in 1916. I was a Fellow in English (maybe that was prophetic) but, as the event turned out, no scholar. I wanted to write a history of Sunday newspaper sections, all about the "Yellow Kid" and "Why Girls Leave Home," but the professors chose a newspaper that had been out of print for two hundred years. To disturb a literary corpse so remarkably quiescent seemed a shame, so I got a job with a trade exposition, which is a combination of circus and business convention, and when that was over, with the New York *Globe*. I was and am the worst salesman in the world, and was trying to sell advertising.

Then the war, which landed me eventually in command of a sub chaser. Getting there I wore every uniform in the navy, missed getting to France on the *Noma* in May, '17, because a bosun's mate thought my name was Sperry—I've never felt so low before or since—just had brains enough to get off the ship before they coaled her, and ran down the dock with my gear wrapped up in a blanket, and that bosun's mate bawling at me to come back and work.

Ralph R. Perry

Stayed at sea during the war, and for a year afterward. Saw fog and ice and France, finally; got shot at in mistake for a sub, and learned something of seagoing from Captain Hugo Osterhaus, who finally decided I could be trusted with a deck watch while we ferried the A.E.F. across the Western Ocean.

Late in 1919 the navy, in peace time, became dull. There were more merchant seamen with ten years' experience against my three than there were berths, so I came ashore. If I'd saved my pay everything would have been swell, but I never could make more than two successive passes in craps. Jobs weren't to be had in 1920, so I began to write. Didn't quite starve, but was pretty glad just the same to land an editorial job in the summer of '21. Four years later I quit to write fiction, and here I am, with a hundred stories back of me, and more interested in writing than ever. Some people think any grandmother could go to sea these days, and five hundred yarns wouldn't demonstrate the contrary too strongly.

Avocation? Building up a run-down Connecticut homestead. There's stone walls to lay, wood to cut, and painting and carpentering *ad lib*. Pleasures—going somewhere far off. Loading the Underwood and my wife into the car or onto a boat, and seeing how people do things two thousand or ten thousand miles away.

www.ingramcontent.com/pod-product-compliance
Lightning Source LLC
Chambersburg PA
CBHW031154020726
47499CB00002B/355